SHADE'S
FALL

JAMIE BEGLEY

Shade's Fall

Young Ink Press Publication
YoungInkPress.com

Copyright © 2014 by Jamie Begley
Edited by C&D Editing, and Hot Tree Editing
Cover Art by Young Ink Press

ISBN-13: 978-0692200018
ISBN-10: 0692200010

PROLOGUE

"Shh... baby, you're going to be fine."

Shade stood in the corner with his brother, Razer, from The Last Riders, standing tensely by his side. He knew Razer had come to care a great deal for his sister-in-law.

Both of them were watching with grim expressions as Lily tried again to get out of the hospital bed. Beth, her sister, prevented her with a soothing voice, murmuring words over and over again that neither men could hear over Lily's cries.

The doctors had relieved the pressure on her brain last night, saving her life. Her broken hand was put in a cast that morning. The trauma combined with the pain and medication left her disoriented.

Every cry and whimper that passed her lips increased his resolve to take his vengeance out on the two men who were responsible for her injuries. The police had them in custody and they wouldn't be getting out any time soon, but Shade had every faith the judicial system would release them on parole. He would be waiting for them when it happened, just like the biker who had dared to touch her and the deputy from Treepoint. Both had disappeared just as Joker and Dale would.

Lily finally slipped into a fitful sleep, tossing and turning on the hospital bed while Beth continued sitting by her side, holding her hand.

Shade stepped forward. "You should both go and get some sleep. I'll stay until you get back."

"I'm not leaving her," Beth protested.

"Go and get a couple hours' rest at Sex Piston's parents' house; it's just a few blocks away. I'll call as soon as she wakes."

It was another hour before exhaustion had Beth leaving reluctantly with Razer.

After they left, Shade sat down in the chair by Lily's bed, looking at the woman who had been on his mind since the moment he had seen her come out of the diner across from the sheriff's office. He and Razer had gone there to get their bikes inspected and the sisters had both appeared eating ice cream. Shade had taken one look at the stunning woman and known that he was going to have her.

His lips twisted wryly. He hadn't known then that he was going to have to wait, but patience was his one and only virtue. He waited, planned and plotted to attain his prize, and Lily was a prize. He hadn't been in her company for more than a few seconds before he'd realized she was perfect for him; however, Lily and her sister both had dreams for her, and Shade wanted her to have that time of freedom before he took it away.

His control had almost broken twice. Once when they had gathered for the Fourth of July picnic and he had looked across the backyard to see Lily holding a toddler while Charles, her high school boyfriend, stood close by, touching her. They had looked, for all appearances, like a happy, young family. If his brothers hadn't held him back, he would have ripped the dumbfuck apart. He could tell Charles thought he was staring into his future with Lily. Shade had planned to show him once and only once that Lily would never have anyone other than him. She would never carry anyone's child but his. Charles still remained to be a thorn in his side, though Shade had a plan to deal with him when the time was right.

No one was going to stand in his way when it came to claiming Lily.

The night of Razer's bachelor party had been another time he'd lost control. She had come to Rosie's bar to talk to Razer; she wanted to protect her sister so badly that she had faced her fear of being around alcohol. He had been in the back of the bar with Bliss on his lap, trying to convince him to let her and the stripper take turns later that night, when one of the brothers had given him the heads-up that Lily had entered the bar. Half drunk, he had barged forward, tired of trying to fuck her out of his mind, but Knox had held him back when he had come close enough to hear her true age. He had gone ape-shit.

He was just drunk and horny enough not to care anymore what anyone said. If he could have gotten to her, Lily would have been the one in his bed that night. Of course, he would have had to lock her in and barricade the door against his whole MC, but he wouldn't have had any compunction about doing either one.

Unfortunately, they had managed to hold him back; however, he'd had the satisfaction of his fists pounding out his frustration on each of them, especially on Razer because Shade still didn't trust that Razer had told the truth of not knowing Lily's true age.

After last night, when Lily had coded, there wasn't anyone who didn't know that he had reached his limit. He was done waiting. He had sworn that if Lily survived, she would be his. No more waiting, no more fucking around. He planned to get Lily the way he would have taken on one of his missions in the SEALS. It was why, behind closed doors, he was known as the deadliest sniper in the US armed forces with over two-hundred–and-twenty-six confirmed kills. Those were just the ones they knew about, not the privately contracted ones by the government that he'd still carry out when the price or the reason was

motivating enough. He had been given the nickname
Shade because of his ability to blend into the shadows,
hitting his targets with cold-blooded precision that others
considered impossible.

Part of what made him so successful in taking out his
target was learning everything about them, knowing their
strengths and weaknesses. Especially their weaknesses.

To gain Lily's trust, he had to find out her weakness.
She and her sister had secrets that they hid from everyone,
refusing to talk about Lily's past. No woman had as many
anxieties and fears as Lily without a reason. To reach her,
he would have to overcome those fears.

Each time he had tried to find out about the cause of
her panic attacks, he had been thwarted. Neither had she
confided in Razer or Penni, his sister, who he had
managed to bribe into transferring colleges to become
Lily's roommate, and not even the therapist Beth had
hired. He had broken into her office several times,
searching, but each time he had read her chart, none of the
reasons had been addressed. The therapist was trying to
build Lily's trust slowly. Fuck that. She was for shit as a
therapist, something else Shade intended to change. The
only thing the woman had done was put a rubber band on
Lily's wrist, teaching her to give herself pain as a way to
relieve her anxieties. Shade had every intention of teaching
Lily the same thing, except in a more enjoyable way.

Shade sat by the bed, watching Lily sleep as the day
slipped into night. When the nurses had checked on Lily
and tried to get him to leave the room, his cold gaze had
intimidated them into silence, sending them scurrying.

When the outside had been completely swallowed by
night, Shade got up from the chair, going to the door and
closing it after the nurse. Determined to find out Lily's
secrets, he only had one option left. Razer had let it slip
that Lily slept with her bathroom door open, depending on
a nightlight. Twice since Razer had moved in with Beth,
their electricity had gone off because of storms during the

middle of the night. Both times, Lily had become hysterical when she had awakened in the dark. Beth had to go in both times to calm Lily down.

Lily was beginning to wake; he had noticed she had begun to move about beneath the covers. He prayed the drugs would keep her disoriented enough that, when he was finished, she wouldn't remember what he was about to do. Shade's fingers flipped the light switch, plunging the room into darkness.

CHAPTER ONE

Lily slid the tape across the top of the box, sealing it closed. Her eyes went to the clock on the wall across the large expanse of the factory, and she swallowed hard. It was almost lunchtime; a time of day she had begun dreading each morning as soon as the metal door closed behind her. The same door that was opening now with Evie carrying in a lunch tray to the main office.

One of the workers seated nearby jumped up to open the door for Evie. She laughed, saying something before going inside and shutting the door with her foot. The poor man flushed with pleasure at Evie's words.

Lily slid off her stool, stretching as she tried to ease the muscles that had become stiff. Her hands smoothed down her loose dress, which had ridden up.

"Lily."

She stiffened, turning toward the office door where Shade stood, framed in the doorway. Reluctantly, she made her way to his office. As she drew closer, Evie came out, giving her a friendly smile.

"How's it going today?" Evie asked.

"Fine," Lily replied, smiling back.

"Cool. You two enjoy your lunch," Evie said as she

started to walk away.

"Why don't you stay and have lunch with Shade today? I'm not very hungry," Lily tried to forestall the woman from leaving.

Evie's eyes went to Shade's before coming back to hers. "I've already eaten. I'd better get back; I left Rider doing lunch by himself," Evie said, leaving before Lily could make up another reason for her to stay, not that it would work. It never did.

Lily slipped by Shade, who made no effort to move away from the door, forcing her to brush her body against his. She then took a seat on the chair, sitting next to his desk.

She had been having lunch with him every day for the last month, and she was determined to put an end to it that day. When he had called her into his office after she had first begun working at the factory, she had thought it was because she was new and Razer's sister-in-law, but she had been here for over a month and he was still waiting to have lunch with her. She had tried everything to get out of the tense situation, yet somehow, every day at twelve she found herself sitting in the same chair.

Shade closed the door then took his seat at his desk. Handing her one of the plates with baked chicken and vegetables, he then began eating his own food.

Lily took a bite of the chicken while debating the best way to tell him that he didn't have to tie his lunchtime up with her.

"How's your arm doing since the cast came off?" Shade broke into her thoughts.

"Fine. The doctor said that it was healed."

"When does school start back?"

"In a month." Lily looked down at her food. It went down easier if she didn't look him in the eyes. Shade was always polite, but he made her nervous. He was friends with her sister's husband; both men had looked after her since Razer and Beth had begun seeing each other.

"How many classes are you taking?"

"Four. They're pretty simple ones. I already completed the coursework in my major area. The only courses I have left are just to give me enough credits to graduate."

Shade continued eating his food silently.

Lily took another bite, swallowing it down as she decided to broach the subject on her mind. Clearing her throat, she played with the food on her plate. "I know you and Razer are friends, and I appreciate the club giving me a job for the summer, but I—you don't have to eat lunch with me every day, Shade. I can eat outside with the rest of the workers." Lily released her breath, proud of herself.

"Don't you want to eat lunch with me?" Shade questioned, his gaze steady on her.

"No. Yes. I don't want you to feel like you have to keep me company because of Razer and Beth being your friends."

"Do I seem to be the type to do anything that I don't want to?"

"No." He definitely wasn't that type.

"Good, then that's settled."

Wait, what did that mean? Lily was confused and, unless she made herself look like an ungrateful brat, she was stuck for another month of lunches with Shade.

"Have you applied for any jobs yet?" Shade asked, changing the conversation.

"A couple. One in Jamestown, and two in Colorado."

"Do you think that you'll really be able to handle a job as a social worker?" Shade's voice held doubt, which he made no attempt to conceal.

Lily stiffened in her chair. "Yes, I do. Why?" Her eyes rose angrily from her plate to find him staring at her mockingly.

"Well, you don't exactly take the best care of yourself. How can you look after someone else that needs your help?"

"None of the situations I've been in have been my

fault," Lily protested.

"You need to learn to take care of yourself before you can help take care of other people that will be depending on you."

"I can take care of myself just fine," Lily snapped.

"You could if I taught you how," Shade said, leaning back in his chair.

"What? How?" Lily tried to keep track of the turn in their conversation.

"I could teach you self-defense. That is, unless you change your mind about being a social worker."

"I'll make a good social worker. I—" Lily argued.

"Good, that's settled. Monday, when you come to work, bring some workout clothes. I'll work with you an hour every day at the end of your shift."

"But—"

"If you're finished, could you ask Train to come here?"

Lily stood up, going out the door and then closing it behind her. *What in the heck just happened?* She had gone into his office to get out of spending a half hour of every day with Shade, not to get stuck for another hour each day.

She found Train, giving him Shade's message before going back to work, still trying to figure out how she was going to get out of the self-defense lessons from Shade.

Shaking the thoughts away, Lily pulled another order up on the computer and began pulling the items before going to the table and packing the order. She worked steadily, and by the end of the day, ended up finishing an additional fifteen orders. It was past her usual time of leaving, but Lily had taken the largest order, sitting there for over an hour on the board where the larger orders were posted. No one had wanted to touch it so close to quitting time.

Taping the box closed, she managed to lift it into the mail cart. Proud of herself, she cleaned her worktable, wiping it down. When her scissors accidently fell to the floor, Lily reached down to pick them up.

She felt his gaze on her as she straightened. Her fingertips grazed over the red rubber band on her wrist, trying not to snap it. He didn't like it when she snapped it. She did it to give herself that small sting of pain that would keep her from retreating into her fear because the therapist had said it diverted her anxieties, describing brain synapses and how they worked. Lily didn't care about the reasons. The red rubber band helped. She had come to rely on it to keep her rooted in the present.

Shade's lips would tighten in displeasure whenever he caught her snapping it, letting her know without words to stop. The problem was he increased the need to rely on the rubber band with his presence. One glance from his striking blue eyes had her nerves so on edge that she needed the small snap of pain to soothe her rioting emotions.

Her trembling hands smoothed down her knee-length dress instead.

"I'm done for the day, Shade." Her eyes didn't meet his, instead going to Rider who was sitting on one of the tables nearby. He and Shade had been talking about the orders while they waited for her to finish so they could lock up.

The other factory workers had left over a half hour ago, yet her speed hadn't increased by much since her cast had been removed earlier in the week. The doctor had warned her it would take several weeks to regain the normal strength of her hand.

She had hurried with the last order because she could tell both men were waiting for their weekend to begin. Her own sister would be arriving in a few hours to spend the night at the house sitting on the hill just above the factory. The Last Riders were a motorcycle club who owned the factory and all the surrounding property, including the huge home where they held their weekly party.

Lily smothered her own hurt feelings that she had never been invited. She knew it was because of her reaction to being around men who drank alcohol, but it still hurt that she was excluded from that part of her sister's life.

Her roommate, Penni, had even attempted to help her overcome her fear by taking her to a few parties in college, but those where alcohol had been served had become a failure. She had always let the fear overcome her, sinking into a paralyzing panic that would inevitably result in her friend practically carrying her back to her car.

Lily was ashamed to admit to herself that she was a coward. She was afraid of everything, and the one person that inspired the most fear was Shade.

When he stared at her with his piercing blue eyes, her mind went into panic mode every single time. Her fears had lessened, however, over the last few years since they had met and her sister had married Razer, his best friend.

"Hot damn. Let the good times roll," Rider said, jumping off the table he had been sitting on.

Lily tried to hide her feelings, yet from the sharp look Shade threw Rider at his insensitive comment, she knew she had been unsuccessful.

Lily picked up the scraps of paper lying on her table, throwing them in the trashcan before going back to the table and picking up her purse.

"See you guys Monday." Lily was going out the door as Bliss was coming in.

"Finished for the day?" The pretty member of The Last Riders was extremely feminine and petite, making Lily feel like a gauche fifteen-year-old. She gave her an open smile until her eyes went behind her back and a frown replaced it on her face.

"Yes, have a good weekend, Bliss."

Lily turned her head and saw Rider and Shade staring back at her with cool smiles. Thinking she had mistaken the worried frown, she started out the door then paused, staring down at the outfit Bliss was wearing. The blue jean shorts were tiny as well as the swimsuit top that tied between her breasts. The tat on her breast drew her attention until Bliss hurried past her into the factory.

Lily waved her hand goodbye, closing the door behind her.

She climbed into her car, whistling, relieved to be away from Shade, who managed the factory and its workers. Being in his presence every day the past summer was getting on her nerves. She couldn't believe she was looking forward to school starting back in a month. She had thought she would dread it with Penni graduating in May, but now it couldn't come soon enough.

Beth and Razer, The Last Riders, and even Sex Piston's crew believed she was a walking, talking disaster waiting to happen, regardless of how many times she reminded them that none of the incidents she invariably became involved in were her fault. She simply always managed to be at the wrong place at the wrong time. It wasn't her fault that it happened a lot.

One incident, three months ago, resulted in her almost dying. Ever since then, Shade had watched over her like she was Typhoid Mary and he was just waiting to see what catastrophe would strike next.

Lily didn't want to hurt Beth's feelings; however, Razer's friend was a real jerk. She felt guilty as soon as the word crossed her mind. She tried to find the best in people, but Shade made it really hard.

The familiar strain of "Girls Just Want to Have Fun" sounded from her purse right as Lily was about to pull out of the parking lot. She put the car in park before she reached inside her purse for the ringing cell phone.

"What's up?" Lily asked, seeing her sister's name on the caller I.D.

"Lily, are you still at the factory?" Beth asked.

"Yes." Lily didn't tell her she was sitting in the parking lot, ready to pull out.

"Is Rider there?"

"Yes, he's talking to Shade and Bliss."

"Oh." Beth paused. "That's probably why he's not answering his phone."

"Yes," Lily said without hesitation.

"Can you do me a favor?" Beth's sister sounded tired and frustrated. "My car is broken down at Ms. Langley's house. Can you ask Rider if he can bring the trailer to pick it up? Razer and Viper are going to meet him here to help. They were at the grocery store when I called. I told him I'd call Rider and get him to meet them at her house."

"No problem. I'll tell him right now," Lily offered.

"Thanks. I'll see you later." Beth disconnected the call.

Lily backed into the lot, parking again. Getting out of the car, she went toward the factory with her thoughts on her sister. Opening the door, she came to a stop.

Rider was standing behind Bliss, his arm around her waist with his hand splayed across her bare stomach. Bliss's face was filled with uninhibited excitement as she looked at Shade who was standing a few inches away, staring back at Bliss. Both men had expressions of desire written plainly across their faces.

A shard of pain went through Lily's brain at the same time that the metal door closed with a loud snap, and the tableau turned to stare at her standing at the doorway.

"Uh, um." Lily had to force herself to focus, trying to get her mind in working order. "Rider, Beth's car is broken down at Mrs. Langley's house. She needs you to bring the trailer. Excuse me," she explained her presence to the three frozen in place before turning tail and running. Her hand hit the metal door rail and the door flew open. Lily ran to her car, her face flaming at overreacting and making a fool of herself as always.

She opened her car door hastily, getting back inside. She was reversing out of the parking lot when she saw Shade, Rider and Bliss come out of the factory. She waved at them before turning her car to exit out of the parking lot.

Lily took deep breaths; a headache was beginning,

making driving difficult. Reaching into her purse, not taking her eyes off the road, she searched for her sunglasses. Finding them, she slid them on, hoping it would help the headache that was threatening to make her vomit.

Her hands tightened on the steering wheel while she continued to take deep breaths then released them several times, focusing on her breathing and not on the look on the two men's faces with Bliss between them. Shards of pain again attacked her at the mere thought.

Starting over, she redirected her thoughts, making herself mentally remember what had gone into each order she had filled that day.

She had just finished reciting her fifth order when she thankfully pulled into the driveway of the house she shared with Beth and Razer. Breathing a sigh of relief, Lily got out of her car, going to the door and unlocking it.

Turning on the lights, the tension lessened as she entered the home she had been raised in since her adoption. Shutting the front door, she grabbed a bottled water from the refrigerator in the kitchen before then going upstairs to her room.

The soothing colors of her room relieved her nerves even further. Going to the medicine cabinet, she took out a prescription bottle and removed a pill, swallowing it with another drink of the bottled water she had carried upstairs.

Returning to her bedroom, she slipped off her shoes before lying down on her bed that she made every morning before she went downstairs. She pulled the small quilt her mother had made for her that lay on the bottom of her bed over her, rubbing her cheek against the soft material, letting the pill she had taken make her drowsy.

Closing her eyes, she drifted off, escaping the migraine and the look on Shade's face as he'd watched Rider hold Bliss.

* * *

Lily awoke from her nap with her headache gone.

Finally feeling well enough to wash the smell of the factory off, she took a shower, washing her long hair. Afterward, she dressed in over-large sweat pants and a large t-shirt that hung on her body then brushed her wet hair, leaving it to dry naturally.

Going downstairs barefoot, she found her sister and Razer sitting at the table, eating dinner.

"Are you hungry? I kept a plate warm for you." Beth's eyes searched hers as she started to rise from the table.

"No, thanks, maybe later." Lily picked up a glass from the counter, pouring herself a glass of tea before going into the living room and curling up on the sofa. Flicking on the television, she searched for a program to watch as she listened to Beth and Razer doing the dishes.

Beth eventually came over and sat down on the sofa next to her. "What are you watching?"

"A cooking show." Lily saw the concerned look on her sister's face. "Is something wrong?"

"No. No, I guess not," Beth answered; her eyes looked over Lily's shoulder then returned to hers. "Razer and I were going to the clubhouse, if it's all right with you?"

"Of course," Lily answered.

Beth sighed, getting to her feet and then going upstairs as Razer sat down in the chair next to the couch.

Lily liked Razer. He was laid back and always friendly with her while being a grouch to everyone else.

"How was work today?" he asked casually.

"Fine." Lily shrugged, not taking her eyes off the television screen. "I'm glad you and Beth are going out. You haven't been to a party at the clubhouse since I came home from the hospital." She'd had the misfortune of stopping by Sex Piston's when both her and T.A.'s exes had decided to rob them.

During the robbery, her hand had been broken and she had developed a hematoma when she had hit her head. Since then, both Beth and Razer had been overprotective. They hadn't left her one night by herself. Before, they would spend most of their weekends at the clubhouse.

Their new home they were building themselves was even situated behind the clubhouse. It was almost finished and Lily hadn't been invited to even see it yet.

Her fingers went to the red rubber band on her wrist, snapping it against her flesh.

"What's bothering you, Lily?"

Razer's concerned gaze met hers. She gave him a reassuring smile but didn't confide her hurt feelings at not being invited to the house. She hadn't wanted to foist herself on them without being invited.

"Nothing that a little rest won't solve, Razer." Lily's eyes went back to the cooking show on the television.

Razer's cell rang and he headed into the kitchen to answer it.

The program was almost over when Beth came back downstairs. Her pale-blonde hair had been smoothed down and she had put on smoky eye shadow, giving her a sexy look. Her jeans and t-shirt with boots were all casual, yet Lily saw her lay a covered dress bag on the stair rail.

"I can't wear my skirt on Razer's bike." She always explained with the same reason each time she carried her clothes to the clubhouse.

Lily picked at the red rubber band. They treated her like a child, and Lily was becoming frustrated that they watched everything they said around her.

"I guess we'll be going."

"Have fun." Lily rose from the couch, giving her sister a hug, her frustration at her sister's over-protectiveness disappearing at Beth's look of concern. "Don't worry; I'm going to spend the night catching up on my reading."

Beth gave her a relieved smile. "What are you going to read?"

"I haven't decided yet. I have one about discovering Alaska that I haven't read. I usually read inspirational." Lily smiled. "It may inspire me to leave the lower forty-eight."

"Alaska?" Beth asked, picking up her dress bag.

"When I graduate, I'm thinking of going there. That's why I wanted to work this summer. I've been saving all my paychecks," Lily said enthusiastically.

"Lily, give me time to get over almost losing you before you start talking about going to Alaska."

"All right." Lily laughed, opening the door for her sister. Beth went out frowning while Razer's amused chuckle had her looking up into his laughing eyes.

"Lil' sis, I think you need to dream about visiting a warmer climate." He followed his wife out the door.

Lily locked the door behind them, already missing their company. She didn't enjoy being by herself. The problem was, she didn't fit in with most groups. People her own age thought she was old-fashioned, older groups thought she was immature; the only place she really fit in was at church.

Lily went to the closet and took out her reading bag that she had placed there when she had come home from the library the other day. Taking the oversized bag to the couch, she took a seat, making herself comfortable before she pulled out the large book she was looking for.

The book had a cover of the Alaskan wilderness, which had instantly stirred Lily's sense of adventure. Opening the book, she relaxed back against the soft cushions, tucking her feet underneath her.

She had just turned to the third page when the doorbell rang. Lily went to the door and checked the peephole, pausing before she opened it.

"Open the door, Lily," Shade's impatient voice sounded from the other side.

Lily did as he'd asked, coming face to face with Shade.

He held out his hand with keys in the palm. "Rider fixed the battery in Beth's car." Lily wondered why he hadn't just left it at the clubhouse—Beth could have simply driven it home tomorrow—yet she stayed silent about that.

"Thanks." Lily reached out, taking the keys from his

palm, careful not to touch him.

"Do you mind if I come in? I want to order some Chinese and they won't deliver to the clubhouse."

"Of course not." Lily opened the door wider, letting Shade inside before closing it behind him.

He pulled out his cell and then Lily heard him ordering his food as she retook her seat on the couch. Picking up her book, she started reading again, ignoring the man that had her jumpy again.

Shade took a seat on the couch beside her, looking at the book she was reading. Unconsciously, she stiffened, about to get up from the couch, but Shade's hand on her thigh pressed her back into the cushions. Taking the book from her, he turned it so that he could look at the pages.

"You like Alaska?"

"Yes," Lily said, remaining still.

Shade turned another page. "What do you like about it?"

"The snow. I love snow. I like how pretty it looks on the mountains in the winter." Lily was aware of how silly she sounded.

"It snows in Kentucky," Shade said absently.

"Not deep like it does in Alaska." Lily looked at the pictures as he turned the pages, sinking back onto the couch.

"I've been to Alaska," Shade commented.

"You have?" Lily asked, staring at Shade in surprise. She had never met anyone who had ever been there before. "Is it as beautiful as the pictures?"

"Yes, but I was too busy freezing my ass off to appreciate it at the time."

Lily laughed at his expression.

He began flipping the pages of the book, describing the places he had been to in Alaska. He was describing Juneau when the doorbell rang.

Lily started to get up, but his hand on her thigh pressed her back down onto the couch once more. He went to the door, opening it to the delivery driver, who handed Shade a large bag after Shade pulled out the money to pay him.

Lily watched as Shade closed the door behind the delivery driver. He set the food down on the coffee table before going to the kitchen where he pulled out plates and forks then took out two bottled waters from the fridge.

He returned to the couch, setting the plates down. He then opened the bag of food and began dishing it out onto the two plates.

Lily sat stunned, not knowing what to do except to take the plate he had made for her out of reflex.

"But I thought—" Lily had assumed that he would take the food and leave.

"Eat, Lily. The food would have been cold before I got it back to the clubhouse."

Lily immediately began eating, satisfied with his explanation. Chinese food was actually one of her favorites, but because Beth didn't care for it, she didn't have it often.

Curiously, Lily questioned Shade. "What other places have you been to?"

Lily ate while Shade talked about the different countries he had been to when he had been in the Navy. Listening, she was amazed that he had traveled as much as he had.

"My dad was in the service so we constantly followed him from base to base."

"I bet that was fun."

Shade shrugged. "I didn't mind, but my mother got tired of it quick. That was the main reason they divorced."

"I'm sorry," Lily said sympathetically.

"Don't be. They both remarried and have happy marriages."

Lily finished her food, setting her plate on the table before curling back on the couch, watching as Shade loaded his plate with food again.

Lily picked up the book about Alaska, flipping through the pages while Shade finished eating then took their plates to the kitchen.

"I was going to do that," Lily protested.

"Finish looking at your book. I'll take care of them."

Lily went back to looking through her book, only half-aware when Shade resumed his seat on the couch, looking through the other books on the couch.

"You have several books here on Texas and Arizona," he said.

"Um, hm." Lily turned another page before stopping. Her hands tightened on the book and her stomach turned. She gasped as a blinding pain struck her head again. She dropped the book to the floor as she tried to get to her feet to run to the restroom, feeling as if she was going to lose the food she had just eaten. That was the last thing she remembered.

CHAPTER TWO

Lily woke to a concerned Shade leaning over her. She was briefly disoriented at finding herself lying flat on the couch, but the realization of what had happened came back quickly.

"Lily, are you okay?"

"Yes, I'm fine." She rose up, embarrassed, and Shade helped her back into a sitting position on the couch.

"What happened?" Shade asked, his blue eyes searching hers.

Lily put her hand to her head, but the pain was gone. "I don't know. I was just looking through the book and suddenly got sick. Maybe I had a reaction to the food?"

"I think if it was the food, it would have just made you sick, not faint."

"I had a terrible headache. I've had them on and off my whole life, but they're getting worse. Do you think it could be from when I hit my head during the robbery?"

"I don't think so. Your doctor did several tests to make sure everything was clear. Beth insisted he was thorough since there is so much new information coming out about head injuries."

"I know. It's just that I've never had two in one day

21

before," Lily said shakily, reaching for the bottled water sitting on the coffee table.

"When did you have the other headache?"

"On the drive home. I took a nap when I got home and felt better." Lily sat the bottled water back on the table before reaching down to pick up the books on the floor, sliding them back into the bag.

"I see." Shade handed her one of the books, giving her a speculative look, which she didn't understand. She slid the book into the bag without looking at it.

"Is your headache gone?"

"Yes." Lily brushed her hair back from her pale face. She felt silly for passing out in front of Shade. She consistently seemed to have some incident or other in front of him, which made her appear to be a weakling.

"Maybe watching something on television will take your mind off it." Shade picked up the controller, flipping the channels until he found a comedy.

Lily sat on the couch watching the screen until the show finally managed to draw her into the silly plot. She was still laughing an hour later when the program went off.

Lily stretched, yawning.

"Go to bed, Lily." The friendly man who had sat and shared his travels with her was gone, and in his place was the same withdrawn man that she knew.

"I am tired. Thanks for dinner, Shade." Lily expected him to get up and leave.

"Go on to bed, Lily. I'm going to sleep on the couch."

"There's no need for you to stay," Lily protested.

"You just fainted an hour ago. I'm not leaving unless you want me to call Beth and Razer. I'm sure she would come home."

"I'm not a child you're babysitting that isn't feeling well so you need to call the parents to come home," Lily snapped angrily. "I'm perfectly fine."

"No, Lily, you're not. People who are fine don't almost do a face-plant onto a coffee table. If I wasn't here, you could have hit your head again, and no one would have known until Beth came home in the morning and found you."

Lily gritted her teeth. She had known he was waiting to throw that at her.

"Shade, I'm fine now," Lily repeated her words, hoping this time he would believe her.

"Lily, go to bed, now. I'll lock up. I'll even be a gentleman and leave in the morning before Beth and Razer get home."

Lily knew from his expression that he wasn't leaving.

"Fine. If you want to sleep on a couch, go ahead." Lily angrily left, going up the steps to his mocking laughter.

When she reached her bedroom, she slammed the door behind her then immediately felt guilty. She had never been one to throw temper tantrums and wasn't about to let that stubborn man make her start now.

She lay down on her bed, leaving her bathroom light on as she curled into a ball, pulling the covers over her even though the bedroom was warm; however, she was too drowsy to get up and turn the air conditioner down lower. She had always burrowed beneath the covers to sleep since she had come to live with Beth and her adoptive parents.

As soon as the thought came to mind, Lily pictured an imaginary door blocking all thoughts of her life from before. It was a trick she had learned when she was a little girl, and she still used it to keep all the memories at bay.

She became angry when everyone treated her like a child, yet she used childish tricks to keep the negative tide of emotions away instead of facing them. She didn't want to remember the memories that were locked away behind that door, though. She fought her fears and anxieties every day, terrified that what was behind that imaginary door would take what little sanity she had left.

* * *

The next morning she woke, sitting up, covered in

sweat with her pajamas clinging to her. She took a shower, washing her hair and enjoying the cool water on her overheated flesh. When she dried off, she dressed in a cool, pink sundress that had little cap sleeves. Lily preferred wearing dresses to jeans, liking the loose feel of them on her body than the more constrictive clothes women of her age preferred.

Going to her bed, she pulled the sheets off then put fresh sheets on, making it carefully. She picked up the dirty ones, carrying them downstairs as she hoped Shade had kept his word and left.

Beth and Razer were sitting in the living room drinking coffee when she came down the steps.

"Good morning," Lily said brightly.

"Good morning," they both replied.

"Can I get you some breakfast?" Beth asked, starting to get up.

"No, thanks. I'll pour me a cup of coffee in a minute."

Going into the back laundry room off the kitchen, Lily started her sheets in the wash before pouring herself a cup of coffee.

"Did you have a good time last night?" Lily asked, sitting in the chair, carefully balancing her cup of coffee.

"Yes," Beth answered. Lily wondered at the blush on Beth's face but didn't make a remark.

"What did you do last night?" Beth asked.

"Read for a while, watched some television and then went to bed." Lily watched Beth's face to see if Shade had told them about her fainting then decided he hadn't when her sister's expression remained the same.

"Any plans for today?" Beth asked.

"No. I thought I would just clean the house."

"I'll help," Beth offered.

Razer got to his feet. "I'm going to mow the lawn while you two clean. I'll throw some hamburgers on the grill when I get finished."

"Sounds like a plan." Lily grinned, getting to her feet.

They managed to get most of the cleaning done before Razer had lunch ready. They spent the remainder of the day taking care of the household chores and relaxing. Lily enjoyed spending time with Beth and her husband, knowing the moment wasn't far away when this time would be gone forever.

"What's wrong?" Beth paused in loading the dishwasher.

"Nothing." Lily smiled. "I was just thinking about how things are changing. I'm graduating in December and your house will be ready. I guess I'm already missing you guys."

"Lily."

Lily took her sister's hand when her eyes filled with tears. "Beth, I didn't mean to make you sad."

"I don't want you to leave Treepoint."

"I haven't made up my mind what I'm going to do. It all depends on where I get offered a job. At one time, you didn't want me to settle for Treepoint."

Both of them knew the likelihood of getting a job as a social worker in Treepoint was slim. It was a small county and state jobs didn't open often.

"Promise me that you won't rush out and make a decision if you get offered a job somewhere else?"

"Of course. I prefer to stay in Treepoint." Deciding to lighten the atmosphere, Lily said, "But I have to go find my cowboy first and convince him to come back with me. Penni is loving Texas. I'm thinking of going to visit her after Christmas. The band she's managing, their tour doesn't leave until February."

"That sounds like fun," Beth said, finishing loading the dishwasher.

"I thought so. Maybe I need to change my mind and go after a rocker instead of a cowboy."

* * *

The next morning, they walked to church, enjoying the pretty summer morning. Lily and Beth walked arm-in-arm with Razer following behind. In church, they sat together with Beth in the middle. Many of The Last Riders had begun going to the church. Viper joined Winter in the front with Evie, Jewell and Bliss sitting along the same pew. Lily wondered how many motorcycle club members attended church regularly, not that it really mattered. She was perfectly happy to have this club at her church.

Shade never attended, though. Lily shook away any further reflection on him. She found her thoughts wandering to him more now that she worked with Shade and shared lunch with him every day. Her eyes went to The Last Rider women, wondering at his relationship with them and which one he was involved with. Lily never asked Beth any questions about The Last Riders. Every time she had previously broached the subject, when Beth had first started getting serious with Razer, Beth had avoided discussing the individual members and their relationships. Lily had shrugged it off, not one to invade others' privacy when she didn't want anyone questioning hers.

After the service, they stopped and talked to Pastor Dean who was standing in the front of the church. Lily smiled at him brightly. He was an excellent pastor who had taken over after her father's death a few years before.

"Lily, how are you this beautiful morning?" he greeted her.

"Just fine, Pastor Dean. I enjoyed your sermon."

"Thank you. I have a favor to ask of you. Several parishioners have made donations which I put in the basement. Since it has a separate entrance, I thought that, if I could get a couple of volunteers to clean out the basement and then organize the donations, I could open it to the public who need our help."

"I think that's a wonderful idea. I would be glad to help," Lily offered.

"I would appreciate it. Rachel has volunteered to help next Saturday. Does that work for you?" Pastor Dean asked.

"Yes," Lily said eagerly.

"I could help," Beth joined in the conversation.

"I think Rachel and Lily will be enough for now, but thanks for offering. If it becomes too much for them, I'll give you a call."

"Oh, okay."

Pastor Dean gave Beth a warm smile. "Beth, you have plenty to keep you busy with our food outreach program. I think that's enough of a contribution of your time."

Beth laughed. "I do stay pretty busy. I've promised Razer I wouldn't take on anything else until we get in our new house."

"I have every confidence that you can accomplish anything you set your mind to, Beth." Lily watched as Beth gave Pastor Dean a bright smile at his response. Her sister was so pretty standing in the sun with her flaxen hair shining and her light-colored, paisley dress. She looked like an angel. Lily turned away, her eyes darkening with torment. *Not like me with my demons constantly chasing through my mind.*

Attempting to shake herself from the feeling, Lily walked to the sidewalk and waited for Beth and Razer. Her eyes drifted across the street to the diner, seeing the motorcycles outside the restaurant.

"Ready?" Beth asked, coming to stand by her side.

"I'm not going to join you today. I thought I would go on home. I'm not very hungry." She wasn't in the mood to go to lunch and watch everyone monitoring their words around her.

"That's fine. I'll go with you and fix us something later," Beth said.

"Don't be silly. Go have lunch. I can manage an hour on my own, Beth."

Beth hesitated. "All right. I'll see you in a little while."

Lily smiled, brushing a kiss on her sister's concerned face. "You worry too much."

Lily waved at the others as she left, walking down the

sidewalk back to their home. It really was a lovely morning and Lily enjoyed the walk on the tree-lined road. They always walked to church and then would have lunch at the diner. The Last Rider members that didn't make it to church would meet them at the diner afterward for lunch.

She had seen Shade's bike outside and knew he would be waiting inside with Train and Rider. Those three needed to go to church more than anyone else. From the way her friends acted, they kept the women population busy.

Several of her girlfriends from high school, who still lived in Treepoint, were constantly talking about how good looking the men were. They had even tried to use Lily to gain an introduction to them. When they saw that Lily wasn't going to perform the introductions, though, they had devised other means. A couple had even succeeded, unable to hide their glee at showing off in front of the others, yet when the others would ask what they were like, a secretive look would appear, and the girls would change the subject.

Lily wasn't a fool. It didn't take a rocket scientist to figure out that the club had a policy about keeping quiet about what took place at the clubhouse. Again, Lily had to smother her hurt feelings. She felt as if each day she and Beth were drawing further apart.

Pushing away yet another bothersome thought, she turned the corner onto her street. It never failed to give her a sense of homecoming when she saw her house.

As she walked, Lily began to feel as if someone was watching her, though. She looked around, not seeing anyone, yet she unconsciously began to walk faster, not sure why. She felt chills crawl down her back and goose bumps rise on her arms.

Thankfully, she came to her house, rushing up the two steps to the door, and quickly slid the key into the keyhole. Once inside, she locked the door behind her, taking a step back to stare at the closed door.

It took several minutes for the quiet sound of the

house to steady her nerves, feeling silly that she had overreacted.

Sitting her purse on the table by the door, she resolved to herself that maybe letting Shade teach her a few moves on defending herself might not be a bad idea after all.

CHAPTER THREE

Lily pulled into the parking lot of The Last Riders. As she parked her car, she saw Train talking to Kaley. She was the sister of a friend of hers from high school, Miranda. Miranda had been worried about her sister since her divorce from her high school sweetheart. Kaley had caught her husband cheating, and ever since then, she had been trying to even the score.

Lily felt terrible for Kaley. She didn't know her that well, but she still remembered the agony that Beth had gone through when she had caught Razer cheating.

Lily parked her car and stepped out. She had to walk by the two as she went to the door of the factory.

"Good morning, Kaley, Train."

"Hi, Lily." Kaley stared back at her with a frown.

"Morning, Lily." Train nodded his head. Of all The Last Riders, Lily knew Train the least. She had been around him as much as the others; he was just the quietest of the group.

Lily continued on to the factory, hesitating briefly when she saw Shade standing in the doorway and holding the door open for her.

"Good morning, Shade." Lily smiled.

"Lily." His eyes went to Lily before moving over her shoulder to Kaley and Train.

Lily brushed by him without stopping, going inside to get busy. Orders were already waiting on the board. She took a minute to look over the orders waiting to be filled and then picked two of the larger ones.

"Going to save one for me?" Hardin asked from behind her back.

Lily laughed, stepping to the side. "I might if you weren't so slow," she joked back at the young man she had met since coming to work for The Last Riders.

Hardin took one of the orders off the board. "Why don't you take one of the work stations next to mine and I'll show you how it's done."

Lily's reply was cut off by Shade's irritated voice. "Lily's work station is the one I put her at; yours is going to be at the unemployment office if you don't get busy."

Lily started to get angry at Shade's rude remark, but she quickly smothered any comment she would have made when his gaze fell on her. She wouldn't use her connection to Beth to say what she wanted to Shade. In reality, he was her boss and she should watch her words. That didn't prevent her reproachful eyes from meeting his when Hardin hurried to his work station.

"Don't look at me like that, Lily. He deserved it. Get to work."

Lunchtime came much quicker than she wanted. Today, it was Bliss who delivered their lunch. Lily kept working, hoping that she wouldn't hear her name. Bliss stayed inside his office several minutes before they both came out. The attractive girl with the short blonde hair was smiling seductively back at him and then waved at Lily as she left.

Lily waved back at her. Bliss was another member who Lily could never figure out which Last Rider she was involved with. At one time, Lily had suspected it was her who Razer had cheated with on Beth, but Beth had never confirmed or denied it. Lily guessed Beth didn't want her to hold it against whichever woman it had been. Lily was glad she didn't know, too. She wasn't sure she wouldn't have held a grudge after witnessing firsthand how badly her sister had been hurt.

"Lily."

Lily set down the box she was working on, going to Shade's office. Her hands clenched at her side, she was determined that today was the day she would put a stop to eating lunch in his office with him.

She didn't miss the speculative look that Hardin and several of the other workers cast her way as she entered his office.

She took the seat next to his desk as he closed the door and resumed his seat, handing her one of the trays with a grilled chicken salad. Lily ate her lunch quickly, wanting to get it over with so she could get out of the office.

"What's the rush?" Shade asked.

Lily finished chewing the bite in her mouth, perturbed. He never let anything slide by his notice.

She decided to quit beating around the bush, which hadn't been working anyway. "I think it's better if I eat lunch with everyone else," Lily delicately began.

"No." Shade took a bite of his own food while Lily sat stunned. She had just told him she didn't want to eat with him. She was caught unaware by his blunt refusal, not knowing how to be blunter, other than becoming mean, and she didn't want to take that route with him.

"But—"

"Did you bring a change of clothes?" he asked, looking at her pink dress.

Lily felt herself flush as his eyes lingered on the tiny buttons at the front of her dress. "Yes."

Shade kept eating while Lily continued to eat more slowly, brainstorming a way out of this ridiculous situation.

"Why didn't you eat lunch at the diner yesterday?"

"I wasn't hungry," Lily snapped.

Shade's stern mouth twitched in amusement.

"If you didn't eat lunch in here, what would you do for lunch, Lily?"

"I would eat lunch outside with the other workers," Lily said honestly.

"You don't need to eat lunch with them. You would become too friendly with them and they will start to take advantage."

"That's ridiculous."

"Is it? They all are aware that your sister is married to one of the owners of the factory."

Lily finished eating her salad in silence, coming to the conclusion she wasn't going to win this argument with Shade.

"I would never use my connection to Razer."

"I think it's better to not put you in that position. Is it so hard to keep me company for lunch?"

"I don't think you lack for company, Shade," Lily teased him wryly as she got to her feet.

"Really, what makes you say that?" His eyes bore into hers.

She speculated, "I'm pretty sure that any of The Last Riders would join you for lunch, not to mention the other women who work here. Several of the women are interested in you. They ask me constantly if you're seeing someone."

"Tell them to mind their own business."

Lily laughed at his disgruntled expression. Opening the door, she glanced back. "I can't do that, Shade. I wouldn't presume on my relationship with you to speak for you." She closed the door before he could say anything else. For once, she actually felt as if she had gotten in the last word.

* * *

Lily worked steadily the whole day, stopping only once for a quick break when she had stepped outside for a breath of fresh air, drinking a bottled tea.

Hardin came outside not long after and they stood

chatting casually.

"What are you two taking such a long break for?" Georgia asked as she walked up to them. Lily tried to like the woman approaching them, but she made it extremely difficult. She had made floor manager, and she used her power to intimidate the others. Lily had begun to notice she picked unnecessarily on those she didn't like, finding fault with their work and often making them redo orders.

"It hasn't been fifteen minutes yet," Hardin replied, his face losing the smile.

Georgia's eyes narrowed in on Hardin. "If flirting means more than your job, then keep on trying to antagonize Shade," she snapped, jerking her head toward Shade who was talking to Rider as he worked on one of the member's bike. Without another word, Georgia turned on her heel, walking back into the factory.

Hardin turned to look at Shade who hadn't turned his attention away from them before turning back to Lily. "If there's something going on between you two, it would be nice to know. That's twice today my job has been threatened because I was talking to you."

Lily shook her head. "He's a family friend, that's all. My sister is married to his friend."

"Uh, huh."

Lily threw her bottle away in the recycle bin. "That's all it is."

"In that case, want to go see a movie with me this weekend?"

Lily paused. She liked Hardin; however, she didn't want to encourage anything further. "I stay pretty busy on the weekends, but thanks anyway."

"I didn't think you would, but I thought I would give it a shot." He grinned at her, holding the door open for her.

They got back to work and the rest of the afternoon went quickly.

"See you tomorrow, Lily," Hardin said on his way out the door.

"Hardin, I need to see you in my office." Shade stood in the doorway, holding his door open.

Hardin cast Lily a glance before going into the office where Shade shut the door behind them. Lily cleaned her workstation and was just putting the last package in the cart when Hardin came out of Shade's office. His friendly expression was gone and his face was pale.

"Is everything all right?" Lily asked.

Hardin didn't speak to her, walking past her to leave the building at the same time that Shade came out of his office.

"Is everything all right?" she asked Shade this time.

"Everything is fine," Shade said with his usual, detached expression.

"Why was Hardin upset?"

"That's none of your business." When Lily would have said something else, Shade forestalled her. "But I'll tell you anyway. I gave him a promotion. We need another driver so he's going to be working on the trucks from now on."

Lily looked out the window as Hardin sped out of the parking lot.

"He doesn't seem to be very happy about his promotion."

"I'm sure he's not," he said grimly. "Are you ready?"

Lily nodded her head and then followed him outside.

"I need to get my clothes."

Shade waited by the steps as she grabbed her small travel bag out of the backseat of her car.

"Where are we going to work out?" Lily asked curiously, as she walked back to his side.

"In the gym in the basement." Shade walked up the path that had been laid, leading up to the side of the clubhouse to make it easier for Winter to walk up instead of all the steps. The concrete path had taken them a couple of months to lay and led around the house to the backdoor. Lily had only been to the clubhouse once and that was when Winter had married Viper, The Last Riders' president.

Instead of going in through the kitchen door, Shade opened another door at the side of the house, leading into what looked like the basement where there was a full-fledged gym inside.

Lily looked around curiously. When she had started work at the factory, Beth had told her there was only one rule: she wasn't allowed in the clubhouse. Lily had been hurt, but she had agreed, hiding the hurt she had felt. Beth had gone on to explain that the men liked to drink sometimes during the day and they didn't want her upset if she inadvertently came in while they were drinking. Lily had agreed, not wanting her sister to feel bad since she had used her connection to Razer to get her the job in the first place.

The room was very large with exercise equipment, and there was a pole set up in the middle of the room like the one Lily used in her pole-dancing class at school. There was also a large couch and a flat screen television.

"You can get changed back here." Shade walked across the room, opening another door. As she approached the room he indicated, she noticed that there was a door on the right, another to the left and then another down at the end of the hallway.

"That room has the hot tub." Shade pointed to the door on the left. "That's the restroom where you can get changed. The door at the end is my room. I'll wait for you in the gym." Shade left her in the hallway.

Lily went into the bathroom, amazed at the space. It was large, with a five-piece set and a shower.

She changed quickly, not wanting to keep him waiting. Taking off her dress and putting it in her bag, she took out her clothes. She would just wear her workout clothes home; she didn't feel comfortable keeping him waiting while she showered.

Her stomach clenched with butterflies, not quite believing she was going to go through with letting him teach her self-defense. Only her determination to become a social worker had her going through with it. If she was going to try to protect others, then she first had to learn to protect herself. Yesterday had proved her vulnerability when she had locked the door against whatever had been following her. If they had gotten in, she wouldn't have known what to do.

She put on her sweat pants and oversized sweatshirt and then her tennis shoes. Taking out a rubber band, she gathered her dark hair into a tight ponytail on the back of her head. Gathering what confidence she had, she picked up her bag and went back outside where Shade was in a pair of shorts and a t-shirt.

She came to a stop. She hadn't realized he would be changing also.

Lily felt his eyes run over her as he took in her clothes.

"What kind of workout clothes are those?"

"It's what I always wear," she said.

"Then you need to get some different ones. Those won't do." Shade motioned for her to stand on the mat. Lily came to stand in front of him where he was pointing. Shade was taller than her, but he was actually the smallest in size of The Last Riders. He was lean, but Lily noticed his tattoo-covered arms were muscular.

Shade had her warm up first by stretching, which he also did, and then he moved her again to where she was standing in front of him.

Shade showed her how to kick out at him, which he blocked over and over again.

"Come on, Lily; you can do better than this."

Lily tried to move, striking out with her foot several times.

"That's enough," he said when she stopped to catch her breath. "At least you're in good shape physically, but you need to do some weight training."

Lily nodded her head. "I agree. Thanks, Shade."

"When we're in here, you call me Sir."

"Okay." Personally, Lily thought he was taking his role of instructor a little too seriously, but she wasn't going to make a big deal out of it. The few tips he had shown her today were enough to make her see that she would be easily victimized as she had been in the past if she didn't continue. Maybe, if Shade taught her well enough, she would be better prepared.

Picking up her bag, she turned to leave, surprised when Shade walked her back out to her car.

"Bye, Shade."

"Later." Shade closed the car door and watched as she pulled out of the parking lot. Lily shivered as the air conditioner kicked on, cooling her overheated flesh. She was not sure what the look she had caught on Shade's face in her rearview mirror meant, yet a sense of foreboding overcame her.

On her way home, Lily decided to stop at the local discount store for a different workout outfit. She was going to the checkout when she saw her friend, Miranda, who was pushing a cart with her young daughter in the basket.

"Hi, Lily."

"Hi, Miranda."

They chatted pleasantly for several minutes before Miranda brought up her sister. "Kaley quit her job at the pharmacy in town. I'm really worried about her."

Lily didn't tell Miranda she had seen Kaley at The Last Riders' clubhouse. She didn't like gossips and made it a point not to do it herself.

"I'm sure she'll be fine. I've got to go, Miranda. It was nice seeing you again."

Lily checked out, feeling guilty for not telling her friend, yet Kaley was a few years older than both Miranda and Lily, and she was sure that the woman wouldn't be happy if she knew her sister was spreading her private business around town.

Lily drove home and took a quick shower before

getting dressed and fixing dinner for herself, Beth and Razer.

When they arrived home, they ate dinner before going into the living room to watch a movie. It was times like this, as they sat and watched television, sharing popcorn, that Lily would miss.

Later, as she got ready for bed, she turned off her bedroom light, leaving her bathroom light on. Snuggling under her covers, she stared at the light coming from the bathroom until she fell asleep.

* * *

The next day was uneventful with Hardin gone. His company had made the time go by faster. None of the other workers made any attempt to talk to her, despite her friendly overtures. Georgia especially would send the workers to do odd jobs if she saw anyone lingering, talking to her. By lunchtime, Lily was beginning to get upset.

She ate her lunch quietly, unaware of the speculative looks she was receiving from Shade.

"Anything wrong?"

Lily shook her head, picking at her hamburger and fries. "No."

"Are you sure?"

"Yes," Lily said glumly.

Shades lips twisted. "You're very emotional, aren't you?"

Lily stiffened in her seat. "I'm sorry if I can't be emotionless like you. I get a little upset when people run like the plague when I approach them."

"Who's running?"

"The other workers. If I try to talk to them, they ignore me and move away."

"I'm sure you're exaggerating," Shade said, eating his own food with a hearty appetite.

"I'm not exaggerating. I asked Gaige if he knew where the pocket flares were, and you would have thought I had asked for condoms. I asked Trent to help me find a packet of seeds, and he walked off while I was still talking to him. And, in case you didn't know, Georgia is a reincarnated Attila the Hun."

Shade burst out laughing and Lily's hurt feelings disappeared a little. When Shade laughed, his appearance softened and he was a very handsome man. Lily had never really noticed before and she wasn't happy about noticing now. She carefully opened the imaginary door in her mind and thrust the thought inside; then her hand went to her wrist, snapping the red rubber band.

"Why did you do that?" Shade snapped.

Lily handed him her partially untouched plate, preparing to get to her feet.

"Sit down." His hard voice had her bottom immediately returning to her seat, her eyes going to her hands which were on her lap.

"Eyes to me, Lily."

Lily's eyes reluctantly returned to his.

"Answer my question. Why did you snap the rubber band?"

"I don't know. It's just a habit. Sometimes I do it without knowing why," Lily said softly.

"I see. I only give instructions once, Lily. The next time you snap that rubber band around me, you better be able to explain why. Do you understand me?" Shade's hard, blue gaze stared directly into hers.

Lily nodded her head. Her hands clenched to prevent herself from snapping the band again.

"I need to get back to work," Lily said, this time succeeding in getting to her feet and going out the office door.

Breathing a sigh of relief, she went back to work, going through the orders so fast that Georgia looked at her strangely, though thankfully, she stayed off Lily's case for the rest of the day.

At quitting time, Lily cleaned her workstation and went to her car to get her workout bag. She reentered the factory to see Shade leaning against the doorway to his office with Georgia talking to him. The usually grouchy expression was gone from her face, replaced with one of flirtation.

Lily didn't interrupt; she personally thought the two of them would be a match made in Heaven.

Shade talked for a few minutes longer before ending the conversation, walking toward Lily. Georgia's face behind Shade's back changed into one that made Lily agree that they were made for each other, and then she felt guilty for wishing Georgia on anyone. The woman wasn't in the least way nice, and while Shade wasn't the friendliest person, he had always watched out for her.

"What has you looking so guilty?" Shade asked.

Lily, as always, tried to be honest. "I was thinking that you and Georgia would make a nice couple."

Shade's face closed off. "Really?"

"That's when I felt guilty. In case you didn't know, she's really not a nice person."

Shade gave Lily a look she couldn't interpret. "I think I can handle Georgia," he said, walking to the door of the factory and holding it open for her.

"That's good to know. Then I think you should go for it. She obviously has a thing for you," Lily said helpfully.

Shade stopped in his tracks. "Lily, have I given you the impression I want to be your BFF?"

"Noo…"

"Good."

Lily followed behind Shade's quick strides, trying to hide her hurt feelings. When he opened the door to the basement, waiting for her to enter, Lily avoided his eyes as she went inside.

"I'll go get changed," Lily said, heading straight to the restroom. It didn't take her long to get changed, but Shade still beat her, already working out on the weights.

He paused when she entered the room, his eyes going to her new workout outfit. Shade didn't say anything, but

Lily could tell he didn't like her choice of clothes.

The black leggings were several sizes too large, and the top was spandex but was also too large with long sleeves.

Shade placed his weights down. "Come here."

Lily moved toward him.

Shade spent the next hour with her weight training, making sure the hand that had been broken started with minimal weight.

"Two more, Lily." She was lying on the bench, lifting weights, when Shade's hand went to the inside of her thigh.

"Keep your legs straight." Shade's hand guided her leg to where he wanted it.

Lily stiffened, almost dropping the weight.

"Keep your arms steady." His hand glided up the length of her arm, steadying it.

Lily forced herself to straighten her trembling arms then almost dropped the weights when his hand lay flat on her stomach. The thin material of her shirt was no barrier against the warmth of his hand.

"Breathe, Lily."

Lily took a deep breath then released it. She was beginning to feel surrounded by Shade.

"That's enough for today." Shade straightened, standing above her.

Lily felt him take the weights from her as she hastily got to her feet. She was thankful that the awkward experience was over.

"Two days a week we'll work on weight training. The other three we'll work on your defense moves."

"That sounds good," Lily said, not looking at him as she picked up her workout bag. "I appreciate your help, Sir." She made herself refer to him the way he expected before she went to the door, not waiting for him, but she was very aware of him watching her as she made her way to her car.

Lily drove home, debating calling an end to their

workout sessions. Her hand constantly snapped the rubber band against her wrist all the way home.

At dinnertime that evening, she was loading the dishwasher when Beth gasped. "Lily."

She looked at her sister, seeing her horrified look, then looked down at her wrist. It was an angry red and was becoming inflamed.

"What have you done to yourself?" Beth exclaimed, becoming upset with tears in her eyes.

"Nothing," Lily demurred, continuing to load the dishwasher. "I hadn't even noticed that I was doing it."

"Something must have upset you. What was it?" Beth asked.

"Nothing. Honestly, I don't understand it, either," Lily said truthfully.

Beth took a deep breath. "Okay, but next time be more careful."

"I will." Lily didn't miss the concerned look that passed between Razer and Beth.

She had to get herself back under control, she thought, glancing down at her wrist. Whatever was triggering her anxiety had to be faced. She couldn't keep avoiding it. Sooner or later, she was going to have to face her fears. Hopefully, she wouldn't lose her mind when she did.

Upstairs, she changed into her pajamas, turning off her light but leaving the bathroom light on.

The wind blew against the window and Lily shivered. The wind was picking up, yet she didn't worry about it. There had been no storm warnings posted.

Snuggling under her covers, she curled onto her side, letting her mind go back to the dinner that evening. Beth had looked so happy with Razer. The love Beth and Razer shared was special. Lily knew she would never find happiness like her sister; however, she would be satisfied if she could find someone to share her life with and have children. She wanted several children, though she feared the likelihood of finding the perfect father didn't exist.

Lily was certain that everything that she loved was eventually destroyed with the exception of Beth. She was the one constant in her life. If she was ever taken away, Lily didn't know what she would do. She was the one person that kept her rooted and sane.

Lily knew that even when she was in college, all she had to do was call and Beth would be there.

God help her if the day ever came that she wasn't.

CHAPTER FOUR

She was able to calm her nerves by Friday, relieved that the weekend was almost here. The day was spent working steadily. She didn't even let eating lunch with Shade faze her. Lily had managed to start loosening up around him slightly since she was spending so much extra time with him every day.

Jewell and Bliss were laughing and cracking up, making jokes as they worked next to each other. Lily noticed that Georgia didn't say anything to the two women; in fact, she seemed to be trying to get friendly with them. While both women were always friendly to her, neither made any real attempt to become better acquainted.

After lunch, Lily went into the back room and was trying to straighten the seeds when several packs spilled out. Leaning over, she was attempting to put them back when the door opened and Gaige came in.

"Need some help?"

"I think I've got it under control," Lily replied. She always felt uncomfortable when he was around. He inevitably managed to make her feel dirty when he looked at her.

Before she could rise up, his hand slid under the hem

of her dress, sliding against her bottom. Lily dropped the seeds she was holding to the floor, jerking away from his touch.

She didn't say anything as she quickly went to the door.

"Hey, I was just joking," he uttered.

As soon as the door clicked behind her, she started shaking; however, her hand managed to slide into the pocket of her dress to pull out her phone. Praying silently to herself, she pressed Beth's number and put the phone to her ear, aware of Bliss, Jewell and Georgia looking at her strangely.

Shakily, she managed to begin the walk to her workstation, becoming more and more upset that Beth wasn't answering. She needed Beth when the darkness was about to hit. Beth could talk to her and calm her down.

Shade was standing by Train in his office, but she noticed his eyes were on her. She ran her fingers through her hair as a whimper passed her lips. She needed Beth!

The door opened and Razer's familiar figure walked through as another whimper unconsciously passed her lips. She took a step toward him.

"Lily!" Lily stopped, her hands going to her hair. "Lily, come here. Now!" Lily's feet changed direction and she moved toward Shade, trying not to whimper again as both men moved out of the doorway.

"Go take your chair." Lily wanted Razer if she couldn't have Beth. He would get Beth for her.

"I need Beth," she managed to get out between chattering teeth.

"Go take your chair," Shade repeated, his expression hard. He took her jaw in his hand. "What did I tell you about me repeating instructions?"

"Shade?" Razer's concerned voice was behind Lily's back, but she couldn't turn to him because Shade still had her jaw in his grip.

"I will handle this, Razer." Lily shivered at the look Shade gave Razer. Shade's hand dropped from her face.

She heard Train mutter, "I'll take care of it," before Shade came inside the office and shut the door.

"Go stand in the corner, Lily." Shade's hard voice kept the darkness from taking over.

"Now," he snapped.

Lily's feet immediately took her to the corner where she stood, facing the office, while Shade took his seat back at the desk and resumed doing his paperwork as if she wasn't there.

Lily didn't know what to do or how to feel. She took a deep, shuddering breath, leaning her head on the wall.

"Stand up straight." Shade didn't take his eyes off his paperwork, pushing a few buttons on his computer before making more notes. Lily straightened, her hand going to her wrist.

"No." This time his eyes looked up, daring her to snap the rubber band. Her hand reluctantly fell to her side. Concentrating on what she could and couldn't do, she eventually drew her mind away from Gaige touching her. The dual pressures of remaining straight and not snapping the rubber band were not letting her focus on the feel of his hand under her dress.

Lily's eyes found the clock, watching it as the minutes ticked by.

It was weird, yet she felt herself gradually letting the stress of the encounter leave her body, feeling safe in the enclosed office with Shade.

"Come here, Lily." Lily didn't hesitate; she went to his side as he pushed his chair back from his desk. His hand reached out to snag her hand, jerking her down to sit on his thigh.

Lily started to go wild.

"Sit still."

Lily quit fighting, sitting stiffly on his thigh. Shade didn't attempt to touch her further, his hand going back to the computer screen, moving the cursor to begin going through the email.

"The Farthings ordered three more cases of MREs. I think they're planning for World War III." He went down the emails, checking them off one by one. Sometimes he would make a remark, sometimes he wouldn't.

"So what happened to get you upset?" Shade finally asked as he scrolled down the list for the next email.

Lily, reading the email requesting survival kits, told him without thinking. "When I was in the back room, Gaige came in. I was bent over the refrigerator and he slid his hand underneath my dress."

"I would be upset if he tried to touch my ass, too," Shade remarked, still working and not looking at her.

Lily laughed. She couldn't believe it, but she laughed.

"Did he try to stop you from leaving the room?" Shade probed.

"No. I probably overreacted. I know how silly I sound."

"You didn't overreact. He had no business touching you," Shade said, his hand going to her hip, adjusting her so that she sat more comfortably on his leg. Several more minutes passed.

"Are you all right now?"

"Yes. Thanks, Shade." She stood up, feeling ridiculous for freaking out over something that women had dealt with for years in the workplace.

Lily opened the door, going back to work, aware that everyone's eyes were on her with Georgia throwing her annoyed glances.

"Are you okay?" Bliss and Jewell both stopped by her workstation as they left.

"I'm fine. I just overreacted."

"Do you need anything before we leave?" Bliss gave her a friendly smile.

Lily hesitated before she asked, "Would you mind getting me a number four green bean pack from the refrigerator?" She felt like such a coward for asking Bliss.

"No problem," Bliss said, turning to go to the back

room to get the item.

"I'll handle it, Bliss. You two go on up to the club." Lily watched as Shade walked up to them. The two women left, giving her a sympathetic look.

"Go get the seeds. I'll wait here," Shade told her.

Lily almost refused but knew she was being silly. Gaige hadn't been around for the rest of the afternoon, and she had gone into the room numerous times before without incident.

She went to the room, passing a gloating Georgia who was really beginning to wear on her nerves. She was mildly relieved when she heard Shade tell her she could leave as she passed.

Lily hurried and opened the refrigerator and found the seeds quickly, closing the door and going back to her station. Shade watched as she finished her order while the rest of the workers left for the day. When Lily had completed the order and cleaned her workstation for Monday, she was relieved that the day was finally at an end.

"Go get your bag while I lock up," Shade ordered.

"But I thought—" Lily protested. She really wanted to go home.

Shade tilted his head to the side in question.

Resigned, Lily gave in. "I'll go get my bag." Lily had thought he would let her slide on working out tonight because of the incident; however, she should have known better. The hard man didn't have an inch of leeway in him. Her conscience argued with her over how he had managed to calm her from a full-fledged panic attack.

Grabbing her bag, she followed Shade to the basement and went to get changed. Shade was warming up on the mat when she returned and Lily sank to the mat to begin stretching. Shade watched her before standing up and turning on the music. He hadn't turned the music on during their previous workouts, so Lily looked at him in question, yet Shade didn't say anything, moving her into position to begin her defense training. He worked on her kick for several minutes, becoming irritated when she didn't connect with him.

Lily began to become distracted; the noise from upstairs was loud. She could tell it was a large group of people from the voices filtering down the steps. She could hear the feminine and male laughter. Lily understood now why Shade had turned on the music to try to disguise the noise from upstairs.

"Pay attention, Lily. If you used more strength, we would have been done ten minutes ago and I would be upstairs drinking a cold beer."

Probably with one of the women by his side, Lily thought, kicking out sharply and managing to catch Shade on the side of his thigh.

"About fucking time." Shade smiled at her proudly.

Lily was amazed at herself and contrite at the same time. "Did I hurt you?"

"No, Lily, you didn't hurt me. Next time a dick like Gaige tries to touch your ass again, try that move."

Lily grinned back. "Okay."

"We're done for the day."

"Thanks, Sir." Lily was finding it easier to address him as Sir when they worked out.

Going for her bag, she picked it up before she hesitated for a moment, twisting the handle of the bag in her hand. "Thanks for getting me to go get the seeds. I would have just avoided the room."

"I know. Lily, let's work on getting rid of the old fears before adding new ones. You're completely safe at the factory and here."

"I know that."

"Good. I'll see you Sunday."

"All right." Lily left with a spring in her step and a smile at her accomplishment. For the first time, she was beginning to feel herself capable of taking control of her physical well-being.

* * *

Lily fielded Beth's concern when she arrived home. Beth was hesitant to leave her that evening, but Lily assured her she was fine. Actually, for the first time, she was looking forward to some time alone.

After Beth and Razer left, Lily showered and put on her pajamas before going downstairs to watch television. A music show was on and Lily found herself dancing around the living room. Penni would often dance with her when the mood struck Lily to dance, which was something she had never done with a boy. She enjoyed dancing when no one was watching, though.

Lily laughed when she finished one song, spinning herself until she was almost dizzy. She didn't often let herself go. Her personality was always held in check, so when she finally did, she did it wholeheartedly.

She was getting a drink of water when the doorbell rang, and she looked down at herself, seeing her dark blue fleece pajamas.

Going to the door, she looked out the peephole before answering it. Shade stood there, holding two pizza boxes and a six-pack of beer.

Lily just stood there with her mouth open.

"Move, Lily, before I drop the pizza."

Unlocking the door, Lily took a step back, letting him enter. Shade came in, setting the pizza and beer on the coffee table.

"What are you doing here?" Lily asked, closing the door before walking barefoot back to the couch.

"I thought you might be hungry." The smell coming from the boxes was delicious. Lily's stomach grumbled. "Go grab us a couple of plates."

She went into the kitchen, getting the plates and her bottled water.

She sat down on the couch as Shade opened the box, putting two slices on her plate. She immediately took a bite of the warm pizza, loving the taste of the melted cheese on

51

her tongue.

Shade put two slices on his own plate and began devouring his. They ate quietly as Lily put a movie on for them to watch. She stiffened when she heard the beer can open, refusing to look his way. Her hand trembled; however, she tried to act as if it was no big deal.

Shade began to talk about the movie they were watching and the two others in the series.

Lily relaxed back into the cushions, but not before taking another slice of pizza. She was full to the brim when she sat her plate back on the table, engrossed in the movie.

Shade had grabbed himself another piece of pizza and she heard another beer open. She crowded herself closer to the side of the couch, not watching as he drank it.

When he finished, he cleaned the table and put the beer in the fridge before relaxing back on the couch. The movie ended and they argued about what to watch next. Lily was through half of the second movie when she dozed off, her head on the side of the couch.

Feeling herself lifted, she was laid next to Shade as he sprawled out on the couch. She smelled the faint odor of beer on his breath and was amazed that she was letting him this close to her. She was simply too sleepy and full to protest his dispassionate hold.

"Go back to sleep."

Getting up early and her long day had combined to make her doze heavily with her head on his arm. Her taut body was relaxed. Her bottom was against his thighs and his upper body didn't touch her. Plus, his closeness didn't set off any of her inner alarms.

She felt safe. The words played softly through her mind. Had she ever felt safe?

When she woke the next morning, Shade was gone and she was lying on her bed, covered in blankets. Lily sat up, confused as to how he had moved her without waking her. She looked at the bedside clock then hurried to the bathroom to shower and dress.

Beth and Razer weren't back yet, so she made herself a piece of toast and left a note saying she was going to the church.

Rachel was hard at work when she got there, already going through the boxes in the basement.

"Sorry I'm late," Lily apologized.

"Don't worry about it," Rachel replied. Lily liked Rachel and owed her a debt she would never be able to repay. The night the town deputy had tried to kill her and Winter, Lily had run into the woods to escape. Rachel had found her and taken her into her home that she shared with her three brothers who were very protective of their sister.

"How's Logan doing?" Lily asked about Rachel's nephew.

"Growing like a weed. He's going to be as tall as my brothers."

Lily moved some boxes around, opening them to discover Christmas decorations. The two women divided the boxes into ones they would keep for the church and those that would be given away in the new store. Stacking the boxes that were for the church's use into the back room, they continued going through the rest until lunchtime.

"Want to grab a bite to eat? I packed lunch for both of us," Rachel offered.

"I can eat," Lily said, laying the bags she was sorting to the side. They went outside to eat in the backyard at one of the picnic tables.

"You go back to school in a few weeks, don't you?" Rachel asked, handing her a sandwich and bag of chips. They had grabbed sodas from the vending machine inside.

"Yes." Lily opened her sandwich, taking a bite.

"You must be looking forward to it being your last semester."

"Yes and no. Now that Penni's graduated, I don't have many friends. I actually have enough credits that I could take my last classes on the internet."

"You don't want to go back to school?" Rachel asked in surprise.

"Not really, but I don't want to put Beth and Razer out by staying. I know it must be hard having me around all the time," Lily admitted.

"I don't believe that. I think she would enjoy having you close to home after you were injured so badly."

"Maybe, I'll talk to her about it after I make my mind up."

"Are you going to the fair tonight?" Lily questioned the pretty redhead. They had gone to school together and knew each other well.

"No, we went last night. Logan rode everything twice. Tonight I have someone flying in from Canada."

Lily whistled. Rachel was becoming renowned for her use of medicinal herbs and her healing touch. Lily didn't know if she believed in it, yet she was happy the sick found some comfort.

"It must be wonderful to help so many people," Lily said.

"It is. My grandmother would be proud I'm using her gift to help others."

"Your grandmother?"

"She was a full-blooded Cherokee, and she taught me everything, from herbal medicine to how to lay my hands. She was an inspiration to me."

Lily smiled sadly. "It must be wonderful to have that kind of heritage."

"It is." Rachel closed her lunch bag. "Do you ever wonder…? Never mind, I shouldn't ask. It's none of my business."

"If I ever am curious about my past?" Lily asked, her hand going to her forehead. "I don't have to wonder; I know. About my mother at least." Lily's hand began to shake.

"Lily, are you all right?" Lily heard the concern in

Rachel's voice.

"Yes. I was adopted when I was eight," Lily said. "My adopted parents said my mother was killed and my father didn't want me, so there's no need to look, is there?"

"I didn't mean to pry."

"I know you didn't." Lily smiled tremulously, getting to her feet. Rachel reached out to steady her and Lily felt the warmth of her hand against her arm. She managed to get herself back under control with that comforting gesture.

When they went back to work, Lily was quiet at first but couldn't remain so for long in Rachel's cheerful presence. Rachel told her how one man had flown in from England so that she could perform her healing on his penis when he could no longer get an erection.

"I thought I would die, I was so embarrassed," Rachel said, describing the incident. "My brothers refused to leave the room."

Lily was laughing so hard she almost dropped a box she was carrying. "Did it work?"

"He's had two children since then. Of course, I got a text from his wife who asked if I could turn it off again."

Lily's laughter bubbled over, enjoying spending the day with Rachel.

As they finished up for the day, Lily got a text from Beth, telling her to meet her at the fair when she was done. They had worked most of the day and only had a fourth of the store completed.

"See you next Saturday?" Rachel asked as they grabbed their purses.

"Absolutely."

They left each other in the parking lot, each heading their own way.

Lily went home and showered, changing into a pale blue sundress then a matching sweater in case the night turned cool.

She drove to the outskirts of town to the fairgrounds, where there was already a huge crowd. She managed to find a parking spot at the end and began the trek toward the fair when Lily heard several motorcycles pull in.

She glanced back, expecting to see some of The Last Riders or even a Destructor, but she didn't recognize the jackets of the riders pulling in. Lily wondered how Treepoint was going to deal with yet another motorcycle club.

CHAPTER FIVE

Lily got in line to purchase her entrance tickets, texting Beth that she was at the fairgrounds. After purchasing her ticket, she wandered through the various booths before Beth texted back that they were on their way to meet her. Lily smiled when she read Beth's text that said Razer had decided to hit the hot dog stand when they'd arrived, thinking it was more likely Beth had joined him in getting one.

Lily stopped at one of the booths, looking over the delicate glass figurines. There was one of a delicate flower with a tiny crystal raindrop dangling from one of the petals. It was beautiful.

"How much?" Lily was in awe of the skill it must have taken to make the beautiful art.

"Twenty," the vendor quoted. Lily reached into the pocket of her sundress for her money, pulling out a twenty, unable to resist the buy.

"Thank you," Lily said, taking the piece, which had been wrapped in tissue paper. Afraid it would become damaged if she packed it around for the rest of the evening, Lily decided to take it back to her car.

Texting Beth that she would be right back, Lily walked back to the parking lot. It was just beginning to get dark, yet there was still plenty of light. She was halfway back to her car when she had the feeling she was being watched. Lily looked around casually. There were several people still coming and going to the fair, so she didn't worry about her safety; however, she began to feel uncomfortable and didn't understand why.

She was almost to her car when a truck door slammed shut. Lily swallowed hard when she recognized who had gotten out of the truck. He was already striding angrily toward her.

"You fucking bitch!" Gaige stopped in front of her, looking down at her angrily. He had a busted-up lip and a black eye that was half-closed.

"Gaige," Lily greeted him, despite his hateful words.

"I hope you're happy. I lost my job because of you. How am I supposed to feed my kids with no job?"

"I'm sorry. I didn't want you to be fired," Lily said, taking a step back at his aggressive stance.

"I was only joking around."

"It didn't feel very funny when you put your hand on my butt," Lily snapped.

"Then you sent Train to beat the hell out of my face."

"I didn't," Lily protested.

"At least I got out of there before Shade came after me. Now I have to leave town for a few days. He's been all over town looking for me today. You need to call that psycho off."

"I'll talk to him," Lily promised.

"You do that, because if he comes after me, when he's finished I'm going to come after you," he threatened.

Ripping the tissue with the delicate glass from her hand, he tore the fragile tissue away. "Well, isn't that pretty." Turning sideways, he threw the glass at her windshield, breaking both in a shatter of flying glass.

Lily gasped as tears came to her eyes at the wanton

destruction of something so beautiful. She didn't care about the windshield; she was more upset about losing the glass figurine. She hardly ever splurged and bought herself something like that.

He caught her arm in a tight grip when she would have stepped back.

"Now is that any way to treat a woman?" a hard voice came from behind her. From Gaige's widening eyes, she could tell it wasn't good. Turning her head, she saw the motorcycle riders that had pulled in after she had arrived coming to her aid.

"I don't want any trouble with you," Gaige said. This time it was him taking a step back at the three men coming toward him, releasing his tight hold of her arm.

"I hate it when pussies start crying before I can even get my hands on them," the biggest one complained. He was huge, almost rivaling Knox in size. While Knox appeared fiercer, this man looked like he would beat the crap out of you while laughing about doing it.

The remaining two, on the other hand, didn't look like they ever laughed. One was blond with a look of hardness and the other was just plain scary with his dark hair and scar down his cheek.

"Pretty little thing here don't need to watch me beat the shit out of you, so why don't we go over here and take care of some business." The huge man slung a meaty arm around Gaige's shoulder, turning him toward a group of trees. Gaige's frightened expression tugged at Lily's conscience.

"Wait, he just lost his temper."

"That's okay, sweet thing, I'm going to help him find it." He was leading a struggling Gaige away.

Lily took a step forward when she felt an arm slide around her waist. "Let Max deal with him. He can't look much worse than he does now," an amused voice said in her ear.

Lily stiffened, beginning to get frightened.

"Lily!" Beth's yell as she drew closer was cut off when Razer grabbed her arm, preventing her from coming any closer.

Lily turned her head as The Last Riders appeared in mass.

Viper, Cash, Razer, Shade, Train and Rider were covering the parking lot with the rest of their members following behind while the women members kept Beth from running to her sister.

"Want to take a bet on which one she belongs to?" the one with his arm around her waist spoke.

"Don't have to. I know," the dark-haired one said in amusement, moving in front of Lily and blocking her from view.

"Let me go." Lily tried to wiggle from the grasp around her waist.

"Calm down. I'm going to let you go."

Viper's harsh voice could be heard over the thrumming of her heart. "Let her go."

The one with Gaige in a stranglehold turned back, moving closer to his friends.

"I have every intention of letting this sweet thing go. We're not out for trouble; just passing through." He nodded his head at Gaige. "Found him giving her some trouble." Nodding his head at Lily's car, he then said, "Decided to step in. Seeing she's yours, we'll step back." His arm slid away from Lily, releasing her.

Lily took a step forward toward Razer while none of the men took their eyes off each other. The one with the scar stepped to the side. When Lily passed him, she brushed against him and his jacket moved to the side. Lily saw the gun clipped to his waist. Terror almost took hold of her, yet Lily knew she didn't want anyone hurt.

"He's telling the truth, Viper. Gaige was angry that he got fired and they made him leave me alone."

"Lily, go to your sister," Shade spoke.

Lily had done what she could, so she went to Beth.

Neither group of bikers was interested in her opinion at this point. It was now a standoff between the two groups.

"Are you all right?" Beth asked.

"I'm fine," Lily answered, turning around to see what was going on.

Seeing the one called Max hand over Gaige to Shade, Lily started to go back.

"Stay here, Lily. Knox is pulling into the parking lot," Beth said, placing her hand on Lily's arm. Knox, a former member of The Last Riders, pulled his deputy car into the parking lot close to the men.

Lily, Beth and the other women watched as the men talked. Knox took Gaige from Shade, putting him in handcuffs before placing him into the backseat of the cruiser. They continued to watch as the men talked to the members of the other motorcycle club. Lily bit her lip, not wanting anyone to get in a fight. The other men had only stepped in when they had seen Gaige bothering her.

"What happened?" Evie asked. Lily told her and the women about Gaige breaking her windshield and grabbing her arm, explaining how the men stopped him.

They stood watching as The Last Riders started back toward them with the men from the other club going to their bikes.

Razer was the first to reach her; however, she felt Shade's eyes running over her, checking to see if she was hurt.

Assuring her bother-in-law that she was fine, they went back into the fair. Lily didn't want to ruin the fun for everyone, so she changed the subject as she walked arm in arm with her sister through the fair.

"Do you want to go back to the booth and get another figurine?" Beth asked.

"No," Lily said, aware of the others' eyes on her. "Let's play some games."

Attempting to prove that she was fine, she walked up to one of the booths where you had to throw a ring around a milk jug, handed the worker some money and he gave her several rings. Aiming, she missed pathetically. She tried again with the other two rings, throwing each one carefully, and missed them all.

Afterwards, the others split up, going to different games and playing. The men went to the shooting game while Lily moved on to another game, shooting water into a clown's mouth. She did well in a race with the other women, jumping up and down when she won, laughing.

They did two more races and Lily finally won a prize, picking a purple monkey. The man behind the counter handed it to Lily.

"Here you go." Lily handed it to Beth.

"Don't you want it?" Beth protested.

"You're the one that likes stuffed animals." Lily didn't like to collect items. The only thing she had let herself get in a long time was the flower and Gaige had seen to its destruction.

With their game over, they went to watch the men play. Train and Rider were shooting at the targets while Viper and Shade stood nearby watching. Razer walked to Beth, putting his arm around her shoulder as they all waited to see who would win. Lily stood to the side near Beth as Evie and Jewell came to stand next to her.

It was fun just watching everyone relax.

"Why don't you take a turn, Shade?" Bliss asked.

Shade's eyes went to Bliss and the small woman seemed to shrink in on herself. Shade was good at that. Lily felt bad for the woman, throwing Shade an angry glance, which he ignored.

"Let's go ride the bumper cars," Bliss suggested.

The Last Riders made their way through the fair, stopping and riding a few rides and playing several more games.

Everyone was waiting in line for a ride that Lily had no intention of getting on.

"I'm going to go get something to drink," Lily told

Beth who was standing in line with Razer, her arms wrapped around his waist. Lily was happy that Beth was so much in love with her husband.

She walked to one of the vendors to get a soda. Unable to resist, she bought a cotton candy, too. Taking a seat at a nearby picnic table, she watched the ride going around and around. Nope, that ride wasn't for her.

Opening her bag of cotton candy, she pulled out a tuft of the soft confection and ate it. The sugar melted on her tongue. She licked the sugar crystals from her lips.

Shade sat down on the bench next to her. "You don't want to ride?"

"Not that one, I don't," Lily replied, smiling, her anger forgotten.

She sat, eating her candy as The Last Riders got on. Then, seconds later, she heard the women's screams and the men mocking them.

She pulled out another tuft of cotton candy, letting it melt on her tongue once more as she felt Shade move restlessly next to her, and she looked at him inquiringly. She licked the sugar crystals from her lips and watched as his blue eyes fell to them. Uncomfortable, Lily turned away, taking a drink of her soda.

When she saw The Last Riders get off the ride, Bliss, Jewell and Evie were walking with Rider; Dawn and Stori were next to Train; Raci was walking with Cash; Winter and Viper were walking hand-in-hand; and Ember was mixed in with the rest of the bikers, teasing Nickel for having a weak stomach.

Lily thought about how happy everyone looked.

"What are you thinking?" Shade asked.

She turned to him with a start, giving him a sweet smile. "I was just thinking how happy everyone looked, like they belong together. I can see you all care about each other." Lily tore another piece of the spun candy off. "You shouldn't be so hard on Bliss. I think she has a thing for you," Lily said, raising the confection to her lips.

Shade's hand snapped out, catching her wrist in a hard grasp. "What did I tell you about me not being your BFF? Bliss knows exactly what I feel for her." Shade brought her hand to his mouth, taking the bite of cotton candy from her fingertips. His tongue licked her fingers, taking the sugar off.

Lily shuddered, her eyes darkening. Jerking her hand from his, she avoided his eyes. She got to her feet and dumped the cotton candy and drink into the trashcan before making a beeline straight for Beth's side.

She refused to let herself think or dwell on the incident. It was just one more memory to lock behind her imaginary door when she couldn't cope with the reaction. She couldn't handle the spark that had lit inside of her when his tongue glided across her fingertips. She was letting her defenses down around Shade, and she had to build them back. He was everything she didn't want in a man, everything she couldn't have. If she failed at keeping him at bay, he could very well be the path to her destruction.

* * *

Shade followed behind the group, keeping a watchful eye on his club members. Lily didn't stray from Beth's side for the rest of the evening, using her as protection against him. Lily used Beth and Razer as her shield against the world; however, naively she thought that they would protect her from him. They would try.

He had thought that Beth would be his biggest opposition but, surprisingly, Razer was playing the big brother and had laid down the ground rules. Shade was willing to go along with it for now.

He watched as she looked back over her shoulder then moved closer to Beth. His gut twisted as he wondered if she would ever turn to him over Beth, if he would be the one she turned to for protection.

He would lay back. He could wait; he was a patient man. For now.

CHAPTER SIX

Lily kept her head down during service, concentrating on her Pastor's words, letting them fill her heart and calm her tumultuous mind.

Beth's hand grasped hers and Lily held it tightly, gathering strength from her sister, as well.

After the service, Pastor Dean's eyes searched hers. "You and Rachel got a lot done yesterday. Thank you for your help."

"I enjoyed it," Lily replied, moving forward to let the other parishioners greet the Pastor.

"Let's get lunch," Razer said.

Lily thought about going home, but she remembered the strange experience from last week and decided against it. Following her sister, Razer, Evie, Bliss, Raci, Diamond, Winter and Viper crossed the street and they entered the diner.

Shade, Rider, Train and Cash were already inside drinking their coffee. When Lily took a seat between Razer and Winter at the end farthest away from Shade, she felt his eyes on her.

After the waitress had taken their table's order and left, Lily listened to the conversation around her, but she didn't participate. The food arrived and Lily ate her salad.

As she ate, she heard the door of the diner open, but didn't turn around until the silence at the table had her raising her head to see the concerned look on the women and the men's hard expressions.

"What's going on?" Lily asked Winter.

"The bikers from last night just came in," Winter answered.

"Oh." She didn't turn around and make it obvious she was staring at them.

Conversation gradually resumed; however, Lily could still see the men were tense.

Thankfully lunch finished and everyone rose to leave. Lily followed The Last Riders to the door, but stopped at the cash register, opening her purse to take out some money.

"What are you doing? Razer already took care of the check," Beth told her.

"I know." She gave her money to the cashier. "I want to pay for the men's ticket by the window."

The cashier's mouth dropped open, yet she took the cash.

"Lily, what are you doing?" Beth questioned in a hushed voice.

"Paying back a favor," Lily said, taking a deep breath, and before anyone could stop her, she approached the men sitting at the table. There were more of them today, but Lily had been around The Last Riders and the Destructors enough that she easily recognized the leader.

Standing in front of the dark blond man, she spoke in a rush. "I wanted to thank you for what you did last night. It could have gotten bad without your help."

The man's eyes went over Lily's shoulder. She knew The Last Riders were waiting at the door.

"Anytime, sweet thing." The man's hard eyes softened briefly when he looked at her, yet they resumed their hardness instantly, so Lily wasn't even sure she had witnessed it.

Lily smiled, turning back to the door, though her gaze was briefly caught by one of the men. His hair was slightly longer and he had a goatee along with several tattoos on his arm. It was the kindness in his gaze, however, that caught her attention.

"Hi, I'm Colton." He put out his hand to shake.

"Hi, I'm Lily." She placed her hand in his, which he shook.

"Hi, Lily. That's Ice." He nodded his head toward the blond. "The big guy there is Max, and the ugly one next to him is Jackal."

"It's nice to meet you." Lily smiled before continuing, "I didn't mean to disturb your lunch. I wanted to thank your friends."

"I'm sure they enjoyed it, knowing them. Take care, Lily," Colton said, his gentle gaze the direct opposite of his bad-boy appearance.

"I will." Lily smiled again, moving away and almost bumping into Shade who had come to stand behind her.

She didn't appreciate the warning glare he gave the men. He ignored her own glare, though, leading her away from the table and back to The Last Riders who hadn't moved away from the door.

They waited until she was outside before giving her hell.

"What were you thinking, Lily?" Beth started.

"I was thinking that I would do the polite thing and thank them for helping me out of a difficult situation."

"You can't get friendly with another motorcycle club," Evie said.

"I don't know why not." When several would have opened their mouths, Lily put up her hand. "I wasn't getting friendly. I was thanking them. I can be friends with anyone I want. I'm friends with Stud." Lily mentioned the president of the Destructors, yet it was a stretch calling him a friend. From the dubious expressions centered on her, she knew she wasn't pulling one over on them.

Lily noticed Viper and Shade were talking quietly to themselves, and when she and Beth turned to walk home, Razer hung back.

"You two go ahead. I'll be there in a few," Razer said.

Lily hesitated, somehow knowing they were going to confront the men inside when they came out, and they wanted her and Beth gone.

Lily faced Viper, touching his arm gently. "Leave them alone, please, Viper. They don't want trouble and I approached them."

"They came inside seeing our bikes were outside," Viper replied.

"Please, Viper."

"I'll give in this time, Lily, but don't ask me to back down again," Viper replied.

Lily reached up, kissing Viper on his cheek. "Thank you," she said before moving away.

"Let's go home." This time Razer's voice was amused as he guided the women toward their home.

Lily looked back in time to see Shade punch Viper in the stomach. Gasping, she turned to go back again.

"Keep going, Lily." This time Razer's voice held definite amusement.

"Why did Shade just punch Viper?"

"I have no idea." Lily could tell that he knew perfectly well what was going on, but he wasn't going to tell on his friend.

Lily looked at her sister.

"Men," was Beth's only answer, rolling her eyes at their strange behavior.

* * *

Lily didn't have to worry about eating lunch with Shade the next day--he wasn't working. It was the first time since she had begun to work at the factory that he hadn't been there.

In his place, Rider ran the factory that day with his

easy, good humor.

Evie brought her a tray of food, which she ate at the picnic table by herself while Rider went to the house for lunch.

As soon as the door closed behind him, Georgia's whole demeanor changed. Lily couldn't help thinking, once again, that the woman was not nice. Her intimidation had turned to a new low; she had begun to manipulate the schedule, giving those that weren't in her favor less hours.

Lily really was still looking for the best in Georgia, but she wasn't making it easy. She was short and curvy; however, her grumpy appearance made her unattractive until one of The Last Riders was in the factory, then she lit up like a sparkler.

At the end of the day, with still no Shade, Lily drove home, strangely let down from not doing her workout with him.

* * *

Joker inserted the nozzle into his bike's tank, keeping a wary eye out as Dale filled his own tank on the opposite side of the pump. When he finished, he got back on his bike, impatiently waiting.

"Hurry up. I want to be at Jake's before it gets dark. That turn-off is hard enough to see in the daylight."

Dale hung the nozzle back up, screwing the lid back on his tank. "Are you sure that nobody is going to think to look for us at your cousin's house?"

"No, I never mentioned him. I never took Crazy Bitch to meet him because he lives at the top of the fucking mountain and she hates heights. She would have pissed herself looking off the side of the road."

His cousin lived on Black Mountain in a home that had been passed down for generations. No one would find them there. They would hide out with Jake and his wife until the law gave up looking for them.

They had decided to miss their court date and make a run for it when their lawyer said they weren't going to get out of the charges. Too many witnesses.

If those fuckers hadn't shown up when they had, there would have been no witnesses left alive to say shit. He had every intention of killing every one of those bitches, even that dark-haired, pretty one. It wasn't his fault she had been stupid enough to hang out with his ex.

He started his motor, pulling back onto the curvy mountainous road. Dale was slightly ahead of him, going around a sharp curve, when he heard the shot. His bike spun out and Joker barely managed to slow his bike as Dale's front tire exploded, sending his bike spinning. His scream as he hit the guardrail raised the bile in Joker's throat as Dale went flying over the mountain's edge.

Before he could bring his own speed down, he heard another shot. He didn't even have time to scream as he felt a warm wetness between his thighs. Joker desperately tried to control his bike as his front wheel exploded. His bike hit the guardrail, the force flinging him from his bike as he followed Dale over the side of the mountain, into everlasting darkness.

* * *

Lily didn't know what to expect the next day, and she definitely didn't want to examine the feelings of relief she felt when Shade was there when she arrived. She got busy and managed to get several orders completed before lunch.

When he called her name, she didn't complain to herself; she merely went to his office and tried not to notice the hateful look on Georgia's face. Lily couldn't understand why the woman disliked her so much.

Shade closed the door after she entered, going to sit at the chair beside his desk where he handed her the chicken salad.

"Thanks, Shade."

As Lily ate, she noticed that he was staying awfully quiet.

"You look tired today," Lily broached.

"Late night."

"Oh." Lily took another bite of her food, playing with it for several minutes, the silence tearing on her nerves.

"Are you mad at me for something?" Lily was angry at herself for caring.

"Yes."

Lily should know by now not to ask Shade a question she didn't want to hear the answer to.

"Why?"

Shade gave her an angry glare, leaning back in his seat. "Why do you think?"

"Because I talked to those bikers?"

"You know better than being friendly with bikers like that. Remember the first time you saw us at the lake? You were petrified, yet you sashayed your ass right up to their table."

Lily winced at his description and then tried to explain. "Because I wasn't scared of them. I knew you were there."

Shade's expression changed. He wasn't exactly less angry, but he did seem somewhat mollified by her explanation.

"They've left town, but if they come back, stay away from them." Shade gave her the warning in a cold voice.

"I will," Lily promised.

She discovered that she didn't want Shade angry with her, though the biggest reason was that she knew Beth could be placed in a difficult position. She would never place Beth in a situation of having to choose the club over her.

Lily got up from the desk, her appetite completely gone. Placing her plate on the tray, she turned the doorknob, about to leave his office with feelings of guilt and anger that her small gesture of gratitude to the other bikers had caused such upheaval.

"Lily." She turned back to face Shade. "Don't ever touch Viper or one of the other men again."

Lily felt a chill go down her back. Without glancing back or giving a word in reply, her hand twisted the knob and she went through hurriedly, closing it behind her. That was one remark she wasn't going to touch. She was smart enough to know that she didn't want to hear anything else he said when it came to that order.

* * *

That afternoon, Shade spent his time walking the floor, managing the huge number of orders. She was forced to watch Georgia flirt and gush over him, which didn't bother her. What did, however, was when Kaley came into the factory with Rider and Train. She was wearing a pair of shorts that made Lily blush and a swimsuit top showing her large breasts. Evie and Bliss were at the door as they tried to convince Shade to go swimming with them.

Lily expected him to go. What man in his right mind would refuse to go with a bunch of attractive women instead of staying cooped up in a factory for the rest of the afternoon?

He stayed, and that was when Lily came to the conclusion that maybe Georgia and he were becoming closer. Lily's hand snapped the rubber band several times as the thought struck her throughout the afternoon.

"You ready?" Shade spoke from behind her.

Lily jumped. "What for?"

"To work out." Shade looked at her strangely.

"I didn't bring my bag. I didn't know if you would be gone again today."

"I left a message for Georgia to tell you that I was out of town yesterday and I would be back today."

"I guess she forgot."

Shade didn't seem convinced, but he went on to say, "It doesn't matter. Winter always keeps extra outfits in her locker. You can have one of hers. You need a new one anyway."

"There's nothing wrong with the one I have," Lily protested.

"Other than it's two sizes too big and meant to be worn during the winter, and you left it at home."

Lily shut up. She was getting tired of losing word battles with him.

"Fine," she snapped. She could tell that he didn't like her tone. "I'm sorry," Lily hastily apologized.

Shade nodded his head, pacified at her apology. "Go outside. I'll be there in a minute."

"Okay."

Lily waited outside by the pathway that led up to the house.

Several minutes later, Georgia came out, and her angry stride ate up the distance to her car.

Shade came out of the factory then, locking the door behind him.

"Why is she angry?" Lily asked as she watched Georgia pull out of the parking lot.

"When I leave a message, I expect it to be delivered."

"Do you always have to be so rude?" Lily knew it was going to be miserable working with the woman from now on. On the other hand, it hadn't been a bowl of cherries up to now anyway.

"Yes." She should have known better than to ask; of course, that was his answer.

When they got to the basement, Shade went to a locker in the corner and pulled out some clothes, handing them to her. Lily then went into the bathroom and looked at the clothes. Biting her lip, she looked at the bright purple top and black shorts. This was not going to happen.

Lily opened the bathroom door, coming to a stop when she saw Shade standing outside the door, leaning against the wall.

"Get changed."

"But I can't wear these," Lily protested.

"Get changed."

She slammed the door.

Pulling off her dress, she pulled on the shorts then the top. The shorts came to the midline of her thighs and clung like a second skin. The top was even worse. It was scoop-necked, showing the tops of her full breasts. There were no sleeves at all; it was a tank and it left her midriff completely bare.

She would never wear something so revealing even to the gym she worked out at in her college town, and it was an all-women's gym. There was no way she was walking out in front of Shade.

She picked up her dress to change back into it when the door opened and Shade came in.

"What are you doing?" she screeched.

"Let's go. I don't have all day."

Taking her hand, he led her into the other room to the mats. "Start stretching," he said, releasing her hand.

Lily stood there, unsure what to do next, while Shade began stretching, ignoring her. She gritted her teeth, started stretching out and gradually loosened as Shade ignored her. She was certain that she was over-reacting. This was the same outfit Winter worked out in. She had seen similar ones in her gym on dozens of women.

"Okay, that's enough," Shade broke into her musings.

He took her through the movements she had learned last week. She became more adapt at kicking him, making him take a step back. Once she had done that enough to make him happy, he taught her a different move where her knee would actually make contact with him.

"But I'll hurt you," Lily protested. She hated the thought of hurting anyone, even Shade.

"Baby, you're not going to get close enough to my balls to hurt me." Shade laughed in her face.

Lily's anger rose and she snapped her knee out, but Shade caught her thigh. The feel of his hand on the inside of her thigh had her taking a step back, her own hand going to the rubber band.

"Remember what I told you about snapping that damn thing in front of me," Shade warned. Lily wasn't about to explain why she felt the need to snap the band, so her hands clenched by her side.

"Come on, Lily, quit being such a wimp," Shade goaded.

Lily's usually non-existent temper soared. Her knee snapped out and she was gratified to see she almost accomplished her mission. Shade had barely managed to save himself as his hand caught her knee, cupping it from behind. Lily's weight was off balance. Her hands went to his chest and her head went back as she grinned up at him.

"I almost got you," Lily bragged.

"Almost doesn't count." Shade raised her leg to his hip and Lily found her mound up against his penis. Their workout clothes were too thin between them.

Lily started panicking, her mind filled with terror.

When Shade's foot came out, sweeping the one she was standing on, she began to fall, landing on her back with Shade on top of her. Her mind began to black out and she opened her mouth to scream. Before a sound could erupt, however, Shade lifted himself off her in one fluid movement. Reaching down, he then snagged her hand and lifted her to her feet.

"Again. This time, I'll show you how to keep me from sweeping your foot out from under you."

Lily couldn't focus, standing numbly.

Shade took her arm, leading her to the corner of the room. "Stand there until you're ready to continue." Shade left her.

Without another word, he began to lift weights, ignoring her. Lily tried to get her mind away from the darkness, her hand going to her wrist.

"No, Lily." Lily was becoming frustrated. Her mind left the darkness and she focused on her anger toward Shade while he worked out with the weights as if she wasn't in the room.

Lily finally managed to get herself together, her breath leaving her in a shuddering sigh. When her breathing slowed and her mind cleared, she started to take a step out of the corner.

"Don't come out of the corner until you're ready to try the move again."

Lily thought that she would get dressed and go home. Obviously, Shade had other plans. She stayed in the corner, debating it over and over.

She couldn't stand for him to touch her so intimately. The feel of his body against hers was more than she could take. Her mind in turmoil, she started tracing imaginary designs on the wall, trying to distract herself.

"Hands to your sides, stand up straight." Lily corrected her posture, hating him, not knowing why she was obeying his demands. Her stubbornness kicked in and Lily eventually decided to simply outwait him. Surely, he would get tired of this and release her.

She was wrong, though. He went to the treadmill and started running. The man was a machine. She didn't even know men could have that much stamina.

As Lily began getting hungry and her legs were getting tired, she took a step forward out of the corner.

"Go to the mat." Shade got off the treadmill, keeping her waiting as he took off his shirt, using it to wipe the sweat from his forehead.

He was covered in tattoos. There wasn't an inch that hadn't been touched. His lean frame was highlighted by the myriad of tattoos. They gave him a menacing appearance that only fueled Lily's fear of him.

She looked away as he approached the mat.

"Eyes to me. Are you ready?"

Lily nodded her head, just wanting to get it over with so she could escape.

As soon as he was in position, she attacked, trying to take him by surprise. This time, when he caught her knee and pulled her off balance, before her mind could spaz out again, Shade gave her instructions to keep her balance and her foot from being swept out from under her. Unfortunately, it involved using his shoulders as a way to balance herself. Her hands gripping his hard flesh sought to drive her away from reality again, but Shade's hands on her hips showed her how to push off from him.

"Good. That's enough for the day." He removed his hands from her body.

"Thank God," Lily muttered.

"What did you say?" Shade questioned.

"Nothing. Sir."

"You can go get changed."

"Thanks. *Sir.*" This time her tone was a little sarcastic; his ordering her around was getting old, fast.

"Would you like a lesson I give when I believe someone is being disrespectful?" Shade snapped.

"No, Sir." Lily rushed to the bathroom, locking the door behind her. She knew the most important lesson in self-defense was knowing when to run.

CHAPTER SEVEN

Vida waited impatiently as she sat on the couch, watching Sawyer pace the floor while twisting a lock of her hair.

She tensed, getting to her feet when the door opened and Colton, Ice, Max and Jackal entered the hotel suite. They were in Louisville, Kentucky, staying in a hotel while Kaden was set to perform a concert there tonight with Mouth2Mouth.

Vida ran into Colton's arms the minute she saw him. "Did you see her?" Vida looked up at her husband with watery eyes.

The door opened and closed again. Vida knew it was Kaden coming into the room; sure Colton would have called him when they were back in town. Kaden had stayed as long as he could before he had gone to the arena for a sound check.

"I saw her," Colton answered his wife's question.

Vida couldn't help it; she started crying, knowing from the sounds next to her that Sawyer wasn't able to contain her emotions any better.

"Vida, you're breaking my heart, please stop," Colton said, holding on to her shaking body.

"I'm sorry." Vida managed to get herself back under control.

Colton sat down on the couch, pulling Vida down next to him.

"Was she okay?" Sawyer asked, sitting on Kaden's lap when he sat down on a chair.

"She was fine," he assured her.

"We want to see her, Colton," Vida and Sawyer both spoke together.

"You two are going to have to wait. Digger's trial comes up in two months. Once he's sentenced and sent to prison, it will be safer for you two to approach her. But it's not going to be easy, Vida." Colton put the brakes on their possible reunion.

"Why?" Vida asked impatiently.

"What little information Penni would tell us about her friend is the truth. She's prone to anxiety attacks and gets easily frightened. Plus her adopted sister is married to a member of a motorcycle club—The Last Riders."

His grim voice had Vida searching his eyes. "Is she in any danger from them?"

"No, honey. She's safe with them. To be honest, it relieves my mind that they watch over her as closely as they do," Colton said, not telling her about the incident at the fair.

"She shouldn't be in any danger from Digger. He doesn't even know she's alive," Sawyer entered the conversation.

"No, he doesn't, and I want to keep it that way. He's not giving up any information on the women he's kidnapped until he gets a deal. I won't feel better about Lily's safety until his whole operation is shut down," Colton told them both.

"I agree," Ice spoke up. "Don't underestimate Digger just because he's in prison."

Sawyer and Vida both reluctantly nodded their heads.

"Did she look—" Vida got her voice back under

control. "How did she look?"

Colton ran his thumb over Vida's cheek, wiping away the tear that clung to her soft skin. "She's beautiful, sweetheart, just like you said," he said softly.

Vida's head fell to his shoulder. "Whatever it takes, Colton, whatever we have to do, we'll do it to keep her safe," she vowed, seeing the same resolve in Sawyer's eyes.

They had waited all these years; they could wait a few more months.

* * *

The week went by fairly quickly for Lily. By Friday, she had managed to get more comfortable with Shade handling her body during her defense lessons.

He refused to let her go back to her old workout outfits, instead making her put Winter's back on after she had washed and tried to return it.

As she left Friday, she and Shade came around the corner of the house to see Kaley walking up the steps in a red leather skirt and a black halter top. Rider had his arm around her shoulders.

"I thought she was dating Train," Lily said.

Shade didn't say anything, silently walking her to her car.

"See you Sunday," Lily said, getting in her car.

"Later," Shade said, turning back to the house.

With that, Lily drove home.

Going inside the house, she saw Beth and Razer getting ready to go out to the party at the clubhouse.

"What are you doing tonight?" Beth asked as they were going out the door.

"I'm having dinner with Charles and Miranda and her husband," Lily replied on her way upstairs to take a shower.

"When did Charles get back in town?"

"Last night," Lily answered.

Charles had spent the last few months opening a new restaurant for his father.

"Have fun. See you tomorrow," Beth called out, closing the front door behind them.

Lily went upstairs and took a shower. She brushed her hair then made a knot on her head. Going to her closet, she pulled out a bright yellow dress that fell softly to her knees. To finish the look, she slid a colorful strand of beads around her neck.

Sliding on her sandals, she was just coming down the steps when the doorbell rang.

She opened the door to Charles's smiling face then let him in while she grabbed her purse and cell phone.

"Miss me?" Charles asked.

"Of course. How was the opening?"

"Really good. Dad's already planning his next one."

"He deserves it. Both of you have put a lot of hours into making your restaurants successful." Lily smiled at him.

"Ready?"

"Yes."

They met Miranda and her husband at the Pink Slipper. Lily always felt uncomfortable there because they served liquor; however, they sat well away from the bar and neither Charles nor Jackson drank.

Miranda talked of her child while the men talked about the restaurant opening in Lexington.

"Who's babysitting for you tonight?" Lily asked, playing with her silverware.

"I asked Kaley, but she was too busy. I know you work for them, and that Beth is married to Razer, but I really wish she wasn't involved with The Last Riders. I'm getting worried about her," Miranda confided.

Lily didn't mention that she had seen her at the clubhouse a couple of times that week.

"She's not even trying to find a job," Miranda said with a worried frown. "I've heard rumors, too, of stuff going on out there, but when I ask her, she won't talk to me about it."

Lily could respect that Kaley wanted to keep her private life private. Lily didn't like it when others tried to snoop into hers. Treepoint was a small town and most people gossiped to keep themselves occupied.

Lily changed the subject, not wanting to hear the rumors about The Last Riders. They had been kind to her, and Beth wouldn't let herself become involved in anything that was illegal. Lily didn't want to be disloyal to Beth by discussing them.

They went to a movie afterward, which everyone enjoyed, deciding to go to the diner for coffee and dessert once it was through. They were sitting there, laughing over the movie, when the door opened and The Last Riders came in, taking several large tables. Beth and Razer came in the door last with Razer's arm wrapped around Beth's shoulders and her hair windblown. They sat down at the large table. Lily noticed that Beth lost her smile when she saw her, but she still came to their table.

Lily noticed that Shade was missing from the group.

"Did you have fun at the movies?"

"Yes, it was good. I see you guys went for a ride." Lily wondered at her sister's bright flush.

"Yes."

"Enjoy it while you can, winter will be here soon," Lily said as Charles paid the waitress their ticket.

"Where's Kaley? Didn't she go on the ride?" Miranda questioned Beth.

"No, she stayed at the clubhouse," Beth spoke as she turned to go to her own table. "See you in the morning, Lily."

"Okay."

Lily could tell that Miranda wasn't happy with Beth's answer.

Following Charles out the door, she waved at the members sitting at the table, seeing Rider was also missing from the group.

"You're quiet tonight," Charles said on the drive back

to her home, sending her a questioning glance.

"I guess I'm just tired," Lily replied, laying her head back against the headrest.

"Lily, is everything all right? I try not to pry, but you know that you can talk to me."

"I know, Charles. You've always been a good friend to me. I'm glad you're back in town," Lily said, looking out the window.

"Where are we going?" she asked Charles as they drove past her house, instantly alert.

"It's still early; I thought we would take a walk."

Lily was ready to go home. Her hand went to her wrist. "I have to be up early in the morning, Charles. I volunteered to help at the church."

"I won't keep you out too late, Lily. I missed you while I was gone, I thought we would be able to spend the summer together. Dad's restaurant took longer to get situated than I thought. Didn't you miss me at all?"

Lily looked at his handsome face as he drove. "I missed our friendship, Charles. I don't really have anyone to talk to since Penni left school."

His lips tightened. Lily knew it wasn't the answer he wanted to hear.

She watched the road, wondering where they were going. They drove out of town, going toward the lake. Lily wasn't frightened. She had dated Charles since high school, so his actions didn't raise any alarms.

Ten minutes later he pulled into a spot within walking distance of the lake. Charles got out of the car, coming to open the door for her. Lily emerged, letting him take her hand.

He searched her eyes. "Do you remember when we used to do this in high school? We would walk for an hour and just talk."

"I remember, Charles." Lily walked next to his tall figure, knowing he was reaching out to her, and trying to reconnect after being away for most of the summer.

However, Lily had felt the loss of closeness before he had left when he had tried to deepen their relationship, and she had to tell him she didn't return his feelings. She thought maybe he had hoped being away would have changed her mind, that missing him would have shown her she cared about him after all.

Lily watched her feet as they walked. She could have told him before he left that she wouldn't change her mind about him. He didn't attract her in that way. No man did.

As soon as the thought crossed her mind, a picture of Shade appeared to replace it.

"Is something wrong?" Charles paused next to her.

"No, I guess someone walked over my grave." She shivered again. Charles placed his arm over her shoulder as they walked further along, losing sight of the car.

* * *

Shade sat in the darkness of Cash's borrowed truck, watching Lily as she walked next to the fucker that was courting a death wish if he didn't move his arm. He relaxed when he saw Lily move slightly away, keeping a few inches between them. He didn't like them holding hands, but he could handle it.

He had planned to come up with another lame-ass excuse to spend the evening with her, but Razer had told him that Charles had beaten him to the punch. He hadn't had to deal with him before now because he had been out of town, but now he was back and thought he and Lily would continue dating.

Shade got out of the truck as soon as they walked far enough away that they couldn't see their car. Keeping to the shadows in case they doubled back, Shade made it quickly to Charles' car, kneeling down by the back tire. He slipped his knife out of his boot, and thrust it into the tire before moving to the front and doing the same. As soon as he heard the hissing air, he returned to the truck, sliding back behind the wheel.

Taking out his cell phone, he gave Rider a call to give

him a head's up that Razer would be calling him shortly, so he needed to finish his business with Kaley. He wanted his ass ready to roll when Razer called to give Lily a ride home.

Shade sat back and patiently waited for the couple to return.

* * *

Lily couldn't hide her yawn as Charles talked about his father's new restaurant.

"Let's head back; I can tell you're tired," Charles broke off.

"I'm sorry, Charles. It's been a long day." She squeezed his hand, relieved when he gave her a smile.

When they got to the car, he opened the door, letting her slide inside. Lily watched as he walked around the front of the car, seeing Charles bend down by the front tire then stand with a frown on his face. She turned as he walked to the back tire and stood, staring down for a minute before getting inside the car.

"I have some bad news. We have two flat tires," Charles said, reaching into his pocket and pulling out his cell phone.

"Don't you have a spare?" Lily asked then felt stupid at the look he gave her.

"I do, but not two. Dad's still in Lexington, so I can't call him. I'm going to try Lyle, but it's Friday, so the chances aren't good that he'll actually answer."

Lyle was the town drunk. Lily hated to refer to him that way; however, he was drunk more often than he was sober. She really didn't want to be stuck in the tow truck with him after he had been drinking most of the night.

"I'll call Razer," Lily offered when Charles had no luck reaching Lyle. She pulled out her own cell phone, calling her brother-in-law. He answered on the third ring, and Lily quickly explained their predicament. He offered to send Rider.

"Thanks, Razer." She disconnected the call, turning

back to Charles. She could tell he wasn't happy she had called Razer, but the problem with living in a town the size of Treepoint was that your options were limited.

"I wanted to spend some more time with you. I guess I got my wish," Charles said wryly.

Lily laughed. Reaching over the console, she kissed his cheek. "I really missed you, Charles."

The tension faded from his face and he relaxed back against his seat. They started talking about the mischief they would get into in high school.

Twenty minutes later headlights pulled in behind them. Rider opened his truck door as another truck pulled up next to him. Shade climbed out of the older-looking truck that everyone in town knew was Cash's. Both Charles and Lily then got out of the car.

"What's going on, Lily?" Rider asked as he walked next to Charles and looked down at the car with the two flat tires.

"We went for a walk and when we came back, the tires were flat," Charles explained.

"I'll get it loaded onto the trailer and drop it off at the garage."

"I'll give you both a ride home," Shade offered, moving forward.

Neither of them said anything as the two men loaded Charles's car onto the trailer. When they finished, Rider climbed back into his truck.

Shade went to the truck he was driving and opened the passenger door for them. Lily climbed into the truck first, holding her dress down as she slid across the seat so that Charles had enough room to sit. Shade climbed into the driver's seat and started the truck, as Lily tugged her dress down over her knees.

When Shade backed up and turned around; she was sitting so close to him the movement of him shifting gears had him brushing his arm against her breasts. Lily stiffened, trapped between the two men with nowhere to go.

The silence in the car could be cut with a knife. Feeling agitated and uncomfortable in the silence, her hand went to her wrist, but before she could snap it, Shade's hand covered hers, preventing her from snapping it.

She slid her hand away, laying both hands on her lap.

"I appreciate you and Rider coming out." Charles broke the silence as they hit the outskirts of town. "We tried calling Lyle, but he didn't answer."

"That's because he was at Rosie's. I saw his truck as I passed." Shade's cold voice filled the cab of the truck.

"That explains it." Charles muttered.

Lily expected Shade to drop her off first, but he kept driving past her house.

"Where to?" Shade asked.

Charles gave him directions and silence resumed in the truck. She had to force herself to keep her breathing even as they turned a corner and she was pressed up against Shade's side. Thankfully, Charles lived close by and it wasn't long before they were pulling into his driveway.

Charles opened the door when the truck came to a stop. "Thanks, Shade. You and Rider come by the restaurant and I'll buy you dinner," Charles said, getting out.

"We'll do that," Shade said.

"Goodnight, Lily. I'll see you in church Sunday.

"Goodnight, Charles."

Charles closed the door and Shade backed out of the driveway, his arm again rubbing against her breasts again. Lily tried to scoot over, but his thigh was sitting on her dress. When her dress started slipping up, she sat still, pinned in place. She didn't make an issue of it, since it was a short distance to her house.

"Did you have fun on your date tonight?"

His harsh voice startled her.

"Yes. We went to the movie and ate with my friend Miranda-Kaley's sister."

Shade didn't respond, stopping at a red light.

"Beth and the others came into the diner when we were having coffee. You didn't go riding with them?"

"No, I wasn't in the mood for a ride tonight."

The light turned green, and the truck moved forward again.

"I'm sorry you ended up having to get out tonight," Lily apologized.

"You would have done better keeping your own ass home tonight."

Lily stiffened next to him. "What do you mean by that?"

Shade turned the truck down her street.

"I mean, you need to be cruel to be kind, and quit leading him on," Shade replied, turning into her driveway.

"I'm not leading Charles on," Lily protested, turning to look at him as he came to a stop.

"Yes, you are. When you went out with him tonight were you planning on fucking him?"

"Of course not," Lily said, shocked at his blunt statement. She quickly jerked her dress out from underneath his thigh.

"Then that's leading him on, in my opinion."

"Well, thank God your opinion doesn't count," Lily snapped, sliding across the seat toward the door. "And you should know about being cruel." Lily opened the truck door, sliding down from the seat then turning and slamming the door closed.

Pulling her house key out of her pocket, she went to open the door and then found herself pressed flat against the door. Shade's body pressed against her, his hand planted against the door, preventing her from moving to put the key in the lock.

"It's not a smart move, not leaving your porch light on, Lily. You think I'm cruel? How was I being cruel by telling you that you should quit fucking with his head? Don't you think that every time he goes out with you he's wondering if this will be the time he actually gets to touch that soft skin of yours." His mouth lowered next to her ear. "If you'll let him touch those firm breasts."

Lily trembled, but while his body kept her pinned to the door, his body didn't touch hers. It was the heat of his body and the smell of his leather jacket that were attacking her senses, keeping her pinned by fright, while at the same time, her breasts tightened in response to his words.

"I'm a man, and I'm telling you without a doubt that he walks out of his door to go out with you, he is planning on spending the night between your thighs. I'm not the one being cruel; you are."

Lily moaned, unsure exactly why as Shade took a step back. It took a moment before Lily could gather herself enough to unlock the door and let herself in. When she turned to slam the door in his face, she stopped when he placed his hand on the door.

"I'll have to teach you how to break that hold." He turned, leaving without another word.

She still slammed the door, but he was already pulling out of the driveway so it lacked the effect she wanted. It did make her feel better, though.

She locked the door before going up to her room to get ready for bed. In her room, she caught sight of herself in the mirror, making her pause before climbing in bed. Her cheeks were flushed and her breasts still felt tight and achy. Her hand went to her forehead, feeling the beginning of a headache.

She opened a door in her mind, thrusting all thoughts of Shade and what she was feeling inside. She couldn't let herself be attracted to him. Earlier, when she had turned to shut the door, she had seen a look on his face before he could disguise it with his usual inscrutable one. She had no trouble recognizing the darkness in his soul that he kept hidden.

She had no intention of falling for him like the other women that constantly surrounded him. She was going to find her cowboy and bring him back to Treepoint, and they would live happily in this house.

Lily laid down, fantasizing about her imaginary man, trying to drive all thoughts of Shade away. She didn't realize when she finally managed to fall asleep his was the last image in her mind.

CHAPTER EIGHT

Lily sat next to Charles in church, holding hands, and she wished she could feel for him the way he felt toward her. It wouldn't be too long from now that she was going to have to talk to him. She had already told him they had no future and he needed to find someone else, but he had just shook his head, saying he would wait.

Lily smiled sadly to herself. He would wait forever for her if she gave him the least bit of encouragement. She didn't want that for him, though; it wasn't fair. He deserved a woman that loved him as much as he loved her. She knew she didn't have the stomach to be cruel to him like Shade suggested; she resolved that she could make him understand without hurting him.

Lily stood up when it came time to sing, her gaze caught by Rachel as she sat with her nephew and brothers. Holly and Mrs. Langley sat in the same pew. She and Rachel had worked long into the afternoon yesterday organizing the basement, talking throughout the long day, and she had found herself sharing things with her that she'd imparted only to Beth. Rachel was easy to talk to and she was Lily's own age, sharing many of the same experiences. She would miss their days together when she went back to college, which she was already dreading with Penni's absence.

After church, Charles went to the diner with her and they sat at the same table with Beth and The Last Riders. It was uncomfortable at first, yet gradually everyone at the table just ignored them as they sat at the end of the table talking quietly. All except Shade, whose eyes she could feel on them even though he had his sunglasses on.

"We're going swimming, Lily. Want to come?" Beth invited.

"No, thanks. I'm going to stay at home and relax." Lily refused the invitation, knowing they would refrain from taking their cooler of beer if she went. She didn't want to spoil the day for them.

"Are you sure?" Beth asked.

"Yes."

Not long after, Charles finished, bending down to give her his usual kiss on the cheek before he left.

A cup smashed on the floor and everyone jumped.

"Sorry, my elbow hit my cup," Beth apologized.

"You didn't get cut by any glass, did you?" Lily saw the smashed cup on the floor by her sister's feet.

"No, I'm fine. Just clumsy."

"I'll call you tonight," Charles said before leaving, ignoring the strained silence at the table.

When they got home a few minutes later, Beth and Razer went upstairs to change into their swimsuits. While they changed, Lily loaded the cooler with cold sandwiches and fruit for when they became hungry. Opening the refrigerator, she found some bottled water and sodas, putting those in the cooler, as well.

As she had taken out the water and soda, she had noticed that the beers Shade had left behind were still inside the fridge. Beth hadn't asked why there was beer in there, so Lily had come to the conclusion that she had asked Shade to keep an eye on her. She felt ashamed that Shade had been put in the position of watching a grown woman.

"You sure you don't want to change your mind and go?" Beth asked, coming into the kitchen.

"No, thanks. I think I'll read for a while in the backyard and get some sun that way."

"All right, if you're sure." Giving Razer a glance, she said, "We may just spend the night at the club, if that's all right?"

"Of course. I'll see you both tomorrow."

Lily watched them leave, remembering the days that she and Beth would go spend the day together swimming. She missed those times with Beth. She didn't resent Razer or the others. It was her own fault she couldn't bear to be around them when they were drinking.

She changed into her bikini before fixing herself an iced tea and going outside into the backyard. She sat down on a lounge chair, putting on some tanning lotion before she lay back to read a self-help book.

She enjoyed lying in the warm sun, especially in the backyard that was completely closed off with a privacy fence and mature trees that prevented anyone from looking into it. It was her own safe-zone of privacy to just be herself since the houses on both sides were one-story and the home behind theirs was empty. It had been that way for years, but it was regularly maintained, and every now and then, they would see a car outside. Their father had told them it belonged to a couple who vacationed there twice a year.

Lily rolled onto her stomach after laying the lounge chair flat. She felt the swimsuit's bottom ride up a little, but she was too drowsy to fiddle with it, knowing no one would see. It was getting a little snug on her and she needed to get a new one. She'd had the same one since high school, though as she seldom wore it, she didn't want to waste the money.

Lily later woke from her nap startled, feeling warm hands rubbing cold lotion into her skin. Her hands went to her side, ready to jump up from the lounge chair.

"Stay still. I didn't want you to burn," Shade's voice sounded behind her as his hands rubbed more lotion onto the backs of her legs.

"That's enough. I was going to go in and get changed," Lily protested.

"Stay and relax. I brought us some steaks to grill. When they're almost done, you can get changed."

Lily wasn't sure, but she thought she felt the faint touch of his thumb against the lowest globe of her butt. She started to stiffen; however, Shade was already up and moving away.

Lily turned her head, seeing that he must have been here for a while since the steaks were already on a plate, waiting to be put on the grill he was heating up.

"How did you get in?" Lily asked.

"I have a key."

"What? How?" Lily asked.

"Beth gave me her extra key when you were in the hospital. She'd asked me to pack some clothes for you."

Her sister had neglected to tell her that it was Shade who had brought her clothes to the hospital. Lily was horrified at the thought of Shade going through her bedroom, opening drawers. She remembered the red panties that had been packed for her. Lily was going to let Beth have it when she returned home.

"You can grab a quick shower. The steaks are almost done."

Lily didn't want to get up from the lounge chair. Her top was indecent and her large breasts were barely held inside the tiny cups.

Fussing at herself for not bringing a wrap, Lily got to her feet and hurried toward the back door, keeping her face averted from Shade's.

A hard arm went around her waist, pulling her toward him.

"Wait a minute."

A finger pressed on the skin just above the flesh of her breasts. "You've gotten too much sun. Put some lotion on before you come back downstairs. I'll keep the steaks warm."

"I'm a grown woman," Lily snapped.

"I can see that for myself." His eyes were on her breasts.

"Jerk." Lily started to wiggle away but was released before she could do so.

"Get changed." Shade grinned.

"I planned to." Lily stomped away, but then walked more demurely after she glanced back and saw his eyes on her butt.

"Don't say anything unless you want to learn my lesson on respect," he said, seeing the fire in her eyes.

Lily muttered something unintelligible under her breath.

"What did you say?" he asked with a warning glint in his eyes.

"I'll be back in a minute."

Lily showered, washing her hair thoroughly. After drying off, she smoothed some body lotion onto her skin before sliding on a pale green maxi dress that came to her ankles. Leaving her hair to dry naturally, she went back downstairs to the smell of the steaks, making her hungry.

Outside, Shade was already putting the steaks onto a platter. He had also packed out the tea pitcher and glasses with ice. There was even a big baked potato placed on each plate.

"Exactly how long have you been here?" Lily asked, taking a seat at the table.

"Long enough." Shade grinned, setting the plate of steaks down onto the table.

"I would complain, but the food looks too good," Lily said with wry amusement.

Shade placed one of the big steaks on her plate before serving himself. Lily cut off a piece of the tender meat then took a bite.

"It's delicious," she complimented.

"You didn't think I could cook?" Shade raised a brow.

"Why would you need to cook? You have a bunch of pretty women cooking and delivering it to you," Lily teased without rancor.

"I'll have you know that we all take turns cooking and sharing chores."

"I bet that's interesting. How often does Winter get stuck doing chores?"

"Not often, unless it's a punishment. She has a way of finagling things to get her way."

"I know. It comes from being a high school principal. She was a mastermind at making the kids do things that they didn't want to do." Lily remembered her own experiences at losing to Winter's machinations.

"Really?"

Lily nodded her head. "The seniors wanted to cut class on the first day of spring—it was a tradition at our school—yet students every year would manage to get into trouble. The previous principal had tried to stop it but wasn't successful. Winter, on the other hand, acted all gung ho for us to have the day off. She told us that if we volunteered to clean the kitchen of the school's chef training program she would let us have the afternoon off. What she didn't tell us was that the students had made pizza the day before and hadn't used pizza pans. It took us all day to clean those ovens. I had nightmares about burnt-on cheese for a month."

Shade had stopped eating. Lily looked at him in question before it dawned on her what the look meant. She couldn't stop the laughter from bubbling from her throat.

"Don't tell me she got you on that one?"

"Let's change the subject before I decide to stuff her into our oven."

They talked the rest of the meal about the different

things people ordered through the factory.

"Knox put Diamond on a budget," Lily said when he described Diamond sneaking into the factory when a new shipment arrived.

"She finally calmed down. She's too busy decorating her new house."

Lily didn't tell him about the two cases of MREs she had bought on his day off.

Cleaning the table, she watched Shade turn off the grill, making sure it was out before they went inside.

"I cooked; you can do the dishes," he said, opening the fridge to take out a beer. Lily stiffened as he went to the living room and turned on the television.

"What do you want to watch? Something scary or something funny?"

"Funny," Lily answered as she continued putting up the dishes.

"Scary it is."

"Don't you dare."

"Then you better hurry up." Lily closed the dishwasher before going into the living room to take the other side of the couch.

He had chosen a romantic comedy to watch, which Lily didn't watch often and never with a male. She became so uncomfortable watching the two main characters fool around on the screen that, during one particular scene, Lily jumped up and went into the kitchen to make popcorn. She filled two bowls, grabbed a soda for herself and hesitantly took another beer for Shade.

"Thanks." He took the beer and popcorn from her, and then Lily resumed her seat.

She didn't even stiffen when she heard the can pop this time while not taking her eyes off the television.

After the movie was over, Lily carried the popcorn and empty cans to the kitchen.

Shade was already at the door when she returned.

"Lock the door behind me."

"I will. Thanks for the steaks, Shade." Lily braced herself and leaned up, brushing his cheek with a soft kiss before stepping back hastily.

"Goodnight."

"Goodnight, Lily."

* * *

Shade sat on his bike in the parking lot of Rick's Pub. The lights inside cut off and the workers exited, casting cautious looks in Shade's direction. Charles came out last, shutting and locking the doors behind him. When he turned to the parking lot and saw him sitting there, Shade didn't see any surprise. He walked towards him. Shade had to give the kid credit, he didn't flinch from his hard stare.

"If you came for that dinner, I'm afraid were closed."

Shade let a wry smile touch his lips. "We both know that's not why I'm here."

Charles looked him over. "If you came here to threaten me to stay away from Lily, I won't. You're wasting your time. Even if you beat me up, all I have to do is show Lily. It would turn her against you. There's no way you can win, Shade." The little shit smiled at him.

Shade smiled back affably before reaching into his pocket, pulling some photographs out and handing them to Charles.

Charles took the photos from him, turning pale. He looked back up at Shade.

Shade leaned forward, taking the photos back, looking at the woman and child in the picture. "Amazing resemblance, isn't it? I think we both know what Lily would do if she found out you knocked up one of her friends. Miranda may have passed your kid off to the dumbass she married, but we both know the kid is yours. Not only would Lily not have anything to do with you, but it would break up Miranda's marriage, and the gossip would get back to your daddy. I believe her husband is a Deacon in the church." Shade leaned forward, resting his forearm on his knee, his eyes pinning Charles in place.

"What do you want?" Charles asked, his jaw tight. Shade smiled in satisfaction.

"What I want is for you to go back to Lexington. I'll even give you a couple of weeks home before you have to leave, just don't try to see Lily anymore."

Charles nodded his agreement.

Shade straightened, starting his motor.

"She won't ever love you. What makes you think you stand a better chance than me?" Charles looked him over as if he was trash.

Shade gave him his moment. Charles knew he had lost all hope of having Lily; he sure as fuck was taking it better than Shade would have. He gazed back at the man, but felt no pity.

"The difference between us, Charles, is I would give my right arm for her. You, on the other hand, didn't take five seconds to put on a fucking condom." Shade drove off, leaving the speechless man behind.

CHAPTER NINE

Lily changed into her workout outfit, no longer worried about its brief coverage. She had become used to Shade seeing her in it after working out with him for almost a month now.

As she beat him to the mats, which was a first, she could hear music playing upstairs, so that meant that the usual Friday party had already started.

She began stretching while she waited for Shade to appear. The time had flown by and she could tell her defense lessons had helped her confidence, combined with the weights making her feel stronger. Her panic attacks had decreased to be almost nonexistent.

She had also confided to Rachel that she had decided to stay in Treepoint and finish her classes on the internet. Lily was enjoying feeling more comfortable in the world, and she didn't want to go back to the insecurities of college life.

She couldn't admit that she would miss everyone too badly if she left, though. She had become used to spending her Saturdays with Rachel, and she liked spending her days at the factory. Georgia was the only fly in the ointment. Her hostility had increased as she witnessed the strengthening friendship between Lily and Shade.

Lily's mind shied away from the mere mention of an actual relationship with Shade, but their friendship had certainly developed. He had spent the last few weekends with her at her house when Beth and Razer had been at the club.

She was so happy that Lily felt as if the weight of her fears was slowly dissolving.

Her favorite music came on the sound system while she was finishing warming up when Shade came downstairs.

"Sorry, there was something I needed to take care of."

"No problem," Lily said, bouncing up and down on the balls of her feet. "What are we going to work on today? Do you want me to try to knee you again?" Her eager face was lit up with excitement.

"You seem anxious to take my dick out of commission."

Lily laughed, her eyes twinkling. Usually this was a side of herself that only Beth saw, but Shade had proven his gentlemanly behavior over time, and she now felt comfortable enough to be herself around him.

"We're going to work on something different today," he said, moving her closer to the wall at the end of the mat. "I want you to try to get out of a specific type of hold. For instance, if you're getting into your car and someone comes up behind you."

Lily nodded.

"You ready?"

"Yes."

"Turn around."

Lily innocently turned around, clueless as to what he was about to do. As Shade moved closer to her, pressing his body against her back, Lily's hand automatically went to the wall to keep herself from being pressed against it, leaving her helpless. She began to panic but managed to calm herself down.

One of her arms left the wall on instinct, going back to try to push him away, and his hand caught her wrist, holding it captured against her lower back. Her other hand automatically went back and it was captured also, leaving her defenseless, pressed flat against the wall.

His lower body was flush against her butt, making her feel surrounded. Her breathing escalated and her mind started to shut down. She went limp, about to pass out. Shade stepped back, and helplessly, she started to slide down the wall.

Shade took her arm, leading her to the corner, and left her there to stand alone. She stood, gasping for breath, her hands going to her head, fighting the darkness descending on her terror-filled senses.

"Hands to your side. Stand up straight. Lily, by now you should know how I want you to stand." Shade's hard voice had her correcting her posture, her shoulders straightening as her hands obediently went to her side. Regulating her breathing, she focused on Shade as he took a drink of his bottled water before he went to the weights and began working out, ignoring her.

Lily wanted to be angry at him for ruining her good mood. She resented him throwing her into a panic attack.

"Lose the attitude, Lily, or my hand is going to be on that bouncy butt."

Lily was shocked that he'd threatened her with physical violence. She had never expected him to lay a hand on her in a personal way.

Shade was sitting on the weight bench with his arm frozen in position at her look of shocked horror. "I didn't say I would beat you, Lily. But I will smack that ass if you don't behave." His blue gaze stared into hers.

Lily gasped, turning her eyes toward the wall.

"Eyes forward," Shade said, continuing his arm curls.

Lily's eyes snapped forward as she attempted to pacify her tumultuous emotions. The shock of him saying that he would smack her butt had her forgetting the feeling of being held against the wall. As she calmed, she was able to start looking at the situation objectively. It took a long time for Lily to work through how dangerous that hold was and why she needed to learn to get out of it. She even realized where she had screwed up.

"I shouldn't have reached back," she said out loud.

"No," Shade answered.

Lily took a step forward.

"Are you ready to go back to the mat?"

"Yes," Lily said determinedly, leaving the corner.

"Turn around."

Lily took a deep breath then, meeting his gaze briefly, she turned around. This time, when Shade grabbed her, pushing her against the wall, she braced herself with her arms.

"What do I do next?" Lily's voice trembled at feeling his body pressed against her own. She felt the panic attack coming; however, she forced herself to listen to his directions. She did exactly as he told her, and while her movements were too timid to work, she knew that if they practiced she could break his hold.

Shade released her. "Enough?"

"Yes." Lily turned around, sliding away from him.

"We'll work on that until you get it right. You need to learn how to defend yourself when someone comes up behind you. Men who attack women are confident that you'll panic, that you'll be too startled to be able to defend yourself."

"I'll work on it until I get it right." Lily was going to prove to him that she could break that hold.

"I know you will. You're learning fast. I'm proud of you," Shade complimented.

Lily took his praise to heart. "Thank you, Sir." Lily reached out and hugged him. She hugged Beth all the time; it was part of her personality to show her affection. "I really appreciate all your help."

Lily turned away from him, missing the hungry

expression on his face.

"I'll get changed." Lily walked away, so happy that she hadn't panicked twice. She was learning to be more capable of defending herself. For a woman who had a history of misadventures, it was a big thing for her to become more confident in the world around her instead of seeing ghosts around every corner.

Lily didn't take long to change; she would shower when she got home, and Shade was waiting for her in the other room when she came out. The noise coming from upstairs was even louder than normal as she made her way across the room. Her eyes traveled up the steps to the closed door.

"It sounds like a football game is going on up there," she remarked.

"Several of the brothers from Ohio are down for the weekend."

"Oh." Lily tried not to sound disappointed, certain that with his friends visiting that Shade wouldn't hang out with her this weekend. She had gotten used to having him around.

She had talked to Charles, telling him as gently as possible that he was a friend, and would always remain just a friend. He had taken it well, but Lily believed that he hoped she would eventually change her mind. She wouldn't, and since she had told him, she didn't feel right asking for him to spend time with her. She had the sinking feeling that it was going to be a lonely weekend.

Shade was walking her out the door when his cell phone rang. He listened for a minute before he replied to whoever had called.

"Give me five. I need a shower and to get changed." He then disconnected the call.

"You go ahead," Lily told him, not wanting to keep him from his fun.

"You sure?"

"My car is just around the corner," Lily said dolefully.

"All right. I'll see you later," Shade said, going back inside.

"Bye."

Lily walked down the path toward her car, checking her text messages to see that Beth had left her one saying that she and Razer had left for the party early and that they would see her tomorrow. She saw Razer's bike already parked in the almost-full parking lot.

She placed her bag in the backseat of her car and was about to get inside when a car swerved into the parking lot. Lily recognized it instantly. Leaving her car door open, she saw Miranda getting out of her car, slamming her door shut before going up the steps to the house.

"Miranda!" Lily yelled, drawing her attention.

Miranda didn't stop. Lily ran after her, catching her halfway up the steps.

"What's going on?" Lily asked, taking her arm.

"Don't you dare talk to me, Lily, after you have lied to my face!" Miranda spat out, trying to pull away from Lily's grip.

"What have I lied about?" Lily questioned, sincerely confused.

"The whole time I told you that I've been worried about Kaley, you knew that she's been here every day and the weekends, too."

Lily hadn't tried to hide that Kaley was here constantly, she just hadn't volunteered the information, and Miranda had never outright asked for it.

"I knew, but I didn't want to butt into her private business," Lily tried to defend herself.

"You're no friend of mine, Lily. Georgia saw me at the store, telling me that she's seen her here drunk and doing God knows what, and you didn't say a thing."

"I've never seen her drunk," Lily protested.

"Why would I believe you? You're one of them. Your sister is in there right now. Well, you might not care about *your* sister, but I do *mine*." She rushed up the steps.

Lily didn't know what to do. Twisting her hands, she now regretted not mentioning to Miranda that Kaley had been there so frequently; however, she had truly believed it was Kaley's private business.

Lily was relieved when she looked up to see that Miranda had been blocked from entering the house. Several men were standing in front of the door, watching them curiously as Miranda stormed back down the steps.

Lily turned to go, but Miranda took a sharp turn, walking across the hilly yard to the path that led around the house and disappearing around the corner.

Lily wished she hadn't left her phone in the car; she could have called Beth. Not knowing what else to do, she followed Miranda.

"Miranda!" The woman's fury made her fast. Lily ran behind her, trying to stop her from making a scene that she would regret, yet she couldn't catch her. The back door that led into the kitchen was open, so Lily ran in behind the disappearing woman. Several eyes from the family room were turned to the other room where Lily could hear raised voices already.

As she moved further into the house, she had expected to see a party atmosphere, and there was, just not the type she had anticipated. Several of the women were in a state of undress. Kaley was rising up from one of the couches next to Cash. Her top was completely off, her skirt was hiked to her waist and she wasn't wearing underwear. Her sister had caught them actually having sex in the open. And they hadn't been the only ones.

Several women were covering themselves, pulling on clothes. Those who did have on clothes were the type Lily had never seen them wearing before.

She was instantly grateful that everyone's backs were to her as she watched Miranda and Kaley have it out.

"You slut. This would kill Mom if she knew what you were doing," Miranda screamed at her sister.

"Make sure you run and tell her," Kaley yelled back.

"How could you fuck someone in front of all these people?" Miranda sounded horrified at her sister.

"Look around you, dumbass. I wasn't the only one fucking. I was doing it because it felt good. I've had more dick in the last two months than I had in five years of marriage and I fucking love it. In fact, you might as well know that I'm joining their club as soon as I finish fucking all the head members."

"What!?" Miranda screeched.

"That's how you get in. You have to fuck six of the eight original members. But I plan on fucking them all," Kaley bragged.

Miranda reached out, smacking her sister across the face as they went into a full-fledged cat fight.

Lily stood frozen, unable to move for a second, unaware that whimpers were escaping her mouth. That was when Razer and Viper came running down the steps with Beth and Winter behind them. Both women looked like they had just thrown their clothes on. Beth was wearing a short skirt and a fringed vest that Lily had never seen before and would never have expected her sister to wear.

Lily wasn't even aware that all the eyes in the room weren't on Miranda and Kaley but her. She was too lost in taking in what Kaley had said. She understood Miranda's shock because she was experiencing it herself. In fact, she was so stunned that she couldn't even turn away as Jewell began scrambling into her shorts at the same time that Stori was pushing Nickel away, breaking his hold on her bared breasts.

"Lily." Beth came down the steps, speaking to her sister quietly.

Lily took a step backwards into the kitchen, and the door to her side opened. Evie came to an abrupt stop when she saw Lily. She wasn't wearing a top and her blue jean shorts had been left unbuttoned. She moved to the side, obviously uncomfortable, and Rider came into view, walking up the steps without a shirt and wearing only his jeans. His hair was wet and his face froze at her expression. He moved to the side and Lily's eyes met Shade's. He had changed; his hair was just as wet, but he was dressed.

His face hardened when he saw her pale one and he approached her. Taking a step toward her, Beth was as white as a ghost as Lily backed away from them. They both tried to speak at the same time, but her whimpers of pain wouldn't let her hear their words.

Lily ran, unable to bear what her mind was telling her.

"Lily!" She heard Shade running after her and Beth's pleading voice, yet she couldn't stop. She had to get away.

She flew down the path, almost falling down several times. She sensed that Shade was close to reaching her as she screamed all the way to her car, barely managing to get in, slam the door shut and lock it before she felt him try to open the door. By this point people were coming out of the house to watch the commotion. Beth and Razer pulled Shade back from her car as she thrust it into gear and drove out of the parking lot.

Lily couldn't go home. She couldn't face Beth and Razer right now, and she knew they wouldn't be far behind her. She needed somewhere she could go and think before the panic closed her mind down.

Lily swerved the car as an idea struck her. She knew where she could go. The only place that was left to her.

CHAPTER TEN

Lily picked up her backpack after the professor finished class. It was only the second week into the class, but Lily could tell it wasn't going to prove a challenge, and she needed a challenge to keep her mind occupied. She honestly wished now that she hadn't saved all the easy classes for her last semester.

She walked slowly back to her dorm room, becoming tired before she was even halfway there. Taking a seat on one of the benches outside, she watched the carefree students on their way to their classes.

She looked down at the plain brown dress she was wearing. She needed to go shopping for some more clothes. She hadn't been back to her house since the day she'd left for work at the factory. That night after she had left Beth at The Last Rider club, Lily had driven back to college. She had then sat inside an all-night restaurant on the outskirts of town until her dorm had opened in the morning.

She had texted Beth that she was fine and that she would see her in a few weeks, but she needed time. Beth had texted back, asking Lily to talk to her. She hadn't replied to her texts or calls, though. She had slept practically that whole weekend, barely managing with her migraine to go to the local discount store to buy her some clothes and toiletries before coming back to her bed.

Lily felt so alone; she didn't know how she could make it without Beth. It was a constant struggle not to call and talk to her; however, Lily couldn't bring herself to break her silence.

She hadn't cared that Beth had become involved in what she considered a sex club. She wasn't so naïve that she hadn't heard of them before, even if she and Beth had never talked about sex. Lily believed that it was her sister's choice to make, just like it was Kaley's.

What hurt Lily and what she couldn't understand were the lies Beth had used to conceal her other life. Lily had thought they had confided everything to each other, and yet, she had become a part of a lifestyle that condoned free sex with every member and hadn't told her, and had actually taken devious measures to keep it hidden from her.

Beth had obviously picked The Last Riders over her. With them, she could be herself while with Lily she had felt compelled to hide her deepening relationships with them. Beth had pulled away from her; it was as simple as that.

The one person she had trusted in the whole world had lied to her on numerous occasions to protect The Last Riders' code of secrecy.

Lily blinked the tears from her eyes, brushing her hair back from her face.

She rose from the bench, continuing on to her dorm. She had to pass the parking lot in front of her dorm where the sun glinted off the parked chrome motorcycles. Lily paused, wishing she had noticed them sooner. She could have turned around before they'd seen her.

Lily kept walking, seeing Beth standing by the doors to her dorm.

"Hello, Lily." Her sister's anxious face watched for her

reaction.

"Beth."

Beth took a step forward, but Lily took a step back, her face twisting into a painful mask.

"Please talk to me, Lily. I can't bear this silence from you," Beth pleaded.

Lily nodded her head. She didn't want to take Beth to her room, yet she didn't want to stay where the passersby could overhear. Lily pointed to a shaded bench under a large tree.

"Are you doing okay?" Beth asked once they were seated.

"I'm doing fine. Classes are pretty much the same," Lily said, shrugging.

"Lily, I'd like to explain what you saw that night."

She winced at her sister's words. "What I saw was self-explanatory."

"Yes, it was." Beth took a deep breath. "But it's not ugly the way Kaley said. We all care about each other, Lily. We're friends that—"

"Have sex with each other," Lily finished, looking down at her clenched hands, determined not to snap the red band in front of her sister.

"Yes—no. I don't have sex with the other members," Beth explained.

"Kaley said to become a member you have to have sex with the original members." This time her hand snapped the band, despite her promise to herself.

"Yes, but I didn't. I became a member because several of them felt they owed me a marker or wanted Razer's vote in the future. Viper gave me his vote when you were hurt in the accident because I didn't freak out on Ton. Some gave me theirs because I helped solve Gavin's murder."

"So you got all your votes that way?" Lily asked.

"No," her sister admitted quietly.

Lily twisted the band on her wrist tighter. "I don't need

to hear this, Beth."

"Lily, I just didn't feel comfortable discussing this with you."

"I understand." And Lily did; it was something she was uncomfortable discussing in detail. "It's hard to talk to someone who freaks out over every little thing."

"You don't, sweetheart." Beth tried to touch her hand, but Lily pulled away.

Lily stared straight ahead, focusing on a tree to her left, not letting her eyes go to the men sitting on their bikes, watching them intently.

"Who are the original members that Kaley was talking about?" Lily asked the question she knew was going to hurt the most.

Beth hesitated, however she answered her low question. "Viper, Cash, Rider, Train, Lucky, Knox, Razer and Shade."

Unconsciously, Lily's hand went to the skin over her heart, rubbing the flesh.

"Your husband is one of the men who gives sexual votes to women who enter the club?" Lily couldn't hide her disbelief that Beth would let Razer have sex with other women.

"He doesn't vote anymore. He hasn't since we broke up three years ago."

"That's why you broke up?"

"No, we broke up because I thought he had cheated on me with Bliss. He hadn't."

"I see. Do Sex Piston and her crew know about The Last Riders?"

"Yes."

"So, everyone you're close to knew, except me," Lily stated. "Me, you didn't tell."

"No. I didn't know if you would be able to handle the life I have with Razer. I didn't want you to think less of me," Beth confessed.

"Instead, you just shut me out." Lily gave her sister a

sad smile. "I would never have judged you on your sex life, Beth. Because I have hang-ups doesn't make me believe others should. What hurt me was the deception. You lied to conceal what was going on." Lily felt tears slide down her cheeks. No, the details didn't matter, but the lies definitely did. "I've never lied to you, ever, and I didn't think you had to me, either. I'm hurt, but I'll get over it probably in a few days. You know I never could stay mad for long." Lily looked at her sister's pained expression. She didn't know what else to say, though. It was like her feelings toward Beth were encased in ice. She couldn't mend her sister's broken heart when her own was broken.

"All right. Will you at least quit ignoring my texts and calls?"

"Yes." Lily got to her feet, picking up her backpack.

"Do you want to go get a bite to eat before you go inside?" Beth's hopeful expression didn't sway Lily. She didn't want to be near Shade ever again.

"No, thanks."

"How about I drive down this weekend and bring your suitcases here? You have to need clothes."

"I already bought some new ones. You can box up what's in my room and give them to the church. I have a test on Monday, so this weekend isn't a good time. I'll see you for Thanksgiving."

Without another word, Lily went inside the building, not letting her gaze return to the parking lot. She wanted to run back into her sister's arms, but she knew she couldn't. She didn't trust her anymore.

* * *

Beth watched her sister walk through the doors before she couldn't hold it back any longer. She buried her face in her hands, heartbroken at the devastation she had caused with her secrecy. Lily was never going to forgive her. She had broken Lily's faith in her. She could see it in her delicate, pale face.

Lily looked like the wind would blow her away; she

looked so fragile.

"Beth, please don't cry, kitten." Razer sat down next to her, pulling her into his arms.

"I've lost her, Razer. I can see it in her eyes. She's so hurt. It's like looking into an open wound."

"She'll get over it."

"No, Razer, she won't. She thinks I've lied and deceived her, and she's right. I should have told her at least parts of it; she could have taken that. What she can't accept is the one person she trusted hiding things from her."

"Did she tell you not to talk to her anymore?"

"No, but she told me to give her clothes away. She's cutting herself off from me."

"Then don't let her," Shade's voice came from over Razer's shoulder. Beth looked back at him.

"She knows everything now, Shade. She knows that Razer and you both are original members. How the women get the votes."

"She was bound to find out sooner or later. When you, Winter and Diamond found out, was it any less painful? But each of you got over it and moved on. Lily will, too."

"No, she won't, Shade. Lily is different. She'll believe that Razer and you took advantage of the women."

"That won't last long when she's around them," Shade said ironically.

Beth got to her feet. "You just don't get it, Shade. She's cut not only me, but us all from her heart. That's what Lily does. Lily doesn't give second chances with her love."

"No, Beth, it's you who doesn't understand. Lily's not going to be given the choice."

CHAPTER ELEVEN

Lily walked back to her dorm from her class the next day. Her mind had not been on the class but on Beth's face. Lily knew the position Beth had been in must have been hard, yet the ice encasing her kept her from reaching out.

Lily stopped, leaning against a tree as a wave of dizziness swept over her. Taking a deep breath, she straightened, just wanting to make it back to her dorm room and crawl in bed. She walked another few feet, seeing her dorm building not far away. Her sole focus was on simply putting one step in front of the other, so she didn't notice the big truck pull up next to her.

"Get in, Lily." Lily looked through the passenger window and saw Shade. She didn't say anything, taking another step forward. "You can either get in or I'll put you in." His dark sunglasses did little to hide his harsh expression.

"Go away," Lily forced herself to talk to him.

She heard the truck door open and Shade get out of the truck, opening the passenger door. "Get in."

"If you don't go away, I'll scream," Lily threatened.

"Try it and see what I do." She could tell he meant it.

Lily sighed. If he wanted to talk like Beth, she would listen rather than argue with him on a busy sidewalk. Maybe then, he would leave like Beth and she could be alone again. She climbed into the truck, and Shade slammed the door closed before going around the front of it and getting back inside.

When he put the truck in gear, driving out of the parking lot, Lily didn't try to talk to him as he drove through the small town. He pulled into a restaurant with a drive-thru, ordering food, and still not a word had been spoken between them.

He didn't ask what she wanted when placing the order, yet she knew he was ordering the food for her. She was equally surprised when he didn't pull to the side to eat. Instead, he got back on the road after the large bag of food was given to him.

The aromas coming from it were making Lily nauseous.

"Don't you dare throw up. Rider will be pissed enough when he sees his truck is gone."

Lily forced the bile back down.

Shade pulled into the parking lot of the local hotel, stopping in front of a block of rooms. Picking up the bag, he walked to one of the rooms and disappeared inside after unlocking the door. A second later, he was back, opening the door by her side.

"Get out."

"Quit ordering me around. I'm not going in there." The words were no sooner out of her mouth than she found herself lifted from the truck. Shade slammed the door closed with his shoulder as she was struggling to get away, and then carried her into the room, slamming that door shut with his foot.

The room was small, but it held two beds, a small table and a dresser with a television. He set her down on one of the chairs by the small, round table in the room. When she would have jumped to her feet, he leaned down, placing a hand on each side of the chair she was sitting in, effectively blocking her in.

"Lily, I am a man with infinite patience, but you are trying me. I advise you to keep your ass on that chair. Do you understand me?"

Lily did. She could hear the threat in his voice.

Shade straightened, going to the other chair and sitting down. He opened the bag, pulling out a small cup of soup and several packs of crackers then set them in front of her with a plastic spoon.

"Eat."

"Will you please quit ordering me around?" Lily asked again, her voice as cold as ice.

"I'll think about it." Shades lips twitched in amusement at her frosty gaze.

Lily took the lid off the soup, and her stomach lurched.

"Eat a cracker first."

Lily's trembling fingers tore open a pack of the crackers, removing one. She nibbled on it until her stomach settled then ate another.

She watched Shade eat the large burger and fries as she picked up her spoon and took a small bite of the soup before she opened another pack of crackers. Her stomach gradually settled.

Shade finished eating, setting one of the drinks in front of her. Lily took a drink. The chocolate shake was delicious. She started to cry as she drank it, remembering the meals they had shared over the summer.

"I hate you."

"I know." Shade removed his sunglasses, letting her see his remorse.

Lily quit eating, sitting there with tears coursing down her cheeks, hating herself for letting him see how weak she was.

Shade stood, picking her up before going to the bed and laying her down. "Sleep, Lily. You'll feel better when you wake up. You're exhausted."

Lily closed her eyes, unable to keep the drowsiness at

bay.

* * *

She didn't know how long she'd slept. Waking, she sat up and she could tell it was dark outside.

"What time is it?"

"Ten o'clock. You've slept six hours."

"Oh." Lily brushed her hands through her hair, trying to untangle the mess.

"There're clothes for you in the bag. Go take a shower."

Lily didn't argue. She had learned it was useless against Shade. So, picking up the bag, she went into the bathroom. She took a quick shower, drying off when she got out, and peeked into the bag he'd given her. Everything she needed was in there. She dressed in the jeans and sweatshirt, putting on the warm socks and tennis shoes. She brushed her hair, leaving it down to dry before putting her dirty clothes in the bag.

She went into the other room to see he had somehow made them sandwiches.

She held up a hand, forestalling him. "I'll eat." She wasn't up to fighting him. If she ate without arguing, then maybe he would take her back to her dorm.

Lily sat at the table, eating her sandwich while watching him lie on the bed on his back, watching the television.

When she was finished, she threw away the trash and the empty milk carton.

"Will you take me back to my dorm now?"

"Later. Come here."

Lily wasn't stupid; she wasn't going near him.

Getting up, she went to the phone on the bedside table instead. Before she could place a call, however, the phone was jerked from her hand and she felt herself falling onto the bed. Lily froze as Shade picked her up and adjusted her until she was lying on the bed with her head on the pillow.

"I'll take you back in the morning in time for your eight o'clock class."

"I want to go now," Lily spoke between clenched teeth.

"Too bad." Shade lay down on the bed next to her, adjusting the pillow until he could see the television.

"You're unbelievable. You think you can do anything you want," she said resentfully.

Shade ignored her, turning the volume up.

Lily crossed her arms over her chest, hating the stubborn man. She lay there, gradually unable to help being drawn in to the old black-and-white movie. She fell back asleep before it ended.

The next thing she knew, Shade was waking her up.

"Move it if you don't want to miss your class."

Lily got up from the bed, following Shade outside. She climbed back into the truck, not saying anything. Shade went through a drive-thru, getting her breakfast and handing it to her as he continued driving back to her campus while she ate. She finished as he pulled up outside her dorm.

Opening the door, she slid out of the truck, slamming the door behind her. She heard the truck finally pull out as she walked into her dorm. She had an hour to get changed and get to class, so she rushed upstairs to prepare for the day.

It was only later, as she walked to class, that she realized he had known what time her class was.

* * *

Shade showed up the rest of the week, taking her to his hotel room every evening. Lily quit trying to argue with him. She had tried to evade him, only to lose. She hadn't spoken to him since the first day, though, and what irritated her the most was he seemed not to care that she was giving him the silent treatment.

Friday, he was waiting for her once again.

She climbed into the truck, expecting him to turn into the hotel again; instead, he headed past it, staying on the road. Lily turned to see his hard profile, wondering where he was going.

A few minutes later, there was no doubt in her mind left.

"I don't want to go home for the weekend. I have a test Monday."

"Your books are in your backpack. You can study at home."

Lily didn't have a temper, but when it was roused, he was usually the cause, and she'd had enough of him deciding what was best for her. It was a good thing he was driving or Lily would have jumped from the truck.

The closer they came to Treepoint, the madder she became at him. She didn't even have her car so that she could drive back to school. She would be forced to have Beth take her back, which she was certain was what he had planned.

When he finally pulled up in front of her house, Lily's hand immediately flew to the doorknob.

Sliding out of the truck, she shot Shade a hateful glance. "Enjoy your Friday night!" She slammed the door, turning toward the house, sick at her behavior.

She opened the house's front door and was about to shut it when a hand prevented her. Shade propelled her forward with a hand on her arm, shutting the door behind them.

"What are you doing?" Lily tried to jerk away, dropping her backpack.

"Doing something I've warned you repeatedly about," Shade said grimly.

He jerked her to the couch where he took a seat then yanked her over his lap.

"What!"

The smack across her butt caught her by surprise. He had threatened several times, but she had never thought he would actually lay a hand on her.

She tried to throw herself off his lap, yet his hand on her back prevented her. She kicked her legs, which earned her another smack across her bottom. She was wearing a dress, which was sliding dangerously high with her lying over his lap. She was mortified and angrier than ever all at the same time.

"You can't do this!" Lily screamed at him.

"Watch me."

His hand swatted her butt several more times until Lily stopped struggling and lay limply across his thighs, defeated. When he was done, he lifted her to sit next to him on the couch, gripping her jaw in his hand.

"Do not ever talk to me that way again. Do not slam doors to show your anger and throw me a fucking look like the one you did, or I will smack your ass with no dress and panties in the way. Do you understand me?"

Lily tried to turn her face away, her lashes hiding her eyes. She was embarrassed at her childish behavior. "I understand."

"How do you fucking address me?"

"I understand, Sir."

As his hand released her jaw, Shade got to his feet, going out the door without another word.

Lily sat there for several minutes, wishing she hadn't lost her temper. In a matter of minutes, Shade had ripped her icy detachment away, leaving her raw and hurting.

Any woman who wanted his vote needed her head examined.

CHAPTER TWELVE

Lily had dinner waiting for Beth and Razer when they came through the door. She could tell they weren't surprised to see her, which wasn't all that shocking.

They ate dinner with Beth asking about her classes. Lily answered her questions, but she continued to keep the barrier between them; the same barrier she had put up against Razer.

While Beth was trying to be over friendly, Razer made no attempt to hide his anger at her. Lily didn't blame him, either. It was obvious Beth was hurting. Lily just couldn't reach out to her yet.

After dinner, Lily got up to clean the table.

"I'll help."

"I've got it. You go ahead and get ready."

Beth looked her in the eye while Razer put his arm around her shoulder.

"Go, Beth. There's no reason to sit around the house, bored to death. Besides, I have a test to study for."

"I don't want to go," Beth said.

Lily sighed, ignoring Razer's angry glare. This was between Beth and her, and while he was angry, it was up to them to settle the problem.

Lily sat back down at the table, facing the couple, doing what she hadn't been capable of doing a couple of weeks ago. Her buried emotions allowed her to discuss the situation detachedly.

"Beth, you enjoy being a member of The Last Riders and their lifestyle. That's your personal business. That's what I tried to tell Miranda about Kaley. You should never take what I think or feel into consideration when it's something you want to do."

"Lily—" Beth protested.

"I am not a child any longer. I have to become more self-sufficient without you, as you are without me." Her fingertips went to the rubber band on her wrist.

The couple didn't say anything this time, listening.

"I think it's best, after your house is built, we sell this house and you keep the money. I have several job applications in and enough money saved up from working this summer that I can rent an apartment."

"Sweetheart, I'm not selling your home," Beth said firmly.

"It's not my home; it's your home. You worked and paid off our parents' debt. You've paid for this house. It's yours."

"It's ours."

Lily shook her head, getting to her feet. "I don't have a home."

"Are you deliberately trying to hurt her?" Razer snapped.

"I'm not trying to hurt Beth, Razer. I'm trying to set her free."

Lily went upstairs, leaving the couple staring at each other.

When she came back down later to study, Beth and Razer were still home despite Lily's protests. She made herself stay downstairs, studying at the kitchen table. She didn't want them to feel like she was avoiding them.

She had trouble concentrating, thinking about Shade at

the clubhouse. She was constantly flipping the band on her wrist when her thoughts would inadvertently go to him.

Finally giving up, she said goodnight and went to bed.

The next morning she was dressed and gone before Razer and Beth could wake. She left a note that said she was going to the church.

She got there early enough that Rachel hadn't arrived yet. Lily felt guilty seeing that Rachel had made good progress on sorting through the donations without her.

She started going through several boxes, managing to empty several before she heard Rachel coming in the door.

"Well, hello, Lily."

"Hi, Rachel." Lily smiled without her usual warmth.

"I'm glad you're here. I don't mind the work, but it's not fun talking to myself."

"I'm sorry I left you in a lurch. I should have told Pastor Dean and made arrangements for someone to replace me."

Rachel looked at her curiously. "Beth said you went back to school and she offered to help, but I told her no. She keeps busy enough. Pastor Dean offered to find someone else, but I was too afraid of who he would replace you with." Rachel shuddered in mock horror.

Lily couldn't blame her; some of the women from the church would be hard to be around for several hours at a time.

"Well, I'm here today," Lily said, trying to infuse enthusiasm in her voice.

They worked steadily for the next few hours before going to the diner for lunch. They returned to work again after the short break.

"How's school going?"

"Good," Lily replied, opening a box of clothing.

"I thought you had decided to stay home your last semester?"

"I changed my mind," Lily replied.

"Did you and Beth get in a fight?" Rachel asked in

surprise.

"Not exactly."

"I'm sorry. It seems I'm always prying. I need to learn to mind my own business."

"You're not prying. I just decided to stay at school and give Razer and Beth the alone time they need. I'm sure it gets old having me around all the time." Sometimes the truth was the hardest thing to take when it involved oneself.

"I don't think Beth feels that way at all. She misses you when you're gone. I saw her last week and she looked terrible, and you don't look much better. I can tell you've lost weight." Rachel's concern for both sisters was evident.

"I'll adjust." Lily shrugged off her own feelings.

Beth had a whole clubhouse of friends and a husband. She was better off without Lily being so dependent on her time and finances.

"I'm sure you will," Rachel said doubtfully then went on to talk about how she could use some space from her brothers. "I want to get an apartment in town, but they keep putting me off."

Rachel's brothers were very protective of her.

"I don't suppose you would take one off my hands," Rachel pleaded. "All three are still single," she reminded Lily.

Lily laughed, shaking her head.

"Oh, well, I like Holly. Maybe I can convince her."

They spent the rest of the afternoon plotting matches for her three brothers as they steadily sorted through the boxes.

Lily was taking a drink of water when Rachel came up with a surprising choice.

"Miranda's sister's divorce became final. I can see her with Greer."

Lily choked on her water and Rachel patted her on the back.

"I think Kaley is seeing someone," Lily told her.

"Darn. Who's she seeing?"

"One of The Last Riders," Lily answered, wishing Rachel would drop the conversation.

"Really? Which one?"

It was everything Lily could do not to say *all of them;* instead, she said the ladylike thing. "I'm not sure which one."

"Maybe it's not serious?"

"I think it's pretty serious," Lily said between gritted teeth.

"Oh, well. How about…"

Lily zoned out, losing track of the conversation as her mind played out visions of Shade and Kaley together.

"Lily, are you all right? You just went as white as a ghost," Rachel asked, stretching out to touch her arm.

"I'm fine." Reaching down, she picked up a box, moving away before Rachel could touch her.

At the end of the day, Lily told Rachel she would see her next week then walked home, refusing Rachel's offer of a ride.

She had just begun to cross the street to get to her block when a loud screech of tires sounded and Lily froze as a black car sped toward her. The next second, she went flying when a person pushed her out of the way. She lay on the pavement with the wind knocked out of her, her palms and knees burning. She turned to see the car speeding down the street then turning another corner.

"Motherfucker." Lily looked up in shock at the profanity coming from the man who had saved her life.

"Are you all right, Lily?" Pastor Dean's voice didn't sound like it did on Sundays in church, nor was the harsh expression the same affable one that she was used to seeing.

"I think so." Lily took his hand, getting shakily to her feet. He then helped her to the sidewalk after picking up her purse from the middle of the road.

"Whoever was in that car was going so fast I didn't

even see them when I started to cross the street," Lily said, brushing her messed-up hair out of her face.

"That's because they were parked," Pastor Dean replied grimly. "I was coming out of Mr. Isaac's house when I saw the car wasn't going to stop."

"Maybe their brakes malfunctioned?"

"No. I saw the brake lights come on when they slowed down to make the corner."

"I'm sure it was just someone out joy-riding then. Anyway, it doesn't matter. It's over now and no one's hurt."

"Your hands and knees look pretty busted up," Pastor Dean refuted her claim.

"I'll go home and put some antiseptic on them," Lily promised, reaching out to touch his jacket with her fingertips, not wanting to get blood on him.

"Thank you. If you hadn't reacted so fast, it could have been much worse."

"That's what I'm worried about," Pastor Dean said, his eyes still searching the empty street.

"Don't be. Accidents happen, and they always manage to find me," Lily said ruefully.

"Keep an eye out, Lily," Pastor Dean warned.

"I'm sure it's nothing," Lily said casually. "I'll see you in church tomorrow."

"Good evening, Lily."

Lily walked to her house, ignoring the burning pain from her knees and palms. As she unlocked the door, she looked back up the street to see Pastor Dean still watching. She waved her hand just before she went in, locking the door behind her.

She went upstairs to her room, carefully washing the dirt and grime from her palms and knees. She then put antiseptic on her knees before wrapping gauze around them. Her hands she left uncovered, not wanting to draw attention to them. She dressed in sweats and a loose sweatshirt, feeling chilled. Brushing her hair, she braided it, wanting the weight off her for a while. She was getting another migraine.

Deciding to fix a light dinner, she went downstairs where she dug her cell phone out of her purse. Beth had texted her that Mrs. Langley was ill and that she and Razer were driving her to the hospital. She didn't know what time she would be home.

Lily shrugged it off. She hadn't really wanted to spend another awkward night with Beth and Razer anyway. She went into the kitchen, making herself some soup and a grilled cheese sandwich.

She was pouring the soup into a bowl when she felt as if someone was staring at her. It was the same feeling she'd had a couple of times before, and it unnerved her.

Going to the back door, she checked to make sure it was locked before lowering and closing the blinds.

Thinking she was overreacting, she started walking away from the door when she saw the handle silently turn. If she hadn't been standing there, she would never have noticed.

Lily let out a small scream, running out of the kitchen to get her cell phone, about to call Knox when the doorbell rang.

"Who is it?" she asked, going to the door. *Would a burglar answer?* she thought uselessly.

"Shade."

Anger had her hastily opening the door. "Next time, come to the front door first. You scared me half to death."

"What are you talking about?" Shade asked, coming through the doorway.

"Weren't you just at the back door?" Lily asked, her fear beginning to return at the look that came over his face. It hadn't been him at the back door.

"Stay here." Shade went to the back door, opening it and going out.

Lily stayed where she was, frightened for Shade. Should she turn the lights on outside for him or not? She stood there indecisively for several minutes, debating whether to call Knox, yet before she could decide, Shade came back with an even grimmer expression.

"Someone was out there; they must have taken off when they heard my bike pull in the driveway."

Lily sat down on the couch before her shaking knees gave out. "Should I call Knox?"

"I will." Shade took out his cell phone and called, talking to him for several minutes before hanging up. "He's on his way."

"Who would try to break in the house?" Lily asked.

"I don't know, but I plan to find out."

It didn't take long for Knox to arrive. Minutes later, Cash knocked on the door as well, coming inside to listen silently as Lily told how she was fixing herself something to eat and had felt someone watching, deciding to lock the door.

"Are you sure you saw the handle move?"

"Yes. At least, I think so. Maybe I was just tense. I don't know." Could it have been just the night playing tricks with her eyes? Lily brushed her hair away from her eyes.

"What happened to your hand?" Shade asked sharply.

"I fell this afternoon when I was coming home from the church."

"How?"

"I was crossing the street and a car was speeding. Pastor Dean pushed me out of the way, and I fell and skinned my hands and knees." Lily shrugged.

The men looked silently at each other before Cash left, going out the back door.

"Where's he going?" Lily asked.

"To check things out," Knox told her. "I'm going to make a report then look around myself before going back to the station. I'll call Razer and let Beth and him know what's going on."

"Okay," Lily said.

129

"Shade?" Knox turned to the grim-faced man. "I don't think it's a good idea to leave her alone."

"I'll stay until they get home," Shade agreed.

"Sounds good. Later." Knox went out the door.

"Do you think they'll be able to find anything?"

"Probably not, but Cash is good. If there's anything to be found, he'll find it."

Lily nodded before going into the kitchen where she put the soup into the fridge. She then forced herself to eat the cold grilled cheese when she saw Shade about to make a remark.

She sat the dirty dishes in the sink, too tired to deal with them now. She would do them in the morning.

"Go to bed. You look exhausted."

Lily turned to the steps.

"Don't you get tired of ordering me around?" Lily snapped.

"No."

Lily started to make another comment when he raised his brow and crossed his arms against his chest, waiting.

"I can't believe I ever thought you were a gentleman."

Shade burst out laughing. "I'm no gentleman."

"No shit." Lily clapped her hand over her mouth. "You've driven me to cussing."

"Lily, cussing isn't going to be the worst thing I teach you."

She fled up the steps, hearing his mocking laughter following behind.

CHAPTER THIRTEEN

Lily came downstairs the next day to Beth and Razer's concern. Assuring them that nothing had happened other than a minor scare, she picked up her purse, ready for church.

She saw Beth looking at her dress without saying anything. Lily smoothed the dark navy dress down, wondering what was wrong.

"I thought we would drive the car to church this morning. I can take you back to the college after lunch at the diner."

"I'll get my backpack." Lily went back upstairs to get the bag while Razer and Beth waited outside in the car.

Church was packed that Sunday. Lily nodded her head toward Rachel and other parishioners in the congregation as they went to take their seats.

Afterward, she talked to Pastor Dean briefly, moving on before he could mention the incident from the day before. She didn't feel there was a need to rehash it.

Lily dreaded going to the diner after the service. If there had been a way out of it, she would have gladly taken it. Seeing the women she had come to know with their clothes off and Cash and Train, whose privates had been

131

exposed, had been deeply embarrassing to her. It would be a long time before she would be comfortable around them again.

She squared her shoulders, walking across the street after making sure she looked both ways several times.

The others were already there when Lily sat down beside Diamond with Beth on her other side. She was facing the door of the busy restaurant, seeing that several families were having lunch. Pastor Dean came in, snagging a chair with Rachel's family.

Lily ordered her food, listening to the conversation as she tried not to meet any of The Last Riders' eyes, which was hard to do with Bliss and Evie seated across from her.

"How's school?" Diamond asked sympathetically.

"Good. How's Knox liking his new job?"

"I don't think he can tell yet. He loves breaking up the fights, but he's not so fond of getting dragged out of bed at three a.m."

As Lily listened to Diamond, her eyes were momentarily caught by Shade's until she managed to tear her gaze away, landing on a small family a couple of tables away.

The little girl had dark brown hair and was sitting with her mother and father as the waitress set their plates in front of them. It was the epitome of the perfect family gathering on a Sunday afternoon.

"We miss having you at the factory. No one likes to fill the big orders," Evie complained.

Lily hadn't minded filling those orders; she had considered them challenging while others considered them a pain.

"I miss it, too," Lily confessed, truthfully. The job had kept her busy.

Her eyes drifted back to the table with the small family. The little girl was lifting her drink to her mouth when the person sitting behind her jarred her, forcing her to spill some of the juice from her glass onto her dress. The look of terror that came across her face had Lily freezing and her heartbeat soaring when the mother's lips tightened. Picking up a napkin, she wiped the girl's dress with rough movements. The entire time the mother kept up her brisk movements, the little girl's eyes watered and she kept apologizing to her mother.

"Lily?" Evie's voice had her eyes leaving the table momentarily.

"Diamond. Please call Knox." Lily's hoarse voice had everyone sitting at the table going silent as they looked at her. Lily's hand went to the rubber band on her wrist, snapping it furiously as a dull headache began to pound at her temples.

Diamond took out her phone, calling Knox and asking him to come to the diner while Beth's voice asking her what was wrong was drowned out by the loud pumping of her heart.

The little girl's lips trembled when her mother's hand disappeared under the table. Her obvious pain had Lily moving to the end of her seat, about to rise when the girl's father spoke sharply to the mother, and he reached out to soothe the little girl. That simple movement brought a flash of pain that had Lily gripping her head, screaming in agony. She bent over in excruciating pain, her head in her hands. The pain felt like it was crushing her skull.

"Lily!" Beth's voice yelled her name, but there was no going back; Lily had placed a barrier between them. She couldn't reach for Beth this time like she had always done before.

Lily blindly rose from the table, trying to escape the pain, when a hand around her waist tried to hold her, but Lily fought free. She needed somewhere to hide and there was no place available. She screamed at the agony that was storming through her mind.

Lily fell to the floor, writhing in torment. She vaguely heard several people calling her name; however, her mind had blocked out everything except the door in her mind that was trying to open. She was too weak to keep it closed; the secrets it held wanted out. She saw herself standing in front of the door, trying to bar it from opening.

"Help me! Help me!" Lily screamed in terror.

She felt her head lifted and placed in someone's lap. She tried to roll away from the agony, yet she couldn't get away from it. It was everywhere around her—within her—suffocating.

"Help me!" Lily's screams were tortured, but she didn't know how to stop them. She was too scared of the door opening. She couldn't let it open.

"What do you need me to do?" the voice, neither male nor female, asked in her mind.

"Help me shut the door!" Lily screamed.

"What's behind the door?"

"Everything. Help me. She can't get out." Lily sobbed as the door opened a small amount.

"I'm helping you, Lily." Lily saw another pair of hands helping her to press the door closed again.

When it was completely closed, she told whoever had helped her, "I have to lock it."

Lily locked the imaginary door while the hands held it closed. After she locked it, she slid down the door, curling into a ball as she rocked back and forth.

"It's okay, Lily. The door is locked again," the voice assured her.

"I can't remember what's behind that door," Lily sobbed, rocking back and forth, trying to comfort herself now that all those memories were locked away forever.

"Not today, Lily, but soon," the voice said sadly.

"Not ever," Lily replied, curling into a tighter ball.

"Soon, and I'll help. Sleep, Lily. Go to sleep."

Lily felt herself relax as soothing warmth spread through her body.

* * *

Lily woke, turning her head on the soft pillow and

rolling to her side before she opened her eyes reluctantly. She closed them then reopened them again, not sure what she was staring at. Surveying the room, she saw the black furniture was modern. The dark carpeting looked thick and expensive in a huge bedroom she had never been in before. To one side there were two large, black leather chairs with a coffee table sitting in front of them, and a flat screen television was mounted on a pedestal on the wall that could be turned toward the chairs or the bed. A small refrigerator sat on top of a dark cabinet and a huge armoire made of dark wood stood against the wall.

Her head turned and she saw a mirrored wall facing the bed. Her pale face and slender body, dressed in conservative pajamas, looked back at her from the huge, California-king, pedestal bed. The wall behind the bed was also mirrored. Lily swallowed hard.

She turned and saw a large dresser with nothing on top and a chair by the bed. The room was immaculately clean. She couldn't see any personal belongings; there was nothing to give her a clue as to whose room she was inside.

A door stood open where Lily could see a bathroom with the light on. Seeing the bathroom made the fullness in her bladder more pressing. Pulling back the soft-as-silk comforter, she raised herself up before sliding her feet out of the bed.

Getting to her feet, she felt a wave of dizziness, but she slowly managed to walk to the bathroom, coming to a stop when she saw the luxurious suite. It had a double sink with dark colors swirling throughout.

Closing the door, she used the restroom. Hesitantly, she washed her face with a washcloth that had been set out.

She looked over at the huge shower, which took up easily half of the bathroom. It was tiled in black and gray and had three steps leading down into the glass enclosure. She saw it had faucets surrounding it with the rain-type one from the top. It also had a tiled bench on one side. It was a fantasy shower. Lily wouldn't be surprised if it had surround sound.

Dropping the dirty washcloth into a basket, she left the bathroom, going back into the bedroom while wondering where she was.

She was halfway to the bed when the door opened.

Lily didn't know whether to be relieved or frightened at his familiar face.

"Where am I?" Lily asked, taking a seat on the edge of the bed.

"My room," Shade replied, coming in and shutting the door, carrying a tray.

Walking across the room, he set the tray on the coffee table. "Come and eat."

Lily got up from the bed, going to the chair and looking down at the tray of food.

"How—did—why am I here?" She looked at Shade, not understanding why she was in his room.

"What do you remember?" Shade asked patiently.

Lily sat down on the chair, trying to remember what had happened before she'd woken up here. She searched her mind, trying to figure out her last memory.

"I was at the church helping Rachel." Lily licked her dry lips. Reaching forward, she took the bottled water and opened it, taking a long drink.

Shade didn't say anything as Lily set the bottled water back down on the tray, keeping her eyes on him.

"Lily, you had an episode at the diner after church on Sunday. That was two days ago," Shade explained gently.

"An episode?" Lily's greatest fear that she would lose her mind had begun.

"You became hysterical."

"Oh, God. Where's Beth? Why am I here instead of my bedroom?" Lily asked, trying to remain calm.

"You had to be sedated, Lily. The doctor felt it was best that someone kept an eye on you. Since Beth works, we agreed this was the best place for you now."

"Where are my clothes?" Lily asked. "I want to get dressed."

"Eat first. Your clothes are in the closet and drawers. I'll show you when you finish."

Lily picked up an apple slice from the plate, chewing on it. Swallowing the bite, she said, "I need to get back to school after I'm dressed. Would you—"

"Lily, you're going to be staying here for a while."

Lily shook her head. "I have to finish school."

"You will. Beth talked to your school and arranged for a medical emergency so that you can complete your coursework on the computer."

"But why can't I go back to school?"

"Lily, someone tried to run you over with a car and then tried to break into your house. We feel it's safer to keep you where we can watch who you come into contact with." Shade talked about events he seemed to think she remembered.

"I can stay at my house," Lily said, trying to take in what he was telling her, becoming frightened that she didn't remember either incident.

Lily picked up the toast, nibbling on it.

"That won't work with Beth's work schedule. We need to figure out who tried to harm you twice."

"I just can't stay cooped up in your room."

"You won't. You can go back to work at the factory and finish your classes."

"I don't want to stay here at the club," Lily protested.

"A few weeks won't hurt you, Lily. By then, we may have some idea who is after you, and it will give you some time to figure out why you forgot the last few days."

Lily looked away, not wanting to admit she didn't want to remember. "Do you know what caused me to have the episode?"

"Yes. Actually, it was Diamond who figured it out. Do you want to know?"

"No." Lily got to her feet. "Where are my clothes? I want to get dressed. Do you mind if I use your shower? I could use the one in the other bathroom; it doesn't look as complicated."

Shade's lips twisted at her attempt of humor. "Use mine. I think you can figure it out."

"All right." She was relieved he stopped trying to jog her memory.

Shade opened one side of his closet, showing her clothes.

Lily took a step back. "Those are the clothes that I boxed up to give the church. I bought new clothes. I was going to buy some more." Lily turned her face away but found her jaw caught in his tight grip.

"Those new rags you bought are the ones being donated. They look like what someone would wear to a funeral—all black, brown and grey. Since I've known you, you've worn dresses with every color under the rainbow. Why have you suddenly stopped wearing color?"

"I don't know," Lily said, confused.

"Yes, Lily, you do. There are some things I'll let you hide from me for a while longer, others I won't."

Lily stiffened, trying to turn away from his firm grip.

"Why the dark colors?"

She mutinously refused to answer.

"We'll stand here all day until you answer me."

Lily didn't answer as her hand went to her wrist to snap at the red band. Her searching fingertips couldn't find it, though, and he wouldn't let her look at her wrist; his hand was still on her jaw, forcing her to look at him.

"I took it." At her look of horror, he spoke before she could. "I'll give it back on two conditions."

"What are they?" She *needed* the rubber band.

"You have to tell me about your clothes, and secondly, every time you snap it, you have to tell me why if I'm there. If I'm not, then you have to write it down in a small book I'll give you. Each and every time."

Lily thought frantically, trying to think of another substitute she could use, but she was also sure that he would have thought of that.

"All right." Lily gave in to his demands.

Shade's hand dropped to his side. Taking a step back, he demanded, "Tell me about the clothes."

Lily licked her dry mouth, wishing she had the water. "I don't know how to explain it. When I wore my dresses, the colors made me feel happy. I would choose the color some days because it matched the sky or the sun or was the color of a flower I saw." Lily shrugged feeling juvenile.

"The new dresses?"

"I don't know. I just guess… I don't know. The color is I—"

"Do you feel sad?"

"Yes, but not like depressed sad, like someone died," Lily tried to explain the deep feeling of loss she had felt the last week or so.

Shade nodded his head, catching her eyes with his. "Who do you feel like you lost, Lily?"

"Beth." A lone tear slid down her cheek.

"Anyone else?"

"Razer." Another tear joined the first.

"Who else, Lily?"

Lily remained quiet.

"Who else, Lily?" Shade's voice became firmer.

"You," her voice was a whisper.

"Why do you think you lost me?"

"I don't know. You were my friend, then I saw you with Evie and Rider and I know that…" Lily took a shuddering breath, "I don't know you."

His thumb traced over her high cheekbone. "You know me, and you sure as fuck haven't lost me, even though I know you want to. Go take a shower then change into your workout clothes. I'll lay them out for you while you're in the shower. I'll meet you in the gym."

"Okay." Lily gratefully moved away, relieved his

questions were over.

She closed the bathroom door behind her, leaning back against it. She would get through the day and talk to Beth tonight. She would convince her sister that she could go back to school. She couldn't stay at the clubhouse, and she was not about to stay another night in Shade's room. Whoever it was out there who wanted to hurt her wasn't as frightening as the man on the other side of that door.

CHAPTER FOURTEEN

Shade was waiting for her on the mat.

"Ready?"

"Yes," Lily replied.

"Today, I just want you to stretch then work on your weight training."

"Okay." Lily warmed up then moved over to the weights.

Shade handed her some weights. "From now on, when you feel uncomfortable trying something or you get scared, I want you to say a word that lets me know you're getting scared and want me to stop."

"All right. What's the word?"

"You make one up. That way you'll remember it better."

"Blueberries."

"Blueberries?"

"Yeah, I like blueberries. Even saying it makes me happy." She smiled at him.

"Christ." Shade returned to work on his own weights.

"What's wrong with blueberries?" Lily asked curiously.

"Nothing," Shade stated, his jaw clenched.

"Then why are you frowning?"

"I don't know. Most women would pick a color or an object, not a fruit."

Lily continued lifting her weights. "I can pick a color. I like pink."

"Lily, blueberries is fine," he snapped.

"Why are you getting angry?"

"I'm not getting mad, you're just distracting me."

"Oh." Lily lifted the weight again. "I like baby blue."

Shade stopped and glared at her. "If you don't quit bugging me, you're going to be using your safe word in the next sixty seconds."

Lily shut up.

By the time they finished, she was tired and needed another shower.

"You finish up while I get showered and changed," Shade told her.

Shade left and Lily did some more stretches, cooling down. It didn't take Shade long to return, dressed in faded jeans, boots and a black t-shirt. His dark hair was still wet.

"Get showered. I laid out another outfit for you."

Lily ignored his last words, going to his room. The sooner Beth showed up, the better.

She went into the bedroom, seeing a pale blue dress lying on the bed with her flat shoes beside it.

Lily showered before dressing. She was brushing her hair when Shade came back into the room.

"Dinner's ready," Shade said. "Let's go."

"We're going out to eat?" Lily asked hopefully. She could get him to drop her off at her house afterwards, surely he wouldn't mind leaving her with Beth there.

"No. We're eating upstairs like everyone else."

"But I'm not allowed upstairs," Lily argued, trying to pull away as Shade took her hand, leading her to the steps.

Shade stopped and looked down at her. "If you're going to get used to living here, that means you get used to going upstairs. You don't want to stay down here all the time, do you?"

"No, but I don't want to go up there, either," Lily insisted.

"Come on." Lily tried to pull away again, her hand going to the rubber band on her wrist.

"Remember our deal," Shade warned.

"I already told you, I don't want to go up there."

"Lily, the club isn't going to hide itself from you anymore. That cat's already out of the bag. At first, you'll be uncomfortable, but then you'll become familiar with how things work around here."

As Shade pulled her up the steps, Lily was afraid to attempt to yank herself away, not wanting to fall. Coming to the head of the stairs, he opened the door to the kitchen, which was full of The Last Rider members. Lily tried to hold back, yet Shade pushed her forward into the big room.

Evie, Jewell and Raci watched in amusement as Lily was then tugged forward to get in the food line.

"Hello," Lily greeted them.

"Hi," they greeted her in return.

Shade pushed her forward when the line moved and she stayed still. Lily gave him a frustrated look.

"I'm hungry. Unlike you, I haven't eaten."

"I'm sorry," Lily said, stricken with guilt that she was being difficult while he just wanted to eat.

"I was joking, Lily. You take everything literally."

Lily lowered her head, her feelings hurt.

Shade's hand wrapped around the back of her neck, using his thumb to raise her head to meet his eyes. "You look very pretty in that shade of blue."

"Are you trying to patronize me?"

"A little," he admitted.

Lily laughed, shaking her head at him.

Taking a plate, she grabbed a few things that she thought looked good despite not having much of an appetite. Shade, on the other hand, filled his plate with much larger servings. Then they sat down at a table with

Evie, Rider, Train and Bliss.

Lily kept her eyes on her plate, not able to meet Rider and Train's amused gazes.

"Have you given Killyama her ride yet?" Lily asked Rider when she couldn't take it anymore.

Rider's amused expression disappeared. "Not yet. I've been busy."

"Pussy," Train goaded.

Rider's hand clenched on his fork. "That woman probably expects me to ride bitch," Rider made excuses for himself.

"If the panties fit, wear them," Train said, dodging the fork that Rider threw across the table.

"I like Killyama," Lily said, cutting into her pork roast. Silence was her only response. "She saved my life, and I heard Star's mother had to have plastic surgery after she got in a fight with her. I can see where she might be too much for you," Lily said, thinking the laid-back man wouldn't have anything in common with the more serious Killyama.

Everyone at the table burst into laughter.

Rider turned to Shade. "Set it up," he ordered, all humor gone.

"Will do," Shade replied, keeping a straight face.

"Make sure you take protection," Train goaded.

"Which one are you talking about? Condoms or my gun?" Rider asked.

"Both," Train said truthfully.

Lily threw Train a reproving look. "I think you should volunteer to give Crazy Bitch a ride, Train. I think you two would have a lot in common."

Evie put her hand on her mouth while Bliss, sitting next to her, asked, "Is she serious?"

"I think so," Evie said, getting to her feet before she broke down into laughter, taking the dirty dishes with her.

Lily got up, taking hers, and Shade followed her into the kitchen. She started to do the dishes, but Shade took her hand.

"It's Raci and Train's week. We take turns." Lily followed him nervously into the other room where everyone was sitting around, talking.

"I thought Beth would have been here by now," Lily stated, noticing Train and Cash were pouring drinks at the bar.

"Beth won't be here tonight. Mrs. Langley had surgery to remove her gall bladder and she's staying with her at the hospital," Evie said, taking a seat across from her.

Lily looked at Shade sharply before her eyes went back to the bar where several members were going back and forth, taking beers.

"But I need to talk to her."

"I'm sure you do, but it's not going to make a difference." Shade replied.

Lily's hand went to her wrist as Viper and Winter came in through the front door. A breath of relief left Lily. Winter would drive her back to college or drop her off at her house.

Viper stopped at the bar long enough to take a beer and the couple came to sit down on the couch, forcing Lily to slide closer to Shade.

Winter sat next to Lily. "I'm relieved to see you up. How's it going?" Winter asked.

"Fine," Lily said, not letting her eyes go to the beer bottle in Viper's hand. "Do you think you could give me a ride back to my house? I really need to get back to school."

"You're going to be staying here. Didn't Shade tell you?"

"He mentioned it, but—"

"Did he tell you why?" Viper asked, looking at Shade.

"Yes, he did. Someone tried to hit me with a car then break in my house, but at school, I'll be perfectly safe."

"Lily, when Cash followed the prints to who tried to break into your house, they led to the house behind yours.

Someone's been watching you for some time."

"That house belongs to a couple who vacation here a couple of times a year. It's usually empty," Lily explained.

"Knox traced the ownership of the house to a corporation and that's as far as he can get. Cash said that whoever has been staying there is watching your house. There were video cameras, Lily."

Lily felt frightened that someone would invade their privacy to that extent.

Winter took her hand. "That's not all."

"Your dorm room had listening devices planted there. There's really no safe place for you to stay other than here, for now. Cash and Knox are both trying to find out who could be doing this, but until they do, you have to be patient. At your home, you would inevitably be alone, but what if Beth or Razer's presence didn't deter them? You don't want them hurt because you didn't take our help, do you?" Viper's harsh words had her shaking her head in denial.

"Of course not."

"Good, then everything is settled." Lily was glad Winter was relieved. She just wished she could say the same thing.

"I was afraid you wouldn't listen to reason. I'm sure Beth will be relieved, too. She doesn't want you unhappy, but she wants you safe," Viper told her.

"I know." Lily didn't know what else to do or say. She really didn't want to stay here. They were obviously used to living a lifestyle that she didn't fit into; however, it was the only option she had available right then.

Viper took another drink of his beer and someone turned the music up louder. Winter and Evie started talking about Mrs. Langley while Lily half-listened as her eyes wandered the room, which had several sitting areas. The members had spread out throughout the large room.

Her gaze caught on Bliss sitting with Cash. She had leaned forward and her top had fallen open at her breasts.

Cash's hands had come out, tracing the outline of a tattoo that Lily couldn't see.

She hastily turned her gaze away, joining into the conversation with Evie and Winter. She felt Shade get up then return. He handed her a bottled water while she saw he had a beer in his hand.

Lily ran her hand nervously through her hair. She desperately wanted to snap her rubber band, yet she didn't want him asking why in front of the others.

She noticed then Cash and Bliss walking up the steps to the upper floor.

Winter leaned sideways, breaking off her conversation with Evie. "The members will watch how they behave around you for a while, but eventually you'll walk into an embarrassing situation. Just do what I do: leave the room." Winter's face was blood red as she talked, letting Lily know she was as uncomfortable as Lily was discussing the topic.

"At least she did the first few times," Viper corrected her, cutting into the conversation.

Winter threw Viper a dirty look.

"Bring it on, pretty girl," Viper warned.

Winter's face went an even darker shade of red.

Evie got up. "Anyone want another beer?"

"I'll take one," Viper spoke up.

Lily started fiddling with the rubber band around her wrist.

"Sorry, Lily. The men might refrain from acting inappropriate around you, but there's no way to keep them from their alcohol." Winter said.

Lily couldn't help it; she burst out laughing. "I guess beer outranks sex."

They laughed in return and Lily began to get as comfortable as she could, which wasn't much, but it was a start. When none of the men drank excessively or acted out of control, Lily had the feeling they were trying to accumulate her slowly. She didn't know whether to be charmed or angry at their behavior.

Evie sank back down in her chair, taking a long swallow of her own beer.

"Don't knock it until you've tried it." Lily's face went pale at Evie's suggestion of her taking a drink. "I was only joking," Evie said in apology.

Shade's hand went to her face. "Stop it, Lily. No one expects you to drink. Okay? Evie was only joking like she would with anyone else."

Lily nodded her head. Would she never be able to act normal? Lily didn't feel like she fit in anywhere.

"I think living here for a while might be good for me." Lily always tried to look on the bright side of things. "I need to get used to being around different people. This will make me quit being sensitive about people drinking around me. I wonder if cowboys drink a lot." Lily looked at Evie this time, being the one to make a joke.

"Like a fish," she answered.

CHAPTER FIFTEEN

Lily stifled her yawn as she looked at her cards. She and Shade had been playing several games of poker with Winter and Viper.

"It's time for bed if you're going to start back at the factory tomorrow," Shade told Lily when Winter reached forward to claim her winnings, which were mainly IOUs for punishments. Lily had been told they usually played for money, but Winter preferred to play for punishments; that way, when she got in trouble and had to pull a punishment, she would cash in one of her IOUs.

"I haven't had to do a punishment in six months," she bragged.

Viper ruffled his wife's hair. "Unless it was the ones you wanted."

Winter slapped his hands away. Lily got to her feet, smiling down at the couple. "I'll probably have to find another way to pay you back for my IOUs. I probably won't be around long enough to pay all those back."

Winter looked doubtfully up at Lily, but replied, "I'm sure we'll work out an arrangement."

"Goodnight," Lily said, following Shade to the door that went downstairs. They went down the steps, Lily feeling terrible about taking Shade's room from him for the next several days.

She went into his room, going to get her pajamas, which were sitting on the chair.

She stiffened when the bedroom door closed and Shade went to one side of the bed, pulling off his t-shirt as he went.

"What are you doing?" Lily asked, shocked.

"Going to bed."

"Oh, where am I sleeping?"

"In the bed next to me."

"No, I'm not." Lily shook her head.

"Yes, you are."

"No, Shade, I'm not."

"I don't sleep on couches."

"Then I will," Lily said firmly.

"What are you going to do if one of the brothers stumbles into the downstairs drunk?" Lily looked at the door fearfully as Shade continued, "This room is off-limits, but the other rooms, not so much. We have an open-bedroom policy."

"Even Winter and Viper?"

"You think you're going to put Viper out of his bed?" Shade asked with a raised brow.

No, she didn't. No one was going to make Viper do anything he didn't want to do, and she had seen the obvious way Viper's hand had intentionally stroked his wife's thigh under the table. It was hard to miss with Winter constantly swatting it away.

"No, but maybe Evie?"

"Evie doesn't sleep alone; none of the women do. Go get changed, Lily. I'm tired. It's not like it's the first time we've shared a room."

Lily went into the bathroom, getting changed into her pajamas. When she was done, she went back into the bedroom to see Shade was already in bed. She came to a stop, knowing she couldn't get in the bed with him.

Sighing, Shade got out of bed, moving the chair out of the corner. Sliding it over, he took her arm and led her to the corner. "This is your safe place in the bedroom. Anytime anything scares you or makes you feel uncomfortable, you can come here. I won't come near you here."

Shade turned and walked away, Lily couldn't tear her eyes away from his lean body. Shade didn't have an ounce of fat on him, but his muscles were firm and lithe.

Shade climbed back into bed, pulling the thin blanket over him.

"Can I have a blanket?"

"No," he said, turning out the light.

The light from the bathroom remained on, keeping the bedroom from being dark. Thanking God for small mercies, she stood there, debating what to do next. She could wait until he fell asleep and maneuver the covers away from him or at least take the pillow, but she really didn't like being sneaky.

After standing for several minutes, she reached out to pull the large chair toward her.

"Leave the chair where it is."

Lily could not believe how mean he was being to her, but she didn't dare take the chair anyway.

She stood there a while before she quietly slid down the wall, sitting on the floor as she waited for him to say something. When he didn't, she closed her eyes, leaning her head back against the wall.

Lily dozed off, waking several times during the night to try to make herself more comfortable.

She woke up completely around six-thirty, stiffly getting to her feet. Not trying to be quiet, she looked in the drawers for her underwear, slamming each one closed until she found what she was looking for, hoping she would wake Shade and deprive him of a little sleep. She then went to the closet, opening the door.

"Wear the purple one."

151

Lily jumped, startled, turning to see him watching her from the bed. Aware she had succeeded in waking him, she took the purple dress and closed the closet with a snap.

Lily went to the bathroom, taking her time in the shower. She had dressed and was blow drying her hair when a knock sounded on the door.

"Unless you want to share, you need to hurry up."

Lily unplugged the hairdryer and picked up the brush, taking her time to brush out her hair.

Finally she unlocked the door. Expecting Shade to move to the side, she found herself pressed up against the bathroom door.

"Lily, I'm coming to the conclusion that you're a little spoiled, and while I won't mind doing so occasionally after you've earned such rewards from me, now is not the time to piss me off."

Lily gasped as she felt his penis behind his shorts press against her mound with just the material of the shorts and her dress between them.

Lily started to panic when he stepped away, going into the bathroom. She could tell he wasn't going to wait for her to leave before he used the restroom, so she shut the door hastily before he could take care of his business. She almost went to her corner, but she was wary of him making her stand the entire morning there. She instead busied herself by making the bed and straightening the room.

Shade opened the bathroom door, coming out with just a towel wrapped around his lean waist.

Lily ran to the corner, not appreciating the mocking laughter as he removed his clothes from the drawers. She turned to the wall when he started to drop the towel. She heard the rustling of his clothes as he dressed and the stamping of his feet as he put on his boots.

"Let's go eat breakfast, unless you want to stand there longer."

Lily moved to follow him, but he stopped her with his hand going to her jaw, making her look him in the face. She didn't try to hide her resentment.

"That's two, for slamming the drawers."

"Two what?" Lily asked in confusion.

"Two smacks on your ass. I'll keep a total and Friday will be the day we clean the slate and start over," Shade said, ushering her out of the door.

"You have lost your mind if you think I'm going to stand still and let you spank me."

"You won't be standing; your ass will be turned over my knee."

"Sure, Shade. Anything you say, Shade," Lily said mockingly, too angry to be scared.

Today was only Wednesday. She planned to be long gone before Friday rolled around. *In the meantime, let him count as high as he wants to; his hand isn't going anywhere near my butt again,* Lily thought confidently.

* * *

"Can't you go any faster?" Georgia complained.

The day hadn't started off the best; she was tired and grumpy from sleeping in the corner and her mind was coming up empty with alternative places to stay. Leave it to Georgia to catch her distraction.

"Yes. I'm sorry I'm taking so long." Lily really wanted to say something unkind, yet she bit back the response. Shade's bad manners were rubbing off on her. She was afraid because she hadn't even been back a full day and Lily wanted to snap back at the woman.

During break, she had called Charles to find he had left town again. She thought about calling Miranda, but she had a small child and Lily didn't really want to endanger them. Besides that, she had a feeling she was still angry with her.

She had one other option and she wanted to talk to Beth before she did. She could stay with Penni; she was sure. It would solve all their problems by getting her out of

Kentucky until they could find out who was watching and trying to hurt her. It would be a win-win situation.

The day ended without further comment from Georgia, and Lily walked with Shade back to his room.

Their workout session and dinner were spent with Lily saying as little as possible to the man. She was disappointed to see that Beth didn't show up again that night, and Winter also was a no-show with a PTA meeting. She was stuck with Shade, who didn't seem to mind her silent treatment.

After dinner, she thought he would go into the main room, and she was about to excuse herself when he surprised her.

"I need to check on some work going on at my house. Do you want to come with me?" he asked.

"Sure." Lily walked out the back door with him into the huge backyard.

Beth had told her one of the reasons Viper's brother, Gavin, had wanted this property was because of the amount of land. Shade's house was being built behind Beth and Razer's. It was nestled up higher than the main house and Beth's with a wraparound porch and a main path, which led to each of them before it divided: one side leading to Beth's and the other to Shade's.

Shade opened the door, coming into what seemed to be the living room and dining room combo. It was an open-concept house where you could see through the whole downstairs. The walls were all dry-walled and the subfloors had been laid.

Shade walked into the kitchen where none of the cabinets or anything had been placed. There was a small, fold-up table and two metal chairs sitting in the room with several books lying on top.

Shade looked around the room, moving from one area to the other.

Lily looked at him curiously. "What are you doing?"

"Trying to figure out where I want the island to go and

which wall for the appliances."

"Start with where you want the sink, which is obviously by the window." She pointed toward said window.

"Why by the window?"

"So you can look out while you do the dishes," Lily explained.

"What about the stove?"

Lily looked around the room and pointed to the wall on the right. "That way you can keep an eye on the room while you're cooking; the other wall you would have your back to the room.

"That's true, but the exhaust fan would break the line of sight."

Lily agreed, temporarily forgetting she was angry at him.

Shade finally decided to place it against the wall Lily had pointed out.

He sat down at the table, going through floor samples, which Lily helped him narrow down to hardwood then the type of wood. Next he picked out cabinets, but when Lily made a face, he turned over several more pages until she found one she thought would suit the style of the house.

"I'm surprised. I thought you would try to talk me into a country-looking kitchen, but you're guiding me into a more modern look."

Lily smiled. "I'm surprised you know the difference. I like the modern look for the clean lines and angles."

"I do, too." Shade closed the books. "That's enough for today. It will take a couple of weeks to get it done then I can pick out the fixtures for the bathrooms."

"Make sure you have one put in like you do now. Your shower is amazing."

"I like it, too, but I was thinking of going a little bigger here."

"How much bigger do you need? It's already big enough for several people." It dawned on Lily as soon as the words were out of her mouth that he had probably shared his shower many times with the women members. Lily closed the book she was looking at with a snap, getting to her feet without looking at him.

"Ready?" she asked. "If you need to stay, I can go back by myself."

"I'm finished," Shade replied, going to the door, turning off the lights on the way.

They walked back to the house, and instead of going through the kitchen, he led her through the door, which led directly downstairs.

Lily went to Shade's room, getting a fresh pair of flannel pajamas before she went into the bathroom to get changed. She was tired. Tonight she wanted to sleep in the bed, yet she knew she was incapable of climbing into the bed with Shade.

Lily opened the door to see Shade was taking off his shoes. He had already removed his t-shirt and his jeans were unsnapped.

He got up from the side of the bed and then went inside the bathroom, closing the door.

Lily stood in the middle of the floor for several seconds. She couldn't do it, going instead for the corner.

When Shade came out of the bathroom, she thought she saw a flash of disappointment before his face became impassive. He got into the bed, turning out the lamp.

Lily stood there several moments before she sat down on the floor. Her mind was thinking she was already stiff from working out and sleeping on the floor was going to hurt her even more. She had to find another place to stay.

As she sat there thinking, several things occurred to her. She had walked across the floor barefoot, and while the carpeting was thick throughout, where she was sitting was extremely padded. She put her hand down and noticed it was thicker. There was extra padding underneath the carpet where she was sitting. The room itself was very warm, which she liked; she wasn't cold and didn't need a blanket to keep warm.

She was staring at him sleeping on the bed when it dawned on her that she could see him clearly. Her head then turned in the direction of the bathroom. He had left the door open and the light on.

CHAPTER SIXTEEN

Lily filled the last order of the day, aware of Georgia's eyes on her. Lily wanted to turn around and stick her tongue out at her. Feeling childish, she packed the items back to the table and began sorting them.

Jewell was on her way out, finished with her last box, when she stopped by Lily's table. "That woman is Jonesing for you."

"She doesn't like me," Lily agreed.

"No shit," Jewell mocked, throwing a glare at Georgia.

Lily almost laughed but didn't think it would help the situation, and it would increase Georgia's hostility toward her.

"I must rub her the wrong way. I don't think I've done anything to make her dislike me."

"I'll tell you why she doesn't like you in one word. Jealousy."

"Georgia is not jealous of me," Lily said wryly.

"Oh, yes she is. She's hung up on Shade. She made friends with me just to get closer to him." Jewell shrugged. "I'm a sucker for a pretty face and a rocking body."

Lily studied the sultry body that always had one of The Last Riders close.

"I assumed—I mean... never mind," Lily trailed off, embarrassed.

"That I'm into dudes? I'm into anyone who makes me feel good," Jewell replied, not in the least bit embarrassed. "I like sex. I *really* like sex."

Lily couldn't help but like the woman who had showed her where everything was when she had first started working at the factory.

"I keep hoping she'll ease up," Lily admitted.

"Georgia isn't going to take a personality pill one day and become a nice person. You have to stand your ground. She can't fire you, so tell her to fuck off."

"I can't be disrespectful. She's everyone's supervisor."

"She's a worker. Whichever of the club's members is over the factory is the boss. That's what counts. You have to learn to take up for yourself, Lily. That's why none of us has said anything to her. This is your first real job, and everyone wants you to learn to handle this situation without one of us stepping in and fixing it for you. You have to stop being such a sweet person all the time. A little bit of being a bitch wouldn't hurt." Jewell advised.

Lily had mixed emotions. She understood what Jewell was saying. She was trying to tell her to stop being a wimp. She didn't want to get in Georgia's face, though. She always avoided confrontations. She *hated* confrontations.

She didn't like that part of herself. She had to get past that fear or she was never going to stop the panic attacks that had plagued her throughout her life.

"I'll try."

"Cool. If you need any help, let me know. I always enjoy a good fight."

"All right," Lily said, getting back to work.

"Finished?" Raci asked Jewell.

"Almost. I just need to give this paperwork to Shade." Jewell left, taking the paperwork to Shade's office, leaving the door open.

Lily continued packing the order, listening to Raci

describe a movie she had watched the previous evening. She saw Jewell sitting on the corner of Shade's desk, talking while leaning toward him. The expression on her face was very explicit. When her hand glided up his arm, Lily tore her gaze away, concentrating on Raci's words.

"Are you going to come to your first party tonight?" Raci asked eagerly.

"What?" Lily asked in shock.

Raci shrugged her shoulder. "Well, since it's not a secret anymore, and you've been at the house all week, I just assumed you would be at the party tonight. I have an outfit you could borrow, but you have to promise to give it back."

"No, thanks. I'm not going to the party." She might have been upstairs several times during mealtimes and during the evenings when most of the members mainly had done nothing more than drink a few drinks, yet none had become drunk. Several of the members had even gone upstairs together, leaving no doubt what was about to happen, but Lily was sure their Friday party wouldn't be so restrained.

Raci grinned infectiously. "I remember the first time Beth and Winter came to our parties. They were shell-shocked. Don't worry; once you've seen it and get over the newness of seeing everyone, it's hot. It's my favorite day of the week, but I enjoy the rest of the week, too."

Raci was open and nice and she liked to keep everyone happy. She would constantly jump in and volunteer when the orders backed up. During the week, Lily had also noticed the men around her a lot.

"Can I ask you a question, Raci?" Lily hesitated. Raci nodded. "Do you have a room to yourself or do you share others'?"

"I have a room to myself now since Knox moved out. Why?"

"I know this is an imposition, but would you mind if I shared?"

"You're giving up Shade's bed? Are you crazy? He's the only member who doesn't let anyone sleep with him. Ever. Do you know how many women have tried to spend the night with him?"

"Um, no. Shh… everyone will hear you."

Raci didn't lower her big mouth. "A lot, including me. He might fuck you all night, but no one sleeps beside him. Damn." Raci shook her head, staring at her in disbelief.

"I don't mind you sharing my room. It'll be fun. Of course, Train and Rider will love it. One of them always spends the night; they love to show off."

"Never mind. I'll stick to Shade."

When Raci looked disappointed, Lily drew the conclusion that the men weren't the only ones who liked to show off. Lily looked toward Shade's office; the door was now closed. Lily began to become agitated and wasn't sure why. Her hand went to her wrist, snapping the band before she went back to taping the package closed.

Raci was describing the new outfit she had purchased for tonight. "I broke down and bought a few new clothes. The women are notorious for swiping the best ones. They steal them out of the laundry baskets." Her eyes traveled down Lily's cream dress. "Of course, you don't have to worry about your clothes," she finished lamely.

Lily realized her taste in clothes had just been insulted. She looked down at herself. She had intended to purchase more clothes. The next time she went into town she would, but she doubted they would be any that they would consider borrowing.

Her eyes went back to Shade's office door to see it opening and both of them coming out. Both of them seemed in a good mood, which was rare for Shade. Lily's teeth clenched.

She began cleaning her workstation with jerky movements.

"Ready?" Shade asked, coming to her side and touching her arm. Lily jerked away from his touch.

"Yes." Lily turned to the door, ignoring his inquiring blue gaze. Opening the door, she blinked briefly as her eyes became adjusted to the light, her temper simmering without cause.

She went to the path which led to the house where Train and Kaley were arguing, making no attempt to lower their voices.

"Please, Train, talk to them." Her voice was pleading against his stony face.

Lily felt sorry for her when she heard Train's negative reply.

She had to pass Kaley on the way to the path, and Kaley's reaction at seeing her wasn't pleasant.

"This is all your fault," she said hatefully.

"Excuse me?" Lily asked, coming to a stop.

"Shut up, Kaley. It's not Lily's fault you didn't keep your mouth shut," Train said.

"No one would have cared if she hadn't been nosing in, like my sister."

"Miranda was worried about you," Lily protested.

"Miranda was just jealous. I was getting plenty of sex and she wasn't."

Her harsh words had Lily taking a step back, coming into contact with Shade. As his arm slipped around her waist, Lily tried to move away, but he held her still.

"That's not true," Lily tried to reason with the angry woman.

"It is true. Neither one of you would know how to have sex other than lying on your back and spreading your legs. And I doubt if you would even lower yourself enough to do that, Lily." She nodded her head at Shade. "He's fucking wasted on you, but he'll get tired of your shit, and when he does, he'll go back to fucking anything with a cunt."

"Lily, go on up to the house," Shade said calmly, his arm leaving her waist.

She took a step forward, going up the path with Jewell

and Raci beside her.

"What set her off so bad?" Lily asked the other women.

"They told her she's not allowed to come to the clubhouse anymore. She broke the rules when she told her sister about the votes."

Lily went in the doorway to the basement while the other two continued on to the kitchen door.

Lily headed to Shade's room to get changed into her workout clothes, though she wasn't really in the mood to work out. Winter had given her an extra pair of black leggings and a new t-shirt to wear so she didn't have to keep washing the other one every day.

Her mind was still on the closed office door and Kaley's words, trying to drive them out of her mind.

She went back to the gym and began stretching, not saying anything when Shade came in, telling her he would get changed and be back.

She felt like pounding something.

When Shade returned, she got into position. They always did a set of maneuvers, switching it up occasionally when she became bored. Shade made one of his practiced moves, and Lily responded with more force than usual, almost managing to knee him in his privates.

"You're getting better. You almost got them that time," Shade complimented her. Lily gritted her teeth. He never really expected her to succeed in getting the better of him.

Lily circled the mat. "You haven't seen anything yet."

Shade lifted his brow at her assertion. This time, when he came for her, Lily responded unexpectedly, using both of her fists to hit him between the shoulder blades when she wiggled away from his hold.

"What the hell?"

"I'm supposed to pretend you're attacking me, aren't I?"

"Yes, but I want you to learn to stop an attacker, not piss them off."

"As long as it works and I get away, that's all that counts," Lily said smugly.

"Is that so?"

"Yes." Lily kept facing him, not letting him have her back like she usually did. She was tired of playing someone about to be attacked. She wanted to see him coming at her.

"Did Kaley go home?"

Shade had started moving toward her, but his momentum stopped at her words. "Yes."

"Do a lot of women try to join?"

"Yes." Shade was beginning to get the message that she was the one who was pissed, giving her a wary look.

"I bet that's fun for the men. Don't the women members resent the new members?" Lily couldn't believe she was discussing this with him.

"No. Why are you interested?" Shade asked, taking his move against her. This time her foot shot out and she managed to nail him in the stomach. The unfortunate part was it probably hurt her more than it hurt him. His stomach was rock hard; however, she did force him to catch his breath. Lily walked around the mat gloating.

"You're getting slow, Shade," Lily said, bouncing from foot to foot. "And no, I'm not interested. You and the other men can have all the women in Treepoint that want to join your club. I won't be one of them. I plan to find me a man who can appreciate one woman."

"That's a joke."

"What do you mean by that?" Lily stopped bouncing.

"That you would ever let a man touch you. Tell me, how do you intend to catch a cowboy or any man when you have no intention of giving them anything? I bet Charles's balls are blue around you, but I'm sure he finds one of his daddy's waitresses to relieve him."

"That's not true. Charles is a gentleman."

"He likes his cock sucked as much as any man," Shade taunted.

"You're disgusting!" Lily screamed at him, turning to

leave the mat.

"What's the matter, Lily? What really set off this little temper tantrum of yours?"

Lily didn't reply as Shade blocked her path.

"Move."

"Make me. I'm already shocked as shit you haven't run to your corner like a scared little girl."

"You're a mean person. I hate you." Lily slammed her hands out, shoving his chest, trying to make him move out of her way.

Lily felt her feet swept out from under her, though, and then she fell to her back on the mat.

Darn, just once she wanted to best the man. Just once, she wanted to wipe the self-satisfied smirk from his face. Her anger boiled. Lily had never lost her temper to the extent Shade could raise out of her, and she didn't know how to deal with the anger boiling through her veins. She was a God-fearing woman, dammit, and Shade made her want to strangle him with her bare hands.

"You lose. Again." Shade looked down at her in triumph.

He always told her to react like he was a stranger, so she did. Without thinking about the consequences of her actions, her hand reached up and viciously grabbed his balls, squeezing them in a vice.

He fell to his knees as his hand went to his balls, trying to jerk her hand away. Her hand tightened even further as she rose up on her knees, squeezing harder. Her satisfied smile widened at his pain-filled expression.

"How's this work for taking the attacker by surprise? Are you surprised? Don't underestimate me. I don't like it." Her hand twisted his balls one last time before letting him go, getting to her feet.

"It's un-cool to talk about Charles like that. It's his private business, just like you and Jewell in your office. I don't care who either of you fool around with," she snapped.

Shade got to his feet and Lily came to her senses, realizing what she had done too late. She wasn't stupid. When she saw the look of retribution on his face, she ran toward the steps and managed to make it up several before he caught her ankle in a hard grip. Lily kicked her other foot out, balancing her hands on the upper steps, nailing him in the jaw and making him release her foot. She managed to escape him, going up the last steps to sling the door open, running into the kitchen and slamming the door in his furious face.

Everyone in line for dinner turned to look at her running into the kitchen.

She came to a stop. She heard Shade slamming through the doorway as he came up behind her.

"Lily?" Beth's voice had her turning to the table. She saw her sister, Razer, Winter and Viper looking at her in shock.

Well, hell.

CHAPTER SEVENTEEN

"Been working out?" Beth asked, her gaze going back and forth between Lily and Shade.

"Yes. I think I'm finally getting the hang of it." She threw Shade a gloating look over her shoulder.

"That's great. I was so worried about you after the diner, but I knew everyone would look out for you, and Mrs. Langley doesn't have anyone. The doctor is going to release her in an hour. I'm going to spend the weekend with her, but I wanted to stop in to check on you."

"I'm doing great. In fact, why don't you stay here and I'll stay with Mrs. Langley? No one will think to look for me there," Lily devised quickly.

"Maybe when she's better, but she needs skilled care after just having surgery."

Darn. Every time she came up with an idea, they shot her down.

"I'm glad you showed up. I have another idea. Since we don't know who was watching me, it makes sense for me to leave Kentucky. I can contact Penni and stay with her until the band she's working for goes on tour."

"I think that's a great idea. I know you would be safe with Penni and I can understand that it's not comfortable for you to stay here." Her sister's eyes went to Shade as he excused himself to go take a shower.

"I'll call her after dinner then let you know her answer."

"I can get Razer to drive you to the airport," Beth said. Lily still felt the barrier of her own making between them, but she was so relieved at having her problem solved that she gave her a genuine smile for the first time in weeks.

Lily fixed herself a plate of food and then sat down at the table next to Beth.

"Any more panic attacks?" Beth questioned as they ate.

Lily had to stop and think. "No." She hadn't had one all week and she had infrequently felt the need to snap the rubber band against her wrist, as well. Shade might not be the nicest person she had ever known, but he did make her feel safe.

He came back upstairs from showering and changing and fixed himself something to eat while Beth kept telling her how good she looked.

"You have color in your cheeks again. I hope being here this week has shown you that they really care about you."

"Yes." Lily knew they were all good people, though she would never be able to understand how they were so free sexually. It was a side of Beth that she had kept hidden; that was what had hurt.

Beth and Razer got up from the table. "Let me know what Penni says."

Lily stood up, hugging both Beth and Razer goodbye. She had to try to let her hurt feelings go. She loved Beth and Razer; she didn't want to damage them with her actions.

Beth gave her a sad smile before leaving.

She ignored Shade as she told everyone else goodnight and then went back downstairs, anxious to call Penni.

She picked her phone up from the nightstand and hit Penni's number. Listening, she heard it ring twice before

Penni's voice came over the line.

"Hello?"

"Penni, this is Lily."

"Hi, I was going to call you. I was missing your voice!" Penni said enthusiastically.

"How's the new job going?" Lily sat down cross-legged on the bed as she talked to Penni.

"Great. I finally got my office organized and the tour set. I can hardly wait."

"That's good. I'm glad you're liking your new boss."

"Kaden is a dream to work for. He can be a bit uptight, but his wife keeps him under control."

Lily's smile disappeared as Shade casually walked into the room, shutting the door and locking it behind him. She barely paid attention to Penni as she talked about her boss's wife and everyone they had introduced her to since she had arrived.

She watched as Shade straightened from the door, going to the dresser where he took off his shirt then his boots, placing them to the side. Walking barefoot, he went to the large closet that was against the wall where her clothes were kept. Lily wouldn't be surprised if he wasn't angry enough to pack for her. Instead, he reached into his pocket and pulled out a keychain, unlocking the other side of the closet that she had assumed had his clothes.

Her mouth dropped open at the vast array of objects in the closet that were neatly arranged. Lily began to get nervous. She had made a terrible mistake in underestimating Shade.

One after the other, he pulled out various items, testing their weight in his hands. He took out a thick ruler, which he smacked against his hand before putting it back in the closet. He then pulled out what looked like a mini-whip with several strands, which he slapped against his thigh before putting it back in the cabinet.

"Lily, are you there?"

"Yes." Lily didn't take her eyes off Shade.

"I thought you would be excited for me." Penni's disappointment sounded through the line.

Lily dragged her mind back to the conversation she was having. "About what?"

"Going to London for a mini-tour on the day after tomorrow. We're going to be gone two weeks."

Oh, God, she wasn't going to be able to go with Penni; she didn't have a passport. She was stuck here with the man who had pulled out a thin paddle that looked like it was covered in leather. He smacked it against his palm, this time seeming happy with his choice. Shutting the closet, he walked to the chair and sat down, staring directly into her eyes.

Lily felt like a predator was watching her, readying itself for an attack.

Her eyes went to the door, judging the distance. She had outrun him once today; surely, she could do it again. She tried to take in all the factors, including the time it would take her to unlock the door. She wouldn't make it. She knew she would have to make a break for the bathroom instead.

Tensing her body, she prepared to make her getaway.

"I'll call you when I get back."

"Make sure you do. I'm planning on coming for a visit."

"That would be fantastic. I'll talk to you later. Bye."

Lily jumped from the bed, making a run for the bathroom. She didn't make it. Halfway there, he had her around the waist.

"Oh, no you don't."

"Don't you dare touch me!" Lily yelled.

"I am going to do more than touch you. I'm going to teach you a lesson that you will never forget, Lily."

She was about to scream, terrified, when he sat her down on her feet in her corner and took a step back.

Not understanding, she watched him as he pulled the chair to face her, taking a seat.

"I think it's past time we straighten out a few things."

Her hand went to the rubber band as she pressed back against the wall.

"Cut it out. You're in your safe zone and I won't touch you when you're there." Shade leaned back against his chair.

"I joined The Last Riders when I left the military. There are eight original members. When we started the club, we decided women would be members, too. Both the men and women have rules as to how they can join. The men, if they want to enter and we want them as a part of the club, pick two of the eight original members to go up against. If they can handle themselves, they become members. The women need six votes from the eight original members to join. To get the votes, the member either fucks them or has an orgasm as a result of their play."

"I don't want to know," Lily moaned.

"Lily, you're going to hear it all. No more pretending. Now, to continue, Beth and Winter earned their votes differently. They earned markers. That's not to say they didn't earn a few votes the normal way, just not the majority of the votes." His dispassionate voice discussed her sister and Winter matter-of-factly.

"I really don't want to hear this," Lily said, feeling sick, turning her face to the wall.

"After they gain their last vote, the women can get their tat with the date they earned their last vote and became a member."

Lily turned back to face him. "Beth doesn't have a tattoo."

"I believe that Beth and Winter both had their tats placed where no one would see them. I wouldn't know. I gave them both my marker. I also have never participated in any of their fun with the club. Diamond also."

"Why?"

"Because Beth is your sister, Winter is your friend, and

Diamond because I could tell that, when you eventually spent more time with her, you would become close friends. I didn't want you to feel uncomfortable around them."

"I don't understand." Lily shook her head.

"Yes, you do. You don't want to admit it, but you do."

"No." As Lily turned her face back to the wall, she heard his deep sigh.

"Lily, I've wanted you since the first minute I saw you coming out of the diner with Beth when we first moved to Treepoint. I took one look at you and knew you were mine."

Lily shook her head, still not facing him.

"Razer unfortunately made his move with Beth first, and I had to lie back and let him see where it was going. I also knew you were young and wanted you to have some time to yourself. I never intended to wait this long for you, but I let Winter convince me to let you finish school. So, I waited."

"You didn't suffer waiting, did you, Shade? With a club full of women at your beck and call," Lily snapped.

"I am no saint. I've enjoyed every woman here at the club, but they weren't you, Lily. Never you. I would fuck them for hours trying to get me through the night so I wouldn't get on my bike and come for you."

"You can't seriously believe I would have gone with you." Lily stared at his harsh expression.

Understanding dawned on her; his clear blue eyes were telling her he wouldn't have given her a choice. She started shaking. He wasn't going to give her a choice now.

"I am no longer going to hide anything from you, and you are going to have to learn to deal with what you can and what you can't. You have your safe space, and I gave you the summer to get to know me."

"I got to know too much. That you're bossy, you're mean, and you have sex with too many women."

"I'm no cowboy," he mocked.

"You're no cowboy," Lily agreed.

"It doesn't matter what I am or not. I will be the one whose bed you will be in, who puts my ring on your finger, my baby in your belly, and you will let me, Lily."

"No." Lily shook her head, denying his words.

"Yes, Lily, you will. You won't be able to help yourself. I'll make damn sure of that. Since I want to make sure there are no more secrets between us, I'm going to tell you that Penni is my sister. Actually, my half-sister, but she says that doesn't count."

Lily sucked in a deep breath. Her sense of betrayal went so deep that she didn't know if she could bear it. Beth and now Penni had kept secrets from her.

"Beth didn't know and Penni thought I asked her to transfer colleges because of Beth. She has no idea of my interest in you."

Lily refused to look at him.

"Lily, look at me."

She wanted to deny him, but she still turned her head to look at his grim face.

"I know that this is a lot for you to take in. You don't do well with surprises; however, there is one last piece of business we need to take care of.

"You have pushed me all week. After I told you that you had earned a spanking, you deliberately tried to raise my temper. I don't lose my temper, unlike you; instead, you have earned several more strokes. I will give you a chance to explain yourself and you may be able to lessen your punishment, if it's good enough. Otherwise..." Shade shrugged.

"I will not take a punishment from you. I'm not one of your women who actually care to please you. You can go to Hell. I'm leaving. If you lay one hand on me, I'll call the police." It was then Lily realized she no longer had her cell phone.

She frantically looked around the room for it, seeing it lying on the floor where Shade had caught her. Shade saw where she was looking and got up from the chair, walking across the floor to the phone and picking it up. Walking back, he handed it to her before going to the drawer, opening it and then handing her an envelope. He resumed his seat.

"Before you make a call, you should open that envelope."

Lily knew she shouldn't, dread filling her at the unopened contents.

Slowly, she tore the envelope open, pulling out the papers and then looking through them. They were ownership papers of The Last Riders, the factory and the house. It showed all the separate names of the corporation.

Her eyes lifted to his, not understanding.

"My name is John Hunter."

Her eyes went back to the papers, going through them once again. Then horror struck. While the name of all the assets were divided equally among the members, the property that everything was built on, including Beth's new home that she loved, was owned by Shade. She looked back up at him.

"When we all got out of the service, we wanted to start the business, but they had no capital. They had the ideas; I had the money. My money combined with what they had managed to save was invested in the business. The land, being in my name, was to ensure I wasn't left without anything since I took the most risk."

"Beth and Razer's home…"

"Is on my property," Shade confirmed her worst fears.

"Oh, God."

"There's no need to be upset. I have no intention of taking their home from them… if we come to an agreement."

"What do you want, Shade?" A lone tear slid down her cheek. She already knew what he was going to say.

"You."

Lily shook her head. "You can't be serious. You have

to know this just makes me dislike you even more."

"Lily, you don't know what you want. You want a man who doesn't exist. One who will never touch you, pretend you don't have something seriously messed up going on inside of your head, and willing to put up with you constantly in some kind of trouble."

"I am not," Lily snapped. Shade lifted his brow at her response and her inability to deny the truth of the other two statements. "The man I want exists and I know you're not him."

"I'm the only man for you." Menace poured from his eyes before he regained control, shrugging and nodding his head toward the phone. "Make your mind up."

"Beth and Razer can build another house," Lily argued.

"They certainly can, but it won't be *that* house."

"Razer and you are like brothers; you wouldn't do that to him," Lily called his bluff.

"Yes, I would."

She thought about his cold-blooded approach to everything he dealt with and knew he wasn't bluffing.

"I can't do this." She pointed back and forth between them.

"I'm not going to rush you. We can go as slow as you want. I'm a patient man." *If he tells me he's a patient man one more time, I'm going to scream*, Lily thought.

"I'm going to talk to Diamond."

"I'll take you to see her tomorrow, after you get finished at the church."

"If I can find a way, I will leave." Lily had every intention of finding a way out of his trap.

"You can leave now, Lily. It's your decision."

"Okay." Lily gave in, left with no choice until she could make sure Beth didn't lose her house. Beth had protected her too many years to let her lose her house without trying to save it. If Shade was true to his word, he wouldn't pressure her, and she could find a way out of this mess. Beth would be angry and make her leave if she ever found out. She would forfeit the house she loved to protect her; Lily couldn't do less.

CHAPTER EIGHTEEN

"Good, now that it's settled, we need to take care of your punishment for nearly ripping my balls off."

"I became caught up in our lesson," Lily defended her actions.

"You were pissed at me for something. Care to tell?"

Lily remained silent.

"All right." Shade leaned forward. "Let's begin with Jewell. She closed the door to my office when Cash called. Kaley broke the rules. I really didn't give a fuck if she tried to join the club or not. She would never have gotten enough votes to anyway, so it's no loss.

"Now, let's talk about your punishment. I'm going to be lenient this time," he paused at Lily's unladylike snort, "and give you your choice of punishment."

"What are the choices?" Lily had no doubt she wasn't going to be happy with any of them.

"You can take the spanking you deserve, or you can sleep in the bed tonight, or you can give me one kiss. Take your pick."

"You're not serious?"

"Yes, I am being more than fair. It hurt like hell when you grabbed my nuts. None of your choices involve excruciating pain."

"That strap looks like it's going to hurt."

"I plan for you to enjoy that." Shade gave her a grin.

Lily shivered, and it wasn't from pleasure.

"Which one?" Shade prompted her. "Would you like me to pick for you?"

"No!"

Lily was stuck. She was going to have to pick one. She really didn't want a spanking with that strap, but the other two were just as bad. The kiss was totally out; she couldn't imagine touching her mouth to his.

"I'll sleep in the bed," Lily said reluctantly.

"You sure?"

Lily nodded her head.

"Fine. You can get ready for bed." Shade got up from the chair, turning the television on.

Lily gathered her pajamas before going into the bathroom. Pulling off her clothes, she walked down the three steps into the shower. She turned it on, feeling the water hit her body at different areas. She took her time, as the shower was becoming an obsession of hers. Each time she took one, she felt absolutely decadent.

Lily bowed her head, confused with why he wanted her when he had a variety of women to choose from, not only in the club but also in town. Every woman in town who was single, and some who were married, had been chasing him since he had rode into town.

Reluctantly getting out of the shower, she blow-dried her hair to take even more time delaying the inevitable. She wanted to flick the rubber band, but she didn't.

Dressed in her thick pajamas, she opened the door, going into the bedroom. She wanted to go to the corner; instead, she forced her feet toward the bed.

Shade didn't take his attention away from the television as Lily climbed into the bed, clinging to the side as much as she could without falling out. Shade then turned the television off and went into the bathroom. Lily relaxed when he left the room, letting herself get even more comfortable when she heard the shower. She drifted in and out of sleep, too tense to slip into a deep slumber.

When the door opened, however, she pretended to be asleep. She felt the bed dip on the other side of the bed and felt Shade reach out to turn off the lights. With her back to him, Lily opened her eyes and saw he had left the bathroom light on. She continued to lie tensely, feeling him move under the covers, getting comfortable.

She was trying not to panic. If he rolled one inch closer to her, though, she would go to the corner. Lily didn't know how long she lay tensed before she realized he was already asleep. She forced herself to relax again, her fingertips lying against the red rubber band as if it would protect her.

Closing her eyes, she drifted off to sleep, thinking she had gotten one over on Shade. This wasn't a punishment; she was glad to be out of the corner.

* * *

Shade forced his body to remain still long after Lily had managed to fall asleep. The whole bed had practically shaken with her frightened tremors. When he was sure she had finally gone into a deep sleep, he rolled closer to her, fitting her against him as his warmth seeped into her chilled body.

He let his fingers play with the wisps of hair on the pillow. He was an expert at moving his body a centimeter at a time. All his years of experience had led to this one moment that he had waited years for: Lily in his bed, holding her close.

After she had been hurt back in the summer, he had purchased a whole new bed. None of the women had lain in the bed Lily was lying on now.

A small smile tugged at his lips. Her temper had surprised him today. Over the last couple of years, he had seen a few flashes of it, but today it had passed her barricade and broken loose. She had been jealous, and she didn't even realize that was the emotion she was feeling, yet he had known it when he'd opened the office door and seen her face.

He hadn't touched Jewell in his office. He had told Lily the truth. He hadn't touched a woman since he had almost lost her and had seen her lying on that hospital bed. The sight of her had made him come to the conclusion he couldn't wait for her anymore. Lily needed him as much as he needed her.

All summer, he had worked toward one goal—luring her to him. He had almost succeeded, too, if not for that bitch Kaley. Now she believed she hated him and he couldn't blame her, but it didn't make a difference because, either way, she wasn't ready to admit to herself that she cared about him.

* * *

Lily woke the next morning to an empty bed. She showered and dressed and then, leaving the bedroom, she found Shade working out.

"I need to get to the church."

"Grab some breakfast while I get dressed," Shade said, setting his weights down.

"All right." Lily went upstairs.

No one was in the kitchen as she prepared herself a bowl of cereal. She had just finished when Shade came in.

"Ready?"

"Yes," she answered, putting her bowl into the dishwasher. "Aren't you going to eat breakfast?"

"Rider and I are going to eat at the diner."

They walked outside and down the path to Shade's bike. Rider nodded at her as he came outside, getting on his own bike. Lily put on the helmet that Shade handed her and then got on behind him. Her car was still at the college. She needed to make arrangements to get it back to Treepoint so she wouldn't have to depend on others for transportation.

The ride down the mountain was spectacular in the fall

with the changing leaf colors. Lily couldn't imagine a more beautiful sight.

Shade pulled into the church's parking lot by the door that led to the room she and Rachel would be working in for the day.

Lily climbed off the bike, handing Shade his helmet.

"Thanks," Lily said, starting toward the door.

"Lily." She paused, turning back toward him. "Call when you're finished."

Lily nodded, going inside the building. She needed her car.

Rachel was already there, sorting clothes.

"Hey, Lily."

"Good morning, Rachel. You're hard at work, I see." Lily picked up a handful of socks that the woman was sorting.

Rachel laughed. "Someone donated a whole bag of socks that had no matches."

Lily looked down at the colorful assortment. "Just bag them into smaller bags. They won't care. Most of the people we'll be helping will just be happy to have something warm on their feet this winter."

"Good idea," Rachel said, dividing the socks into smaller piles.

The women worked steadily, talking about their week. Lily felt Rachel's hesitance at broaching the subject of her breakdown.

"Were you okay when you woke up?"

Lily paused before opening another bag. "Yes, but I couldn't remember what had set off the panic attack."

Rachel nodded, reaching out to open the bag for her. "I've never seen anyone have a panic attack before. It was scary for me to watch. I can only imagine how Beth and Shade felt."

Lily looked at Rachel. "Shade?"

Rachel looked her in the eye. "It's obvious he cares about you, Lily. The man never lets you out of his sight unless you're with Beth and Razer or at church."

"I don't like him… sometimes."

"Why not? It certainly can't be his looks that don't attract you. I was in town last week when a woman practically walked into a parking meter while she was watching him."

"He's too... well... too..." Lily couldn't think of the word she was looking for.

"Much?"

Lily nodded. "He's too handsome, bossy, aggravating, and he can be mean, too."

Rachel started to get angry. "He's mean to you?"

"Not exactly," Lily conceded.

Rachel gave a relieved sigh. "Thank God. I wasn't looking forward to kicking his ass for you."

Lily giggled. "You don't have to; I can do it for myself." She told Rachel what she had done the day before.

"Stop. I'm going to pee on myself if you don't." It took several minutes for Rachel to get herself back under control. "You actually grabbed Shade by the balls?"

Lily nodded her head.

"Why?"

"Because he made me angry with the way he treated Kaley." Rachel gave her a wry glance before she began to fold the clothes from the bag.

"Are you sure that's all there was to it? You weren't just a little bit jealous?" Rachel probed.

"No, I wasn't. Shade's just Beth and Razer's friend, that's all."

"Um, hm… I think the lady protests too much."

Lily tossed one of the t-shirts at her and Rachel laughed, dodging her.

The door opening had both women turning to see who had entered.

"Hi, girls."

"Hi, Willa." Willa Weeks was in her early thirties. She was a caterer who specialized in cakes. Her creations had even made a few food magazines. Her cupcakes were also just as delicious-looking, more like little creations of art that didn't deserve to be eaten.

"I have several bags of old clothes to donate if you can use them. I also updated my kitchen if you need any kitchen appliances. I have the clothes in the car, but the appliances are in my garage at home. I couldn't move them by myself, so if you can get them picked up, the church can have them."

"That's great. The church could give them to someone who really needs them," Rachel said.

"I thought of a couple of families who I know are cooking on hot plates because they couldn't afford a new stove," Willa said.

"I'll tell Pastor Dean and he can get some volunteers to pick them up," Lily said.

"Okay. I'm usually home unless I'm making a delivery so anytime is convenient," Willa responded. "I'll get the clothes out of my car."

"I'll help," Lily offered.

"Let me," Rachel said. "I need to work off my dinner from last night."

Rachel followed Willa out the door. Lily continued to sort clothes while they packed in several more bags.

"That's a lot of clothes," Lily commented.

"I cleaned out my closets. I'm afraid my baking isn't helping my figure any." Willa was a pretty brunette who both Lily and Rachel had to glance down at because of her barely five-foot frame. "I keep telling myself they'll invent a diet that will make cupcakes an option."

"When you find one, let me know." Rachel laughed.

"There's one more bag. I'll get it," Willa said, going back out the door.

Lily put the bags of clothes to the side for them to work on next. The way everyone was donating, it was going to take several weeks for both her and Rachel to get everything organized.

"Are you thinking what I'm thinking?" Rachel asked.

"I'm afraid so," Lily answered. "If we're going to get this shop opened anytime soon, then we need another volunteer or we have to work days during the week."

Willa walked back into the store carrying another bag of clothes and a small box.

"We appreciate the donations." Rachel smiled at Willa who laid the clothes on the counter and then the small box, which she pushed toward Lily and Rachel.

Lily opened the box to see two cupcakes, which looked like little clouds of perfection. The pink frosting with chocolate chips was immediately grabbed by the women.

"I thought you two deserved a treat for the time you are donating," Willa said, watching the two women eat her cupcakes.

"None for me?" Pastor Dean said, coming into the room from the church entrance.

Lily watched Willa's face flame red in embarrassment.

"I'm sorry, Pastor Dean. I didn't think you would be in the store."

Pastor Dean eyed them enviously eating the remains of the cupcakes.

"It was delicious," Lily complimented.

"I wouldn't know," Pastor Dean said woefully.

Lily and Rachel laughed while Willa looked embarrassed.

"I better go. I have an order I need to get started." Willa edged closer to the door.

"Wait a minute, Willa," Rachel forestalled the woman. "Pastor Dean, Willa has some appliances to donate, but she needs some help getting them here."

"I'll take care of it. When would be a good time?"

"Anytime would be fine. I'm usually home," Willa told him.

"This evening around five sound good? I should be able to round up a couple of men to stop by and pick them up."

"That's fine."

"I appreciate the donations to the church."

"You're welcome. Well, I better go. See you tomorrow, Rachel and Lily. Pastor Dean."

Willa left and Lily looked at Pastor Dean.

"I think she thought you would break into a spontaneous sermon the way she took off from here," Rachel said.

"She always acts like that. I don't know why. Am I one of those preachers who puts the fear of God into you by being in the room?" he asked with a frown. "None of the other women in the church act like that. They like to make desserts for me, but she has a kitchen full of baked goods and never brings me anything." If Lily didn't know better, she would have thought the Pastor was pouting.

"Those women bring you food trying to catch you. They want to impress you with their cooking skills," Lily told him.

It was no secret that Pastor Dean was the most eligible bachelor in town. Ever since he had taken over the church after her father's death, the single women in the congregation had been vying for his attention.

"Willa doesn't need to worry that she'll give me that impression. She doesn't give me the time of day if she can help it. I think if there was another Baptist church in town, she would have left ours already," Pastor Dean said.

Lily could hear the concern in his voice. "I don't think that's true at all. She was probably in a rush."

"Could be," Pastor Dean said, yet he didn't sound like he believed his own words.

Rachel and Lily shared a glance. It was unusual to see Pastor Dean unsure of himself. He was loved and respected by the whole congregation. Lily was sure he had over-thought Willa's reaction to his presence.

"How soon do you think we'll be able to open the store for the community?" Pastor Dean asked, changing the conversation.

"We were just talking about that," Lily answered. "We think we need another helper or we need to do an extra night."

"I don't want to impose on your time, but I've already asked several to help out and been given every excuse they can come up with."

"I don't mind. How about Wednesday, Rachel? We could do it after service."

"I think that will be fine. I have the time."

"If you're both sure?" Pastor Dean asked.

"We're sure," Lily answered. It would give her a few extra hours away from the club a week.

"I'll see you both in the morning then," Pastor Dean excused himself.

Lily and Rachel spent the rest of the day making headway with the large job ahead of them.

They were going through the last bag when Rachel pulled out a sheer nightgown. She stared down at it then broke out laughing. "Do you think it was a mistake or do you suppose they were trying to give Pastor Dean a message?"

Lily blushed, folding clothes on the table next to her. "What should we do with it?" Lily asked.

"Put it out. We'll have to watch and see who takes it." Rachel raised it up so Lily could see it better. "Are you sure you don't want to take it home?"

"I wouldn't need it. I don't believe in premarital sex."

Rachel just stared at her in disbelief. "Good luck with that."

"What does that mean?" Lily asked, insulted.

Rachel just shook her head. "I'm not going there."

"I don't know why you think it's strange. I don't see you getting any man past your brothers."

Rachel grinned conspiratorially. "No one's tempted me enough to make me want to go against those knuckleheads, but believe me, when I do, I'll have no problem saying yes."

Lily looked at her in surprise. Lily had thought as religious as Rachel was that she would share her own view.

"You would?"

"Oh, yes. I've been looking forward to losing my v-card. I just can't find the man worth giving it up." Rachel grinned. "You should see your face, Lily."

"I want my first time to be special," Lily said, looking down at the clothes held tightly in her hands, not sure why she wanted to cry all of a sudden.

"I do, too," Rachel said, reaching over to touch her hand lightly. "I didn't say I wouldn't love him with my whole heart, just that I don't need a piece of paper saying it's all right to express my love in a physical way."

"But I would want my minister's blessing."

"I'm sure Pastor Dean would know and give his blessing if he was aware that you cared about him." Rachel's hand tightened on hers before letting go. Lily missed the soothing warmth of her touch.

"I want to wait."

"Then you should. No one is pressuring you, are they?"

Lily thought hard on Shade's words from last night. He had told her he wanted her, but he hadn't demanded anything from her sexually. The man was going to need the patience of Job if he thought she would ever marry him and have his children.

"No."

"There you go then. Don't worry about something before you have to. Life is stressful enough."

"You're right. I won't. I'm sure that whoever I pick to spend my life with will understand," Lily said confidently.

"I wouldn't go that far, but I believe you've got to roll with what life gives you," she said, nodding her head to the window, seeing Shade pull up in front. "Just remember that promise to yourself when that bad boy is tempting you."

Lily looked out the window. "He's not the type of man I pictured my life with."

"Still hung up on getting a cowboy?"

"Yes," Lily replied, stubbornly determined to find a way to save Beth's house.

"Well, all I can say is, I hope he can shoot as good as he can ride a horse."

CHAPTER NINETEEN

Lily got on the motorcycle behind Shade. "I need to get my car from school," she told him as she put on the helmet.

"I've already taken care of it; it's parked at your house," Shade told her before starting his bike.

Lily was happy it was already in town. "Can you drop me off to pick it up?"

"Later," Shade replied, driving off the parking lot as Lily stiffened at his noncommittal response.

Shade drove through town, turning down a side street and then another before pulling up in front of a pretty two-story home.

"What are we doing here?" Lily asked.

"This is where Diamond and Knox live. I'll wait here while you talk to her."

Lily was angry at herself for not remembering she needed to talk to Diamond.

Getting jerkily off the bike, she handed him the helmet, but before she could turn away, he reached into his jacket pocket and pulled out a now-familiar envelope.

"You might need these."

Lily snatched the envelope from his hand, ignoring his

confident grin. His sunglasses hid his eyes, but she was sure they contained amusement that he was making no effort to hide.

She headed up the walkway and rang the doorbell. It took several minutes before she heard someone approaching from the other side of the door.

The disheveled woman who answered was not the cool and calm lawyer she was becoming acquainted with.

"Lily." Her eyes went to Shade sitting in the driveway. "What can I do for you?"

"I'm sorry to bother you, but I have a legal question to ask, if you're not too busy."

"Not at all. Come in." Diamond opened the door wider for her to enter.

"I'm sorry. I should have made an appointment at your office."

"I wasn't doing anything important," Diamond protested.

"Yes, she was," Knox said, coming into the room as he buckled his gun belt around his waist.

Lily wanted to die of embarrassment at what she had interrupted.

"I'm sorry. I should have called first." Lily's face flamed.

"It's all right. She can make it up to me later. I need to get back to work anyway." Knox teased his wife before bending down and kissing her goodbye. Lily looked away as the kiss became passionate before breaking apart.

"Bye, Diamond. Lily, everything okay?" Knox asked.

"Yes, I just need a piece of legal advice."

"All right. I'll leave you with Diamond then. Take care."

"I will," Lily responded to the huge man who didn't need the uniform to make him look frightening as heck.

Diamond waited for the door to close behind him before asking, "What's up?" Lily handed her the envelope. "I have a feeling I'm going to need a cup of coffee for this," she said, leading Lily into the kitchen.

"Have a seat."

Lily took a seat at her counter while Diamond poured them both a cup of hot coffee.

Diamond opened the envelope on the counter and read as she sipped her coffee. "What am I looking for?" she asked. "Everything looks straightforward."

Lily pointed to a section that showed the property. "That's where Beth and Razer built their house."

Diamond flipped back through the paperwork. "Fuck," she said. That pretty much summed up what Lily had been afraid of; she was in trouble.

"Do you know who John Hunter is?" Diamond asked, looking up from the paperwork.

"Shade."

"Well, that's a relief. I was worried for a moment." Diamond turned away to freshen her coffee.

"Why?"

"Because if the house is built on his property, then technically it's his home. As are all the buildings on the property. They're pretty smart. If there was a lawsuit, it could tie whoever is suing them in court years to separate the two."

"I see," Lily murmured.

"Is there anything else?"

"No, that's what I needed to know," Lily said, standing up.

"Lily, are you sure? You don't look like you're happy right now. Is there anything you're not telling me?"

"No, I was just worried about Razer and Beth. Sometimes even best friends get in arguments and I was worried they might lose their home if there was ever one in the future."

"To be honest, Razer and Beth should have thought about that before they decided to build their house where they did, but if Razer isn't worried about it, then you shouldn't be, Lily. Let Razer and Shade deal with it."

"That's easier said than done."

"That's why I'm such a good lawyer; I can give plenty of advice." She walked Lily to the door. "If you need anything else, let me know. If you're really worried about it, talk to Shade."

"I will. Thanks," Lily said, going out the door. She felt Shade's eyes on her the minute she walked outside.

"Can we go get my car now?" Lily put on the helmet, getting on behind Shade.

"Yes."

Lily held on tightly as they drove toward her home. She had ridden with Shade several times and had never worried about her safety. If anything, she felt that Shade was overly-cautious when she rode on his bike. She wished that sometimes he would crank up the speed and let her ride without the helmet to feel the wind through her hair. Instead, he pulled up behind her car and cut the motor.

"You need to pick anything up while you're here?"

"No." Lily took her car keys from his hand before going to her car and sliding inside. She was afraid if she went inside, she wouldn't come out again. She wanted to run and hide from whoever was watching her... and Shade. She wasn't sure which one to be more afraid of at the moment.

Shade followed her back to the club. As she drove, the sky darkened with storm clouds. Lily hated storms. Her hands tightened on the car wheel as the strong winds buffeted the vehicle. She pulled into The Last Riders' parking lot, driving toward the back of the lot where Shade motioned for her to park as he parked his bike toward the front with the rest of them.

Shade walked over to her car when she got out, carrying a car cover. He pulled it over the car and Lily had to question, "Why cover my car?"

"Just being careful. If someone is looking to find out where you're staying, they'll either have to follow you or come onto the property to see if this is your car."

"If they do?"

"Then we'll see them." Shade pointed to the cameras.

It was a relief to see they could possibly catch whoever was watching her. That way, Knox could handle it without anyone getting hurt.

"We placed a few in your home, too, so if they try to break in again, an alarm will go off at the sheriff's office and here, also.

"Maybe they gave up and moved on?"

"Possibly, but I don't believe so. Whoever's been watching you has been doing so for a while." Lily tried to hide how worried she was becoming, but she wasn't successful. Shade tried to ease her fears. "Don't worry; we'll find out who it is and deal with it."

"You'll turn them over to Knox?"

"Maybe. Let's get some dinner." His evasive answer renewed her fears. Lily didn't want Shade to get into trouble trying to protect her, no matter how infuriating he could be.

They walked up the pathway to the kitchen door. She could see that most of the large crowd had already been served. Lily took a plate before handing one to Shade and getting into the buffet line. When she finished, she saw Winter and Viper sitting at a table with Bliss and Raci. Going to their table, she took a seat next to Winter and Shade sat down across from her, next to Bliss.

Lily ate while she listened to Winter and Viper argue over him donating money, so she could buy her students at the alternate high school where she was principal, the computers they needed.

"It's not fair, Viper. They deserve the computers as much as the high school students do."

"If they had kept their asses out of trouble, then they wouldn't have gotten thrown out of the school district."

"That's unfair. Both schools should have the same standards," Winter argued.

Viper shrugged. "I gave you two large chunks of

money already this year. You've reached your limit with my generosity, but that doesn't mean you can't hit the other members up for donations. Their pockets are deeper than mine since you've already robbed me twice."

Winter turned her eyes to the members sitting across from her. Lily wanted to laugh at their deer-caught-in-the-headlights looks.

"Raci?"

"Don't ask me. I'm not an original member; I earn a paycheck like everyone else."

Lily was convinced Raci didn't have any money from her pathetic expression. She was about to offer her a loan when Winter's words had her changing her mind.

"I do the payroll; I know what you make." Winter gave the woman a narrow-eyed stare. Lily could have told her it would be a waste of time to out-maneuver Winter.

"I can buy a couple," Raci conceded reluctantly. Since Lily had been around the club, she had learned Raci loved clothes and shoes. Expensive purses were said to be her greatest weakness. Lily didn't know why; she had never seen her carry one in all the time she had known her.

"Bliss?"

"Put me down for two." Bliss wasn't even going to fight the inevitable.

"Thanks. Shade?"

Shade paused with the fork halfway to his mouth. "No."

Lily shot him a reproachful look.

"Don't look at me that way, Lily. I've already bought that school two pieces of expensive equipment for their auto shop, a confection oven for the cooking class and paid the salary of the auto shop teacher, so no computer from me. Maybe next year, if you don't hit me up for something else before then." Shade had no problem returning Winter's stare, giving her one of his own.

"Have you asked Razer?" Lily broke into the staring contest.

"No," Winter said.

"Why not?" Lily was sure Razer would be willing to donate.

"Because he coughed up the money to pay for the afterschool tutors. Her chances of getting any money out of Razer are nil," Shade answered, taking a drink of his beer. Lily sent him another reproachful look.

"Rider and Train?" Lily asked.

Winter remained silent.

"New bus to drive the kids, and lab equipment," Shade replied after Winter's continued silence.

"Knox?" Lily asked hesitantly.

"Media library."

"Ouch. I could buy two. I have some money saved up," Lily offered, finally understanding that Winter had tapped her money well dry for the time being.

As everyone at the table looked at her, she felt self-conscious.

"No, Lily. I couldn't take your money. I have one other member I haven't hit up yet."

"Who?" Lily asked.

"Lucky."

"I haven't met him yet," Lily said, glancing across the table to see that Bliss was giving Shade a furtive look from under her lashes. She glanced back down at her plate, her hand going to the stinging pain in her chest.

"Are you all right?" Shade asked, looking across the table at her with a frown.

"Yes, I must have eaten something that gave me indigestion," Lily said, getting up from the table.

"Yeah, I feel a little nauseous myself," Winter commented with a warning look at Bliss, sitting across from her.

"You're probably stressed out, worrying about coming up with the money for the computers. Let me know how much they cost and I'll write you a check for two of them. I wish I could do more," Lily said, not looking at the people sitting at the table.

"I'll ask Lucky. If he doesn't, then I'll pay for them," Viper conceded, taking Lily's hand as she reached for his plate. "We'll take care of it. Keep your money, Lily." Lily gave his hand a squeeze before letting it go and picking up his plate then Winter's.

"Okay, but if you decide you need it, let me know. I'm going to bed. I'm tired tonight. Goodnight, everyone." Lily left everyone sitting at the table, carrying the dirty dishes to the sink.

Jewell was rinsing and stacking the dirty dishes into the dishwasher. Lily quietly helped her finish the dishes until Nickel showed up to help.

Wishing them goodnight, Lily went downstairs to Shade's bedroom where she carried her pajamas to the bathroom, took a quick shower, and then took her time blow-drying her hair.

For once, she was glad she was downstairs as the wind howled from outside. She hated storms. She had noticed the storm was moving closer when she had been upstairs. The rain was beginning, and from the sounds of rumbling coming through the house, there was thunder starting.

She turned off the blow dryer and then went to the bedroom door where she paused at seeing Shade removing his t-shirt, having already taken his boots off.

Lily started to go to the corner.

"Bed, Lily."

"But—"

"You agreed when you chose your punishment last night," Shade reminded her.

"I thought that was just for last night," she protested.

"No. Go to bed. I'm going to take a shower."

Lily was feeling too tired to argue tonight. She climbed into the bed and attempted not to play back the image of the expression on Bliss's face when she thought she wasn't looking.

Bliss was a very attractive woman with a sexuality that

even she couldn't help noticing. The men's eyes were constantly on her and she wasn't shy about returning their gaze.

Lily did what she always did; she locked it away where it wouldn't bother her anymore, moving her mind toward the fantasy of traveling the many places she wanted to explore instead. Gradually, she fell asleep to the sound of the water from Shade's shower.

Lily awoke later, surrounded in warmth with the blankets pulled snugly around her. She could hear the wind howling, sounding like screams in the night. Her eyes lifted open to complete darkness and she jerked straight up in the bed, screaming in terror.

"Lily." She heard Shade's voice next to her in the darkness. "The power went off. The generator will kick on in a minute. Just take a deep breath with me and let's count."

She couldn't concentrate enough to count; the door was trying to open.

"Lily! Concentrate. Count with me. One... two... three..."

"Four... five..." Lily focused on the sound of Shade's reassuring voice as she counted. She took a sobbing breath and resumed counting. "Six... seven..."

As the lights flickered briefly then came on, she turned to Shade, who was also sitting up, and lay her head on his shoulder, crying in relief.

"I have you, Sweetheart. Shh... I have you."

The rocking motions of his body soothed her as her arms circled his neck and she burrowed closer to him, trying to get warm. She was always so cold. So cold.

Fine tremors shook her body while his firm hand stroked her back as he continued to rock her with his soothing words, repeating over and over that it was a storm. She gradually relaxed, exhausted, lying limply against him and falling back asleep.

A man stronger than the shadows of her memories had

held her demons at bay.

CHAPTER TWENTY

Lily woke the next day, feeling like she hadn't slept. She glanced over at the clock, realizing it was going to be a rush getting ready for church. As she started to slide out of bed, she noticed Shade was lying on his stomach, where she could see his bare back covered in a large tattoo.

In the middle of his back was the Navy Seal emblem with a large snake coiled around it from top to bottom with the head actually appearing as if it was about to strike. At the base of the tattoo were two revolvers that had a chain wrapped around both barrels. To the side and higher up was a pair of brass knuckles. Lily also saw a hand of cards and a long-handled razor. The entire tattoo had a shaded appearance.

While the tats on the rest of his body were clustered together, he only had that single large one on his back. Lily had a sense of its importance to him.

Pulling her attention away from the tattoo, she got off the bed, rushing around the room to get ready for church. Sliding on a navy dress and flats, she brushed her hair, ready to leave.

"Ride in with Evie and Winter." Shade didn't rise, merely rolled over in the bed with his arm over his eyes.

It was then that Lily realized that not only had the overhead light been on but the two lamps on each bedside table and the bathroom light. She took the time to turn off the lights before leaving the room.

Pulling out her phone on the way upstairs, Lily saw that Evie had texted her that they were in the car with Bliss, Jewell and Raci all waiting for her. She rushed out and climbed into the backseat next to Bliss.

"The storm was terrible last night," Evie remarked as she turned onto the road. Lily thought she must have slept through the storm.

"I didn't notice," Bliss said. "Train and Cash kept me too busy." Lily saw Evie throw Bliss a warning glance in the rearview mirror.

The car grew uncomfortably quiet. When Winter looked over her shoulder at her, Lily turned to look out the window as they drove down the mountain. Gradually, conversation resumed with Raci breaking the silence, discussing the Halloween party for next week.

Lily tuned out the discussion, trying to remember back to the night before. Her head started aching, and she wished she had thought to put some ibuprofen in her purse.

The church was already filled when they walked through the door. Looking around, Lily saw Beth and Razer had saved her a spot next to them, so she slid onto their bench.

Beth searched her face, reaching for her hand. Lily—forgetting her resentments for a while—held her hand throughout the service, listening as Pastor Dean presented an eloquent sermon on giving to the community. He ended the service and went to the doorway as usual.

As everyone filed out the doors, Willa was in front of Lily, and she was glad to have the opportunity to speak with her.

"Thank you for the cupcakes yesterday."

Willa smiled back as the line moved forward. "I enjoy

baking."

"Obviously," Georgia said from behind Beth, making no effort to lower her voice.

Lily rushed to talk so that Willa wouldn't overhear the rude woman, but she didn't need to worry as the sound of several motorcycles coming from outside was loud.

"I hear your friends arriving at the diner. It's nice to always have them save a table for you before church lets out," Willa teased.

Lily laughed. "They usually beat us and get the biggest table. Would you like to join us? We could give you a ride home afterward." The line moved forward and Willa reached out to shake Pastor Dean's hand.

"Like her fat ass would fit on the back of a bike," Georgia snidely commented.

When Willa's face turned bright red, Lily had to give the embarrassed woman credit for not losing her composure. Pastor Dean started to speak to her, but with a quick word, Willa moved away, not letting him finish.

Lily bypassed her Pastor, quickly going after the humiliated woman. "Willa."

She stopped, turning back to Lily. "I'm sorry, Lily. I didn't mean to ignore your invitation, but I have an order to get out. See you later."

"That's all right. Stop by the store next weekend if you get time."

"I will." With that, the woman rushed down the sidewalk toward her home.

Lily spun around, furious. Beth and Razer were waiting for her, but Lily walked back toward Georgia and her friends from work, who were just then leaving the church. She could tell that Pastor Dean had already said something from the expression on both of their faces. She had known he would. She admired and respected Pastor Dean for just that reason; he didn't let acts of unkindness go by unnoticed.

"That was terrible." Lily stepped in front of Georgia,

blocking her path.

"What business is it of yours?"

"We were in God's church, Georgia. Why do you go if not to be a better person?"

"I wouldn't talk about people being in church who shouldn't be there. Hell, half of the congregation is headed for God's judgment and your sister is one of them."

As soon as the words were out of Georgia's mouth, Lily could see she realized she had gone too far. It was one thing to insult an acquaintance, but not the hand that pays the bills and puts food on the table. Razer was one of the owners of the factory who gave her a paycheck every week, and she had just insulted his wife.

"I'm sorry, Beth. I let my mouth run away with me," Georgia said as Beth came up to stand next to Lily.

Beth nodded her head but refused to respond. On the other hand, Lily was happy to see Razer had no problem voicing his own displeasure.

"Georgia, no one cares about your bullshit apology. I would fire you here and now, but despite your ignorant belief that we're all going to Hell, I'll give you one more chance. If I hear your ugly-assed comments again, you'll be on the unemployment line." Razer's harsh expression left no doubt he was delivering her a promise.

As Razer took Beth and Lily's arms, leading them across the street, Lily was still simmering with anger at the woman. Willa hadn't deserved her ugly comments. Georgia had wanted to humiliate her and she had succeeded; it had been completely uncalled for.

Lily took a seat next to Beth, avoiding Shade's sharp gaze as the others talked about Lily confronting Georgia. His expression remained passive as he let Razer grumble about firing her.

Thankfully, the waitress taking their order succeeded in changing the topic of conversation, yet Lily had a hard time getting her temper back under control. She couldn't understand why her temper was flaring lately when she had always been so calm and never let anyone bother her before. Usually, she was an extreme pacifist; however, it had hurt something deep inside of her to see that wounded look on Willa's face. She hadn't been able to stand back and let Georgia get away with hurting the kind-hearted woman.

She took a sip of her iced tea, her fingertips rubbing her temple after she placed the glass back down, and caught sight of the rubber band on her wrist. She was becoming less and less dependent on it since she had begun staying with The Last Riders. Lily was happy she needed it less frequently, but wondered if it was because she was becoming more confident in herself or because of the sense of safety The Last Riders provided.

The food arrived hot, yet Lily just picked at her salad. Shade and Razer had both gotten burgers and fries while Bliss and Raci had both ordered breakfasts, though they were complaining that the men's food looked better. As Bliss reached onto Shade's plate, taking a French fry, Lily took a bite of food, ignoring Bliss.

"How much longer before the church store will be able to open?" Beth questioned.

"A few weeks. Not only are Rachel and I sorting through everyone's recent donations but also years of clutter. We've boxed things up for Pastor Dean to decide whether to throw them away or store them."

"Dad was a closet hoarder—he saved everything—and I'm sure Pastor Dean didn't want to throw things away immediately," Beth said.

"Dad saved every sermon he ever wrote. I expected to find all the video tapes he recorded, but I haven't come across them yet. I was looking forward to destroying them," Lily commented.

"I'm sure you'll come across them before you're finished." Beth's lips tightened as Bliss took another French fry from Razer's plate. She then turned her attention back to Lily. "If you find them, let me know. I want to help you burn them."

Lily smiled ruefully. "I'm sure there will be enough for both of us. How's Mrs. Langley?"

"She's having a harder time recuperating than I had hoped. I'm going to stay with her for the rest of the week. Razer and I are staying in her guest room. Logan and Holly have both moved in with his father so that she can get plenty of rest.

"Are you sure you don't need me to sit with her during the day or night to give you a break?" Lily offered.

"No, I have it covered. I don't want to have to worry about your safety and I know at the clubhouse you're protected. Have you managed to get any school work done?"

"I'm going to make a start on it tonight."

"Let me know if you need anything. We should be getting back. Holly sat with her so we could go to church." They stood up from the table as everyone finished. Lily hugged her sister and brother-in-law goodbye.

As they also headed out of the diner, she started to go back to Evie's car, but Shade caught her hand as she passed his bike. Not feeling like arguing, she climbed on the back, tucking her dress around her so it wouldn't blow up as they rode.

It didn't take long for them to get back to the clubhouse. Once there, Shade let her use his computer as he worked out so that she could get caught up on her schoolwork, which took her a couple of hours to complete.

She hadn't been paying attention when Shade had come into the room and gone into the shower, but she found her attention wandering as he reentered the room shirtless.

"Hungry?"

"A little, but I want to finish this."

"Go ahead and finish. I'll bring you a plate."

"Sounds good, thanks," Lily said absently.

Shade left the room and Lily continued working. She was almost done when he returned, setting the plate down in front of her. When he did, she smelled the faint scent of perfume on him as he leaned close to her. Lily's concentration was broken, and she had to force herself to finish the work.

"Is the television distracting you?" Shade asked when she gave a frustrated sigh at a stupid mistake she had caught when she was rechecking her work.

"No." She hadn't even realized he had turned it on; her mind had been so unfocused.

Eating her food, she ignored Shade. The food was good, but again, she had no appetite. If she didn't begin feeling more like herself, she was going to have to see a doctor. Maybe she was getting an ulcer or becoming allergic to certain foods? She couldn't understand why she had lost her healthy appetite. Shrugging it off once more, she told herself it was only worry from the unknown identity of the person watching her.

She stood up, grabbing her plate from the desk. "Do you need anything while I'm upstairs?"

"A beer would be great." Lily wanted to refuse, yet he had been nice enough to bring her dinner; she didn't want to come across as petty. She was so tempted to snap at him that whoever's perfume he was wearing could bring him his darn beer, though.

Going upstairs, she opened the door to the kitchen and went inside. No one was in there, so Lily placed her plate in the sink and was about to rinse it off when a noise from the television room had her head turning in that direction. The unobstructed view let her see exactly what had made the soft noise.

Bliss was riding Train's cock, sliding up and down. Train hadn't paid attention to her in the kitchen, but Bliss had—her eyes were on Lily as Train suckled her breast— she was watching Lily for her reaction.

Lily bolted back downstairs, making sure her eyes

didn't return to the two on the couch.

"Where my beer?" Shade asked when she returned empty-handed.

"I forgot it." Lily, a second too late, realized she had forgotten to get him the beer he requested.

"I'm going to take a shower," Lily said, grabbing her pajamas and then disappearing into the bedroom. She took her time trying to wash away the memory of what she had seen.

When she went back out to the bedroom, the first thing she noticed was Shade drinking his beer.

"It's a little early to go to bed, isn't it?"

"I have a headache. I guess it's from staring at the computer screen."

"Possibly. Will the television disturb you?"

"No." Lily was about to climb into bed but stopped herself, going instead to Shade.

"You need to let me go. I'm never going to fit into this club."

"What makes you say that?"

"You know why." She waved her hand at the beer. "Bliss doesn't try to hide that you both have shared a relationship. She doesn't want me here. She belongs here, I don't."

"You will."

"No, Shade, I won't. You're only going to hurt everyone involved. I'm never going to adjust to your lifestyle. You're not a one-woman man."

"I already am," Shade said softly.

Lily wanted to kick the stubborn man. "Don't claim I'm the woman for you when you smell like another woman's perfume."

"I smell like perfume?" Shade asked, not trying to hide his amusement.

"Yes," Lily said angrily.

"That's because Winter hugged me when I told her I would pay for the computers for her school."

"Well… heck." She was going to have to apologize. She felt terrible he had done something so nice and she was jumping on his case. She felt ashamed. She was no better than Georgia.

"I'm sorry," Lily apologized and meant it.

"You were awfully harsh to me, don't you think? I mean, I was nice enough to fix your dinner and bring it to you, and then you forgot my beer. Then you rant at me about other women. I'm beginning to think you're jealous. I never took you for the jealous type."

"I'm not jealous," Lily snapped.

"I believe you are, and I don't believe you're sorry. Do you know how much those computers are going to cost me?" Shade tried to appear affronted.

It isn't a good look for him, Lily thought. The man didn't have a humble bone in his awesome body. Lily nodded her head. That didn't mean she had been wrong to jump to conclusions, though. "I am not jealous and I apologized."

"I don't believe you." Shade gave her a reproachful look, which did make her feel bad.

"I really do."

"Prove it."

"How?"

"Kiss me and make it better."

"No." Lily shook her head.

"I knew you didn't mean your apology," Shade said, turning back to the television.

"I did—I do," Lily corrected herself. "But I'm still not going to kiss you."

"Why? You've kissed before, haven't you?"

Lily didn't say anything.

"Lily, have you kissed before?" His surprised eyes stared into her embarrassed ones.

"No," Lily admitted.

"What about Charles?"

"Just on the cheek or a brief peck on the lips. I guess I could do that," she said unenthusiastically.

"Don't knock yourself out. I've been told I'm a good kisser. I could teach you how," Shade offered, this time trying to appear innocent. Another not so good look for him.

"I bet you could," she said sarcastically. Then, before she could help herself, she asked, "Who told you you're a good kisser?"

"I don't kiss and tell," he said, grinning at her wickedly. Now *that* look worked for him.

Lily gritted her teeth in aggravation.

"Come on, Lily. What's a little kiss between friends?" He rose to his feet and put his hands behind his back. "I won't touch you with anything other than my mouth. You can experiment and see how you like kissing."

Lily froze, tempted. She had never been kissed. She had been too afraid Charles wouldn't stop when she wanted him to. Shade was more experienced and older. A simple kiss wouldn't make him lose control, and she had no doubts he would stop when she wanted him to.

He was sinfully good looking, trying to appear like a mild-mannered sheep; however, she was well aware that she was in the room with a cunning wolf.

Lily took a timid step forward. Shade didn't say anything, appearing bored. It took several seconds for her to take another step. Shade never became impatient as she steadily drew closer until a mere inch separated them.

She looked up into his cerulean blue eyes, feeling as if she was drowning in their clear depths. She cautiously raised herself onto her tiptoes and then her mouth briefly touched his before breaking away and taking a step back.

Like a moth to a flame, she fluttered closer again. This time, her hands rested on his chest as she touched her mouth to his, letting hers linger a mere breath of a second before leaning back to study his face. The impassiveness of his expression had her leaning forward again, pressing harder against his mouth before she lifted herself away, but she didn't move away from his body this time. Her tongue licked her lips faintly, tasting him on her mouth. Her lashes lowered as she looked at the sensuous mouth he was letting her play with. She pressed her lips harder against his mouth until he opened to her slightly.

Lily jumped away.

"That's enough for tonight. You're not a fast learner. It may take weeks for you to catch on to how it's done." He stepped away, going back to his chair.

Lily felt frustrated, wanting to keep kissing him, but his attention had already been redirected to the television.

She turned away, going to the bed and sliding down underneath the covers. She then rolled onto her side, repeatedly thumping her pillow. She thought she heard Shade laughing, but when she jerked her head around, his attention was concentrated on the television screen.

He was probably regretting his decision to teach her how to kiss. His breathing hadn't even changed. He had all but fallen asleep.

One thing was for certain: if he was going to teach her to kiss, the man was going to have to show more interest than if he was getting a dental exam.

* * *

Shade gritted his teeth trying to get his body back under control, forcing himself to keep his eyes on the television screen. Out of the corner of his eye, he saw her hitting her pillow in frustration. His hands clenched by his side. The woman didn't know the meaning of frustration, but he was about to show her if she threw him another one of her pissed-off looks.

He was trying to go slow, not frighten her away, but even he had his limits. That innocent kiss he had gotten from her had nearly been his undoing.

When he was sure she was asleep he got up, leaving the room. He didn't trust himself to climb into bed with her now. He had to calm his body down.

Going upstairs, he grabbed a bottle of whiskey and poured himself a generous amount. His wall of patience was crumbling. It was time to heat up his efforts with Lily. He didn't think it was fair he was the only one suffering. Lily needed to discover exactly what she was missing out on, which was him fucking her until she begged him for mercy.

Shade poured himself another whiskey, This time his hand shook as he picked up his glass.

* * *

Lily woke the next morning to an empty bed. She showered and dressed for work and was going out the bedroom door when Shade entered the room. His eyes were bloodshot. Lily took a step back from the stench of alcohol.

When she had fallen asleep, he had still been watching television. The way he looked now made it apparent he had been up all night drinking.

"You've been drinking!" she said accusingly.

"Don't worry; I'm not drunk." She paled at his words, flinching away as he brushed by her.

"Aren't you going to work?"

"I'm taking the morning off. Rider is managing the factory until this afternoon."

Shade went to the side of the bed, taking his shoes and t-shirt off. He started to take his pants off, obviously expecting her to leave the room so he could finish undressing. Lily didn't leave, unsure why.

"Um… you must have started drinking after I went to sleep." She didn't know why she was pushing the issue.

Shade cocked an eyebrow at her question. "Yes, I went upstairs for another beer and Cash and Rider were having a card game, so I joined in. I wasn't ready for bed as early as you."

Lily fiddled with the rubber band on her wrist. "I didn't expect you to be. I guess I'll see you this afternoon." She started out the doorway but turned at his next words.

"It was just us; none of the women were there."

Relief flooded through her tense body.

"I didn't ask."

"You didn't have to," Shade mocked.

Lily fled out the door without bothering with breakfast, going straight to the factory. A few of the other workers were slowly trickling in. Georgia was already there, talking to Rider who didn't look in much better shape than Shade. She figured he was the one who'd lost the card game.

Lily pulled a work order and got busy filling it. She worked rapidly throughout the morning, her mind kept occupied on filling orders, distracting herself from dwelling on the kisses she had shared with Shade the night before.

She touched her fingertip to her mouth, remembering the feel of his lips against hers before catching herself. She pulled another order, not even stopping for lunch.

When Shade came in that afternoon, Rider looked like he was going to be sick as he headed out.

Shade went inside his office, ignoring Georgia who was trailing after him and shutting the door in her face. Lily's mouth twitched in amusement and Georgia saw it, giving her a vindictive glare.

Lily sucked in a sharp breath. The woman had never made a pretense of liking her, but the hatred she didn't try to conceal in that moment concerned Lily.

Georgia walked toward her, coming to a stop at the table where she was working. "You think you're hot shit, don't you? Well, let me tell you something. I don't give a fuck how pretty you are, when Shade gets tired of fucking you, you'll be just another worker like every other woman he's laid."

"Georgia, I haven't done a thing to deserve—"

The hateful woman cut her off. "You want to know why I can't stand you, Lily?"

Lily stiffened her shoulders. "Go ahead."

"Don't worry, I will. You pretend to be this helpless little girl so everyone takes care of you. You think that because you're pretty everyone should jump through hoops to keep you happy."

"That's not true." Lily tried not to let Georgia see how her cruel words hurt.

"It is true. I have two kids to support; I need this job. Every one of the workers here needs this job except you. You don't need it and you're taking it from someone who does. My brother was supposed to be the next one hired when a position opened. He's been laid off from the mines for a year and has three kids and a mortgage. I bet you don't even have a car payment for that fancy vehicle you drive."

Lily paled. Her words brought back Beth's words from the summer when Lily had first asked for a summer job, that it was unnecessary for her to work since Beth herself provided her with money. It was only after she had been hurt that the job at the factory had been offered.

She felt terrible, understanding Georgia's predicament at wanting her brother to have a job he desperately needed. To then have to see Lily daily was understandably difficult.

"I'm sorry," Lily said, miserable that a family was doing without because of her selfish desire for a job.

"I don't need or want your pity, just stay out of my way. When you get bored with this job, my brother will get hired and I won't have to see your sanctimonious face anymore." Having said her piece, Georgia turned, giving Lily her back.

Lily went back to work, thinking on the altercation. If she mentioned this to Beth or Razer, she had no doubt after Razer's warning that the woman would be fired. Lily didn't want to be responsible for more kids losing their breadwinner.

Coming to a decision, she went to Shade's office. She was going to get Georgia's brother the job he needed. All she had to do was quit.

CHAPTER TWENTY-ONE

"Can I talk to you for a minute?" Lily stuck her head in the door after knocking briefly.

"Come in." Shade was sitting at his desk going through papers. Lily came inside, closing the door as Shade laid the papers down and leaned back in his chair.

"I want to quit."

"Why?"

Lily didn't want to lie, however she didn't want to tell the truth and get Georgia in trouble either.

"Well?" Shade asked after several minutes of continued silence.

"Give me a minute, I'm thinking."

"Shouldn't you have done that before you came in here?" Shade asked, studying her closely.

"You're right. I'll be back later." Lily turned to go.

Shade sighed in frustration. "What's up, Lily?"

"I don't think it's fair that I take a job from someone who needs it," she blurted out.

"I see. And who needs a job?"

Lily waved her hand evasively. "Most of the town are unemployed."

"That's true. Do you have someone in particular in

mind for your job, though?"

When Lily remained silent, Shade gave a long suffering sigh, getting to his feet and going to the cabinet, opening a drawer. Pulling out a green folder, he opened it as he moved to sit on the corner of his desk, reading it silently. It didn't take long before he closed it and then laid it on his desk.

"Come here."

Lily didn't want to move closer, but her feet carried her near to him anyway.

"What did Georgia say to you?" he asked, reaching out to twine a lock of her dark hair around a long finger.

Lily sighed; she wouldn't evade a direct question, and Shade knew that. "That her brother needed a job because he has three kids and a mortgage."

"Is that all? That's a big guilt trip."

"Not if it's true. I have some money saved up until I graduate. I don't need spending money. I can wait on the new clothes I was going to buy. I don't have any bills and he needs the job."

"You're right; he is the next to be hired. I'll give him a call and tell him to come in."

"Thank you." Lily was going to miss her job. She had been pleasantly surprised by how much she'd liked it.

"Send Georgia to my office," Shade said, releasing her hair.

Lily stopped. "Why?"

"Because she stepped over the line. Razer warned her about that yesterday."

"But…" Georgia had kids also. She didn't want them to have an unemployed mother.

The hard look on Shade's face had her mouth snapping shut.

"The reason we didn't hire her brother was because we didn't want two family members working together, especially not those two, not because you were hired. They both have attitudes, and working together wouldn't be conducive to a cohesive work environment, but since I plan on firing Georgia, that will no longer be an issue."

"I didn't take anyone's job?" Lily asked in relief.

"No. You're a fill-in for days when Bliss wants to sleep late, or Raci wants to go shopping, or Jewell won't get her ass out of bed, or any one of the many reasons they give me. It gives them time off without worrying about getting our orders out."

"Oh." Lily was relieved she hadn't kept someone from a salary they needed.

"Send Georgia in," Shade repeated.

"I don't want you to fire her."

"Why? If the tables were turned, she wouldn't spit on you if you were on fire."

"That doesn't matter."

"What does then?" he asked gently.

"I don't want her to hate me," Lily admitted.

Shade's hands reached out, circling her waist before drawing her near until she stood between his thighs. "Sweetheart, it's already too late for that."

"I know," Lily said miserably.

"Lily, you're too kind for your own good. You take everything to heart that anyone says, and you feel compassion for every living thing. You'll drive yourself crazy if you don't stop."

"I can't."

"Why?"

Lily shrugged, her hands going to his arms. "I guess I like to be needed."

"I need you."

Lily blushed, shaking her head. "You don't need me; you want me. There's a difference."

"No, there isn't."

"Yes, there is." Lily pulled away. "Razer found out the difference when he broke up with Beth. One lasts, the other is temporary. You'll change your mind about me. I see how comfortable the women are with you. You're used to having relationships and remaining friends. I couldn't be with someone then watch them be with someone else. I certainly couldn't remain friends and pretend it doesn't hurt. Beth and Razer were both willing to change. Neither of us can change who we are, Shade," Lily said sadly, going to the door. "Please don't fire Georgia. I should have left things alone."

Lily left his office, going back to work without telling Georgia that Shade wanted to see her.

At the end of the day, when the other workers left, Lily didn't linger, leaving before Shade was ready.

She changed into her workout clothes, deciding to stretch then do weight training. Shade came in, going to the bedroom, and she ignored him. Not long after he had come through, the upstairs door opened and Bliss came downstairs holding a laundry basket with Rider carrying another behind her.

Shade returned and began working out as the other two sorted clothes then sat on the couch as the clothes washed. Lily felt self-conscious as the two talked. Every so often, she could sense their eyes on her when she changed positions. She was glad she had worn the most conservative of her workout clothes.

"That's enough for the day," Shade said, halting her when she would have continued.

Without acknowledging him, Lily went into the bedroom to shower and change for dinner. By the time she was done, she had thought Shade would have come in to get changed, but he hadn't appeared.

Lily left the bedroom, deciding to go upstairs to see if they needed any help with dinner. She walked back into the gym and Shade was still talking to Bliss and Rider as they put clothes in the dryer. Lily felt their conversation cut off as she entered the room. She didn't know how Shade could miss that she didn't fit in with their group when they wouldn't even continue a discussion with her in the room.

As she got to the kitchen, dinner was all ready, but Lily wasn't hungry. Going to the fridge, she grabbed a bottled water and then went outside the kitchen door, wanting a breath of fresh air.

After being in the factory all day then working out, she wanted to feel the sun on her the few minutes she had until it became dark.

She walked to the patio but didn't want to sit down, so she walked forward onto the grass, her feet unconsciously taking her closer to the house of Beth and Razer.

She had never been inside it before; Beth had never invited her. She drew closer and saw it was beautifully surrounded by the forest while Shade's house behind and higher had a view of the whole compound.

She and Beth had talked about her house when they had drawn the plans. She remembered Beth saying she had wanted a small front porch, more like a cottage. Lily had told her a wraparound porch would give her a better view of the mountain. She had tried to talk her into a bay window like Shade's had, yet Beth had wanted two smaller ones, saying it would be much warmer in the winter. Beth wanted her house to be an extension of Razer's and her love for each other, and she had succeeded.

Lily walked up the short flight of steps to Shade's house. She sat down on the top step and looked out at the view. It was breathtaking. She remained there until the sun went down.

Darkness had always been her enemy, but she didn't feel afraid as she sat there in the dwindling daylight. She felt a tear slide down her cheek, not knowing why. Thinking on it, she realized she had never fit in anywhere; not with Beth's family, not college, and now not there at the clubhouse. It was like always being a guest in someone else's home and never having one of her own.

The beauty of the mountains had always comforted her and moments like this were very profound to Lily; she was grateful God had created such beauty. It soothed something torn and broken inside of her that she didn't know how to fix.

Right then, gazing out at the mountains—for that fraction of a moment—she felt like she belonged.

Reluctantly, Lily got to her feet and returned to the clubhouse. She heard music as she went down the basement steps, and when she got to the bottom step, she saw Raci and Cash dancing by the pole, Rider and Bliss kissing on the couch, and Shade sitting next to them as he watched Raci and Cash with a beer in one hand.

Raci was dancing seductively, grinding her butt back onto Cash's pelvis. His arms were on the pole, trapping her between his arms.

Lily took a shuddering breath and tried to rush through the basement to Shade's bedroom, but as she passed he reached out, snagging her wrist and pulling her down on the couch next to him. She started to protest, but his low words forestalled her.

"You can sit out here with me or you can run and hide in the bedroom, wondering what I'm doing out here with them."

"I don't care what you're doing," Lily snapped.

Shade straightened away from her. "Then run away." He lifted his beer to his mouth, leaning back against the couch.

Rider was sitting with Bliss on his lap, his hand under her t-shirt, the tanned expanse of her stomach showing.

Lily almost got up and ran into the bedroom, not wanting to witness anymore, but no one was really paying any attention to her.

Cash's hand went to the waistband of Raci's short skirt, his fingers sliding underneath.

Lily tensed, turning her head away to see Rider's mouth sucking on the flesh of Bliss's neck while his hand had slid further up her top.

Lily tensed, ready to fly off the couch.

"Look at their faces, Lily." Shade's words had her eyes

flying up to his.

He was leaning closer to her, his chest just brushing against hers. Her breasts tightened and her breathing accelerated. This went against everything she believed in, to sit there as the two couples made out in front of her, but the look Shade was giving her held her in place.

Lily turned her head, her eyes going to Raci as Cash's hand had now completely disappeared under her shirt.

"Does she look frightened?" Shade asked.

Lily's eyes lifted to Raci's face. The woman wasn't scared; her face showed her excitement as her hips wiggled back against Cash and her head fell back against his shoulder.

Her eyes moved away, going back to Bliss whose breasts were now uncovered, Rider was twisting her nipple. She saw her tattoo with four daisies and a date in the middle. Lily remembered Shade telling her that the women got tattoos after they got a vote from the last member. She looked closer at the daisies, realizing that it was formed into a chain. Lily wasn't so innocent that she didn't realize the significance. She paled as her mind went through The Last Rider members, which of them were the ones that had sex with Bliss the day she had earned her tattoo.

Lily tried to get up, but Shade's body had her sinking further back into the couch cushions.

"You understand that tattoo, don't you?"

"You disgust me," Lily spat.

"You're not even going to ask me if one of those daisies is me?" Shade mocked.

"I don't have to." Lily tried to turn away, but was pinned in place, her hand covering the flesh over her heart.

Shade moved her hand away, his replacing it. "I was, and Winter wasn't any happier to find out Viper was, too. Evie and Cash were the other two." His hand rubbed against the flesh his hand covered as if he knew the stabbing pain his words elicited. "Bliss likes to show off so it was a matter of time before you saw it, now that you're living here."

"For now." Lily was more determined than ever to find a way to save Beth's house and find an escape for herself. No wonder her juvenile kisses hadn't excited him.

Raci's moans drew her attention. Cash picked the woman up, throwing her over his shoulder before carrying her up the steps.

"I'm not stopping you; you can leave anytime, Lily. I'm sure Beth won't be heartbroken for long. On the other hand, you could start enjoying living here. Look at Bliss. I don't think there's any place else she wants to be."

Rider's hand was no longer under her shirt; it was now under her skirt, which had ridden up to show the woman wore no underwear. He was rubbing her between her splayed thighs. Her hand had gone into his jeans as she unzipped them. Lily thought she might black out from watching them until Shade placed his mouth against her throat.

"See how wet she is. She isn't afraid to let him touch her. She's enjoying every minute of it." One of Rider's fingers slipped inside of Bliss and the woman moaned. "She loves to fuck."

Shade stared at Lily as he ordered, "Give her another finger, Rider."

Lily watched helplessly as Rider followed Shade's directions. Bliss moaned louder when Rider's two fingers glided in and out of the woman's slippery sheathe. "See. She's enjoying his fingers in her pussy," he said as his mouth whispered against the shell of her ear before he pulled away and directed to Rider, "Rub her clit harder, Rider. She enjoys a little pain."

Lily's own thighs pressed together.

"Shade…" Bliss moaned

"Let her come, Rider."

Lily tried to tear her eyes away as Rider's fingers stroked even faster and Bliss raised her hips before plunging herself down on his hand. Her small scream had Lily jumping up from the couch, unable to watch any longer.

"Run, Lily. It's not going to change the fact that you're mine. And the next time a woman moans my name, it will be you."

Lily took his advice, running from the room and the look of dark desire in his eyes, aware she was escaping because he let her.

* * *

The next morning, she dressed in the bathroom then went back into the bedroom where Shade was still getting dressed. The silence between them was uncomfortable. She had gone to bed early the night before and had left Shade in the other room, her mind tortured with thoughts of him touching Bliss after she had run from the room.

"Do you mind if I take the day off? I have a few things I need to take care of today." Her cold voice drew his warning gaze. She couldn't bear to be near him in the factory today; she needed a respite to get her body and thoughts back under control.

"No, go ahead."

"Thanks." This time she was smart enough not to let her own feelings show.

Lily left him getting dressed, going upstairs where she poured herself a cup of coffee. Most of the members were rushing around to get to work on time.

Winter rushed in, pouring some coffee into a huge mug she carried to work.

"What are you doing today? You usually beat me out the door," she asked, pausing in her rush.

"I took the day off. I have a few things I need to get caught up on."

"That will be good for you. You haven't taken some time for yourself in a while."

Lily nodded.

She felt Winter's gaze as she sat down next to her at the

table. "I remember when you went to high school."

Lily looked back at Winter and smiled. "I do, too. You were new and all the kids were giving you a hard time because you looked as young as they did."

Winter shuddered. "Don't remind me. I'm still amazed I made it through that first month. But you made it more bearable for me. I'm here if you need me, Lily."

"Okay."

"When I first came here, I wanted to be here even less than you do," Winter told her.

"That bad?"

Winter nodded her head. "I tried to escape several times."

"Really?" Lily was shocked. She hadn't known. She remembered back to when Winter had first moved into the clubhouse after her attack.

"Really. I was miserable, and I was jealous as hell of the women and Viper's relationship with them. It was an adjustment, but I have really come to care about all the members. We're a family and I love Viper. We all just fit together."

"I can tell." Lily tried to keep the envy out of her voice.

"That doesn't mean there isn't room for you," Winter said softly, reaching out to touch her hand.

Lily looked down, swallowing hard. "The problem is, there's room for too many women in this house."

Winter laughed. "That's very true, but there's only one Lily." Winter got to her feet and Lily looked up at her. "Give it a chance. You may find a part of yourself that you didn't know existed. I did."

That was what Lily was afraid of.

After Winter left, she cleaned the kitchen before going downstairs. Bliss and Rider had washed and dried the clothes, but they had left them sitting around. She quickly folded them before washing and drying her and Shade's clothes. She then cleaned the whole downstairs as she did the laundry.

She loved cleaning, unlike most people, and had changed into a pair of loose sweats as she worked. She had the flat screen on as she was folding the last of the clothes. She had gone upstairs earlier, started a huge pot of chili and had made cornbread, which was sitting on the counter cooling.

She was tired, but she felt better than she had in a long while. She had enjoyed having the house to herself for most of the day. She was used to being on her own. Living with so many people was an adjustment and having the house to herself had been relaxing.

The television had been on a cable news show, and as she was only watching it while she folded the clothes, she hadn't bothered to change the channel. Now she was done, Lily watched as the story of a felony trial beginning unfolded on the screen.

What had made the story take the national spotlight was that the man involved was a crime lord who had been trafficking women. The camera panned the surrounding crowd.

Lily's head burst with pain and her breath started catching with an oncoming panic attack.

Lily managed to get to her feet, instinct driving her as whimpers tore through her throat. Her mind felt consumed by pain. Flinging open the basement door, Lily ran outside barefoot and down the path toward the factory.

It was the end of the day and the parking lot was emptying of cars as Lily flew down the path, half-blinded by the pain.

She managed to spot Shade and Rider standing by the door, both of them staring at her in shocked surprise, and Lily went right to Shade as he started to move to her. He held out his arms and Lily threw herself into them, clutching him tightly and shaking. She tried to burrow into him as tightly as she could, desperate for the pain to go away.

"What's wrong?" He held her to him tightly, giving her the security she needed.

"I don't know." Lily cried, needing to be closer to his warmth.

"Couldn't you get hold of Beth?" he asked.

"What? I didn't try," she said, trembling harder.

"You didn't try to call Beth? You came to me first?" Shade's hand smoothed her tumbled hair away from her face.

Lily nodded her head against his shoulder, whimpering. "My head hurts," she moaned.

Shade lifted her up into his arms, handing Rider a clipboard. He then carried her back to the house, closing the door she had left open in her terror. In the bedroom, he sat down with her on the bed. Lily curled into the safety of his arms, laying her head on his shoulder.

"I think I'm losing my mind," Lily confessed.

"No, you're not." Shade's hand rubbed the back of her neck, easing the tension from her shoulders. "Lily, your attacks are coming less, but they're becoming stronger. I think your mind is trying to tell you that you're strong enough to remember."

Lily jerked upright, her hands going to the sides of her head.

Shade's hands went to her wrists. "Look at me, Lily." Her violet eyes lifted to his. "Look at me," Shade repeated his words.

She stared at him mutely, trying to tear her eyes away from his but unable to do so. Giving in, she sank into his blue gaze, really seeing him for the first time: a man who wasn't afraid of anything—who was strong, skilled and patient.

"What's in here can't hurt you anymore." Shade's finger tapped the side of her head. "The world around you," his hand circled the air around her body, "I've got that." His hands went back to her hands, holding them in his. "No one will ever hurt you again."

Lily heard the truth in his voice and saw it in his eyes.

She had once played a game in school where the teachers had lined the students up into two lines, one facing forward while the other line stood backward. The teacher had told them to fall backwards and trust the person behind them to catch them. She had excused herself to go to the office, getting out of the exercise because she had known that she didn't trust anyone that blindly, which was what Shade was asking of her now.

To fall, knowing that he would catch her. Even with Beth, she had never accomplished that.

CHAPTER TWENTY-TWO

Lily was putting the dishes in the dishwasher when Beth and Winter came in the kitchen after dinner. The whole house was a hub of activity as they prepared for the Halloween party.

The week had gone by fast. The members were filled with anticipation. Even Beth had the night off from caring for Mrs. Langley. Lily had dreaded tonight, though.

"I didn't think Holly would ever get there." Beth carried two bags in that she laid down.

Lily dried her hands, coming to her sister's side. "What did you decide to be?"

"A hippie." She lifted her outfit with the bright fuchsia shirt and yellow shorts out of the garment bag. Lily admired the colorful outfit, thinking it suited Beth's sunny disposition.

Winter had already told her that she was going to be Little Red Riding Hood. As a matter of fact, all of the women had shared which costume each was planning on wearing. Lily could tell they were planning on having fun that night.

"I picked this up for you." Beth raised the other

garment bag and began unzipping it.

"I'm not going to the party," Lily protested.

"We all talked about it and decided you're not going to miss out on all the fun. The downstairs will have a smaller party with just a few of us and we all promised to behave. Then, later, we can go upstairs. Come on, Lily."

Beth opened the garment bag, showing a gypsy outfit in bright purples and blues. It was very pretty. The top had long sleeves and the skirt would flow to her ankles.

Beth had managed to allay all her protests, so she saw no reason not to participate. "As long as you promise that, when you get bored, you'll go back upstairs."

"No problem." Winter and Beth both laughed.

"Cool." The women banded together, taking several snacks downstairs to set around the couch area.

"After I get showered and changed, I'll bring the drinks down. You can tell Shade to put some music on the sound system while we get ready," Beth told her.

"Okay."

Winter and Beth went upstairs to get changed. The music had already been turned on upstairs, and from the amount of voices filtering down, the party had already begun. Shade and Rider were both still at the factory loading a truck.

Lily showered and dressed with the beginning of excitement curling in her stomach at the party and how they were willing to share some of their fun so she could participate.

She was brushing her hair out in the bedroom when Shade walked in.

She twirled her skirt around her legs, showing off her outfit. Her black hair was long and loose, and Beth had included several chunky necklaces for her to put on.

"You look great. What are you supposed to be?"

"A gypsy."

"How is it any different than what you usually wear? You should have at least been adventuresome enough to raise the hemline above your ankles," he said, taking a change of clothes out of a drawer.

Lily looked down at herself.

Shade walked to her, cupping her cheek. "You look gorgeous. Who got it for you?"

"Beth," Lily said, twirling away.

Shade looked at her dress closely. "Remind me to thank her."

"Why?"

Shade just shook his head, going into the bathroom. "Never mind. I won't be long."

Lily shrugged his words off, going into the other room. Winter, Beth and Evie were already there, sitting around and munching on snacks while Viper and Razer were talking and drinking beers. Lily didn't let the beer bother her anymore. She had learned they could handle it, and the sight of the bottles no longer made her frightened.

Beth choked on a pretzel when she saw her before Winter and her both shared a glance.

"What's wrong?" Lily asked.

"Nothing. You look great," Beth assured her, jerking her wrist until she sat down next to her on the couch.

Viper went to the sound system, turning on the music. Someone had taken up the mats, leaving the area clear for dancing. Viper took Winter's hand, moving her toward the dance floor.

"Knox and Diamond wanted to come tonight, but he has to be on duty," Beth explained before Razer sat down next to her, pulling her on his lap.

Shade came in, taking a seat on the opposite side of the couch.

"How was Georgia this week?" Beth asked, putting her arm around Razer's shoulder.

"Fine." Lily didn't mention what had happened Monday. Shade had talked to the woman that afternoon, and since then, she had given Lily a wide berth. Lily still felt guilty over Georgia's brother, however at least she knew she wasn't responsible for his not having a job at the factory.

"Lily, would you mind getting me a beer?" Shade requested.

Lily happily got up from the couch to go to the table the beer had been set up at and got him a beer. He never asked her to do anything for him, so she didn't mind doing so now.

When she handed it to him, and would have gone back to her side of the couch, Shade reached up and pulled her down on his lap. Lily tried to wiggle off, embarrassed. She had never sat on his lap before—unless she had been upset—and Beth was just a few inches away, staring at her in amusement.

"Sit still," Shade ordered. Lily quit wiggling, sitting stiffly on his lap. Shade ignored her stiff posture, resuming his conversation with Razer about the production of one of the tools that was selling well.

"The only way to increase production is to go with another manufacturer," Razer said.

"How is the store coming along?" Beth asked, growing tired of the guys' shop talk.

"Good. Now that Rachel and I are working on it an extra day, we're hoping to open it in a couple of weeks. We talked to Pastor Dean; he's going to start searching for someone to manage it for the church."

"It's going to be hard to find someone who will give it the commitment it needs without pay," Beth remarked.

"I don't know why. Think of how much good it's going to do. The items are going to be free. I suggested he do it based on income to those in need to keep out those that would take advantage of the generosity of the church."

"I agree, so it needs to be someone familiar with the community. That way, they won't be too embarrassed to ask for what they need. A lot of the people who will need the store won't even use it because their pride will stand in the way."

Lily nodded in agreement. "They'll have to be completely trustworthy, also. You wouldn't believe some of the items donated. Rachel found a diamond ring and I found cash in several pockets. We always check if we know where the items come from to make sure that it wasn't a mistake. Mrs. Graver's ring had fallen off when she had bagged the clothes."

"I didn't think of that."

"We were glad we found it for her." Lily unconsciously relaxed back against Shade as they talked, enjoying the warmth of him at her back.

It wasn't long before Train and Jewell came downstairs and started dancing alongside Viper and Winter. Train wasn't wearing a shirt, but he had on a bandana over his hair and a patch over one eye. Jewell was wearing a pirate wench outfit, which left most of her breasts bare, and the short skirt showed the long length of her shapely legs.

As the song changed, Razer got to his feet. "Let's dance." With that, Beth and Razer joined the couples dancing.

Halfway through the song, Evie came downstairs dressed as a French maid with Cash dressed as himself.

Lily laughed, looking into Shade's eyes. "Train is the only one who dressed up?"

Shade shook his head. "Rider dressed as Tarzan, but I threatened to kick his ass if he came down here."

Lily's giggles were cut off as Shade got up, setting Lily on her feet before taking her to the dance floor. She tried to get away, but he snagged her around the waist, pulling her close.

"Dance with me, Lily."

"I don't know how," she protested.

"That's okay. They don't either." Shade pointed his hand at Evie and Cash.

Lily watched the others. They were all just having a good time. They had come down here to make her feel more comfortable while, even over the music, she could hear the sounds of the others partying upstairs.

She began moving, trying not to feel self-conscious about her awkwardness. By the third dance, she was relaxed and moving much more comfortably. The other members came and went, moving back and forth between the two floors, everyone seemingly enjoying themselves.

Shade had pulled her closer and someone had turned off a couple of the lamps, dimming the room without making it too dark. Beth, Razer, Winter and Viper had gone upstairs while Cash, Evie, Train and Jewell were still dancing.

"Are you having a good time?"

Lily smiled up at Shade. "Yes, I am."

"Don't seem so surprised," Shade said, his thigh sliding between her legs as his hand dropped to circle her waist.

"I just thought it would be wilder."

"It is, upstairs."

She blushed, turning her eyes away. "If you want to go upstairs, I won't mind."

"Shut up. I'm exactly where I want to be."

Lily smiled, relieved that he didn't feel like he was missing out.

When Shade lowered his head, his lips briefly touching hers, Lily didn't move away from the brief encounter. The seductive movements of his body and the music heightened her awareness of him.

As Shade's mouth lowered again, lingering against hers, Lily felt the pressure of his lips, enjoying the feel of them. When his tongue then slid along the seam of her lips, she gasped. Shade took advantage, sliding his tongue inside of her mouth.

Lily's hands grabbed his t-shirt, but she didn't push him away. She thought the tangy flavor of the beer he had drunk would repulse her, but it didn't. The silky warmth of his tongue against hers had her indecisive about what to do next. Before she could decide, Shade lifted his head, continuing to dance as if nothing had happened.

She didn't know what to think or feel; she then decided she didn't have to do either. She had to learn to not over-think everything. She should take Rachel's advice and roll with whatever happened between her and Shade. It had just been a kiss, something girls her age did every day without even thinking anything about it.

It was just a kiss, she kept telling herself. *Then why does it feel like so much more?* she asked herself. Why did it feel like a tiny seed of desire had been planted and was waiting to grow into a special something? It was miraculous that she had believed herself incapable of ever wanting or needing something like that.

The music ended and Shade stepped back. "Want to get something to drink?"

"Yes." It was becoming hot downstairs all of a sudden.

As Lily moved off the dance floor, Evie plopped down on the couch out of breath next to Jewell.

"I love your outfit, Lily. It looks all demur; then when you move, it shows that rockin' body of yours. I might need to borrow it for the next party," Jewell complimented.

Lily's mouth dropped open. Now she understood that look on her sister's face and Shade getting her to get up and get him a drink. Lily glared at Shade.

"The drinks are all gone. I'll go get some more," Shade said, the coward making his escape.

As Train and Cash both went upstairs, saying they were going to grab some pizza, Jewell got up from the couch, going to the floor, and began dancing. When she twirled on the pole, Lily realized the women did use it to pole dance.

Evie glanced at her when Jewell really got going, sliding up and down the pole.

"I bet the men miss that with me living down here now," Lily remarked ruefully.

"Forget the men. The women miss it. It's great exercise for us. It'll take me months to get rid of the inch I've

232

gained on my thighs.

"I'm used to exercising on one, too. I might use it when no one is around. I know a great exercise that will take that inch off in no time."

"Really? What is it?" Evie's interest was sparked and she urged Lily to show her the exercise.

Since all of the men were out of the room, Lily got up, going to the stripper pole. Jewell moved back a step, watching curiously.

Lily started spinning, wrapping her leg around it. Not lifting it high, just winding her leg around it. Carefully tucking in her loose skirt, she leaned backwards, arching her back as she let her thigh hold her weight. Rising up unconsciously, she timed her movements with the beat of the music then leaned back again.

"It's great not only for the thighs but your stomach muscles, as well. Just don't let your arms do the work for you; let your tummy and thigh muscles do it," Lily informed Evie. When she didn't make a remark, Lily rose up, noticing her eyes were on the foot of the steps.

She turned to see what Evie was staring at. Shade stood there with his hands full of beer and sodas while Cash had a plate of pizza that was about to slide off with his mouth hanging open, and Train was right behind them, crushing a bag of chips in his hands.

"I was just showing Evie an exercise I learned in my pole class," Lily said, jerking her leg down from the pole and straightening her skirt.

"Could you show me that move again? I have a few pounds I need to lose," Train asked seriously.

Lily didn't miss the threatening glare Shade gave him as he set the drinks down on the side table.

She went to get one, picking an orange soda. Before she could take a seat, Shade pulled her back down on his lap. This time she didn't try to wiggle away, afraid she would spill her drink.

As she got settled, Stori came down the stairs dressed

in a bunny outfit that was even more suggestive than Jewell's. She began dancing with a member from Ohio— who Lily wasn't really familiar with—and the biker put his hand on her butt, grinding her closer to his hips.

Lily looked away, seeing Jewell and Train resuming their dancing. Evie and Cash also started dancing.

"You never told me you knew how to pole dance."

Lily turned bright red. "My gym at college taught an exercise class using the pole."

"Lord have mercy," Shade muttered.

Lily couldn't help herself, laughing at his expression as she playfully hit his chest. Shade's hand went to the back of her neck, tugging her head down to his and catching her mouth. She relaxed against him, letting him have it. When his tongue slid between her lips, her head fell to his shoulder; Shade moved slightly until he leaned her backward against the arm of the couch and he was above her.

Her arms slid around his neck as she thought about the fact she was actually kissing him with the other couples in the room. They were in a dark corner and no one was paying attention; nothing more was happening than what she had seen at the few parties she had attended. This time, however, she was part of the couple necking in the corner.

Before she had time to think any further about it, Shade's hand flattened against her flat stomach then slid up to her shoulder, raising her back up to a sitting position. "Let's dance."

"Okay." She got to her feet and they went to the dance floor, spending the remainder of the evening dancing.

The rest of the members spent the night continuing to go between the two floors. Beth and Winter both showed up a couple of more times before eventually telling her goodnight.

"Night," Lily told her sister.

Beth and Razer had turned to go, but Beth turned back,

giving her a tight hug. "I don't think I've ever seen you look so happy." Beth's voice sounded tight.

"I've had fun," Lily said. "I'm going to use the picture of Rider to blackmail him with later when he's bugging me at work." Beth had taken a picture of Rider dressed as Tarzan as he did the dishes upstairs and had texted the picture to Lily.

"You do that. Just don't tell him who sent you the picture."

"I won't."

Shade was talking to Train and Evie as Lily yawned, finally growing tired.

"I'm going to bed. I have to be up early to go to the church store."

Everyone told her goodnight, and then Lily went into the bedroom. Her mind played back over the evening as she changed into her pajamas and went to the bed, stretching out over it.

She was almost asleep when Shade quietly came to bed not long afterwards. When he reached out underneath the covers, pulling her to his warmth, she didn't pull away. She just let her body sink against his, falling asleep with a tiny smile on her lips.

It was funny how one simple Halloween party had given her hope for the future.

CHAPTER TWENTY-THREE

"Wake up, Lily!" Shade was shaking her awake from a deep sleep.

She jerked upright in the bed. "What's going on?"

"Get up. The basement's on fire." He jerked her from the bed.

She slid her feet into her shoes while Shade ran to the bathroom, coming back with a fire extinguisher. She heard the sounds of screams from upstairs and running feet as the fire alarm went off.

"How are we going to get out of here?" The windows in his room were nonexistent. They were trapped inside.

"The brothers will get us out," Shade said grimly.

Going to his dresser, he pulled out a long piece of material and then ran to the bathroom again. He came back with the wet cloths, tying one across her face then his own. Just as he finished, they heard the sounds of a fire hose and an extinguisher from outside their bedroom door.

There was a loud bang on the door and Shade opened it. Viper stood on the other side with just jeans and boots on. "Let's go," he yelled.

Shade took Lily's hand, pushing her behind Viper as he

followed. It was pitch dark except for the dying embers of the blackened walls. Viper was carrying a flashlight and the men putting out the fire with water hoses were spraying the smoking couch. The steps to the upstairs were destroyed, the blackened door closed.

Viper led them out the side door as Lily choked on the smoke, starting to cough. Shade picked her up into his arms, carrying her into the living room before removing the cloth he had tied around her face.

The screams, the smoky smell and the dark basement she had walked through combined to send Lily into a terror-filled haze she didn't know if she could fight.

She quit coughing, drinking the water that someone thrust into her hands. The smell of the smoke was attacking her senses. This wasn't the first time she had smelled that odor or had seen how flames could destroy.

The door so tightly locked in her mind snapped open.

The glass in her hand dropped to the floor as her skull filled with a blaze of pain there was no way to escape any longer.

Shade dropped down to his knees in front of Lily. He knew it was bad. He had witnessed the gradually spiraling ferocity of her panic attacks, and was certain this was the worst he had seen. Seeing Beth's terror for her sister, his assumption that it was indeed the worst was confirmed.

"Razer, call Rachel and tell her to get here as fast as she can. Beth, call her doctor." Shade could do nothing except hold on to the woman he loved more than life itself as her tortured screams scored his soul with the agony that he couldn't help her.

His friends stood back, giving him space as she fell to the floor. All he could do was hold her, calling her name repeatedly as soothingly as possible.

Beth returned, falling to her knees beside him, calling for Lily as she held her hand. It seemed like forever, each minute ticking by endlessly, until Rachel ran through the door that Cash was holding open.

"Move out of her way," Cash ordered everyone.

Shade didn't make a move to release Lily whose voice had broken from her screams of terror.

Rachel motioned Shade to move over, and he complied shakily. She sat down on the floor by Lily's head, pulling her head onto her lap. Her graceful hands went to Lily's temples, pressing her fingers along them, rubbing in soothing circles.

Everyone went silent then as Rachel's hushed voice spoke to Lily. "Lily, what do you need me to do?"

* * *

Lily heard the voices calling to her, but she didn't know how to reach them; she couldn't find them in the darkness. The flames were preventing her from reaching them. How could it be so dark yet be filled with flames? She was adrift. She was one of those people you hear about who died when they're lost because they wandered away. Then, when their lifeless body was found, help had been invariably just a few feet away.

She needed to stay still so they would come and get her. Shade would come.

Where is he? Shade? Shade! Where are you, Shade? Was I bad? Is that why you're not here? Shade, please help me. I'm so scared.

Beth, please, I won't be mad at you anymore. I'll be good, I promise. Please, Beth. I want to go home. Please. Beth! Shade! Help me!

Razer? Razer! You promised me no one would hurt me. You broke your promise. Razer, please help!

Shade! Shade!

Pastor Dean!

Please help me?

Vida?

Sawyer?

Where are you? Why did you leave me? Vida! Sawyer! Please help me.

Shade… Shade…

"Lily." At first, Lily thought she was imagining the calm

voice from the other side of the flames. She quit screaming, listening again.

There it was. Someone was there.

"I'm here! I'm here! Help me!"

"What do you need me to do?" The voice was coming closer. Someone was there!

"Help me! I'm lost! I can't find my way back!"

"Yes, you can."

"The flames won't let me pass, and I'm afraid to go the other way in the dark. I'm afraid I'll get lost."

"I won't let you get lost, Lily."

"But you're on the other side of the flames," Lily cried out then watched as Rachel walked through the flames without them touching her.

"How did you do that without getting burned?"

"They're not my memories, Lily. They can't hurt me, only you."

"I want to get out of here." She whimpered, "Can you help me?"

"Yes, but you have to lead the way, Lily. I don't know where we are."

"Then we're both lost. I want to go home." Lily started crying again.

"Listen to me. There is only one path home and that's through the flames. You have to be brave enough to take those steps, Lily."

"I can't go through there!" Lily screamed.

"Then you're going to stay lost. You can do this, Lily."

"No, I can't!"

"Lily, your memories have broken free. There is no locking them away anymore. The only way to avoid it is to stay lost. You have to go through the flames."

"They'll hurt me again!"

"No one is ever going to hurt you again. Didn't The Last Riders save you tonight? They're not going to let anyone hurt you again. You know that deep in your heart." Rachel turned her to face the flames.

"I can't," Lily sobbed.

"Not alone, but together we can. I'm beside you. I won't let you go. Shade is here and so are Beth and Razer." As Rachael spoke the words, Lily felt Shade standing behind her, and Beth and Razer each taking a hand, holding tight. "We're all here for you, Lily. Lead us home."

Lily cried, taking a hesitant step forward, one after the other, each of them holding her, not letting go.

Lily's tortured scream filled the dark-filled silence as she stepped into the flames, the pain consuming her.

"The pain will lessen as you go through the flames. You'll leave the pain behind, Lily, because they can't hurt you anymore. Keep walking."

Rachel was right. The flames were reuniting her with long-lost memories. The pain was there, but it wasn't devouring; stinging but not burning.

Lily walked through the hell she had barely survived once, enduring it now for a second time to find her only way home. She emerged on the other side, unscathed and free at last of the monsters she had been hiding from for so very long.

"You can open your eyes now, Lily. You're home."

CHAPTER TWENTY-FOUR

Lily opened her eyes. She was lying on a soft bed in another strange room. She turned her head on the plush pillow at a slight sound to discover Beth sitting on a chair by the window. Shade's room didn't have a window, so they must be in one of the bedrooms upstairs.

"You're awake."

"How long was I out for this time?" Her voice was hoarse and her throat felt raw.

"Just a few hours, actually," Beth said, getting up from the chair and coming to sit next to her on the mattress, taking her hand in hers.

"There was a fire last night." Lily looked down at herself and saw she was wearing a white nightgown.

"Yes. Thank God for Viper's security system. If not…" Beth broke down crying, laying her head down on Lily's chest. Her hand reached out to smooth down her sister's silky hair as she wept.

"I remember, Beth," Lily said softly. Beth raised her head, looking into her eyes. "I remember," Lily whispered, turning her face away from her sister's searching gaze.

"Did you know?" Lily asked.

"During your worst panic attacks, you would let a few things slip past your guard. Over the years, I pieced together what happened."

Lily turned back to her sister. "Did you…" Lily licked her dry lips. "Did you tell Razer?"

"No, Lily. I swear I didn't tell anyone. No one." Lily saw the truth in her eyes. "But Razer and Shade have both been around you a couple of times during your panic attacks and I think they've guessed some, if not all, of it."

Lily squeezed her eyes tightly closed to prevent herself from crying. She refused to cry anymore. Tears were useless and weak like she had been.

She sat up in bed, leaning back against the headboard.

"I laid some clothes out for you. Yours all smell like smoke."

"How bad is the basement?"

"The front part is gutted, but because we live so far out of town, Viper had several water hoses and the factory had fire extinguishers. If they hadn't been so prepared, you and Shade would have been trapped."

"That's twice I've almost died in a fire," Lily said softly.

"Do you want to talk about it? Your doctor came out and checked on you last night and I called your therapist. I can take you to her today if you want," Beth offered.

"No."

"Okay." Beth stared back at her.

"Beth, I want you to know I couldn't have asked for a better sister. I love you."

"I love you, too." The sisters hugged, thankful they were able to do so. The night before could have easily separated them forever.

"Now, I'm going to get dressed. You go take care of what you need to. I'll be fine."

"I just need to do a few patients then I'll be back. If you need anything, there's a cell phone on the nightstand."

Lily nodded her head as Beth got up from the bed,

going for the door.

"I was supposed to help Rachel in the store this morning, could you...?"

"I'll give her a call," Beth promised.

"Thanks."

Lily got up from the bed, pulling on a pair of jeans and a bright pink sweatshirt that fit well, if not for being too short. A pair of sneakers was there, also. They were tight but not painful.

A shopping trip would definitely be on the agenda now with her clothes damaged. She didn't think it would be easy to get the smoke smell out of them and most of them were old enough that it wouldn't be worth the bother.

Going downstairs, she found the house was eerily quiet. She was beginning to think she was the only one home until she went into the kitchen.

The women members were sitting around the kitchen drinking coffee. There were none of the usual smells of cooking food, though.

When Lily walked through the doorway, they went silent and everyone's eyes turned toward her.

Lily hated being the center of attention. She wiped her sweaty palms against the side of her pants and said, "I was going to get a cup of coffee."

Jewell and Evie both turned toward the coffee pot. Raci started to get up, but sat back down when she saw the other two women doing it. Bliss got up from her chair, motioning for Lily to take a seat.

"That's okay. I..." Seeing the crushed look on Bliss's face, Lily took the seat. "Thanks, Bliss."

"No problem."

Jewell sat the coffee down in front of her.

"Thanks." Lily took a sip.

"Well, that was some party. I think I'll give next year's a pass," Lily joked, trying to lighten the atmosphere.

The women chuckled, but Lily heard several sobs mixed in. Looking up, she knew they had all witnessed much more than the fire. Lily's eyes watered and she clenched her hands so tightly that her nails dug into her palms.

"Where are the men?" Lily asked, determined to lighten the atmosphere.

"Downstairs ripping out the damaged wood. They took pictures of it before they did anything. Knox came out early this morning," Evie informed her.

"Knox?" Lily questioned.

The women stared at each other before Evie replied, "Someone deliberately set the fire."

Lily absorbed the shock of someone trying to kill a whole houseful of people.

"Do they know who yet?"

"Knox and Shade are looking into it."

At that, the men came through the basement door, carrying with them the smell of smoke. They were covered in soot and grime, so Evie ordered them upstairs to shower before eating lunch.

Lily looked around the kitchen at the mention of food. "We ordered pizzas," Raci answered her unspoken question.

As if on cue, the front door opened and closed, and Shade and Knox came in carrying pizza boxes. Shade glanced at her before setting the pizzas on the counter, quickly coming to her side.

"Hungry?"

"I could eat," Lily admitted, getting up from the table while avoiding his concerned gaze. Getting in line, she took a slice of pizza before resuming her seat. Shade, on the other hand, filled his plate before sitting down next to her.

"Evie said someone deliberately set the fire," Lily told him.

"Yes. Knox came out this morning and took the evidence he needed. Whoever it was slipped into the party last night with a hanger-on. We have a description. It's only a matter of time before we find her."

"Her?" Lily repeated, shocked.

"Yes," Shade answered.

"Why?"

"We think it was another attempt on your life," Shade told her.

Knox sat down at the table and she asked, "Why does someone want me dead? I don't understand." Lily looked for answers from the two men.

"We don't know yet, but when we find who started the fire, we will."

She shivered at the cold look of purpose on both men's faces. She almost felt sorry for the person who'd set the fire. Only the knowledge of how many could have been killed had Lily keeping her mouth closed.

Everyone finished eating then Viper organized them all into one team as a cleanup crew and another to put up new drywall. Lily got up to go downstairs.

"No. You stay up here and start dinner for everyone." She didn't argue with Viper. She hadn't looked forward to going downstairs and seeing the destruction while everyone was present.

Shade hung back once the other members had left. "You need anything?"

"No. Shade, maybe it would be better if I left. I don't want to endanger anyone." Lily didn't want anyone hurt because of her.

"You're not going anywhere," he said, pulling her to him. "It's because you were here with all the security we had that it wasn't much worse. We slipped up because we didn't think someone was brave enough to actually make a move on you in the house. We won't make that mistake twice."

Lily bet they wouldn't. Anger had poured off the men in waves. They wouldn't make a deadly mistake twice.

"Beth will be back soon. Go shopping, get out of the house for a while. Razer will go with you two."

"That sounds good. I'm ready to get out for a while."

Shade touched his mouth to hers briefly before going downstairs.

Lily texted Beth with the plans then quickly threw together two crockpots full of stew to simmer while she and Beth were gone. She had just finished when Beth returned to get changed out of her uniform.

"Give me a minute while I get changed."

It didn't take long and then they drove into town with Razer following behind on his bike.

Treepoint wasn't large, but it had two sizable stores that Lily should have no problem finding a new wardrobe of clothes from.

She tried on several dresses at their first stop; however, nothing was making her happy. She left disappointed. A few doors down, they went into the second department store. After they had been looking around for a while, Beth stopped.

"You go on ahead. I have a call I need to make."

Thinking she needed to check in with her patients, Lily continued to go through the women's department, searching through the racks. She picked out several dresses that she thought could work and a new pair of jeans before going to the fitting room.

Beth showed up as she was about to enter. "Those are very pretty. I'll wait out here while you try them on."

Lily tried one on after the other, unsatisfied with any of them. She pulled off the pair of jeans, the last item she'd had to try, and folded them back up. Giving the clothes to the attendant, she went out to Beth empty-handed.

"No success?"

"No. I don't know what's wrong. I'll just go to the discount store and pick up a few things until I find something else," Lily was explaining when several women stared through the aisle at the convoy of women entering the department store.

Lily turned to Beth with a suspicious look. Beth merely

grinned back, not trying to hide the fact she had called in reinforcements.

"I thought we could use a little help," Beth admitted.

No sooner had she said those words than Sex Piston and her crew stopped in front of them. "Well, I'm glad someone finally had the sense to ask me for my fashion advice."

Lily stared at the obviously pregnant biker woman dressed in leather leggings and a bright red top with a metallic Harley studded on the front. Her baby bump was emphasized by the tightness of the red shirt that should have clashed with her red hair; instead it only highlighted the deep, rich tones of it.

Killyama pulled out one of the dresses from a nearby rack, shuddering before hastily putting it back. "No wonder the bitch couldn't find anything. My mom wouldn't buy anything here and she's stoned out of her fucking mind."

Lily heard the saleswoman a few feet away gasp at the insult.

"Let's get out of here," Sex Piston said, leaving without waiting for any objections.

Lily and Beth followed the women down two blocks to a newer store that had opened recently. Sex Piston flung the door open, strutting inside as if she was the one who owned it.

Lily watched as the women spread throughout the store, searching for clothes for her. She could only stare helplessly at her sister who was going through the racks, ignoring her incriminating glances. Lily decided she had better get busy going through the racks or she would be talked into buying clothes that she would never dream of wearing.

After she had searched fruitlessly, finding nothing that she considered would do, Fat Louise came and led her to the dressing room where everyone was waiting. Each woman handed her clothes to try on, despite the saleswoman's protests that only a certain number of clothes were allowed.

"Get lost. We'll take care of her." Killyama's threatening glare had the woman retreating back to the cash register just as Sex Piston barged into the dressing room, pulling a chair up outside her changing room door.

"If you don't come out and show me, then I'll come in there," she threatened. Lily nodded half-heartedly.

She tried on several items but was too embarrassed to open the door.

"Are you crying?" Sex Piston asked, astounded.

"No." Lily's voice wobbled when she answered.

"Open the fucking door and let me see."

Lily slowly opened the door. "I'm not crying." She wasn't. She had kept her promise to herself; she was just having a hard time keeping it.

Sex Piston took a look at her face then looked up at the ceiling. Lily thought it was strange, but she waited several seconds before Sex Piston looked back down at her.

Sex Piston's eyes were filled with unshed tears. "I'm more emotional now that I'm pregnant. Now, we're going to pull on our big-girl panties and get this done or I'm going to pick everything out for you myself. Okay?"

"Okay." Lily took a deep breath and tried on a dress. She opened the door.

"No," Sex Piston said firmly, running critical eyes over the dress on her body.

Lily shut the door and changed again before opening the door.

"Fuck no."

She tried on a skirt with a matching top.

"Yes."

She closed the door again, also happy with the clothes. She tried another.

The gagging noises Sex Piston made when she opened the dressing room door were self-explanatory. Lily shut the door with a snap.

She tried on a form-fitting dress with a swirling skirt in a soft cranberry color.

"Yes." Lily smiled at her response.

She tried on a pair of jeans and a blue iris sweater that showed a hint of flesh at the top.

"Yes."

Lily tried on a jade-green sweater dress, which was too tight. She didn't want to open the door.

"No, it doesn't suit you at all." Thankfully, Sex Piston agreed with her own opinion.

Lily tried on several more outfits, letting Sex Piston pick and choose. Thankfully, she agreed with most of her choices since she was going to be the one wearing them. She picked up the ones she would be purchasing, setting them aside, and then straightened the rest back onto the hangers.

Going outside the dressing room, she carried the clothes she was going to buy on her arm.

"Can you grab the others to put on the rack so they can restock them?" Lily asked.

Sex Piston took the ones that were going back in stock, hanging them on the rack. All except for the green dress. Lily raised an eyebrow at her.

"What? I said it didn't suit you, but it will look hot on me," Sex Piston said unashamedly.

They checked out.

"Thanks for going with us," Lily said as they shoved all the bags into Beth's SUV.

"Hell, we aren't done. You need shoes." Sex Piston pushed her toward the local shoe store.

The store had a lone salesclerk and he was male. The women had him making trip after trip to the back.

Lily liked this much better. All she had to do was sit and try on pair after pair of shoes.

"No way," Lily refused, seeing the price on the side of the box the clerk was showing her.

"Hell, yeah. Your sister can pay for them. She's married

to Mr. Moneybags," Killyama said, taking the box away from the clerk while giving him one of her flirtatious smiles.

Lily stifled her laughter. The man looked scared enough to wet himself.

Reaching forward, she took the shoes from Killyama, trying on the high heels that she was sure would break her ankle if she ever dared to wear them.

"She'll take them," Beth spoke up with a mischievous look in her eyes.

Lily shook her head, not wanting to spend her sister's money.

"Don't worry about it. They'll be worth every dime when I see Shade's face."

Beth took the six pairs of shoes to the register before Lily could change her mind. Lily walked out of the store overwhelmed by the amount of money Beth had spent carelessly that day. Guilt kicked in, making her decide to take some of the things back next week and return the money to her sister.

"Let's get some dinner," Sex Piston said.

"I'm paying," Beth offered. Since when did Beth become so free with her cash? Her sister, while not broke, had always been frugal with her money.

Razer, who was leaning against the SUV after having helped the women load the car, gave a twisted grin.

"Where at?" Fat Louise asked, excited.

"Let's do it up right. The Pink Slipper sound good to everyone?" Beth mentioned the most expensive restaurant and bar in Treepoint.

"They won't let us in the door." Fat Louise reminded Beth they hadn't been allowed in the restaurant since the fight they had started when Razer and Beth had temporarily broken up.

"I happen to know it's under new management," Beth happily said, spreading the good news.

The whoops and hollers drew the attention of

customers leaving the stores that were closing. No one other than Lily seemed to notice, though, and so they each got in their separate vehicles, driving the short distance to the restaurant.

Inside, Razer went to sit at the bar, leaving the women at a table on their own.

Sex Piston and her crew ordered the most expensive items on the menu. Lily was sure it was because they knew Beth was paying with Razer's money. They still held a grudge against him for breaking their friend's heart. The women were loyal to Beth and even treated her like a sister because of their affection for her.

They all ordered tea and water to drink, except for Crazy Bitch and Killyama who drank beer, telling Sex Piston she was driving.

"Wait until you're knocked up. I'll drink a fucking six-pack in front of you," she said vengefully. Lily thought that by the time Sex Piston's baby arrived, it would be born with an extensive vocabulary.

The diners at the other tables kept giving them censuring looks which they ignored.

T.A. leaned forward. "So, has the hunk of burning love made his move yet?"

"Who?" Lily asked, dumbfounded.

T.A. rolled her eyes. "You know who I'm talking about. Shade."

"Kind of." 'Hunk of burning love' was not how she would describe Shade's stern demeanor.

"What the fuck does that mean? Yes or no?" Crazy Bitch snapped.

"Well, we kissed last night," Lily confided, embarrassed she was talking about something so intimate in front of her sister.

"You kissed?" Crazy Bitch asked, looking at her like she had lost her mind.

"Was it too soon?" Lily asked. The women at the table just stared at her then burst into hysterical laughter. Even

Beth almost fell out of her chair when Killyama whacked her accidentally with her elbow.

"What's so funny?" Lily asked sharply.

"N…N…Nothing," Sex Piston said, wiping the tears off her cheeks. "Beth, if I have a daughter, I'm sending her to live with you when she reaches puberty."

"Hell, she damn sure doesn't take after her sister. Beth gave up the whole shebang quicker than that." Crazy Bitch slammed her beer down on the table.

"Shut up," Beth hissed.

"You go, sister," Sex Piston said, raising her hand for Lily to high-five. "Make the motherfucker work for it." Lily lamely hit her palm against Sex Piston's.

"Are you crazy? Why make him work for it? I'd have given it up before he asked for it. By the way, when you find out how far down those tats go, will you let us know? We've got a bet going," T.A. confided, leaning sideways in her chair to whisper in Lily's ear.

The food arrived, and Lily was glad when they settled down to eat. When the check arrived, Lily tried to take it to pay Beth back for some of the clothes, but Beth wouldn't let her.

"I've got it." She laid the card down on the ticket.

Lily glanced down, expecting to see either Beth or Razer's name on the card; instead, it bore another name she recognized.

"He said to make sure you had a good time. Have you had fun?" Beth teased.

"Yes… but—"

"Don't worry; he can afford a small dinner." Beth patted her hand.

"But—"

"A few pairs of shoes, too," Beth continued, her smile widening.

Lily hid her face in her hand.

"And a whole new wardrobe," Beth finished, then teased, "I'm thinking he might deserve more than a kiss."

CHAPTER TWENTY-FIVE

When Beth pulled her SUV into the parking lot of The Last Riders, cutting the engine, Lily sat relaxed in the seat next to her as Razer opened Beth's door, helping her out. Her sister looked exhausted. Lily felt guilty knowing Beth had given a full morning working then spent the rest of the day shopping.

"I'm sorry you're so tired," Lily said, coming to Beth's side.

"Don't be ridiculous. I enjoyed spending the day with you. We haven't done it in a long time."

As Razer opened the back of the SUV, they all three stared at the small mountain of bags.

"I think we may have overdone it a bit," Beth said jokingly, turning to Lily.

"You think?" Lily laughed. "I'm already planning on taking most of it back."

"Don't you dare," Beth reprimanded her.

"She won't," Shade spoke up from behind them, reaching inside the vehicle to take several of the bags. Razer reached inside also, pulling out a large number for himself. Lily and Beth split up the remaining packages and then they all carried them up the steps to the house.

Lily watched as the men carried the packages up the steps to one of the rooms upstairs. Beth motioned Lily up to the room she had been in that morning, the nightgown she had worn still lying across the chair.

When they set the bags on the floor in front of the bed, Lily didn't know what she was supposed to do with the clothes.

"I'll see you at church in the morning." Lily hugged and kissed her sister goodbye.

Razer gave her a tight hug. "Goodnight, lil' sis."

"Night, Razer."

The door closed behind them.

"I'm not staying in the basement anymore?"

"No. If someone tries to hurt you again, they'll have to get past every brother in the house with you up here."

"I see." She took a deep breath. "Beth told me at dinner that you paid for all this. I'll pay you back."

"No, you won't, and you won't take anything back. Quit worrying and go get your shower."

Lily went to the bathroom, taking the gown. The bathroom wasn't as large as the one in Shade's room, but it was just as nice. The Last Riders were bikers who most definitely enjoyed their creature comforts.

She showered and washed her hair, blow-dried it then brushed it out. There had been at least six different shampoos and a whole smorgasbord of toiletries to choose from.

There was a robe on the back of the door that Lily put on over her gown before opening the door. She had been expecting the room to be empty; instead Shade was already in bed.

Lily climbed in bed, relieved. She had thought he would remain sleeping in the basement. She pulled the covers over her, giving him a smile.

"What was that for?"

Confused her brow furrowed. "What?"

Shade turned off the bedside lamp. The bathroom light

254

was on with the door left half-open. "That smile you just gave me."

"I don't know. I was just happy you were here. I thought you might be sleeping in your room."

Shade rose on his side. His serious face cast in the shadows of the bedroom. "Lily, the only bed you'll be in is the one I'm sleeping in." His finger traced down the fragile line of her cheekbone.

He bent down, kissing her lips. When Lily parted her lips, his tongue entered her mouth, searching its depths. Her tongue timidly touched his, and at her response, he sucked her tongue into his mouth, sliding his own against hers, tempting her to explore the warmth of his mouth.

When her arms slipped around his shoulders, Shade raised his head, breaking off the kiss.

"When I kiss you, it's like touching perfection." Shade placed soft kisses on her neck.

Lily's arms dropped to her side. "I'm not perfect," she replied, turning her face away.

"You're perfect for me," Shade corrected her.

"Shade…" Lily began hesitantly.

"Not tonight, Lily. Tonight, I want to hold you in my arms, knowing that you're taking one breath after another. That when I wake in the morning, your beautiful face will be on the pillow next to mine, and tomorrow night, when I go to bed, you'll be by my side again. Day after day, night after night." Shade's vow expressed how seriously he had taken almost losing her.

Lily's lips smiled against his throat. "What about when I snore?"

"Angels don't snore."

* * *

Church was packed the next day; the closer to the holidays, the more the parishioners made the effort to attend. Lily kept her head down, sitting next to Beth and Razer, only talking when one of them spoke to her. As soon as the service ended, Lily got up from the pew.

"I'll meet you outside." Before they could say anything, Lily left the church before even Pastor Dean could make it to the door.

Lily was the first one in the diner after church. She already was looking over the menu when Shade, Ryder and Cash came through the door.

"What are you doing over here by yourself?" Shade asked, taking a seat next to her.

"I left church a few minutes early," Lily said, staring at the menu.

"Why?"

"I didn't want to stand in line today. Does it matter? Everything's fine." Lily raised the menu higher, ignoring his questioning gaze.

Beth and the others came in from church, asking her the same questions.

"What happened?" Beth asked.

Lily shrugged, avoiding the question by placing her order. They had just been served their food when Pastor Dean came in the restaurant with Rachel and her family, taking a table across the restaurant.

After lunch, Lily was ready to leave. She didn't want to linger like she usually did. She turned to Shade who was still drinking his coffee.

"Ready?" Her fingers were tearing the paper napkin to shreds. She wadded the mess up, placing the pieces on her plate before handing it to the waitress.

"Sure." Shade got up from the table, laying the money for both of them down.

"Are you coming to the house?" Lily asked Beth who nodded her head.

"I'll see you there."

Lily fled the restaurant, not waiting for Shade, missing the worried glance Beth gave Shade and his shrug.

"What's the hurry?" Shade asked when he caught up with her outside.

"I need to get some work done on my college classes

today."

Shade got on the bike and Lily climbed on behind him, her arms circling his waist. The drive home didn't take long. The weather was already turning cooler and the sun was as cloudy as her mood.

She didn't want to sit and talk while everyone was giving her looks like she was going to break any minute. Her memories were back. She wasn't going to hide from them any longer, but neither did she want to talk about them. Lily hoped, given time, something new would occur and her episode would fade from memory, and they would forget she had been a basket case.

She was determined to become stronger, both physically and emotionally. Every day she would work on it until she was as strong as Beth, Winter or anyone else other than herself. Her dream goal was really to be as strong as Sex Piston, but she didn't want to set an unrealistic goal for herself.

Once they got back, Lily spent the rest of the day doing her coursework on the computer, finally pressing submit when she finished.

Shade and the other men had spent the afternoon working in the basement. They had packed out the burnt furniture and workout equipment. The cleanup had been completed and new drywall painted. All that was left was to replace the destroyed items and get new carpeting.

At dinner, the women decided that Evie and Ember would go into town tomorrow and replace the furniture; Viper had already ordered the workout equipment.

Lily ate, listening to everyone making plans. Going into the kitchen afterward, she stood at the counter as Rider and Train argued over the size of the television that would replace the one downstairs. She had never understood the need for men to have such large televisions.

Jewell caught her amused gaze, correctly deciphering its cause. "It's like their dicks, they think bigger is always better." Lily had taken a drink of water and almost choked on the snide comment.

When Train and Rider went to the couch off the kitchen, continuing the argument, Shade and Viper joined them as the women congregated in the kitchen.

"I think bigger is better, too," Bliss said, grinning while stacking the dishes in the sink.

Beth came to stand next to Lily at the counter. Beth's phone gave out a tiny ping and she reached into her pocket, pulling it out. Lily looked over when Beth started laughing.

"Sex Piston and Stud eloped this morning. They're on their way to spend their honeymoon on Knox and Diamond's island."

The whole group of women were happy for the couple. No one was surprised that Sex Piston had eloped. That woman would have a hard time being romantic and giving vows of love in front of a crowd.

"I would never elope. I want a big summer wedding with all the bells and whistles. It will be so big that it would take two years to plan," Raci said dreamily.

"I want a quiet wedding with a short dress and just a few guests," Evie said, pouring herself some tea.

"I loved my wedding," Beth said with a soft sigh.

"Me, too," Winter added. "I loved having it in the backyard."

"I'm not getting married. I'm having too much fun." Stori grimaced at the other women's dream filled expressions.

"What about you, Lily?" asked Jewell.

"Me?"

"Oh, Lord!" Beth shook her head at the other women, giving Lily an affectionate glance.

"What was that?" Winter asked, looking back and forth between the two sisters.

"Do not get Lily started on her fantasy wedding," Beth warned.

The other women turned to look at an innocent Lily.

The girl never spent a dime on herself if she could help it; they were having a hard time believing that she'd want something elaborate.

"Dream wedding?" Evie asked curiously.

"Lily is a hopeless romantic. She's planned it since she was sixteen and saw a wedding on television."

"There was a wedding in December and it was snowing just a little bit. They got married in the backyard of a tiny church. It was beautiful," Lily breathed with dreams in her violet eyes for once.

"What kind of dress?" Evie egged her on.

"My mother's. I have it packed away. It's stunning with long sleeves made of lace, but they're off the shoulder, and it has a long lace veil."

"How do you know it would even fit?" Raci asked.

"Oh, it fits. I wanted to wear it, too, but I couldn't get my big butt in it. It fit Lily perfectly," Beth replied.

Lily playfully swatted her sister for telling she had tried on the dress.

"I would have thought you would have wanted a spring wedding," Jewell said thoughtfully.

"No, I love winter. I love seeing snow on the ground, and when it's snowing, I don't think anything is more beautiful," Lily breathed.

"I know of one thing," Beth said softly to Lily, taking her sister's hand. Lily was grateful when she changed the subject, turning to Evie. "I'll go into town with you tomorrow and check on the carpet I ordered for the house. I want to move into the house next weekend if it's delivered on time."

The women agreed, eager for any reason to shop.

Beth didn't release Lily's hand. "Let's go look at my house. You can tell me what you think." Beth then tugged Lily out the door to the path.

They walked up the steps to the small porch and Beth opened the door, flicking on the lights.

Lily was amazed at how much the house suited Beth. It

was much larger on the inside than the outside made it appear. It had a sizeable kitchen, and while she hadn't wanted a large living room, she had extra space off the kitchen with a family area and a fireplace. It was a house that, even without carpet and furniture, was very homey.

Beth led her down a hallway into the four bedrooms. The master bedroom had its own private bath and Lily could see that Beth and Razer would be very happy there.

"It's beautiful, Beth. You and Razer have built a home to be proud of."

"It's everything I've ever wanted. Lily, I'm sorry I haven't let you see it before now. I was so afraid about you finding out about the club that I didn't show you so I could protect you."

Lily nodded, still a little hurt, but she understood. Beth had wanted to avoid hurting her. Besides, Lily was aware she hadn't taken it well when she *had* found out.

"You should have put a shower in like Shade has in his bedroom," Lily said, staring at her sister's small shower.

"I haven't seen it," Beth said curiously.

"It's the bomb. Of course, it's too late now with all your tile-work laid, but his should be in a magazine."

"Really?"

"Yes!" Lily enthused.

They walked back to the clubhouse where the women members were still in the kitchen; the men were drinking beer and relaxing in front of the television after working on the basement all day.

"I'll be right back," Beth said, going down to the basement.

Razer gave Lily a curious look. She shrugged back, giving him an innocent expression. She knew what was going to happen. That shower was freaking awesome.

Winter's cell phone went off with a text message. A look of surprise crossed her face before she put it back in her pocket and went downstairs. This time, it was Viper giving her a questioning glance. Lily shrugged again, taking a few nuts out of the bowl sitting on the counter. It didn't take long. Both Razer and Viper's cell phones went off next with text messages. Reading the messages, both men went down to the basement with grim looks on their faces.

"What's going on?" Evie asked.

"I told Beth about Shade's shower," Lily confessed.

"Uh-oh," Evie moaned. "Do you know how long it took for her to pick out that tile?"

Lily shook her head. "I told her it was too late."

"What's going on?" Shade asked, coming up behind her.

"She told Beth about your shower and then Beth told Winter. Winter's wanted to redo the bathroom in Viper's room. Want to bet he's going to be shelling out some cold hard cash?" Evie answered.

Shade looked down at her and Lily couldn't resist giving him a mischievous smile.

"You're not causing trouble, are you?" His arm went around her shoulder.

"Can I help it if that shower is a work of art?" Lily said jokingly.

Winter and Beth came back upstairs with determined expressions on their faces. The men, on the other hand, sent accusing looks toward Lily who tried to hide her laughter. She didn't want to speculate how much it would cost to put in a shower like that.

"I can't blame them. That shower has given me many pleasurable moments," Jewell joked.

"Me, too. That rainfall showerhead is gold-plated," Evie agreed "Shade designed it himself when he moved to the basement after Beth moved into the club."

"I love the music that plays to the beat of the water," Dawn shuddered.

Lily stiffened at the second comment, and by Dawn's comment, Lily pulled away; all her amusement had died.

"It's getting late. If I'm going to work tomorrow, I need to get some sleep," Lily excused herself. "Night everyone."

She left the room to mumbled goodnights and went upstairs.

Opening the bedroom door, she saw the new clothes she had purchased. Going through the bags, she picked out one of the least-expensive skirts and blouses, a pair of jeans and another top. Both outfits would do her until she could return the others and had the money credited to Shade's account. She would get enough money out of her checking account to pay him back for the two outfits she was keeping and the pretty plum dress she had worn today.

Lily was hanging the outfits she was planning on keeping in the closet when Shade walked into the bedroom. "What are you doing?"

"Hanging up my new clothes," Lily replied, stepping back from the closet and closing the door.

"Why didn't you hang up the rest?" Shade asked, eyeing the numerous bags still on the floor.

"Because I'm not keeping them." Lily turned away from him, going to the dresser to brush her hair.

"Why not?"

"Because I can't afford them."

"I paid for them."

"Exactly. *You* paid for them, I didn't."

Shade's mouth tightened. "If you're angry, that's fine, but you're keeping the clothes."

"No. I. Am. Not! I'm taking them back." Lily went to the chair, picking up the nightgown and robe before going to the shower, barely managing not to slam the door behind her.

She was angry that she even cared how many women had been in his darned shower.

She washed her hair, picking out a different shampoo than she had the last time. The fragrance was vaguely familiar to her; then it dawned on her that she had smelled the scent on Ember's hair when she had sat next to her at dinner. She rinsed her hair off and realized there were so many shampoos because all the women had used the bathroom.

Lily pressed her forehead against the shower wall, remembering Shade's own well-stocked bathroom closet. She had been a fool for not realizing it sooner, that the women were in his bedroom enough to keep a regular stock of shampoo in his shower.

She slowly stepped out and dried off. She would have rewashed her hair, but she didn't know whose shampoo was whose. She was going to the store tomorrow when she got off to buy her own toiletries and return all the clothes at one time.

When she went out into the bedroom, Shade was sitting at the desk, going through his email. Lily saw the empty store bags sitting on the chair. She lifted one of the bags and the tags fell to the floor.

She stormed angrily to the closet, opening the door and seeing all the clothes hanging up. The shoe boxes were even neatly stacked on the floor underneath the hanging clothes.

"I can't believe you did this! I told you I was taking the clothes back."

"And I told you that you weren't," Shade replied coldly.

Lily stood with her hands on her hips. She would just keep the clothes and give him the money for them. At least she could take the shoes back. They were the most expensive items and there were no tags that he could remove that would keep her from returning them.

Lily bent down, opening one of the boxes and staring in shock at what he had done. One of the shoes was missing. Going down on her knees, she opened each of the boxes and saw each one contained only a single shoe.

She rose to her feet, holding one tennis shoe in her hand. "Where are the other shoes?"

"I've put them away. When you want to wear a particular pair, I'll get you the match."

"I'm not keeping the shoes."

"Doesn't look like you have much choice, does it?" Lily

could hear the satisfaction in his voice.

"You think you have it all figured out. Fine, I'll keep them and the clothes, too. In fact, I'll share them with all the women in the house. They all share clothes. They'll love the shoes."

Shade had the audacity to laugh. "They wouldn't be seen dead in those clothes."

Lily had a temper-flare, believing he was shoving her face into the fact that there was no comparison between her and the other women.

"That's fine then." Lily did an about-face. "I'll give you the money for everything. I don't want to share anything with them, either. Not their clothes, not their shampoo, and certainly not you." With that, she threw the tennis shoe at his stunned face and he barely dodged it. He probably hadn't believed she would actually throw the shoe at him until it had almost hit him in his face.

Lily crossed her arms over her chest, proud of herself, wishing she had the other one to throw at him, too. "Do you mind getting me the match?" Lily unwisely mocked him.

Shade got up from the chair, his face impassive. "That robe belongs to Bliss. She didn't need it because she doesn't wear it."

Lily shrieked in anger, jerking the robe off before she threw it at him. He grabbed it, tossing it to the chair.

"The nightgown belongs to Raci. She sleeps in the nude, so she lent it to you."

Lily wasn't so far gone that she was about to tear the gown off. Instead, she went back to the closet, getting one of the new pajama sets she had bought. Jerking it off the hanger, she turned back around and ran into Shade's chest, who had come up behind her while she was going through the closet.

"I thought you didn't want them?" This time he was mocking her.

"I don't, jerk-face, but I have to wear something."

"I don't see why." His hands went to her hips, clenching the material of the gown in his hands, bunching it up until it came up to her calves.

Lily released her last remnants of temper and used one of the moves that had worked for her in the past. She raised her knee.

"Oh, no, you don't." Shade moved his thigh, blocking her knee and then throwing her off-balance so her body fell against his.

She became determined to take that smug look off his face. Using another move that had worked successfully before, she reached out, resolving to crush his nuts and make him useless to any woman.

"Nuh, uh, you little wildcat." He used his leg to swipe her foot out from under her, making her begin to fall to the floor; however, he twisted so that he fell first and she landed on top of him.

"You're a mean, mean person. I don't even know why I like you." Lily beat on his chest with her fists. "The only women you haven't been with in Treepoint are the ones who are either happily married or dead." He laughed in her face, rolling her onto her back and then lying between her thighs as he took her wrists in one of his, locking them above her head and holding her in place beneath him.

"You don't hate me; you're jealous," he said smugly.

"I'm not jealous of you. You're a… a—"

"Exactly what am I?" Shade's face was amused above her own.

"A manwhore," Lily spat angrily. "I do not think you being promiscuous is funny. I don't care who you have sex with as long as you leave me alone."

"But you're the one I'm the most interested in, Lily. I wouldn't want to leave you out in the cold."

"Leave me in the cold! Better yet, why don't you forget all about me?"

"Forget about you? That's not going to happen, especially since I've thought of nothing but fucking you since the moment I saw you. Don't you get tired of sitting on that moral throne of yours? Don't you want to come out and play?"

Lily stiffened underneath him as his hand slid under her nightgown, going toward her panties. She couldn't believe what he was doing. Her eyes widened, expecting him to stop at any second, that he was just paying her back for losing her temper. She should have known better. When Shade taught a lesson, he didn't stop until you had learned that lesson.

His hands slid under the wispy pink underwear she was wearing, his finger sliding through the dry skin of her pussy.

Lily arched, not knowing what to do next.

"I'm going to play. Feel free to join in anytime."

She opened her mouth to tell him to take his hands off her, but his mouth closed over hers before she could gather her stunned thoughts. His tongue thrust into her mouth as his fingers began playing with her clit, stroking the little nub with an experienced touch that had her freezing at the pleasure it created. A rush of wetness that she couldn't explain made his finger glide slickly against her sensitized flesh.

Embarrassed, she tried to wiggle away, only his fingers moved with her, bringing a flare of arousal she hadn't expected. Lily lay still, her hands gripping his shoulders as he continued to play with her clit. She wiggled her hips experimentally and was struck by another rush of pleasure. Shade's mouth left hers, going to her neck and sucking a tiny amount of skin into his mouth.

Lily's hips rose off the floor at the sparks that flew through her pussy when he sucked on her neck. His finger slid wetly along her flesh as she began twisting beneath him. He sucked harder on her neck then pressed between the folds of her clit.

Lily shuddered, her thighs clenching his hand closer to her pussy as she felt explosions go off. When she lay still,

Shade raised his head from her throat, removing his hand from between her clenched thighs. He brought his fingers to his mouth and sucked the nectar of her from them.

Lily pushed him off her, going to the bathroom.

"Lily, *now* I've had every pussy in town that's not happily married or dead." Lily slammed the door on his mocking words.

CHAPTER TWENTY-SIX

Lily washed up in the bathroom, disgusted with herself. She had never let Charles touch her that way and she had caved to Shade within seconds of him touching her intimately. She was disappointed in herself that she hadn't been able to resist his touch.

She put up her chin, determined to face the conceited man who thought he had proven his point. Well, she was about to shove his point up his butt and show him the bedroom door.

Lily opened the bathroom door, having the wind taken out of her sails by seeing him already in bed with the light out.

She walked barefoot to the side he was on. "I want you to leave. I'm not sleeping with you anymore. There's nothing wrong with your bedroom, so go sleep down there."

"Lily, get in the bed and go to sleep. You're mad because you lost our first fight, but it's over." His patronizing tone set her nerves on edge.

She tugged at his arm. "I am not sleeping with you."

"That did it, Lily. You're going to learn your next lesson in how to behave with me." As Shade flipped the

268

covers from the bed, Lily took a step back, expecting him to storm from the room.

I really have to learn to stop underestimating him, she thought seconds later.

He sat up on the side of the bed, and before she could get away, he flipped her over his knees. Lily screamed in surprise, but she wasn't frightened.

His hand smacked down on her butt, her thin gown and underwear no protection against the pain of the swat.

"Don't you dare!"

Another smack on her bottom showed that he did. Another and another rained down on her flaming bottom.

"Stop it!"

Another hard smack.

Lily thought quickly. "Blueberries!"

"Don't you dare use your safe word to get out of a punishment," Shade snapped.

Another hard smack and she quit struggling and lay quietly across his lap.

Thwack.

"I'm sorry!" Lily wailed.

The spanking stopped immediately, and she was flipped up and set down hard on her stinging bottom on his lap.

His hand grasped her face, making her look up at him. "Don't think you can order me out of your bed when you get mad at me." Shade's voice was coldly furious.

"Okay!" Lily yelled.

Lily found herself flipped back over his thighs, receiving two more punishing smacks.

"I'm sorry." This time her voice was tearfully remorseful. She was again sat upright on her stinging bottom, staring into his cold face.

"Apologize to me correctly."

Lily was confused. "I'm sorry?"

"I'm sorry, *Sir.*"

Lily's face turned mutinous. She wasn't about to give him that title of respect. Shade began to flip her again and

Lily hastily changed her mind. "I'm sorry, Sir."

"I give you a lot of leeway, Lily—more than I have ever given any woman—but I'm also not going to let you twist me around your finger like you did Charles."

Lily opened her mouth.

"I advise you to go to bed before you say something else that makes me angry. You'll learn what I'll allow you to do and what I won't. It'll just take a little time."

Lily thought her temper would explode again at his bossy attitude, but due to the fact that her butt was already stinging, she would wait until tomorrow to prove he wasn't going to treat her like the other women.

Shade released her and Lily crawled into the bed, not looking at him, afraid her angry expression would give her away.

Shade lay back down, pulling the covers over both of them.

She punched the pillow under her head, wishing it was him. It took several minutes before her temper cooled enough that she remembered she had experienced her first orgasm.

"Are you crying?" Shade asked, rolling closer, his hand going to her butt, rubbing the flesh that was no longer hurting; however, she wasn't about to tell him that.

"No."

"All right, why aren't you crying?"

Lily shrugged in the darkness.

A loud sigh of frustration filled the room. "Lily…"

"It was the first time I…" She couldn't bring herself to finish.

Lily felt his laughter against her back. Insulted, she started to climb out of bed, but his arm circled her waist, preventing her from getting out of bed.

"Go to sleep, Lily. I promise it won't be the last."

* * *

Orders were coming in at so fast a rate that many of the members were working overtime, trying to get them out in time. Lily felt guilty taking off Wednesday to work at the church store, but Shade told her to go. He even drove her into town, telling her to call when she was finished and he would pick her up.

"Do not leave, even to go to the diner to pick up a drink."

"I won't," Lily promised, going inside, but she was unable to resist a final look at him riding off the lot on his bike.

Rachel was already hard at work once Lily got inside. The woman was amazing in what she had gotten accomplished.

"I can't take all the credit. I called Willa on Saturday when you couldn't make it. She worked a couple of hours until Pastor Dean showed up. I can't understand why she doesn't like him."

"Oh, I think she likes him," Lily said.

"You think so?"

Lily nodded her head. "It would be hard having a crush on your minister, don't you imagine?"

"Especially Pastor Dean. Every single woman in the city, whether she goes to this church or not, is chasing after him."

"Ouch, I know how that feels," Lily admitted—for the first time—out loud to herself and someone else, her feelings for Shade.

"Shade?" Rachel asked, stacking the dishes someone had donated, putting them on a shelf next to the rest.

"He's not exactly the type of man I pictured myself with."

"A biker?"

"No, not that, either," Lily said ruefully. "I meant someone who doesn't take part in church regularly. It's a big part of my life. Razer goes to church frequently with Beth. He takes the time because it's important to her."

"You don't feel Shade would do the same for you?"

"Shade in church? No, I don't see him sitting in church

every Sunday like Viper and Razer." Lily packed another stack of dishes to the shelf.

"My mother went to church three days a week. Other than her children, it was the most important aspect of her life. The day we buried her, Lily, it was the most beautiful day I had ever seen. The sky and the mountains looked like they could be a picture on a calendar. I think it was God welcoming her home." Lily turned as Rachel recounted that day. "My father, on the other hand, had a little bit of the devil in him." Her voice turned rueful.

Lily laughed. That was putting it mildly. Rachel's father had been the meanest man in the county before he had died. He sold pot to anyone, anywhere, outsmarted the law on numerous occasions, and bragged about it. His three sons were determined to follow in his footsteps.

"My mother would beg him to go to church with her, but he would just laugh and say life was for living, not spending time in church praying about dying. It was just as pretty the day my dad died. I think God was looking forward to some payback."

Lily laughed so hard she almost broke the cups she picked up while Rachel laughed with her. After their laughter died down, they both got back to work; they were getting closer to the store being ready to open.

At lunch, Rachel went across the street to the diner, bringing back burgers and fries, which they demolished. As they were getting up from the table, Lily reached out and touched Rachel's hand.

"I want to thank you for what you did."

Rachel's own hand covered hers. "If you want to talk, I'm always here for you."

"I know you are. You've been a good friend to me. I remember everything now," she continued, turning away from Rachel's compassionate gaze. "I don't want to talk about it. I don't know if I ever will, but at least now I'm not hiding from the memories."

"Don't lock them away again, Lily. Sooner or later, you

need to talk to someone."

"I will, eventually. Just not today." Lily smiled, repeating Rachel's own words.

"Not today," Rachel said. "I can agree to that." She raised her face to the sun.

"What are you doing?" Lily asked, stunned by the serene peace on Rachel's face.

"I was saying a prayer, Lily."

"What about?" Lily got up from the table in the backyard of the church, ready to go back to work inside.

"That God gives us the strength to face that basement again." Rachel smiled at her. Lily turned to go into the basement, missing the words she spoke beneath her breath. "And to grant you the peace you deserve."

* * *

Pastor Dean came down just as they were finishing for the day.

"Shade called and said he was still tied up at the factory. I offered to give you a ride home."

"That's all right; Rachel can give me a ride. She won't mind and I need to make a stop on the way." Lily sent Rachel a pleading glance.

"That's right. I can take care of it and make sure she gets home safe," Rachel agreed, giving Lily a questioning glance.

"I don't know. I told Shade that I would." Pastor Dean seemed uncertain.

Lily kept organizing the boxes, keeping her face averted from Pastor Dean.

"We need to take care of some girl things," Rachel confided, earning Lily's gratitude.

Pastor Dean kept his eyes on Lily, yet she refused to look at him. Her fingers whitened on the box she was holding.

"That will be fine then. I'll see you two Saturday"

Lily let out a sigh of relief when Pastor Dean left.

"What was that about?" Rachel asked.

"I need to make a stop at my house on the way home. I didn't want to inconvenience Pastor Dean. Do you mind?"

"No."

"Thanks." The women finished for the day, shutting and locking the door behind them.

Rachel drove Lily to her house where Lily went inside while Rachel sat in the car. Lily hastily gathered her toiletries and her favorite pajamas. She then rushed back outside, not wanting to keep Rachel waiting any longer than necessary.

The ride to The Last Riders' house was spent with Rachel talking about Logan's adventures since his moving in with them. They were laughing when she described Logan showing his dad his new pet kitten when it had actually been a baby skunk he had found in the bushes.

Their laughter died when they pulled into the lot and found Shade waiting.

CHAPTER TWENTY-SEVEN

Shade opened the car door as soon as the vehicle stopped, taking the bag out of Lily's hand.

"Thanks, Rachel," Shade said. Before the stunned woman could say anything, Shade shut the car door, ushering Lily up the steps to the house and straight to the bedroom they were sharing, shutting and locking the door behind them.

"What's the matter with you?" Lily asked at his pushy behavior.

"Didn't Dean tell you I asked him to give you a ride home?"

"Yes, but—"

"But what? Someone almost killed you the other day! I asked Dean to bring you home because I knew he would be able to handle anything that could happen. If I had wanted you to ride with Rachel, I would have called Rachel."

Lily twisted her hands together as he continued in his rant.

"Not only did you not come straight here, you went by your house and Rachel sat in the car. Someone could have been waiting and killed you inside the house and Rachel wouldn't even have known."

"I didn't think," Lily confessed.

"You sure as fuck didn't. What was so important? Beth and Razer could have picked it up for you."

"I wanted to get a few of my things," Lily told him.

"I asked you days ago if there was anything you wanted. What was it?"

Lily felt stupid. "Shampoo."

"Shampoo?! You got to be fucking kidding me!" His raised voice was interrupted by a knock on the door.

"What?" Shade opened the door to see Beth's white face.

"Is there a problem? Maybe I—" Beth was cut off.

"No, Beth, I don't need your help. Lily and I are having a discussion. You can see her at dinner."

"But—"

When Shade opened the door wider, Lily was relieved; she thought he was going to let her in, but her hope was dashed immediately.

"Razer!" His shout could have raised the roof.

Seconds later, Lily heard footsteps running up the steps and saw Razer in the hallway.

"What's going on?" Razer asked, seeing his wife's pale face and Lily standing in the middle of the bedroom.

"Your wife is interrupting a discussion I'm having with Lily. Out of respect, I'm letting you handle your woman, but she needs to understand that when Lily and I are arguing, she needs to back the fuck off."

"Razer, he was yelling at her," Beth defended herself.

"I'm not that crazy-as-fuck father of yours. I am not going to hurt her, but I am going to spank her because she took an unnecessary risk."

Beth gasped. "Are you listening to him, Razer? He is not going to spank my sister. She's a grown woman."

"Yes, she is, and it's time you realized that. Razer and I are brothers, and you and Lily are going to be sharing this house and our lives together for a long time, so we need to set some boundaries. One is that, when our door is closed and we're arguing, you mind your own business. She can cry on your shoulder later, but you do not interrupt me again. I keep my nose out of your shit; you need to keep your nose out of mine."

Razer put his arm around Beth. "He's right, Beth. Deep down you know he's right. I would be pissed as hell if Lily or Shade came knocking at our door when I was giving you hell." Beth looked up at Razer.

Lily felt terrible for being responsible for bringing about this heated confrontation. "It was my fault," Lily admitted. "I asked Rachel to drive me home after Shade had already asked Pastor Dean. Then I stopped at our house."

"Lily, it's not safe there for you." Beth's worried face gazed back at her from the doorway.

"I wasn't thinking about that. I wanted my shampoo."

"Your shampoo?" At Beth's dumbfounded expression, Lily felt like an idiot.

"I didn't want my hair to smell like Jewell's, Bliss's or Evie's. I wanted it to smell like mine."

Beth's eyes flew angrily to Shade, her mouth snapping open.

"We're leaving," Razer said in amusement. "I'll handle her. Your door is off-limits when you're pissed. Got it. Later, brother." He turned a red-faced Beth away from the door, closing it behind them.

"I will never understand you, will I?" Shade said, crossing his arms over his chest.

"How would you like it if I doused you in Charles's cologne? If every time you breathed in, you smelled like him?" Lily saw Shade wince at her words as she drove her point home.

She was instantly proud of herself. She didn't need Beth's protection; she could handle him on her own. She was quickly learning his weaknesses.

She took a step forward, sliding her arms around his

waist and laying her head on his chest. "I'm sorry. I didn't think. I'll be more careful in the future."

Shade's arms tightened, drawing her nearer. "Next time, will you at least call me and tell me there's been a change in plans? I almost had a heart attack when the silent alarm went off and I saw you on the camera."

"I will. I'm sorry, Shade." Lily looked up at him, smiling in apology.

"Let's go eat dinner. You can sit there and gloat while Beth throws me dirty looks," he said in resignation.

* * *

The Last Riders were exhausted by the time the week before Thanksgiving arrived. They had been busy with the factory since there had been several natural disasters and they had all pulled overtime to fill orders that would benefit hundreds of suffering victims.

Lily could tell by the sense of excitement in the air that it was Friday. The last few Fridays, everyone had been too tired to do anything other than drag themselves to bed, but now the orders were finally caught up, everyone wanted to blow off some steam. Lily resigned herself to spending the night in her room after dinner.

Bliss and Raci practically ran out of the factory after their shift, and Evie wasn't far behind. Only Jewell, Lily and Georgia remained. Shade and Rider had left to go into town, saying only that they needed to pick up some refreshments for the brothers.

"That's it." Jewell taped down the box she was working on.

"Finished?" Lily asked, finishing up her own package.

"Yes. I didn't think this day would ever end. If Cash hadn't taken the edge off at lunch time, I wouldn't have made it to quitting time."

Lily blushed, hoping the woman wouldn't go into detail about how exactly Cash had taken the edge off. The woman talked about sex incessantly and had long since lost her reserve about discussing it in front of her. Lily always managed to turn her thoughts away, but every now and then, a comment would get by her, sending Lily's own imagination running wild.

Shade hadn't touched her since the first night they had switched bedrooms and Lily was both relieved and frustrated. She was watching him incessantly now; how he sat, how he walked. She had even woken early a few times and had lain there, watching him sleep.

She pushed her dark hair out of her eyes. Her body was feeling things she had never felt before. Last evening, they had lain on the couch watching television together when an unusual feeling had built inside of her until she had gotten up and gone to bed, only to feel him behind her in minutes. She was sleepy now because she had tossed and turned most of the night, not knowing how to relieve the building ache in her belly.

"Ready?" Jewell asked, looking at her curiously.

"Yes." Lily gathered herself, setting the package into the cart.

Georgia came out of the office. "You two go ahead. I'll lock up."

"Okay, see you Monday," Jewell replied, waving as they went out the door.

The men were pulling into the parking lot as Lily and Jewell walked outside. Lily waited for Shade as Rider got off the bike, taking a bag out of his saddlebag. Shade got off his bike, opening his own bag and taking out a brown bag.

"What's that?" Lily asked curiously. She had expected him back with beer or liquor, not a brown bag.

Rider gave her a grin before heading up to the house.

"Lily, this can go one of two ways. I'll leave it up to you. If you ask me again, I'll tell you, but I'm warning you, you won't like the answer."

Lily swallowed. She really didn't want to know. "Do you use what's in the bag?"

"Occasionally. Not since I've been in your bed,

though."

"As long as it stays that way, I don't need to know what's in the bag," Lily said stiffly.

"Lily, occasionally I'm going to want to smoke a little. It's legal in Colorado now," Shade said with a twisted smile.

"When it's legal in Kentucky, we'll talk about it," Lily said huffily.

"Hell will freeze over before pot becomes legal in Kentucky. There are some counties that still aren't allowed to sell alcohol."

"Well, I guess you've got a long wait," Lily teased, running up the steps. Shade laughed, running up behind her.

Lily opened the door, going inside where several members were already standing around with beer or a glass of liquor. Lily went upstairs, watching as Shade tossed his bag to Cash.

Lily smiled down at Shade as he started up the steps. "Are you sure you don't want to stay down there?" Lily teased, leaning over the rail.

"Oh, I think I know exactly what I want right now," Shade teased her back.

Lily skipped down the hallway to their bedroom door. She saw the bedroom across from hers had the door open. Raci was bent over the side of the bed while Train powered inside her with his cock. He had her breasts in his hands and was pinching her nipples until her breasts stood out from her chest. Her face was filled with ecstasy as Train kept pounding into her from behind. Raci then reached between her thighs, moving her hand back and forth.

Lily turned away, embarrassed at herself for watching even for a second when a few short weeks ago she would have been hysterical at the sight of them having sex.

Shade's arm went around her waist, studying her face. She tried to hide by turning away.

"Don't be embarrassed. They left the door open so that if anyone wants to watch, they can."

"I don't want to watch." Lily broke away, opening the bedroom door and going in with Shade right behind her.

"Are you sure? You seemed pretty interested." Shade's amusement was obvious.

"I'm sure," Lily said, taking off her shoes. "Leave me alone. I need to get changed and eat my dinner before the downstairs turns into the bedroom across the hall."

Shade held his hands up in the air before throwing himself down onto the couch.

Lily showered quickly, pulling on a soft pair of sweatpants and a t-shirt and then pulled her up into a ponytail.

"Ready?" Lily asked after putting on her shoes.

"Yes." Shade got to his feet, following her to the door.

Lily opened the door a small amount, peeking out.

"What are you doing?"

"Making sure they're finished. How long does it take?" she asked, looking back at him.

"Are you asking me how long it takes Train to fuck? How the hell should I know?"

"Shh... they'll hear you," Lily snapped.

"Move and I'll look. The way you're going, all the food will be gone and Rider will be fucking Evie on the table." Lily moved aside, letting Shade open the door.

He opened it wider. "The coast is clear," he said mockingly.

She cast him a worried glance. "Shade, they really don't have sex on the tables, do they?"

CHAPTER TWENTY-EIGHT

Lily ate her dinner while Shade watched her, laughing at her silently. Over the last few years she had known Shade, she hadn't realized he had a sense of humor; a warped one, but he still had one.

Lily helped Beth and Winter with the dishes, trying not to blush when Viper walked into the room and threw Winter over his shoulder, leaving with her yelling at him to put her down. She winced in sympathy when she heard a loud whack from the other side of the door.

Beth took the dish from Lily, placing it in the dishwasher. "You doing okay with everything?"

"Yes." From the hesitant expression on Beth's face, she knew what subject she was referring to.

"Lily…"

"Not tonight," Lily said hastily.

Beth sighed. "All right. On a brighter note, the bathroom is finally done and they laid the carpet, so Razer and I are going to spend the night in our new home."

"I know. Jewell told me they delivered the carpet today."

Lily dried her hands before going to the refrigerator. Opening the door, she reached inside and took out a bucket of Champagne on ice with a ribbon tied around the bottle. Turning, she handed it to Beth. "I wish you many years of happiness, sister."

Beth took the Champagne bucket, her eyes watering. "Lily, I couldn't have asked for a better sister. I love you."

"I love you, too." The women hugged.

Razer got up from the table, throwing down the cards he had been dealt. "Ready? I'm done with these card sharks. If I don't leave now, Cash will be riding my bike tomorrow."

He walked to Lily, pulling her close for a hug. "Thanks for the booze, lil' sis. Thanks for the green, Shade. We'll see you guys Sunday." He grabbed a squealing Beth into his arms and Lily rushed to open the side kitchen door for them.

"You're joking about the green, right?"

Razer winked on his way out the door.

Lily shut the door behind them, throwing the dishcloth at Shade.

He caught it midair. "What did I do now? Did I say anything about you giving booze to your sister?" Before she could say anything, he added, "I know, I know. It's legal."

Lily went toward the living room, taking a few steps forward before she realized she hadn't escaped upstairs early enough and now the party was in full swing.

"I don't think that's legal," Shade said from behind her as they watched Jewell giving Rider a blowjob while Train was sitting behind her, smacking her on her bare bottom.

Lily walked sedately to the steps, determined not to run. She almost made it through the crowded room before two stunning blondes, one short and petite and the other long and leggy, descended on Shade with smiles of welcome.

"We've been looking for you. Jewell said the kitchen was off-limits, and your room. What's up? We've missed you, Shade. Hook us up with a room and give that flogger of yours a workout. The last marks you put on us are gone, we need a refresher."

Lily didn't think the woman would ever shut up, each sentence more damning than the last.

Lily's fantasies, which had been burgeoning, withered and died.

"You can have the third bedroom on the left; no one is using it anymore." Lily spun on her feet, heading back toward the kitchen. Shade caught her within a few steps, lifting her up into his arms, and then carried her struggling body back to the steps.

"Shade?" one of the blondes tried again.

"Cash!" Shade snapped.

"I'll take care of it." Cash ushered the women away from Shade, giving him room to pack Lily up the stairs.

Lily tried to get away as soon as they were away from the steps. When she saw she wasn't going to get away, she froze in his arms. As soon as the door closed behind them, he set her down on her feet. Lily hurriedly moved away from him.

"Lily."

Lily held her hand up, stopping whatever he would say. She sat down calmly on the bottom of the bed, facing him. "What do you want from me, Shade?" She could tell her blunt question startled him. "Are you wanting a platonic friendship, friends who have sex, or were you wanting me to fall in love with you? Exactly what do you want?"

"I told you. I want *you*."

Lily nodded her head. Standing up, she went to the dresser, pulling out her ponytail holder and then started brushing her hair while looking at herself in the mirror.

"You don't even know who you want." Lily reached out and briefly touched the mirror she was staring into. Her lips twisted ironically. "You want me because you think I'll be the perfect submissive for you. That weak-minded Lily can be guided and manipulated into being exactly what you want."

She strode angrily across the room to stand in front of

him, sinking to her knees. In perfect posture, she knelt with her back straight, her head lowered, her hair falling against her face. Her hands lay palm-up on her lap.

"I could be everything you ever dreamed of having in a woman." Lily's impassive voice didn't show an ounce of emotion. "You and those women downstairs play games for a few nights a month, but I have dreams and they don't include being your little pet."

Lily got to her feet. "I hope you enjoyed that because I will never," she pointed her finger in his chest, "ever do that again, you big jerk."

Lily started to gather her pajamas.

"Those blonde Barbies are more plastic than the dolls." She turned to look at his face as she was about to go into the bathroom.

"What are you doing?"

Shade was standing with his arms across his chest, watching her as she ranted at him. "Watching your ass jiggle."

"My ass? That's all you can say?" Lily's mouth opened and closed. "If I said what I really wanted to, I would have to pray for forgiveness every night for a week." Lily went into the bathroom, pulling off her clothes and throwing them down on the floor. She turned on the shower before stepping underneath the water. She soaped her body and was rinsing off when the shower door opened and Shade came in.

"What are you doing? I'm naked."

"I can see that." Shade's voice turned seductive. Lily covered her breasts with her hands, unable to keep her eyes from traveling down his lean body. His whole body was covered in tats, everywhere except his dick, which was long and hard, pointing upward toward his belly.

Shade grinned when he saw what she was staring at. "Ignore it. Come here."

"Ignore that thing. You're joking, right? Get out! Didn't you understand a thing I just said to you?"

Lily was torn between keeping her breasts covered and covering her mound. Shade, on the other hand, had no trouble.

Reaching to the side, he picked up the body wash and began washing his body.

"You're seriously not getting out?" Lily screeched.

"No. You take forever in the shower."

"Fine, you can have the shower." Lily tried to pass him, but he refused to move, blocking the door.

"Move your hands." Shade's voice deepened. Lily's hands trembled against her wet flesh. "Eyes to me, Lily. Move your hands." Lily couldn't help herself; she lowered her hands to her side.

Shade crowded her closer to the shower wall, his chest brushing the pointed tips of her breasts. His mouth lowered to her breast, gently licking the drops of water away from her nipple. Lily felt the tip tauten and become a nub. Shade sucked the nipple into his mouth, and her breast was lifted with his hand squeezing the plump flesh. Lily felt her stomach clench, yearning for his touch.

She turned her head to the side and Shade lifted his. "Look at me while I suck your breast. I don't want you to take your eyes off me."

Lily nodded her head.

Shade's mouth went back to her breast and Lily moaned as he teased the tip with his teeth.

"You wanted to know what I want. I want these breasts to suck." Shade lifted his head from her breasts and then went to his knees, his face going between her thighs as he used his hand to widen her stance. "I want this pussy." His tongue went to the cleft of her pussy, sliding between the folds, searching the moist warmth of her silky flesh.

Lily closed her eyes. A flare of pain struck between her thighs as his teeth bit down on her clit briefly before releasing the tortured flesh.

"I told you not to take your eyes off me." He licked at the flesh, taking the sting out and filling her with a pleasure she didn't know could possibly exist. The more he licked at her, the more she wanted.

His tongue went to her opening, entering a tiny bit then withdrawing. Shade's hand slid up her leg, going between her thighs, parting her flesh and finding the wetness his tongue had been playing in.

"You're nice and wet, Lily. Do you know why?"

It took Lily a moment to find her voice. "Yes."

"Tell me why."

"Because I want to come."

"That's right, baby, and I'm going to let you. Do you know why?"

"No," Lily whimpered, her hips arching into his touch.

"Because you're mine and I take care of what's mine. I don't need a pet. I want a flesh-and-blood woman, and yes, Lily, you will kneel in front of me again because it will be one of my needs, just like I plan to satisfy all of yours. Every single one."

As his finger slid deep inside her, Lily's legs almost gave out, but Shade stood up, bracing her body with his against the shower wall. His finger slid deeper and her hands went to his chest, her nails digging into his flesh as his finger began to pump in and out of her slick pussy. She kept her eyes on his blue gaze, seeing that he was in complete control of not only her body but his own. His cock was pressed against her belly, but Lily wasn't frightened.

"Those other women downstairs are no comparison to you. I fucked them, made them beg for me, but they weren't you. No matter how hard I tried to pretend they were." Lily began beating at his chest when he started talking about his women.

His finger slid in faster. "Not one of them could give me as much pleasure as you're giving me now with just my finger inside of you." Lily's heart ached at the tormented expression on his face. Her hands quit beating at his chest, rubbing the smooth flesh instead.

"It hurt so bad waiting for you, Lily. I thought I would

lose my mind. No amount of liquor, women or pot drove you from my mind. I would ride on my bike all the way to your dorm and sit outside just to watch you go to classes in the morning, then drive home and start the whole fucking thing over again.

"That night you were stuck in Sex Piston's beauty shop was the worst night of my life. I didn't get stuck in that traffic jam because I was already on the way to your dorm when Razer called me and told me what was happening.

"I swore when you were in the hospital ER that I was done waiting. Everyone knew I was waiting for you but you. I'm still waiting," he groaned against her neck.

Lily shuddered and cried out as her body convulsed in a series of climatic explosions that had her clinging to him while the water showered down on them.

Shade got out of the shower, drying her shivering body and then helping her dress in her pajamas before sliding on his shorts.

Lifting her, he carried her to the bed, lying down next to her before he pulled the covers over them, wrapping them in a snug cocoon and keeping her close to his side.

"Shade?" Lily whispered.

"Yes?"

"Can I see your flogger?" Lily giggled.

"Not tonight."

CHAPTER TWENTY-NINE

Vida stared out the window, watching for Colton's bike.

"He's not going to get here any faster with you watching."

"I know. I'm just nervous." Vida paced the living room from one end to the other.

Sawyer wanted to join her, yet she remained sitting on the comfortable couch, fiddling with her glass of tea.

A door slam sounded from outside and then the sound of motor bikes coming down the quiet neighborhood street sounded loud until the motors were cut off. Sawyer set her glass down on the table, standing up, unable to hide her own nervousness any longer as the door opened.

Kaden and Colton entered, followed by Ice and Jackal.

"Well?" Sawyer asked as soon as the door closed behind them.

"He got another postponement," Kaden said, unable to hide his anger.

"How much longer is this going to last?" Vida said. "We've been patient, but I don't think this trial is ever going to end." She sat down on the chair in the living room of the house she and Colton had bought.

The holidays were here, and she was miserable. This should be the happiest time of her life, and yet, neither she nor Sawyer could move forward in their own happiness until one last part of their past was resolved.

Callie.

"The state is still trying to cut him a deal, and his fucking lawyer is taking advantage of every loophole there is," Ice said grimly, leaning against the fireplace.

"There's another piece of bad news," Jackal spoke up. "Rip said Callie has moved into The Last Riders' Clubhouse. Penni's brother has laid claim to her."

Sawyer and Vida both turned to look at the scary biker.

"What does that mean?" Vida asked.

"It means The Last Riders aren't going to let you waltz into town and endanger their brother's woman."

"We don't won't to hurt Callie. We just want to talk to her," Sawyer protested.

"Until you can be sure that Digger won't figure out who she is, you'll be endangering her." Jackal's words had both Vida and Sawyer coming to the same reluctant conclusion.

"As soon as Digger's trial is over, we're going to Treepoint," Sawyer said sharply. "His lawyer can't drag it on for much longer."

"Maybe someone will take him out in prison. King's owed a lot of favors," Jackal said, looking down at his boots.

"If it wasn't for those women he's kidnapped, I would have killed him myself to keep Callie safe," Sawyer said, admitting her dark thought.

"What are you going to do if it comes down to them or Callie?" Ice asked.

Sawyer and Vida were quiet for several moments until Sawyer said, "I hope it doesn't, I really do, because I would pick Callie without hesitation. Digger would kill Callie if he could; those other women, as long as they're alive, would have a chance."

"Sawyer…" Vida went to her friend's side.

"It's the truth, Vida. Callie deserves to be happy and safe, and this time we're old enough to do something. I'm going to talk to Penni again and make sure Callie is okay." Sawyer shook her head when she saw the men were about to protest. "I'll be careful not to rouse her suspicions, but I want to make sure she's happy with The Last Riders."

"And if she isn't?" Ice asked Sawyer, but it was Vida who answered.

"Then I guess we'd have a fight on our hands."

* * *

Lily woke up early Thanksgiving morning to put the turkey on to cook. The factory had been closed all week to give everyone a chance to go home for the holidays. She had spent those days with Rachel, preparing to open the church store on Friday. They would take turns working in the store until Pastor Dean found someone to work full time.

Lily hummed to herself as she moved around the kitchen. She had volunteered to help cook the dinner, but Beth would come over when she woke to help. Pouring herself a cup of coffee, she blew on it as she walked across the kitchen to sit at the table.

Bliss came into the kitchen wearing a t-shirt that barely came to the top of her thighs and her short, spiked hair was messed. She was halfway across the kitchen before she realized it wasn't empty.

"I didn't know you were down yet. I was just getting a drink."

"I woke up early to put the turkey on," Lily explained uncomfortably.

Bliss went to the fridge, taking two bottled waters. Lily expected her to leave; instead she came to the table and took a seat in front of Lily.

"I want to apologize."

"For what?" Lily asked.

Bliss bit her lip. "For flirting with Shade in front of you.

I know you caught me a couple of times; I wanted you to."

"Why?" Lily lowered her eyes, not wanting the woman to see she had succeeded in hurting her.

"Because I was having Shade withdrawal," Bliss admitted regretfully. "Truthfully, I was hoping you'd get mad enough to leave and everything would go back to normal."

"With you and Shade back together again?"

"Yes, but not like you're thinking. All of us enjoy having sex with each other. When Razer, Viper and then Knox quit fucking us, it didn't bother me. To be blunt, there's plenty of dicks around here to scratch an itch if a girl gets one. The thing is, Shade scratches a particular itch of mine that none of the others do."

Lily sat there listening quietly to Bliss discuss her and Shade's sex life. Her stomach churned, however she couldn't bring herself to say or do anything to hurt Bliss's feelings.

"I even acted out with Razer, hoping Shade would... but he didn't." Bliss paused. "I was wrong, and I apologized to Beth and Razer. We're cool now. Beth understood and I hope you do, too."

Lily smiled at her. "Of course. I didn't mean to come between you and Shade's... um..." She didn't know how to continue.

Bliss smiled. "You can say I'm a submissive. It doesn't bother me. Lily, you do know that Shade isn't your typical man, don't you?"

Lily turned bright red, almost knocking her coffee cup over. "Typical is not a word I would use to describe Shade."

"No, he's not," Bliss sighed then caught herself, giving Lily a rueful smile. Standing up from the table, she picked up her water bottles.

"Can I ask you a question?"

"Go ahead." Bliss paused, waiting for it.

"What made you change your mind about trying to

break me and Shade up?"

"The night of the Halloween party. I'm not going to lie and say I won't miss Shade, but I can say that I don't mind so much if it's you."

Lily had to clear her throat. "Thanks, Bliss."

She left Lily sitting alone in the kitchen, not knowing exactly how to feel about herself and Shade. The kitchen door opened again and Beth came in, still half-asleep.

"Tell me why we volunteered for this again."

"Because we enjoy cooking for the holidays," Lily suggested.

"That's true." Beth yawned as she poured herself a cup of coffee.

"And because we're nuts."

"I won't disagree with that, either."

After they both finished their coffee, they began cooking all the dishes that the members had requested. It was a massive task, but Evie soon showed up to pitch in and the morning passed quickly.

Lily had set the turkey on the serving platter when Pastor Dean walked into the kitchen with Viper.

"The smell of turkey and stuffing… ask and the Lord shall provide," Pastor Dean said, gazing down at the turkey in admiration.

When Beth teased him that he could eat the twenty-pound bird by himself, the pastor replied, "I don't know about that, but I hope one of those legs has my name on it."

Evie picked the turkey up. "You can take that up with the other men. The Lord only gave this turkey two legs."

Lily picked up a casserole, carrying it out to the dining room where Ember and Stori had decorated the table and all the members who had stayed were already seated. Lily took a chair at the opposite end of where Pastor Dean took his.

Lily sat quietly eating her dinner, not joining the conversation around her unless someone spoke directly to her. After dinner, the desserts were fought over as much as the turkey and stuffing had been. Lily ate a small portion and then began carrying the dirty plates into the kitchen. Shade followed her into the kitchen, packing another stack of dishes.

"You were quiet at dinner."

"Just tired, I guess. It's been a long day," Lily said quietly.

Shade leaned against the counter, watching her face carefully. "Bliss said she had a talk with you this morning. Did something she said upset you?"

"No, we're fine," Lily replied as she loaded the dishwasher.

Shade nodded his head, yet she could tell he sensed her disquiet.

"Ready for some football?" Rider asked as the rest of the club came through the kitchen to go into the television room.

"Go ahead. I'm going to head to bed when I finish," Lily urged, waving her hand at Shade to go.

"I'll be up after the game."

"Okay."

Shade left, going into the room to find a space on the already overflowing couch.

"Need any help?" Beth asked.

"Nope, I've got it covered. I'm almost finished. Go watch the game."

"I think I will. I'm exhausted." Lily watched as her sister sat down on the arm of the couch next to Razer. Reaching up, he tugged her down onto his lap and then Beth laid her head on his shoulder. The love between them brought a lump to Lily's throat.

She finished the dishes, wiping her hands on the dishcloth before folding it and placing it on the counter. Instead of going to bed, she slipped out the kitchen door while everyone's attention was on the game. Taking a deep breath, she walked across the backyard, taking the path to

Shade's house. She climbed the steps to the porch then sat down on the top step. Sitting there, she looked out over the vast expanse of the mountains, not feeling the temperature drop as night began to fall.

"You're going to get sick sitting out here in the cold without a jacket." Pastor Dean walked to the bottom of the steps, looking up at her.

Lily tensed; she hadn't seen him approach from the house.

"I was just about to go in," Lily replied.

When Pastor Dean walked up the steps, taking a seat next to her, Lily turned her face away from him.

"Why have you been avoiding me?" Pastor Dean asked quietly.

"I haven't been avoiding you. I saw you last week at the store and Sunday at church."

"You hide behind Rachel at the store and you take off as soon as church is over, and you haven't said two words to me today. What's wrong, Lily?"

She leaned her head against the wooden rail next to her, not letting him see her face in the darkness. "Because I'm so ashamed," Lily's voice trembled.

"What on earth have you got to be ashamed of?" His stunned voice only made Lily want to hide from him more.

"Because I don't belong in your church." Lily licked her cold lips. "I'm not the person you think I am. I've done things, Pastor Dean. Things I know that God's not going to forgive me for."

"Lily, don't. Please don't think like that." He reached out to touch her shoulder, but Lily moved away, not wanting him to touch her. She was too unclean to even be sitting next to him.

"It's true. I...I..." Lily's voice firmed. "Before I came to Treepoint to live with Beth's parents, I lived with my mother. She... she wasn't a nice person. She had me do things, Pastor, to men she would bring to our apartment." She shuddered, remembering the revolting things she had been forced to do. "I didn't want to, but she would make me drink liquor so that I wouldn't fight them. I quit fighting what she wanted me to do so she wouldn't make me drink it anymore. Do you think God will forgive me for that? She told me that, if I told my friends, she would kill them. I knew she would because I was her daughter and she didn't care if I was dead or alive. She just wanted the money they would give her for me."

"Dear God. Lily, stop…" Pastor Dean's voice was hoarse, yet Lily continued. She had to make him see that she didn't deserve to be in his company, that he wasn't the one at fault for her not being the Christian he believed her to be.

"If she couldn't find someone for me, she would send me to apartments where she knew that the men lived alone and make me ask if they wanted company for the night. I learned how to do what she wanted or she would beat me so bad, I couldn't go outside and play with my friends until I healed. If anyone came to ask about me, she would tell them I was too sick to play."

"What happened to your mother?" Pastor Dean's voice was harsh.

"Her boyfriend moved in with us. He was nice for a while. He paid the bills and gave her money to spend. He even bought me my first doll, but she would get mad at him because he wouldn't give her extra money for her pills, so she would wait until he went to work and sneak men into the apartment.

"One day, he came home early and saw me in bed with a man. Marshall pulled a gun out and made them sit on the bed, and told me to get dressed. I heard him call someone, but I was too scared to listen. He made us all sit there until someone knocked on the door."

"Who was it?"

"I don't know. I'd never seen him before, but he was big and scary to me because, when Marshall told him what he'd seen when he came home, he took the gun and killed my mother and the man on my bed." Lily took a deep breath. "Then he turned to me, asking me if Marshall had ever touched me and when I told him yes, he killed Marshall. He lit a fire on my bed and made me leave with him. I didn't try to scream; I was too scared."

"I bet you were," Pastor Dean said grimly.

"He took me on a long drive. I slept most of the time. When I woke up, I was in Beth's house and he was gone. Her parents told me they were adopting me and to forget about my mom and the life I had before, so I did. I made myself forget every dirty thing that I had been forced to do. I forgot the men. I forgot my mom. I forgot Marshall. I forgot my sitter who always smelled like chocolate chip cookies. I forgot my friends, Sawyer and Vida, who were like sisters to me. I forgot every single ugly detail of my life until I forgot me."

CHAPTER THIRTY

"Lily, look at me." Lily didn't want to see the look of disgust she was certain would be on his face.

"Please, look at me." Lily turned her head to see his face in the darkness. Instead of seeing the disgust she'd expected, she saw compassion and love.

In that second, Lily broke. She cried for the child who had never been a child, for all the years she had spent afraid of her own shadow, and most of all, she cried for a future she was afraid to begin with Shade.

Pastor Dean put his arm around her shoulders, letting her cry until she lay quietly against him.

"I promised myself I wasn't going to cry anymore," Lily said, embarrassed at her lapse.

"I think that one was well deserved. That's why you wanted to become a social worker, isn't it, to help children like yourself?"

Lily nodded her head. "Yes, I think so."

"Lily, do you plan on judging children if you find them in situations like you were in?"

"Of course not," Lily said, shocked that he thought she would.

"When people start coming into the church store

tomorrow, are you going to judge them for being in need?"

"No," she repeated. "They need our help."

"Yes, they do, like you needed help, and no one was there for you. You chose to survive, Lily. You're the kindest, most compassionate woman I know, and it's a true miracle that part of you wasn't destroyed. As your pastor, I couldn't be more proud. You make my Sundays worthwhile because, when I look out into my congregation and see your face, I know that God has graced my church with your presence.

"You have done nothing to feel ashamed of. The ones who should be ashamed are the ones that are responsible for hurting you. You don't have any lessons to learn from me, but I have many to learn from you, Lily, because as God is my witness, I would have killed every single one of the bastards who touched you."

"Thank you, Pastor." Lily smiled at him, relieved he hadn't thought less of her.

"Go on inside. It's freezing out here. I'll see you in the morning."

She stood up, pausing when he didn't follow. "Aren't you coming in?"

"In a minute. I want to say a prayer."

"Would you like me to stay and pray with you?"

"No, you've been out here long enough. I won't be long."

"Goodnight."

"Goodnight, Lily."

* * *

"You don't deserve her."

"I know," Shade said, walking out of the shadows, not taking his eyes off Lily as she walked back toward the clubhouse.

"It's a good thing they're all dead or we would be riding tonight."

"It seems they're all dead but one," Shade said

thoughtfully, turning to his brother.

Dean frowned at him. "Which one?"

"The one who gave her to Beth's parents."

"You think that something from her past may be why someone is trying to kill her?"

"Whoever has been watching her house has been doing it for years. Who else could it be?" Shade said, coming to the only conclusion that made any sense.

"Damn."

"Talk to Knox, tell him what we found out tonight. I'm going to talk to Beth and see if she remembers anything from when Lily first came to live with them. At this point, any adoption papers, even fake ones, would be a lead." Shade's only hope of finding the papers was Beth.

"I'll talk to him before he leaves tonight."

"Let's get inside. I don't want Lily alone tonight."

They walked up the path together. Shade was about to go inside when Dean's hand on his arm stopped him. "Promise me one thing."

"What?" Shade asked.

"If we find out whoever took her could have stopped that shit, I get him first."

* * *

Lily wearily climbed into bed, pulling the covers over her as she shivered. The click of the door opening and closing barely drew her notice; she couldn't stop her teeth from chattering.

The covers were briefly pulled back and Shade's warm body enveloped hers as he pressed against her back. His arm circled her waist, drawing her closer. The covers were pulled over them, wrapping her in a cocoon of warmth.

"Shade?"

"Yes?"

"That day in the diner when I had that panic attack, there was a little girl at one of the tables. What happened?"

"I had left with you, but Knox told me that Diamond had seen you staring at the family. Knox talked to them.

The little girl was placed in her grandmother's custody."

"It's funny how things turn out, isn't it?"

"I don't think it's funny at all," Shade said, pulling her tighter.

"I believe sometimes it's meant for us to have to bear trials so that we can recognize how to help others." Lily's voice grew drowsy.

"Go to sleep." Shade's voice was soothing in the darkness. It was then Lily realized the room was encased in darkness. She hadn't turned the bathroom light on.

Her hand laced through Shade's, confident he would keep her safe while she slept.

* * *

When Lily beat Rachel to the store in the morning, there was already a line forming outside. Pastor Dean was waiting for her inside. He looked as if he hadn't slept.

"Are you sick?" Lily asked.

"No. I just woke up this morning with a headache. I'll be fine as soon as I get my coffee. Rachel's stopping by the diner before she gets here."

"Great." Lily stood by the door, anxious to let the people in. They had already taken applications earlier in the week and had decided how everyone would be allowed to take things they needed, giving each family a limit of store credit based on their financial need.

Rachel maneuvered through the crowd, bringing each person a steaming cup of coffee.

"Are we ready for this?" She grinned when she finally came inside.

"Yes." Lily was fired up, ready to help those who stood waiting.

"I have a feeling this is going to be a long day." With that said, Pastor Dean opened the door.

At first, they were nearly overwhelmed by the number of those coming in; however, Lily had organized the paperwork over the last week, and because they were the ones who had stocked the store, they were able to help the customers find the items they needed quickly.

They easily worked out a method for moving people through: Rachel and Pastor Dean worked the store, and when people found the items they needed, they would then be sent to Lily at the counter. She would check the amount of aide they had available for the month, then bag their items for them. It was a rewarding experience for Lily, seeing those in need were given simple basics that would make their lives easier.

By midday, the customers had slowed to a trickle, so Pastor Dean excused himself, explaining he was scheduled to give a counseling session.

"If I didn't know better, I would think Pastor Dean had a hangover." Rachel's speculative voice drew her attention from filing paperwork.

"I'm sure you're wrong. He told me he had a headache this morning."

"I have three brothers; I'm very familiar with the signs of a hangover. Pastor Dean has all the symptoms. Did you see his face when I handed him his sandwich?"

"Yes, but I'm not a fan of meatloaf sandwiches, either. I'm sure it gets old having to eat other's cooked food all the time."

"Maybe." Rachel's tone still sounded doubtful.

Lily didn't get the chance to talk about it further because the door opened and closed, bringing in more customers. Lily worked steadily as a member of the congregation came in searching for winter coats for her children. Lily knelt in front of the little five-year-old, helping her zip a jacket up.

Her little hand tugged the fur collar up, brushing her face with the soft fur. "Can I have this one, Mama?"

The mother looked inquiringly at Lily.

"Of course you can." Lily smiled at the little girl's excited face.

Standing up, she searched through the racks until she found one for her older brother. Going through a plastic tub, she then found each of them gloves.

She bagged everything up, handing the mother the large bag.

"Thank you." The woman started to say something else then gripped the bag tighter in her hand.

Lily knew what the woman wanted to ask without being told. Coming out from behind the counter, she put her arm around her shoulders.

"I think Mom needs a little something for herself." Lily led her to another coat rack, going through several before the woman found one that would fit.

"There. Now everyone has a new coat." Lily reached out, hugging the smiling woman. "Come back the first of December. We'll have the Christmas section open and you can choose some toys for them."

The woman nodded. "I will. I don't like to take help, but Brian was hurt on a construction job. He's been looking for something that's not as strenuous, but he hasn't found anything yet. I have several applications out, but no one's hiring."

"That's why we opened the store. We're happy to help," Lily said matter-of-factly, sensitive to the woman's pride.

"Thank you, Lily."

"Bye, Christy." Lily watched the small family leave, filled with a sense of satisfaction.

"It makes all of our hard work worth it, doesn't it?" Rachel said, straightening one of the clothes racks.

"Yes, it does."

Rachel went to lock the door, staring out the window. "Now that's one man I wouldn't mind fighting my brothers over," she said.

Lily kept filing the paperwork but glanced up briefly, noticing Rachel still staring out the window. "Who?" Lily asked curiously.

"There's someone new in town. He's talking on his cell phone. The hood to his car is up. Jeez, Lily, he's dressed in a suit. I bet he was driving through town and his car broke down. Darn, why can't someone who looks like that move to town?"

"That good?"

"Oh, yeah. If I knew anything about cars, I would have been gone five minutes ago. That car looks expensive, too. Good looking and has money. What else could a woman ask for?"

"Maybe he's a jerk," Lily warned.

"I wouldn't care," Rachel said reverently.

Lily laughed, coming out from behind the counter and walking toward the window.

"Where?" she asked Rachel, gazing out the window.

"There." She pointed out the window. "He's going inside the diner."

Lily saw a tall, broad shoulder man walking into the diner. She only managed to catch a brief glimpse of his back as he walked inside. He had jet-black hair and even Lily could tell the suit he wore was expensive.

The car parked in front of the diner was one of the luxury models she had seen advertised on television.

"Maybe it'll take a couple of days for him to fix his car," Rachel said hopefully.

Lily grinned at her friend before turning away. "You could always go to the diner and get us some coffee," Lily suggested.

"You think?" Rachel grinned back.

"Go for it."

Rachel grabbed her purse, taking off out the door before Lily could suggest it twice.

Lily went back to work, and Rachel was gone quite a while before she walked back into the store carrying the coffee.

"How did it go?" Lily asked curiously.

"We were right. He was passing through when his car broke down. He's even better looking close-up, too, but he's older than I thought. My brothers would lock me up and throw away the key if I tried to get to know him better."

"Did you get his number?" Lily wanted to know how bold Rachel had gotten with the stranger.

"No, but I did get his name," she said triumphantly.

"Oh, what was it?" Lily asked.

"King."

CHAPTER THIRTY-ONE

"Well, that's different."

"I know. Isn't it cool?" Rachel said, setting the coffee down on the counter.

"Did he say where he was from?" Lily pulled a stool up to the counter, taking one of the coffees.

"I forgot to ask." Rachel looked nonplussed for a second. "Oh, well, it really doesn't matter. He already has two strikes against him: he's too old and he's from out of town."

Not long after, Lily saw Shade pull up outside. She threw her empty coffee cup away in the nearby trashcan. "I'll see you next week."

"Bye, Lily."

Until Pastor Dean could find someone to run the store, it would only be able to stay open on Wednesdays and Saturdays. The store really needed to be open more frequently during the winter; she worried about so many going without their basic needs during the winter months.

Lily climbed onto the bike behind Shade after putting on her helmet, noticing the broken-down car was already gone.

When they got back to the clubhouse, she recognized

Sex Piston and her crew's car. Killyama was leaning against it with her arms folded, glaring at Rider as he talked to her.

Train was working on one of the bikes, watching the argument with an amused expression.

Lily got off the bike and Shade took her helmet from her hand. Lily greeted Beth's friend as she drew closer.

"Hey, girl." Killyama didn't remove her glare from Rider.

"What's going on?" Shade asked.

Lily listened curiously; she had been too polite to ask, but obviously, Shade didn't have the same hesitation.

"I was supposed to give her a ride today," Rider nodded his head sharply at Killyama, "but my bike won't start. She thinks I'm fucking with her."

"Babe, if you were fucking with me, I'd hope I would know it." Killyama grinned evilly at the furious Rider.

Lily had to look away to keep from laughing at Rider. The laid-back man didn't stand a chance against the biker woman.

"I meant that I wasn't trying to get out of giving you a ride." His choice of words didn't make the situation any better; he kept digging himself into a bigger hole.

"I know what you meant. Do I look stupid?"

Silence met her question.

Killyama was dressed in leather pants and a black t-shirt that had a skull with a dagger in the eye. It read "Come and get me." Her make-up was dark and smoky, and her biker boots had metal spokes sticking out. She didn't look stupid, yet she did appear scary as heck. Especially for a man who loved women who were very feminine. *At least he makes an attempt to be a gentleman*, Lily thought when he ignored her question.

"We'll have to make it another day. I have to order a part," Rider hedged.

"You've already put me off three times. I'm tired of this shit. Forget it." She turned around, opening her car door as she gave Shade a smirk. "The Last Riders don't know how to keep their word. Good to know for future reference."

Shade stiffened. He was the one who had promised Killyama a ride for saving her life. Lily didn't even want to know what Shade had held over Rider's head to make him come through.

"I'll give you a ride myself," Shade said, giving in to the woman's demands.

"No offense, but I don't ride with a man who's got a woman at his back." Lily took that to mean she wasn't going to ride with Shade because of her. In that moment, Lily knew she liked the woman.

She heard Shade's teeth grinding at her answer.

"I'll give you a ride," Train said, setting down the tool he was holding.

This time Killyama remained quiet, tilting her head to the side as she studied the man like he was a side of beef. *Oh, heck*, Lily thought, noticing Train's eyes narrowing on Killyama.

Since moving in with The Last Riders, she had learned one thing about Train: the man was a wild card, and you never knew how he would react. He was the calmest of the men, yet he actually had the worst temper. You could never be certain if he was going to respond with a smile or a fist until it was too late.

"Deal." Killyama shut the car door.

As Train led the way to his bike, getting on, Lily watched as Killyama got on behind him, snuggling close as she wound her arms around his waist.

"Do you think they'll kill each other?" Lily couldn't resist asking as they turned onto the road.

"I think there's a fifty-fifty chance." Shade's mocking remark had Lily unable to hold back her grin.

"You know you're going to owe him big time." Lily felt like she needed to give Rider a heads-up.

"It'll be worth any price," Rider said fervently.

"That wasn't nice. She's a really sweet woman."

Both men looked at her dubiously, but neither of them disagreed with her out loud.

Lily strode away, leaving both men to follow silently behind her. She walked through the front door and went straight upstairs to get changed into her workout clothes. She needed to wash a few clothes and she wanted to exercise so she could accomplish both goals at the same time.

Her favorite workout outfits needed washing, so she had to resort to the more revealing one she hated to wear. She changed and was organizing the clothes when Shade came into the bedroom.

"Rider is going to work with me at my house for a few hours."

"All right, I'm going to take care of the laundry."

"I'll pack them down for you."

"I can handle a basket of clothes," Lily told him.

Shade picked up the basket anyway, waiting for her by the door. Lily heaved a frustrated sigh then gave in, going out the door and down the steps. She felt self-conscious in her outfit, even though she knew she was being ridiculous. She didn't even know why it bothered her; most of the members had gone home for the holidays, and those who had remained were getting caught up on their shopping and sleep.

"Thanks."

"No problem. If you need anything, just call."

"Okay." Lily rolled her eyes as he left. He was taking her protection too seriously. She wasn't used to being constantly surrounded by someone; even Beth gave her space.

She started a load of clothes then began her stretching and floor exercises, enjoying working out. It served to relieve a lot of her tension and she liked how it made her feel.

She did another load of clothes after putting the others in the dryer, turning on the sound system before beginning her weight routine. She took her time as she worked with the new weights that had just been delivered that day. When she was finished, she checked on her clothes, putting the last of them in the dryer and then folding the other ones. She was still full of energy as she then went to the exercise equipment and stared at the treadmill then at the pole. She hated treadmills; they were boring.

Since she was alone in the house, she stepped toward the pole. She began her routine, one movement after another, following each other seamlessly. She worked herself to the top, and with her arms giving her leverage, slid her legs out from the pole. Her arms were shaky after just lifting weights, yet she managed to keep a firm grip before circling the pole with her thighs. Sliding down, she stopped her momentum a few feet from the floor, and using her thighs, she held onto the pole, going backwards until her hands touched the floor. Releasing her grip on the pole, she flipped her body, doing a brief handstand before continuing to flip until she stood straight, facing the steps. The buzzer for the dryer went off and she moved to finish folding the clothes.

Shade was there, sitting on the couch and staring at her with a look that made goose bumps rise on her arms. He had come in and hadn't even let her know he was there.

"How long have you been there?" she asked suspiciously.

"Long enough to see you climb then come down the pole."

"Oh." Lily went to the dryer, pulling out the clothes and putting them in the basket. She would fold them in the room.

"Come here, Lily."

"Uh, no," Lily said firmly.

"Why?"

"Because I can tell by the way you're looking at me that… you're in a mood," she finished helplessly.

"You're right. I'm in the mood to fuck. Come. Here."

Lily's trembling hands set the basket down on the dryer. She slowly walked toward him. "Shade..."

"What do you call me when we're down here?" he reminded her.

Lily stopped in front of him. She wasn't going to play his games.

His hand came out, cupping the back of her knee, touching the flesh below her workout shorts.

"Answer me." Shade's firm expression wasn't harsh; however, he left no doubt that he expected her to obey him.

"Sir." Lily felt the word leave her lips.

He raised her knee, pulling it toward him until she had to raise her other knee on the other side of his hip or she would fall on top of him. This position wasn't much better. She was kneeling over him while he looked up at her. His hands slid up the sides of her thighs, sliding around toward her butt until his hands cupped her bottom, pulling her toward him.

"Kiss me."

Lily bent down, touching her mouth to his. Shade parted her lips, sucking her tongue into his mouth. Lily explored his mouth, tasting the hint of mint on his breath.

His hand slid forward from behind, rubbing her crotch through the thin material of her shorts. The place he was rubbing teased her flesh with a brief touch before sliding back, not giving her a full caress, only a promise. Lily moaned, unable to help herself. He slid his hand back and forth until her butt was pushing back against his hand and her arms circled his neck.

Shade leaned forward, rising to his feet with her thighs clenching his hips as he carried her back to his bedroom. He opened the door, and then closed it with his foot. Bending down, he laid her on the side of the bed before rising and standing between her spread thighs.

He turned to the bedside table, turning on the small lamp. The light switching on was like one going on in her brain, asking herself what she was doing.

In a split second, she had turned and scrambled off the other side of the bed, breathing heavily. Her breasts lifted and fell with her erratic breathing. Pushing her hair back from her face, she noticed where his attention was directed.

"Cut it out, Shade." Lily blew out a deep breath, unconsciously rubbing her tummy. "I can't do that." She motioned to the bed.

"Why not?" he asked, staring at her in amusement. His eyes dropped to her hand's tell-tale movements.

Lily quickly dropped her hand to her side. "Because I'm not ready yet. I haven't made my mind up if I want to and…" she paused, "I've always planned to wait until I was married." Lily lowered her eyes to the floor. "It means a lot to me," she finished lamely, aware her face showed her embarrassment.

"I see." Shade walked toward the door, opening it for her.

Relieved, she walked toward the doorway. "Thanks, Sir." She gave him a relieved smile.

"No problem."

Lily gave him a curious look as she went through the doorway, surprised and a little hurt. She hadn't expected him to take it so well. Was he planning on finding sex elsewhere if she didn't? It wasn't like he would have to search far.

Morosely, she followed him up the stairs to their bedroom where she showered and changed while he used the shower in the hallway. She had to grit her teeth when they went downstairs for dinner and he actually whistled.

Evie had fixed a huge roast with all the fixings. Lily ate as she watched Shade talk to the others at the table. It took her by surprise to see that someone was missing.

"Train isn't back yet?" Lily asked with a frown.

"Who are you worried about? Killyama or Train?" Rider questioned with a grin.

The whole table cracked up. Lily wanted to throw something; they just didn't understand the abrasive woman. She wanted to think that underneath Killyama's gruff attitude lay a sweet woman, but there wasn't. That was Sex Piston. Killyama was as fierce on the inside as she was on the outside. Lily actually liked that about her; she was loyal and she wouldn't take anyone's bull. Her best feature was the one that had saved her life—she would protect anyone she cared about.

The door opened and closed with a slam. They all sat watching as Train fixed himself a plate, piling on food and then sat down at the table.

"Well?" Rider asked.

"Well what?" Train asked with a glare.

"How did it go?"

"How the fuck do you think it went? The woman is a fucking lunatic. She thought I would let her drive my bike."

"What happened when you told her no?" Lily asked, dreading his answer.

"She tried to climb in front of me. I almost wrecked my bike." He tore the top off his beer, taking a long drink. "When I brought her back here to her car, she actually thought I was going to fuck her." He shook his head in disbelief.

"What happened when you told her no?" Lily asked apprehensively.

This time Train remained quiet.

The shocked silence had Train lifting the beer to his mouth, finishing it in a long swallow. Lily tried to smother her laugher, yet she was unsuccessful.

"Did you manage to tame the bitch?" Rider asked with a smirk.

At that, all hell broke loose. Train's fist flew out, hitting Rider in the jaw and knocking him backwards, toppling the chair and him over. Lily screamed, standing up from the table, about to go to Rider's aide, but Shade took her arm, pulling her away.

Train threw himself on Rider when he attempted to stand up. The two fought on the floor, throwing their fists viciously at each other, striking whatever body part they could reach while Viper and Nickel tried to pull them apart.

"Stop!" Winter yelled. "You two are scaring Lily." Everyone except Winter froze, looking at Lily in trepidation, waiting for her to have one of her panic attacks.

Beth relaxed first, familiar with Winter's machinations. Lily's twinkling violet eyes had the other members turning to Winter suspiciously. She shrugged, sitting back down at the table, and then continued to eat. Lily joined her with the others gradually retaking their seats, as well. Finally, Train held his hand out to Rider, helping him to his feet. Both returned to their seats to finish their own dinners.

Gradually, the atmosphere relaxed and no one else dared to ask about either of Train's rides.

Lily and Beth cleaned the table, leaving Winter and Ember to do the dishes. Shade, Train and Rider began a game of cards while several others began a game of pool in the corner of the room. Since everyone was behaving well, Lily lingered downstairs, talking with Stori. When Raci and Jewell came down, though, Lily knew it was time to disappear.

As she passed the card table, Shade reached up, pulling her down to sit on his lap while he continued to play cards. Lily's back was to the room so that she was unable to see what was going on behind her. She relaxed against Shade, looking down at his cards. Someone put some music on and she heard them moving the furniture so they could dance. Lily was determined to go upstairs when they finished the hand they were playing. When Shade won, she clapped for him. Then they began another game.

"Do you want to play?" Shade asked.

"I don't know how," Lily said regretfully.

"I'll teach you."

The next hour Shade taught her how to play. Rider got up from the table, going into the kitchen and then coming back with beers for the men, placing a soda in front of Lily.

"Unless you want a beer?"

"No, thanks." Lily opened the soda, taking a drink. A moan sounded behind her back and she started to get up.

"It's your turn," Shade reminded her.

Lily took her turn, trying to ignore the escalating moans.

She forced herself to watch their game. From the sounds behind her it was too late to leave anyway. Gradually, the moans died away and Lily was able to concentrate once again.

She was winning steadily with a pile of cash sitting in front of her. She couldn't help thinking of the people at the church it would help this close to Christmas.

She scooted her latest winnings into the pile sitting in front of her.

"Sucker." She grinned at Train across the table.

"Beginner's luck," he mumbled, dealing another hand.

Lily looked down at her cards, stifling the grin that threatened to break loose.

"Can I join?" Jewell came up behind Train, circling his neck. He reached around to pull her down onto his lap and then he dealt her a hand.

"Ante up."

Lily tried not to notice Train's hand slide across Jewell's thigh. *It's time to cash in and leave*, Lily thought.

"I don't have any money. How about we play for favors?" Jewell's hand went to Train's lap.

"Okay with me. I need my room cleaned," Train teased, pulling at her top. Jewell playfully hit his shoulder.

"Okay with you, Lily?" Shade asked, his arm circling her waist.

Lily could just see all three of the men sitting in church

315

this Sunday. "I'm in."

"I don't like that vindictive look in your eyes, but I'm in," Rider agreed.

Lily looked expectantly up at Shade.

"Are you sure you want to play?" he questioned her.

She eagerly nodded her head.

"Deal."

Train dealt the cards. Lily gazed down at her cards, still smiling. She had to hastily place an impassive expression on her face or she was going to lose before she'd even started.

When it came time to place the bets, Jewell got a pad and paper and wrote household services. Ripping the paper off, she threw it onto the middle of the table.

"Of course that means a lot of services that I can perform in the house."

Train wrote on the paper "An hour of my time," throwing the slip of paper into the pot as well.

Rider did the same then Shade. When they handed her the paper, she wrote what the men had, "An hour of my time," not wanting to perform any of the services that Jewell probably had planned. Lily tore off the paper, throwing it in the growing pile.

The game continued. When it came time to bet again, the pen and paper made the rounds again. Everyone's IOUs stayed the same except for Jewell. Lily's mouth dropped open when she described what she had written. She was about to throw it into the pot.

"Uh, excuse me. It's nothing personal, but I don't want that."

"Are you sure?" Jewell didn't try to hide her disappointment.

"I'm sure," Lily replied firmly.

"Perhaps you should just bet what we are?" Shade suggested.

Jewell wrote down "An hour of time." The game resumed with more calls to ante up. Lily was practically bouncing on Shade's lap; her cards were so good.

Then it went to hell. Slowly but inexplicably, Lily realized she was going to lose. Minutes later, Shade grinned as he raked his winnings across the table. Lily didn't know what made her more upset, that she had lost or that he had Jewell's IOUs.

"I'm done for the night. Good game," Shade said. His hand on her hips had her standing so that he could rise to his feet. He reached down onto the table, stacking his papers then sliding them into his pocket before reaching back to collect Lily's winnings and handing them to her.

"Thank you," she said, taking the cash from him.

"It was my pleasure. Later." Shade nodded to the table. Lily turned to go upstairs.

"Lily." She turned her head to see him shaking his. "We're going downstairs for a couple of hours first." Lily stopped. "Unless you want to renege on a bet?"

Everyone at the table paused, looking at her.

Lily cleared her voice. "Of course not."

"I knew you were honest, going to church as often as you do."

Lily reluctantly followed Shade downstairs, lagging slightly behind. She was still trying to figure out how she had landed in her current predicament when Shade closed and locked the door.

"Shade…"

"Take off your clothes."

Lily didn't move.

"So you don't plan to keep your word."

She sucked in a sharp breath. "Yes, but choose something else."

Shade reached into his pocket, pulling out the slips of paper, flipping through them. Opening one, he showed her the piece of paper.

"There are no exceptions or exclusions on this paper. You should have made that clear."

"I thought stuff like that would only count when it was

worded like Jewell did. I didn't…"

"Then you should have asked. Again, there are no exceptions. I won several hours of your time. Do you or do you not plan to keep your word?"

"Yes," Lily finally answered.

"Good. Now take your clothes off." When she didn't move, only stared at him helplessly, he sighed. "Lily, do you trust me? I mean, really trust me?"

Lily thought over the time she had known him, how he had always been gentle and kind to her despite the suspicion she'd had that he wasn't a kind man. In fact, she believed he was exactly the opposite. He hadn't shown it to her even when he had threatened Beth and Razer's home, yet he hadn't taken advantage by making her have sex with him. He had made her sleep in the bed, and if she was honest, she had been pretty sick of the floor after two nights. She remembered the extra padding on the floor in her safe corner. At that, her thoughts snapped in place. She had a safe place in the room she could go. He had promised that he would never touch her there, and she'd believed him. She still did. She had her answer.

"Yes, I trust you."

"Good, now take off your clothes. This time, I'll let you leave your bra and panties on. Will that make you feel better?"

Lily nodded her head, relieved he had relented on her being naked. She undressed, pulling off her clothes and laying them on the chair.

As she undressed, she saw Shade pull off his t-shirt and remove his socks and boots. When she turned back to face him, the door to his closet was open and he was going through his items.

"Lay down on the bed."

Lily climbed on the bed, sitting on her knees waiting. Shade turned on his stereo; the room filled with soft music. When Shade got on the bed beside her, his finger traced her cheek down to her throat. She swallowed as his hand lowered and he traced the edges of her bra above her breast. Her breathing escalated at his touch.

"You have beautiful breasts." Shade's lips traced the same path his fingers had followed, from her check to the flesh above her plain white bra. He lifted her hand and then Lily watched as he buckled a fur lined leather cuff onto her wrist. Her mouth opened to protest.

"No exclusions, Lily," Shade reminded her once again.

She closed her mouth. Another leather cuff closed over her other wrist.

"Lay down."

She lay down on the mattress as he reached for something else on the bedside table. He brought out chains, which he clicked into the side of the cuffs. One at a time, he locked each of the chains to a hook positioned on the bottom of the headboard that the mattress had kept hidden.

As Shade sat on his knees, looking down at her, Lily dreaded to see what he was reaching for on the nightstand this time. The plain silk scarf was anti-climatic and not as scary looking as the flogger she had thought he would have.

After Shade tied the silk scarf around her eyes, his hand slid across her stomach where her muscles quivered. He didn't say anything as his hand traced over her body, lingering at her ankles before she felt the brush of his lips. His hand then traveled to her hips as his lips brushed where his hand had been. Over and over, he explored every area of her body with his hands and mouth.

When his hand slid to her panties, pulling them off, Lily tensed. His hand went between her thighs, exploring her as he slid easily across her damp flesh until her legs tried to close to press his hand harder against her. His light touch wasn't going to be able to bring her over the edge to reach the climax she had been waiting for.

The music started getting louder, the beat faster, as she tried to catch that wisp of a touch that was about to drive her crazy.

"Shade, please…"

A sharp slap against her pussy had her almost climaxing. Lily shuddered.

"How are you supposed to address me when we're in this bed?"

"Sir."

"Now ask me how you're supposed to."

"Sir, please, I want to come."

His hand left her immediately and Lily wanted to ask what she had done wrong this time; however, his body moving between her legs forestalled her. With no warning, she felt his mouth on her pussy, his tongue finding and sliding between the lips to her clit, rubbing it into a frenzy that had her arching upwards. The wet warmth of his tongue moving on her was an unbearable pleasure. Lily couldn't think of one thing that had ever felt as good or would ever feel as good as what she was experiencing now.

He first licked and then sucked her clit into spasms, which had her screaming her climax out as the music rose and then ended abruptly before going back to a soothing rhythm as he stroked her body, bringing her down from the orgasm while still leaving an ache. She wanted more inside of her. He rose over her, releasing the chains and taking the cuffs off before removing the blindfold.

"Thank you for trusting me, Lily." He brushed a tender kiss against her cheek.

"You're welcome, Sir." Shade grinned at her, helping her off the bed and into her clothes. He dressed as she put her shoes back on before storing everything back in his cabinet, locking it and then leading her from the room with an arm around her shoulders to their room upstairs.

Lily changed into her pajamas, climbing into bed, drowsy but unable to fall asleep until Shade came to bed, pulling the covers over them both. She lay, staring up at the ceiling in the dark room, understanding how Bliss had become addicted to his games. She was terrified she would, too, and unlike Bliss, she would never recover from the loss once he was gone.

CHAPTER THIRTY-TWO

Lily had to force herself out of bed Monday. In the two weeks since Thanksgiving, she had been working full-time at the factory and then on her days off, she'd worked at the church store.

Pastor Dean had tried three parishioners who he had thought would do well running the store, but they had proven either incapable of gossiping afterword about everyone's income, or thought that what came out of the store would come out of their own back pockets, or they hadn't been giving them enough aide. They even turned some in need away. Luckily, Pastor Dean had started each new prospective manager with either Lily or Rachel present and they were able to prevent all of the harm they could have caused the burgeoning program.

Lily carried her coffee cup to the factory. Opening the door, she was aware that she was ten minutes late when Georgia gave her a malicious smile as she placed a red mark on Lily's time card. Ignoring her, Lily set her coffee cup on her worktable before going to the work board where she saw no orders posted. Everyone coming in had eagerly taken them with it being Monday. By Friday, the board would still be half-full. She went to the computer, pulling up the next order and making a copy.

With the order in hand, she began moving around the room, filling it. By midday, she had completed several orders. Lunch was spent with Shade on the phone most of the time, talking with a manufacturer.

She had been in an uncharacteristically bad mood this morning, and after lunch, it grew much worse. Since that night two weeks ago, Shade hadn't touched her. She had begun wondering if he had cashed in his other IOUs, including Jewell's, which was the only one she really cared about.

"Lily." Shade came to the doorway of his office with a cell phone in his hand. "The coffee pot isn't working; could you go to the house and get me a cup?"

"Get it yourself!" she snapped, slapping the tape dispenser down onto the worktable. The room went silent at her sharp remark.

"I'll get it for you, boss," Georgia offered with a fake, sweet smile.

"No, thanks, Georgia. I'll take care of it. Lily, come here." Lily started to refuse that request, too, but figured she had pushed her luck enough for the day.

She went into his office, closing the door behind her. Shade had resumed his seat behind the desk and swiveled his chair to face her in the doorway.

"Want to tell me what burr has crawled up your ass?"

"No, I don't."

Instead of him getting angry like any normal man, he gave her a grin that had a shiver running down her back. "Lock the door."

"Fine." Lily went to the door, about to make her escape.

"From the inside, Lily. And if you think to disobey me, have no doubt I will punish you in the other room in front of every man and woman busy working. We really don't want to disturb their work even further, do we?"

"I don't suppose so." Lily reluctantly locked the door.

"When I asked you to close the door, you knew which side I wanted you on, didn't you?"

"Yes." Lily slowly turned back to face him.

"I see. You were being cute. I like cute; you being a smartass is not cute. For future reference, it pisses me off."

"I'm sorry, Sir." Lily thought to head his anger off, however she had a bad feeling it was too late.

"Good try, but I appreciate the effort."

Yep, it's too late, Lily thought when his hand went to the ruler he kept on his desk.

"Come here." Her feet carried her around the desk, standing next to his chair. "Lean over my desk." Lily was going to refuse him then remembered his words that he could handle it in the privacy of his office or on the work floor.

Lily leaned over his desk, which was almost empty since Shade kept the top immaculate. When he would come in after another member had been in the office and had made a mess, he had made them clean it before they left.

"Now, if you answer my question, you'll get a pass. If not, well, your bottom will tell you that answer, won't it?" Lily nodded her head. "Why were you snippy with me?"

"Because I didn't want to get your coffee?" Lily couldn't help the sarcastic reply.

When she felt his hand behind her back, raising the back of her skirt, Lily threw a glare in his direction.

Shade stood up, looking at what he had uncovered. Nothing happened. Lily turned her head to see his expression. She shot straight up, her skirt falling back in place before going to the corner of the room.

Shade burst out laughing. "Smart move."

He sat back down at the desk, leaning back casually, linking his hands together over his flat stomach. "You're quite a surprise with your sexy, little panties. Those red ones of yours always drove me crazy imagining them on you. Now that I've seen you in that pair of purple lace, I have a new favorite color."

Lily gritted her teeth. Everything he was doing and saying was grating on her strung nerves.

"So are you going to tell me what's wrong or are you going to stand there the rest of the day?"

"I don't know what's wrong with me," Lily burst out. "Everything is bugging me; you, Georgia, Jewell, the church. Name it."

Shade leaned back further in his chair, his smile widening. "How about we take one issue at a time. How am I bugging you?"

Her mouth opened and closed. "You're getting on my nerves, bossing me around. You never do what I expect you to do."

"Like what?"

"Like not cashing in my IOUs, not touching me, and when you come in a room you just set my nerves off," she finished, trying to think of something he did that really made her angry and coming up with a blank. How could she expect him to understand what she was trying to say when she realized how stupid she sounded to her own self?

"Okay, we'll tackle that problem last. What has Georgia done now?"

"She made a face at me this morning when I came in late. She's not a nice person."

Shade nodded. "I can agree with that. She isn't, but she is a good worker. Were you late?"

"Yes," she said sulkily.

"Why?" His eyes narrowed on her face. Lily knew she looked tired. She had put a faint pink lip gloss on and a brush of blush to give herself some color. She was sure both were long gone by now, though.

"I was tired," Lily admitted.

"So you're angry at Georgia because you were late and she made a face at you when some bosses would have at least said something to you about being late."

Lily thought about it for a minute. "I may have been

wrong," she admitted, already not liking the direction the conversation was taking.

"Now that's settled, let's move on to Jewell. What did she do?"

"Nothing."

"Then how is she bugging you?"

Lily didn't know how to get out of the sticky situation other than telling the truth. "You have her IOUs." She stopped talking, narrowing her eyes on his expression. "Or do you?"

"I do, and that bothers you?"

"Yes."

"All right." Shade opened the desk drawer before reaching in and pulling out the slips of paper. Opening them, he counted out several before putting the remaining ones back in his drawer. "Here, you can have them." He handed the slips of paper over. Lily stepped out of the corner, taking the papers before hastily returning to her safe space.

"Next up, what's bothering you at the church?"

Lily looked down at her hands. "Pastor Dean can't find anyone to run the church store. No one outside the church wants the position because it doesn't pay. No one in the church that would do okay at it wants it because it doesn't pay, and the few people who did volunteer did terrible. Jordan Douglas told everyone in her bible study class how much money someone made who came in the store. Marie Newman told Lark Jackson he didn't need a new coat, that the one he had was just fine. He had on a thin jacket! Laverne Thomas told Willa to keep the clothes she was donating because the way her weight fluctuates, she would probably need them again in a couple of months." Lily blew out an angry breath.

"So the job needs someone that is qualified to judge based on financial need if the people coming in require help, be sensitive to their privacy, and work five days a week all for free?"

"Yes! Oh, and they need to be nice."

"I know the perfect person," Shade said with a rueful expression.

"You do?" Lily asked hopefully.

"Yes: you. I can't think of anyone more qualified."

"Me? I can't take the job," Lily protested.

"I don't see why not. It will give you the opportunity to use your degree in a way that will really benefit those in need, especially children, which is what you wanted to accomplish. You'll have a better sense of what's going on in their homes than a social worker with limited time. Anyone who arouses your suspicions, you can tell Knox. You would be sensitive to their privacy and you never gossip. But most of all, you have the most important qualification—you're extremely nice."

Lily smiled at his compliment.

"But what about the pay?"

"I have enough money for the both of us." He held up his hand before she could interrupt. "But since I know you want your own money, I'll ask the brothers to each donate enough money to pay your salary for the year."

"I couldn't ask them to do that."

"You won't, I will. Anyway, I already have a couple of their IOUs."

Lily thought hard for a second before stepping back out of the corner, giving him Jewel's IOUs back. "Don't forget to ask the women members," she reminded him.

"I won't. Feel better?"

Lily nodded then bit her lip.

"What?"

"There is a family who comes into the store. They have two kids. Could the father have my job? I know there is a wait list, but since you said my job is extra, could you?"

Shade groaned. "Give them my number."

"Okay." Lily happily went toward the door.

"Lily, we aren't finished. Come here."

She let out a sigh. Yeah, now she remembered. There

had been one issue he had saved for last. She started to go back to her corner but didn't want to appear churlish. Instead, she walked back around the desk, coming to stand next to Shade.

He stood up, causing her to lean backward until her hands went behind her back to press against the desk. "I think I've also figured out what it is about me that's setting your nerves off."

"You have?"

"Yes, I have. You see, sometimes when a woman wants a man, her body lets her know by becoming… how shall I put it delicately? Horny. Yes, that's the word I'm looking for. You're horny."

"I'm not horny!"

"I can prove that's what's bothering you," Shade said smugly, leaning over her, pressing her back against his desk. His hand went to her thigh, bringing it up around his hip. "And, I can fix that problem for you, too."

"How can you fix the fact that you're an arrogant ass?"

"I can't, but I can fix it where you won't care."

As his mouth covered hers, cutting off her smart-aleck reply, Lily literally drowned under his touch. She had been craving his mouth on hers so much the past few days that she immediately opened hers wider, letting him take what he wanted and she needed to give him.

His hand slipped under her skirt, pushing it up to her waist. He stepped back, pulling off her panties before his hand moved to her pussy. Lily wasn't even embarrassed for him to find her wet and needy for his touch. A couple of strokes against her clit had her close to coming. She pushed harder against his hand as he took his mouth away from hers.

Gasping for breath, Lily ran her hands through his short hair, drawing him closer to her. His hand left her cunt, lightly snapping the waistband of her skirt against her taut stomach before sliding her loose shirt up, exposing her matching purple bra.

Shade tugged her breasts out of her bra, his startling blue eyes gazing down at her. He bent over and placed his mouth over her nipple, sucking it into his mouth, laving it into a pointed tip.

"Am I still bothering you?"

"Not so much," Lily moaned as he teased her nipple.

Shade rose, standing straight. Lily could see herself reflected in his clear gaze. His face was a mask of tortured need.

His hands went to his belt buckle, unbuckling and unzipping his jeans, and Lily froze, her memories dragged from her lust back to the present.

"Eyes to me, Lily."

Her dreams of a perfect wedding night intruded, but she didn't protest when he leaned over her. She needed him. She wouldn't be the first, nor the last, woman who had given up that particular dream.

When Shade's cock brushed against the flesh of her pussy, Lily tried to lift her hips so he could slide deep within her, but his hard hand held her to the desk, pinned in place. With his cock sliding back and forth against the outside of her cunt, her desire spiked, wanting him inside her while he denied her that fulfillment.

The feel of his cock butting up against her clit had her climaxing as his hands held her tightly. Her scream was stifled by his mouth as she felt his cock pulse against the outside lips of her pussy. She trembled with the last remnants of her orgasm as he reached over his desk, pulling several tissues out of the box.

She lay across the desk, looking up at him with wonder as he gently cleaned her before throwing the tissues into the trashcan and then helped her into a sitting position. He then cleaned himself before zipping his jeans.

Lily looked down at herself, pushing her breasts back into her top and then pulling her top back down to cover herself.

His hand went to her jaw, tilting her head back, his kiss

brief and gentle. Stepping back, he helped her to her feet.

"Ready to go back to work?"

Lily nodded happily as she slipped off the desk. She was almost around the desk when she turned back, looking around the floor.

"What are you doing?" Shade's resigned voice had her looking swiftly to his eyes, a flush coming to her cheeks.

"I was looking for my panties." Her eyes swept the floor again.

Shade's hand came out of his pocket. "These are now mine." His hand pushed the panties back into his pocket.

She started to argue, not wanting to go back to work with no underwear; but from his predatory gaze studying her unwaveringly, she decided it would be worth the quick trip to the house for her underwear.

She went through the door, reaching back to shut it when he said, "By the way, while you're at the house getting another pair of panties, could you get me a cup of coffee? Please."

Lily's only response was to slam the door.

CHAPTER THIRTY-THREE

After Church on Sunday, Lily had told Beth and Razer to go on to the diner ahead of her. She wanted to talk to Pastor Dean in his office where he readily agreed to give her the job of running the church store. When they walked together to the diner afterward, she was so happy she felt like she was walking on air.

She slipped her arm through her pastor's as they crossed the street, heading into the diner where she thanked him again, hugging him enthusiastically. Laughing, he pulled away at the same time that Lily invited him to sit with them for lunch and saw him pale as his eyes went over her shoulder. He said he remembered leaving something in his office and left her, practically running out the door.

Lily stood with her mouth open as she watched through the diner window as her pastor sprinted across the street. *It must really be important*, Lily thought. Turning back around, she walked to her table, seeing Viper standing behind a red-faced Shade with his hand on his shoulder.

"What happened?" Lily went immediately to Shade's side, her hand going to his forehead.

"He's fine now. He choked on his breakfast," Viper

331

said, resuming his seat by Winter.

"Thanks, Viper. I'm glad you were here," Lily said with concern.

"Me, too," he said grimly.

Lily told everyone the good news about Pastor Dean letting her run the church store and received their congratulations.

"Are you sure that's what you want to do?" Beth asked, leaning closer to her side.

"Yes, I do. I'm happy we settled it before Christmas. Do you think we have enough time to push for another toy drive? The store is already running low."

"I'm sure we do," Beth said above the groans at the table.

"I'm going home and hiding my wallet. Not only do we have Winter constantly after our money, now we have Lily after it for toys. Jeez," Rider moaned.

"It could be worse," Lily suggested.

"How?"

"If I don't get enough toys, I was going to ask Killyama if she could help take donations," Lily said, taking a drink of her hot chocolate.

"How much do you need?" Razer asked, reaching for his wallet.

Lily felt comfortable joking and sitting around the table. In a few weeks' span of time, she had grown more relaxed among them; though she didn't participate in their parties and made sure she avoided the sexual aspects of the club unless she inadvertently blundered into one of their sessions.

After lunch, Shade asked her to go furniture shopping with him. The others went back to the clubhouse as she and Shade went to the only furniture store in town. Luckily, they had a vast assortment of furniture to choose from.

After only a couple of hours, he had managed to find furniture for the entire house and appliances, too. She had liked most of his choices, but when he had been unsure, he would ask her opinion and invariably go with her decision. The sales clerk looked like he was in seventh heaven and Lily was sure he was with the commission he was most-assuredly making.

"Is that all I can help you with today?" Leonard asked, carrying the handheld computer that had rung up Shade's purchases.

"That will be it," Shade replied, putting his arm around her shoulder when she would have kept looking at the furniture.

"But you haven't picked out your bedroom furniture," Lily reminded him.

"I don't need bedroom furniture; I have bedroom furniture."

"The set in the basement?" Lily questioned, looking up at him.

Shade nodded before turning to follow the clerk to the cashier. Lily hung back, her feet not moving.

"But that furniture won't match the furniture in your house," Lily protested. "Just look at the bedroom furniture. You might find something you like better."

"I like what I have," Shade said, again trying to follow the sales clerk.

Lily refused to move, looking down at the floor. "It won't match."

Shade gave a frustrated sigh, motioning for the clerk to wait for him at the register.

"Eyes to me, Lily." She reluctantly raised her eyes to his. "Are you crying?" he asked, obviously stunned.

"No, I don't cry anymore. Haven't you noticed?"

"I can't say that I have," Shade replied.

"Well, I don't," she snapped.

"Okay. We'll debate that later. Why won't my bedroom furniture match the rest of the furniture I bought? That happens to be an expensive set, which I custom-ordered," Shade explained.

"I don't care how expensive it is, it's still different from the rest of your furniture."

"How?"

"It isn't new."

"It isn't new?" Shade repeated.

"It's not freaking new!" Lily whisper-screamed so no one would hear her, though she noticed Leonard turn his back so she wouldn't see him laughing at her.

Understanding dawned on his face, and he bent down to whisper in her ear. "I bought that bedroom set after you were hurt last summer, Lily. It's still new."

Lily's eyes widened.

"It's *all* new?"

"All of it, including the mattress and sheets. And, before you can ask, everything in my cabinet."

She turned red but didn't try to avoid his amused gaze.

"Then I guess it matches after all."

* * *

Lily locked the door after the last customer had left, looking out the window. It had been a long day giving out the Christmas baskets and turkeys. She watched the snow flurries struggling to fly; the tiny ice flakes were more granules than anything else.

"Ready?" Beth asked, coming to her side and looking out the window with her.

Beth had told her Shade had asked them to pick her up because he had something important to take care of. Razer was waiting for them at the diner while Lily closed.

"Yes." Lily turned to Beth. "I have a favor to ask. I know we're supposed to go straight home, but I want to run by the store and pick out Shade's Christmas present."

"I'll call Razer and tell him." Beth reached into her pocket, pulling out her cell phone. While she made the call, Lily put on her coat and took her purse out from under the counter, going back to Beth at the doorway.

"He says that's fine. He'll wait outside the store in the SUV."

"Thanks."

They went outside and Lily locked the door behind them.

"Have you decided what you want to get him?"

"It took me a while to figure it out, but yes, I know what I want to get him," Lily said, unable to hold back her smile.

* * *

A knock sounded on the door.

"Come in," Pastor Dean said, setting his pen down on the desk.

Shade walked into the room, dressed in slacks and a button-down shirt. His expensive shoes were shiny and new.

Pastor Dean sat, uncomprehending exactly what he was staring at. As understanding dawned, an unholy grin came across his face, and he sat up straighter in his chair.

"Before we start, I'm warning you that if you make one wisecrack, you'll be giving your own eulogy."

"Shade, you have to at least give me one."

A warning gleam appeared in his deadly eyes. "Like I said, it's your funeral."

"It might just be worth it," Pastor Dean replied, hastily raising his hands in surrender when Shade took a step forward. "I promise I will behave to the best of my ability."

"You do that," Shade said, still not relaxing his threatening manner.

Pastor Dean stood up, coming from around his desk. He reached out his hand for Shade to shake. "I told you I didn't think you deserved Lily. Let's see if you can change my mind, John."

* * *

Lily woke on Christmas Eve filled with excitement. She had always loved Christmas and this one was no exception.

The day before, she had finished her Christmas shopping and had come home to find Shade still gone. She had eaten dinner and gone to bed all alone, wondering where he was, and had only woken briefly when he had finally slid into bed with her, pulling her to him.

Excitement infused her as she jumped out of bed, going to the window and pulling the curtains back. "It snowed, Shade."

"I know. It started getting heavy last night," he grumbled from the covers.

Lily jumped back on the bed. "I love snow."

"I know. You told me." Shade grinned, pulling her back down. Lily circled his neck with her arms.

"Does your family open presents on Christmas Eve or Christmas Day?"

"What?" Shade asked, not understanding what she was getting at.

"Each family does it differently. Some families open their presents on Christmas Eve, others Christmas Day. We always opened them on Christmas Eve because I couldn't wait."

"We opened ours on Christmas Day."

"Oh." Her face fell in disappointment.

"But I can open it on Christmas Eve."

"No, I'll wait until tomorrow. I don't want to break tradition. It might be bad luck."

"I don't believe in bad luck."

"I'm still not giving you your present until tomorrow," she taunted.

Shade got out of bed, going to the bathroom to shower and dress, telling Lily she took too much time, so he was going first. Lily lay on the bed, waiting for him to come out.

He came out of the shower cleanly-shaven, wearing a nice pair of jeans she hadn't seen before and a dark blue muscle shirt.

He went to look out the window. "It's supposed to quit snowing this afternoon. Come here, Lily."

Lily climbed out of bed, determined not to let his

bossiness on Christmas Eve bother her. She stood by him in front of the window and then Shade went to the bedside table and opened it, removing an envelope before coming back to her and placing it in her hand.

"This present isn't technically for you. Open it."

Lily tore the envelope open, reading the words on the paper. She looked back at him with pure joy.

"Look at the date."

The paper signing over the land that Beth and Razer's property was built on had been signed the day after she had visited Diamond at her home.

"I don't know what to say, Shade. Thank you."

"You're welcome." Taking the papers away and setting them on the chair by the window, he reached into his pocket and pulled out a tiny box, placing it in her hand.

"This present is for you."

Lily's fingers trembled as she slid the ribbon off and then opened the box. Inside, a diamond ring lay on a bed of velvet.

"Will you marry me?" Shade was down on his knees in front of her.

She began crying, telling herself this time didn't count because it was so special. For once, she didn't have to think about her answer. "Yes, I'll marry you."

Shade stood up, kissing her so passionately that it had her arms circling his neck. He raised his arms, pulling her away. "Good. Now you need to get showered and dressed. We're getting married in two hours." He walked to the door and started to open it.

"Wait. What are you talking about? We can't get married in two hours. Weddings have to be planned and—"

"I've already planned everything and what I couldn't, Beth and Winter took care of. You want a snowy, winter wedding. Look out the window. You know Kentucky weather, it could be another year before it snows again. I'm not waiting a year to get married. Besides, how do you schedule snow?"

"I don't know," Lily said in bemusement.

"I don't either. So everything is a go for today, even the snow. I talked to Pastor Dean and got his blessing."

"You did?" Lily was in awe of that accomplishment. She didn't think Pastor Dean liked Shade.

"I did. So are we going to do this?"

"Yes. Do you need me to do anything?"

"No, everything is ready. The brothers and I spent half the night getting it set up. But I do have a quick question."

"What is it?" Lily asked.

"Do I have to invite Sex Piston and her crew?"

CHAPTER THIRTY-FOUR

"Are you sure about this, Lily?" Lily turned from the doorway where they were waiting for the guests to get into position.

"Yes. Look out that door, Beth. How could I not marry a man who did that for me?" The sisters stared out into the winter wonderland that Shade and The Last Riders had created for her. It was everything she had dreamed about and more.

The snow in the backyard of the church was virtually pristine except where the guests were standing. They had waited for the ceremony to begin to go outside into the yard so they wouldn't have to be cold long.

"Shade's been planning this since the weather forecasts came in. I didn't think he would wait for the last second to ask, though." Lily felt Beth scrutinizing her face. "Lily..."

Lily turned to her sister, taking her hand in hers. "I want to marry him, Beth. I don't know if I would have made it the last few months without him. I love him."

She looked outside to where Shade was standing in his black tuxedo; he didn't even seem cold. She saw her reflection in the glass door, standing in her adopted mother's lace wedding gown and veil that lay on her black hair and fell to the floor in a beautiful train that would brush the snow as she walked to Shade.

"I can't even cry; I'll smear my make-up," Beth said, smiling tearfully.

"Are we going to get this show on the road or not? They're freezing their asses off out there." As if on cue, Killyama opened the door for them. She was the only one from Sex Piston's crew able to make it to the wedding on time. Stud had refused to have his wife on the road during a snowstorm and the others had been snowed in by unplowed side streets. Killyama was the only one near cleared roads.

The woman who had showed up was not the one Lily was familiar with, though. The biker bitch had been replaced with a feminine woman whose hair, which hadn't been teased within an inch of its life for once, lay against her shoulders in loose curls the color of rich, dark bourbon. Without the crazy eye shadow, she had hazel eyes that didn't look nearly as scary, either. She wore the tight green dress that Sex Piston had bought the day they had gone shopping, which accentuated a figure that would make a fitness trainer cry. She looked smoking hot, but Lily didn't care how she'd come dressed as long as she was there.

Beth took a deep breath. "Ready?"

"Yes." She looked toward the arch filled with fairy lights where Pastor Dean and Shade were waiting. "I'm more than ready."

* * *

The freezing guests left immediately after the wedding. Shade had invited only Pastor Dean and Killyama back to the clubhouse for the private reception; both had refused. Pastor Dean had Christmas Eve service that evening and Killyama wanted to get back to Jamestown before the weather made the roads even worse.

Lily said goodbye to Killyama before climbing into Beth's SUV. She saw Train approach the woman before she could get in her car. She couldn't help hearing them argue as the other women climbed into the back of Beth's SUV. The men were riding their bikes except Shade and Train who were riding in Rider's truck. Winter and Viper were bringing the overflow in their SUV.

"You had your shot; you didn't want it. Now fuck off." Lily winced when she heard Killyama's harsh words; however, she had no doubt that Train probably deserved much worse.

She watched as Killyama got in her car, ignoring the man while he was trying to talk to her. Train had to jump out of the way to avoid being hit by her, finally giving up and climbing into Rider's truck.

She didn't blame the woman; Train was all over the women at the house. He was... a sudden thought struck Lily. She turned in her seat to look at the women crowded in the backseat as Beth pulled out of the parking lot.

Raci, Bliss, Evie, Jewell, Ember and Stori stared back at her.

"Who's the worst?" Lily asked, staring at the women. "Is it Train?"

The women didn't even question what she meant; they knew what she was asking. Their eyes went back and forth between each other.

"Lily, don't do this. It's your wedding day," Beth said.

Lily turned, facing the front again. The silence coming from the backseat was deafening. Shade was the worst. Lily thought back to every incident that she had witnessed since she had moved into The Last Riders' Clubhouse and knew it wasn't that long ago that Shade also had been participating... and now she knew he had been considered the worst among them by the club itself.

Her mind whirled as they drove home where Beth turned into the parking lot. When she parked and cut the motor, the women members used the opportunity to escape.

Beth turned to her. "Talk to him."

Lily gave her a smile, trying to regain the same cheerfulness she had possessed before she'd left the church. "I will. Let's see if we can make it up those steps without breaking our necks."

The men ended up carrying them up the steps then several went back out to clear them and the pathway for anyone who came by later. As soon as Shade set her back on her feet, she escaped to their bedroom to change. Lily pulled on soft brown slacks and a green sweater.

Dressed, she went back downstairs where the men were standing at the bar congratulating Shade. She watched the men from the stairway, her mind not on what they were drinking but the camaraderie they shared. A bond like theirs was unbreakable; they would die for each other without a second's hesitation.

Shade saw her standing on the steps and came to her. His hands circled her waist, lifting her off the last two steps and holding her against his chest.

"What are you doing?" he asked.

"Watching you." She smiled, touching his cheek.

"Why?" Shade smiled down at her.

"Shade, we need to talk. We should have talked before we were married this morning." Her serious tone wiped his smile away.

"Not today."

"But, I really need to tell you—"

"Not today, okay? Today is Christmas Eve—our wedding day—and we're not going to talk about anything else except that today."

"Okay." Lily gave in to his demand.

"I'm going to go get out of this get-up. I'm never going to live this down."

"I think you'll survive," Lily teased. Shade bent down, brushing his lips with hers.

Before he could start up the stairs, a knock sounded on the door behind them, and Shade gave her a quick grin.

"I have another surprise for you," he said, turning to

open the door.

As it opened, Lily caught sight of Penni standing on the porch. When she saw Shade, she threw herself into his arms. "You big doofus. Only you would give me a day's notice to get here. My stupid flight got cancelled, and I didn't think I would ever get through the roads from Lexington. I didn't even know you two were seeing each other. How come neither of you told me?"

Shade set Penni back on the floor. "Slow down, Penni. If you hadn't been so occupied with your new job, you would have known," he told her.

Penni saw Lily when he took a step back. "Lily!" She grabbed her, pulling her into a tight hug. "I missed seeing you in your wedding dress. I was supposed to be there," she wailed.

"It's all right. Razer took a video for us." Lily tried to keep the reserve out of her voice, yet she was unsuccessful. Penni's eyes flashed her hurt, but she wasn't one to take anything without giving it right back.

"I know you're probably mad at me for not telling you Shade was my brother, but he threatened to take the car back if I told." Lily saw Shade's face go blank at his sister's revealing words.

"Your car?"

"Yes. The one he bought me for transferring colleges so that I could be your roommate because he didn't want Beth to worry. You'll be part of the club now; they'll watch out for you like they did Beth. I'm glad, too; you tend to be a little accident-prone." Penni finally stopped for a breath.

"I'm not accident-prone," Lily denied, trying to process her friend's words. She was coming to the conclusion that Shade was a devious man.

Penni rolled her eyes at her denial. "Anyway, it doesn't matter anymore. You have my big brother to watch out for you now."

"Your half-brother."

"That doesn't matter. Our families both get along. It wasn't an ugly divorce. Our mom was just sick of moving every couple of years. Our parents are pretty cool; Shade's dad especially."

"We'll save that for another day. He couldn't make it to the wedding. He and my stepmother are in Florida taking a long vacation. He just retired," Shade explained to Lily. "Why don't you take Penni into the kitchen and let her see everyone while I go get changed."

"You've met them before?" Lily asked, surprised.

"Of course, since I was little; sometimes a few of them would come home with him when he visited."

Lily took Penni's coat, hanging it in the closet as Shade went upstairs. It was hard to be angry with Penni for long; her personality wouldn't let you remain aloof unless you were willing to be outright mean to her. Her effervescent temperament was always in direct contrast to Lily's own more solemn one.

As soon as they set foot in the kitchen, Penni's appearance created pandemonium as everyone tried to greet her at once.

Lily pitched in to help cook while Penni sat at the kitchen table, telling all the members about her new job.

"I absolutely love it. Right now, it's mainly all paperwork while I set up the venues for the concerts, but once they go on tour, I'm hoping it gets to be more exciting."

Shade came back in his normal jeans and t-shirt.

"There's the brother I know and love. I almost didn't recognize you in that suit, or with that smile you were wearing," Penni teased.

"Food's ready," Beth told everyone. Lily and Shade ate while Penni described all the places she had booked the tour that started next month.

"Kaden Cross has even agreed to do a couple of the venues. We'll even be in Lexington and you all better come. I'll introduce you to Kaden and his wife. I've become friends with her and her friend."

"I'm glad you met new friends."

Penni nodded enthusiastically. "Her friend is married to a member of a motorcycle club. Can you believe it? I actually know two clubs now. Of course, you guys could probably kick their asses." She was quiet for a whole second. "Maybe."

"What's the name?" Shade asked, his eyes on his sister. Lily smiled at the big brother in Shade coming out.

"The Predators." If she hadn't been watching him, Lily would have missed the slight change in his expression and the shifting of his eyes to Viper.

The Last Riders had heard of the Predators, and Lily could tell they didn't like them. She didn't need to hear his next words to know that.

"Stay away from them, Penni, far away."

"That's going to be hard to do," she protested.

"I don't care, just do it," Shade ordered, glaring at her.

Penni stared at her brother as Lily sat watching the contest of wills.

"I'll stay away from them as much as possible," Penni conceded. "I don't even know why we're arguing. I've only been around them a couple of times." She averted her eyes and some tiny part of Lily told her there was something she was holding back. Shade picked up on it, too. Penni was his sister; he would catch something just as easily as Lily.

"What?" Shade asked.

"Nothing. I just think you're being over-protective. Most of them seem to be good guys. They helped my boss out of a jam this summer. They provide security sometimes."

"A rock star needs that kind of security?" Shade questioned, and Lily noticed all the men at the table were listening intently.

"They did when I was doing my internship. Kaden was attacked by a crazy man who wanted something from his wife."

"Were you hurt?" Shade's whole demeanor changed; he was obviously protective.

"No. When I came to, it was already over," Penni said, filling her plate again.

"You're quitting."

"No, I am not. I'm a big girl and I can take care of myself. The dude who knocked me out is in prison, so calm down."

"Let me know if he gets out."

"I will." Penni's sparkly personality wasn't going to let Shade intimidate her. "Now can I finish my dinner?"

"Yes, but you're still quitting."

"No, I'm not," Penni repeated.

"Cut it out, you two. You're both giving me a headache," Lily cut in between them. "Quit worrying, Shade. She works for a band. I wouldn't worry about another motorcycle club and Kaden's wife's stalker. It's all the drugs, sex and parties she's going to be in contact with on the tour that you should be worried about," she said sagely.

"Traitor," Penni hissed.

"I couldn't resist," Lily replied, taking the beer Penni was drinking away. "I think it's kind of funny Shade's warning you away from a motorcycle club when he helped found one, and he's well aware that sometimes you can be in the wrong place at the wrong time. I'm sure your employer was just going through a bad time. You said yourself that the man responsible is in prison now." Lily turned to Shade. "Your sister is smart enough to get out of a situation in which she could get hurt."

"That's right." Penni grinned at her brother. "I think I'm going to enjoy having Lily as my sister-in-law. She might be able to keep you off my back."

"All right, I'll leave it alone for now, but if anything happens, leave."

"I'll be out of there like a shot," Penni agreed.

"Good, now that it's settled, can we enjoy dinner? I have to get ready for Christmas service," Lily said, reminding Shade.

"The brothers and I are going to stay here and take care of a few things while you're gone."

"All right." She hadn't really expected him to go anyway. He had never attended church before; she didn't presume to think that their marriage would change that aspect of Shade's behavior. Church was a large part of her life, not his.

She wondered what parts of his behavior their marriage would change, if any. She should have thought of that before she'd said yes and married him today. It was too late now, though. Well... really, it had been too late from the moment she had realized she had fallen in love with him, despite knowing of his past.

He hadn't told her he loved her, but she was deathly afraid he was. She didn't want him to love her because, until he knew her past, the woman he loved was an illusion.

It was past time for Shade to meet his real wife, Callie.

CHAPTER THIRTY-FIVE

There weren't many parishioners at Christmas Eve services when the women got there. Lily sat on the pew between Penni and Beth as Pastor Dean gave an eloquent service that moved everyone in the audience. Afterward, they had their church supper where Lily had accepted the surprised congratulations of those who hadn't attended the wedding.

They didn't stay long; the women all wanted to spend the evening with their husbands. Lily felt like pinching herself every time she referred to Shade as such.

"I hear you managed to get Shade to put a ring on your finger. When's the baby due?" Lily's head turned in shock at the harsh words that spewed out of Georgia's mouth.

"I'm not pregnant," Lily gasped.

"Why else would he marry you? You've been giving it to him for months, living in sin. You should be ashamed, coming to church, being around good Christian women," Georgia's spite-filled voice carried throughout the entire room. Heads turned to listen unashamedly as Georgia continued on her rant.

"Shut up, Georgia. You can't talk to her that way," a normally timid Willa spoke up for Lily.

348

"I can talk to her any way I want to. She's a slut and everyone in this church knows it. Both her and her sister. Their father would roll over in his grave to know his daughters had lived in sin before they were married. "

"Lower your voice." Willa made another attempt to silence the woman.

"Don't tell me to be quiet again. The only reason you're not out there whoring with your friends is because none of those bikers would want your fat ass."

Lily stood and took Georgia's verbal abuse, but she wasn't going to let her defame Willa.

"Georgia, you need to go and take your nosy friends and walk out that door right now." When Beth and the other Last Rider women finally managed to get through the crowded room, Lily could tell they thought they were coming to her defense. She didn't need their help, though; she could take care of herself.

"What are you going to do if I don't?" Georgia braced her feet apart. The woman actually thought Lily would start a fight in her place of worship.

She honored her God too much to stoop to her level; however, she had turned the other cheek too many times to do it again. Tonight, Willa was the one who had been hurt because she had tried to forgive Georgia's previous verbal attacks.

Lily took a step forward, looking directly into Georgia's eyes. She lowered her voice as much as she could so that the fewer parishioners who heard, the better. "Georgia, you are not a nice person and I, as a good Christian, have tried to ignore your repeated slander against myself and my sister. Whereas your comments are pure lies and you have spread them throughout the entire congregation, the comments I am about to tell are the truth.

"My father was this church's pastor for many years, and while he did not spread gossip within the church, he did, upon occasion, discuss certain parishioners with my mother." Georgia paled.

"Yes, Georgia, I know. Beth knows as well, and neither of us has opened our mouth to tell another of your own year in a rehab center, which my father helped your parents find when they dragged you off the streets where you were selling yourself for a few pills. Do not ever think that you have the right to throw any stone at women like Beth and Willa."

"What's she talking about, Georgia?" one of her loudmouth friends asked.

Lily stepped out of the way so that Georgia could grab her coat and escape the questions her friends were barraging her with as she left the fellowship hall.

"Remind me to never get you mad at me," Bliss said in awe. "You do remember that I did apologize, right?"

"Wow, I'm impressed. I see you don't need me anymore," Penni gloated.

"I wish I had a video of that so Razer could have watched," Beth said proudly.

Lily put her coat on. She wasn't proud of herself, yet if Georgia hadn't lost control enough to have attacked Beth and Willa, she would have continued to ignore the woman. Lily couldn't understand what had brought the woman to lose control like that. She had to have been aware that Razer and Shade would find out and fire her.

Willa was putting on her coat when Lily interrupted her leaving. "I'm sorry she was so hateful to you because of me."

"She wasn't mean to me because of you. We went to school together, and she's always hated me. She made high school miserable for me," Willa told her.

"I hope she leaves you alone from now on." Lily tried to sound encouraging.

Willa shook her head. "Georgia will never change. Goodnight, and congratulations again."

"Thanks, Willa." Lily hugged Willa goodbye, wishing she had Rachel's gift for just a second to make Willa feel better.

* * *

The women talked about Lily shutting Georgia up all the way home. When Beth pulled up at the clubhouse, they all climbed the now-clear steps.

"It's been a long day, hasn't it?" Beth said as she was going in the door.

Lily caught her arm. "I'm going to stay out here for just a few minutes and get a breath of fresh air. I'll be in shortly."

Beth paused then nodded her head. "Don't stay long, it's cold."

"I won't."

Lily walked back down the steps, turning onto the path that led behind the house. As she passed the house, she heard the voices of the members inside. She paused for a brief second, listening to the excitement and laughter from within. She didn't pay attention to the words they were saying, only to the caring in their voices. They belonged, even Penni, who had known them for years. Only Lily was still an outsider.

Lily started walking again, taking the now-familiar path toward Shade's house. Going up the steps, she wanted to sit down, but she didn't want to get her church dress damp and go back inside with a wet butt. She leaned against the porch's post instead.

"Why are you out here?" Shade asked, coming to the bottom of the steps, looking up at her.

"You couldn't have picked a better spot for your home. The view is... perfect. When I stand here from this viewpoint, I feel like I could reach out and touch the sky. It sounds silly, but it's so high here that I think God might hear me a little better." She gave Shade a wry smile. "When I was a little girl, I would pray and pray at night. My real mother wasn't much of a church-goer. If it wasn't for my friends, I wouldn't even have known there was a God. They told me about Him. My mother didn't believe, explaining as much to me."

351

"Lily, stop. I told you, not today. Not on our wedding day."

"I have to tell you today, Shade. Today's the day you made me your wife." Her arms circled the post she was leaning against, trying to find the strength to tell him so he would understand.

"I didn't know what a daddy was, so my friends tried to explain it to me. When they told me, I started crying because I wanted one. I didn't have a lot; no dolls or toys, but I never cried for those. But when they told me what a daddy was, I really wanted one of those. My friends didn't know what to do, but then one of them ran into her apartment and came out with a Bible and they told me about God, how He was everyone's Father. I would talk to Him whenever… whenever I needed Him. I don't know if He could hear me. I don't think I was close enough.

"That's why I love the mountains. I feel closer to God. When I came to the mountains, He gave me parents who loved me. He gave me Beth and He gave me you, Shade. My husband.

"Do you know why I didn't want to have sex with my husband before I married? Because I wanted it to be clean and new, because I'm dirty, unclean—"

"Don't you ever fucking say that again!" Shade's foot came up on the first step.

"It's the truth, Shade. I've slept with more men than any woman in that house, and you deserve to know that. I can't give you my virginity; I lost it long ago and everything else from that life that I forgot until Halloween night."

"I wish you had never remembered." Shade's quiet voice didn't hide the anguish in his voice.

"I don't. It was destroying me, Shade."

"There was nothing worth remembering." His harsh words had her straightening from the pole.

"Oh, yes, there was. There were three little girls who were like sisters. When my mother would finally crash and sleep, she would take me to a babysitter. I know my mom didn't pay her; she spent all her money on anything other than me. I was raised with two beautiful little girls. They loved me enough to see that I had food to eat, that I had toys to play with, that I had a normal touch. They would hold my hand constantly when we went out. They were constantly afraid they would lose me. We would sit on the playground and pretend that we would run away when we grew old enough. Vida was sweet and sensitive. She loved animals. She wanted to live on a farm. Sawyer was more adventurous. She wanted to have fun. She chose Disneyland, and I wanted to see the Northern Lights."

"That was why you wanted to go to Alaska." Shade's soft voice drew her attention from the past.

"I had the furthest to run," she said softly. "That night we were looking through those books must have triggered a memory. My mind was trying to remind me of my past. A past that I don't belong to any more than I belong here."

She stood straight, standing on the top step, looking down at him. "You thought I was a young, innocent woman, that I've never touched alcohol. You don't know that I was sold for pocket change. I've done things that make me sick. How can I belong anywhere when I know how disgusting I am?"

"Lily, look at that house behind you. I built that house for you—every room, this porch, these steps, for you, for us and the children we will have." His passion-filled voice showed strength enough to help her bear the burden of her past.

"I love you. When I say it, I don't say it lightly. I say it because when I look at you, I see an angel who God let slip through his fingers to leave behind just for me.

"Lily, you belong. You belong to me. You will always belong to me." Shade walked up the steps, sweeping her up into his arms. "Always."

He took her to the front door of their house, carrying

her inside and slamming the door behind them. Reaching beside the door, he balanced her while he flipped on the lights.

Lily stared around the living room filled with furniture. "When did you do this?" she asked, seeing the furniture they had just picked out the day before.

"While you were in church tonight. The brothers and I busted our balls getting this done while you were gone."

"How did you get the furniture delivered so fast?" She was amazed at how well they had done, matching the house with the furniture.

"I threatened Leonard, but I also gave him a big tip," Shade said ruefully.

"We did good," Lily said, trying to wiggle down so she could look closer at her kitchen. "Let me down; I want to see the kitchen," Lily said, exasperated.

"Later. I'm going to show you the bedroom first." His wicked grin melted her heart.

Shade packed her upstairs to the bedroom where the door was already open. Shade carried her through, setting her down in their new bedroom. All of his bedroom furniture had been moved inside and there were candles set in various places throughout the room, giving it a soft glow. The bed was made up with the covers pulled down. On the bed was the present she had bought Shade yesterday.

"Beth made me promise to have it on the bed waiting for you."

"What time is it?" Lily asked.

"Eleven-thirty."

"That's close enough. I think it's time I gave you your Christmas present."

Lily went to the bed, picking the package up, and then headed toward the bathroom.

"Wait. I thought you were going to let me open it?"

"I will. Give me ten minutes." Lily disappeared into the bathroom.

This bathroom was even better than the one in the basement, if that was possible. Instead of one rain showerhead, it had two, and the bench was longer and wider with a black marble that she could see her reflection in. She showered and blow-dried her hair before she opened the package, taking the contents out. Getting dressed took only a few minutes. She nervously looked at herself in the mirror, took a deep breath for courage, and opened the bathroom door.

Shade was already lying on the bed waiting for her. His different-colored tats were highlighted in the candlelight.

"That is the best present I've ever had. Come here and let me open it." His intense blue eyes didn't lift from the gift she had bought.

Lily slid into the bed next to him, self-conscious that he was naked.

"Come here." Shade put his hand behind her neck, drawing her closer to him. The white lace corset she was wearing had no straps, hugging her breasts in sweetheart cups that pushed her full breasts up and showed how tiny her waist was in comparison to her flared hips. The lace ended just above the tiny white lace panties.

His mouth went to her breasts, grazing against the top.

"I don't get a kiss?" Shade lifted his head, his lips giving her a brief, hard kiss before returning to her breasts.

Lily burst out laughing, her fear and nervousness disappearing. "You can't do better than that?" she teased.

"Angel, these breasts are... I'm trying to think of a word that's good enough to describe them." His hand went to the tiny hooks that went down the lace corset, unfastening them. When he'd finished, he spread the corset apart. "Fucking magnificent." His hand pushed one globe up, finding the tip with his lips. He sucked just the tip of the nipple into his mouth before releasing it. His hand then went to the other breast, grasping it before he lowered his mouth to the tip, sucking it into his mouth then releasing it. "Fucking gorgeous."

"I take it you're a breast man."

"All men are breast men," he replied, looking at her breasts in awe.

Lily lay down on the bed, stretching before her arms reached out to him. Shade bent down, his mouth covering hers, giving her the kiss she'd desired. She needed that kiss from him to show her it was Shade and no one else in their wedding bed; the nightmares of her past weren't present now.

He parted her lips with his tongue, seducing her with the wildness of his taste and the gentle glide of his against her own. His mouth then went to her neck, exploring her flesh with tiny flicks of his tongue while his hand slid up her thigh, gliding straight to her pussy, finding her nub and rubbing it with strokes that were already close to making her climax.

"Shade, I need you." One of her legs rubbed against his as she tried to tell him what she needed.

"You're not hot enough yet." Shade's mouth moved to her breast again, taking her nipple back into his mouth.

"Yes, I am." Lily heartily disagreed with him. If he kept rubbing her pussy, she was going to come before he'd even entered her.

Then understanding dawned on her, what he was trying to tell her. She was just lying there, letting him have sex with her. He wanted her to make love *with* him.

Her hands left his shoulders, exploring every inch of his skin, discovering his body; how he trembled when her lips grazed the flesh at the base of his throat, how his lean body had stone-hard muscles.

As her teeth grazed his nipples, she learned how his body felt when he shifted to lay between her thighs. Her palms slid along his ribcage, circling his waist to hold him tighter as he slid his cock deep within her. Lily memorized how her breasts felt when she arched them against his chest, then when he crushed them beneath his chest.

She didn't want to forget any moment from her

wedding night, so when her monsters tried to threaten her, it would be Shade's touch—his kiss, his image—that would drive every hurtful memory away until all that was left was him and this night. Their wedding night. Their first time.

Lily turned her head to whisper in his ear, "I love you, John Hunter."

"Lily, I didn't know a man could love a woman as much as I love you. I don't deserve you, but I'm never going to let you go. I couldn't survive without you in my life. I wouldn't want to."

His mouth covered hers as his thrusts increased, carrying them both into a climax that gave as much as it took. It gave them a way to express their love and took a part of their soul as it receded, crashing the two into one, forever entwined.

* * *

Shade rolled over, pulling Lily onto his chest.

"That was beautiful," Lily said, nuzzling his neck.

"Did you enjoy it?"

"Yes, I never expected… Yes, I enjoyed it a lot." She laughed against his neck.

"Good. That was for you. This time is for me," Shade said, sitting up.

"What are you doing?" Lily asked curiously.

Shade slid out of the bed, picking her up and carrying her into the bathroom. There were three steps that led down into the massive shower. Shade turned the water and music on, and the water began to pulse to the music.

"Oh, heck no," Lily said, giggling as she tried to get out of the shower. "I just blow-dried my hair."

"I'll help you when we get out, if I'm not too tired." Shade's hand went into her already-wet hair, turning her mouth up to his. His hand was already going for the lotions on the side of the shower.

"Lean up against the shower wall," he ordered her, lifting his mouth and stepping away. With a grin, Lily went to the shower wall, leaning back against it.

He opened the bottle of lotion, spilling some of it on his hand before reaching out and rubbing it into her tiny, black curls.

Lily tried to smack his hand away. "What are you doing now?"

"I'm going to shave you," Shade said, his hand returning to the tiny curls.

"Oh, no, you're not," Lily protested.

"Yes, I am. Now stand still or I'm going to go get my paddle. It's my turn."

Lily stood still, feeling his hand on her pubic hair, trying to decide whether to go along with him or not.

His hand went to the shelf again, pulling out a long, old-fashioned razor. That answered her question. She was not going to let him near her sensitive flesh.

"Let me do it. I'll get a regular razor," Lily attempted to stop him.

"But that won't be any fun for me." Shade went to his knees in the shower. "Don't worry; I'm good at this. Not as good as Razer, but almost as good." He scraped the first few curls away. "See. That didn't hurt, did it?"

"What do you mean, *as good as Razer*?" Lily asked, his sentence making her pause in getting away from him.

"This is how Razer got his nickname." Shade scraped away even more curls.

"Eww, that's TMI. I didn't need to know that about my brother-in-law. Wait a minute; does Beth know how Razer got his nickname?"

"What do you think?" His wicked voice was muffled with laughter.

"That's definitely TMI, Shade. He used to shave the women in the house?" Lily couldn't resist asking.

"Yep." Shade continued at his task.

"So you're almost as good as him now. I guess I don't need to know who took over for him, do I?" Lily asked snidely.

"Nope." Shade spread her legs, one at a time. Lily would have jerked away when he started shaving her, but once that lethal-looking razor was pressed against her crotch, she froze in place. When he finished, he took the showerhead, spraying the now clean-shaven pussy.

"Damn," he said in appreciation.

"I thought you were a breast man?" Lily teased.

"I don't play favorites."

"Let me do you now," Lily said with saccharin sweetness.

"No, it's—"

"Not my turn," Lily finished for him.

"Angel, when it's your turn, you can do anything to me you want." His eyes dared her.

"I'm going to hold you to that." Her thoughts of revenge were side-tracked by his mouth going directly to her pussy. One second she was talking to him, the next he was devouring her, sliding his tongue through the fleshy pink lips of her cunt.

Lily's hand grasped the back of his neck, pulling him closer as his tongue teased the opening of her pussy, plunging deep inside of her then pulling out before plunging back in again. He tongue-fucked her until her thighs started trembling.

Shade then stood up, dragging his tongue away with a final sweep across her clit. He turned her until she was facing the shower bench that was against one wall of the shower. "Bend over," he groaned.

Lily bent over, placing her hands on the bench. His hand on her back pushed her down further until her face lay on her hands.

Shade rubbed the tip of his cock through the silky wetness of her pussy, sliding the long length between the lips. She felt the tip touch her clit, nearly making her come, but then he changed directions. On his next forward thrust, the momentum sent his cock tunneling through her cunt, burying himself deep within her. He leaned over her back, pushing himself inside of her to the hilt.

Lily screamed over the loud blast of the music as he pistoned inside of her, driving himself in and out until her screams became whimpers. His foot moved her stance wider, taking him deep enough so that she tried to adjust herself.

"Stay still." His mouth found the tender flesh of her neck. "I'm going to fuck you deep and long enough that you're going to always remember tonight. I'm going to leave my mark on your pussy so you will never, ever doubt in your mind that you belong to me. Do you understand me?"

"Yes," Lily gasped, her next orgasm driving her back on his cock.

His hand slid around her ribcage then upwards, grabbing her breast in a tight hold to pull her back onto his thrusting cock.

"How long, Lily?" he demanded.

"Always, Shade. I'll always belong to you."

CHAPTER THIRTY-SIX

Lily bit her lip as she stood on the porch of the clubhouse. It had been her turn to cook dinner and she had come outside to tell the men that dinner was ready.

The men were down in the parking lot below. It was freezing out, but they stood watching as Rider rode a new motorcycle he had just bought, saying his other one was headed for the scrap heap.

Several of the women had gone down to see his new bike also. Bliss and Jewell along with Evie stood watching Rider on the bike. They were taking turns getting on behind him, while Viper, Shade and Train were talking. Shade was sitting casually on his bike with his back to the house. Raci was on Rider's bike at the moment, and jumped off when the bike came to a stop. She looked gorgeous with her flushed cheeks and tight jeans. She was wearing a thin cream top with one of the men's leather jacket on. She wondered whose jacket she had on, since she had never seen Beth wearing Razer's the whole time they had been married.

When Raci turned, Lily saw the back of the jacket and knew instantly whose it was. It was like a knife had been stabbed in her heart.

She went back inside without telling them dinner was ready, going back inside to the kitchen. She stood at the kitchen several minutes staring out the window as she tried to catch her breath. She began praying hard.

A few minutes later, she heard the front door open and the voices of the members. She quickly busied herself, placing a calm expression on her face.

"That bike makes me want to get a new one." Train was the first in the kitchen with the rest following behind.

Evie and Jewell took advantage of the men talking to get in the food line to fix their plates. Lily saw Shade come into the kitchen with Viper, Raci and Bliss trailing behind them. Raci was no longer wearing Shade's jacket.

Lily was tempted to go back to their house, but she was just as determined not to run. She fixed herself a plate, taking a seat at the table next to Evie and Jewell, forcing herself to eat while Shade and the others fixed themselves plates.

Shade finished filling his plate and took a seat across from her. When he would have said something, Lily picked up her plate and stood up.

"I'm done, Raci. You can have my seat." Lily walked away from the table as Raci sat down.

Placing her plate in the sink, she went to the kitchen door.

"Lily?" Shade's questioning voice had her shoulders stiffening. She reminded herself she wanted to be more like Sex Piston and her crew. She knew exactly what Sex Piston would do.

Turning around, she went back to the table, ignoring Beth and Winter who had come into the kitchen, just now getting off work. She walked up behind Rider and gave him sweet smile.

"Rider, it's cold outside, and I left my jacket at the house. May I borrow yours?"

Rider paled, his eyes going to Shade's.

"This isn't going to be pretty." Lily heard Beth's

amused voice behind her back.

"Uh, Lily. Shade's jacket is in the other room; would you like me to get it for you?" Raci's face was as white as Rider's.

Lily turned toward Raci. This time the smile didn't reach her eyes. "No thanks, Raci. Rider?" Lily turned back to Rider who hadn't taken his eyes off Shade's grim visage.

"Is there a problem?" she continued. "It's not like your jackets mean anything, do they? It's not like a wedding ring is it? I'll give it back when I'm done with it." This time Lily didn't try to hide her anger at the knowledge that she had been right in the importance of the jackets. "I thought you men were all about sharing."

"There's the Lily I know and love," Winter said, making no attempt to keep the amusement out of her voice.

Rider reached for his jacket, which he had hung on the back of his chair.

"Touch that jacket, and you won't sit for a week," Shade's coldly furious voice had everyone tensing.

"Never mind, Rider. I'm sure a few minutes out in the cold won't bother me." Lily turned on her foot, going out the kitchen door

She was halfway back to their house when she was jerked to a stop. "What the fuck?" Shade's angry face stared down at her.

"Don't you dare ask me why I'm mad." She wrenched her arm away from him and rushed toward the house. She opened the door and turned to close it, but Shade prevented her by coming in behind her, shutting it himself.

Lily ignored him as she turned on the lights.

"So what is this? The silent treatment?" Shade mocked with his arms crossed over his chest.

Lily threw him an angry look, turning to face him. "There is nothing to say, Shade." Staring back at him, she buried her hands in the side of her dress. Even angry and hurt as she was, he attracted her like a moth to a flame, and just like a moth, she had given him the power to destroy her.

He was wearing dark jeans and boots with a black muscle shirt that showed his body to his best advantage. How could she blame Bliss or the other women for wanting him when the only thing she could think of was touching him?

Lily sighed going to the steps. "I fell in love with The Last Rider that's the wildest? I knew you were bad, but I had no concept of just how bad, did I?"

"No." Shade didn't try to evade her question.

"Go have your dinner." She climbed the steps to their bedroom, aware he was following her.

Her mind went back to after her wedding ceremony and the women's faces when she had questioned them. She should never have lost her temper. Now she was regretting letting it rattle her that she had seen Raci in his jacket. Lily didn't want to be jealous of other women; it would affect her marriage. She had to trust Shade or their marriage was never going to work.

In the bedroom, she gathered her pajamas and went into the shower, taking a long time, hoping Shade would go back to the clubhouse and finish his dinner. It would give her time to soothe her hurt feelings without wanting to throw something at him. Lily even thought of calling Sex Piston for advice.

When she finally came out of the bathroom, Shade was leaning against his cabinet with his shirt and boots removed.

Lily came to an abrupt stop, looking at the determined expression on his face. Shade took out a slip of paper she recognized. It was her IOU.

"I'm going to give you a choice. Either you can apologize or I can cash in my hour of time. Your choice, Angel."

Which was really no choice at all.

Stubbornly, she mimicked him, crossing her arms over her chest. "The IOU." Lily trembled when he gave her a lethal smile. "I'm not the one who should apologize."

"Take off your nightgown."

Lily jerked off her gown, throwing it at his smug face, her eyes throwing violent sparks.

Shade went to his cabinet, opening the side where he kept his toys, she was sure. He pulled out a paddle then sat it back down. Next, he took out a flogger. Lily swallowed hard when he sat that back down. He paused several seconds before he opened a sliding compartment to the side, taking out what she had only seen in old westerns that looked like a whip.

Lily lost her confidence.

Scanning her new bedroom, she picked the closest corner and ran to it, shivering when Shade laughed.

He sat the whip down on the chair next to the cabinet then went back to his cabinet and pulled out leather cuffs.

"Get on the bed, Lily."

"I'm sorry. I overreacted." Lily's temper had fled when he had pulled out the flogger.

"You're not sorry yet, but you will be." He pointed to the bed. "Bed. Now."

Lily tried one more time to escape her punishment. "Blueberries."

"What did I tell you about using your safe word to get out of a punishment?" If it was possible, his frown became even more ferocious. Her mouth snapped open. "If you're about to tell me you hate me, I would seriously think about it." Her mouth closed.

Lily wanted to cry, but channeled her inner Sex Piston and stubbornly lifted her chin. Leaving the relative safety of the corner, she went to the bed and lay down.

"On your stomach." Lily paused then rolled onto her stomach.

As soon as she was on her stomach, she heard him move. He took her wrist and placed the leather cuff around her wrist then moved it to the headboard and slipped the ring into the hook on the bottom, snapping it closed. He moved to her other side and did the same. He then moved to the foot of the bed and buckled another cuff around her ankle before doing the same to the other. She was now bound and spread-eagled on the bed.

His hand brushed her calf as he picked up the whip.

"I can understand you being angry about Raci wearing my jacket. I wouldn't have said a thing if you had tore me a new asshole. What I didn't think was cool was you trying to get Rider killed. If you had touched anything of his, he would have been in the morgue tonight, brother or not.

"I don't think that you have quite grasped the fact that you are mine, Lily. Mine."

She heard the swish of the whip and gave a startled scream, waiting for the burning pain. She lay there, paralyzed with fear, not knowing what to do. When the tip of the whip touched the hair on the back of her shoulder, it actually felt like he had brushed it away with his hand. She felt only the faintest touch against her skin.

Thinking he had missed, she heard the sound of the whip again, this time feeling it against her other shoulder, the barest touch as if he had touched her with a gentle finger. She lay tense as another series of flicks had her feeling as if he was caressing her with fluttering touches. Her fear lessened and she relaxed against the mattress, a tear of relief she couldn't hold back slipping from the corner of her eye.

The whip started striking her faster, moving from her shoulders to different areas of her back. This time Lily felt the strikes going from caresses to tingling, waking her nerve endings until she felt a light buzz across her skin, almost like when she felt static electricity. She felt the tiny flicks as he moved to her lower back then her buttocks, down her legs to her ankles. Her whole body was tingling.

Shade moved between her thighs, his fingers sliding into the moisture she had felt beginning when the whip had been striking her buttocks. Two fingers plunged into her passage.

"Are you doing okay, Lily?"

"Yes," She mumbled.

Shade's fingers slid out of her, giving only a faint brush against her clit. He went to the nightstand and Lily heard the music as he switched it on. He walked back to the foot of the bed where she couldn't see him again.

"I didn't give Raci my jacket. She was joking around and picked it up and put it on. I told her to take it off several times. I controlled my temper and didn't jerk it off her the way I wanted because I knew she had smoked some pot and thought she was being cute. I told her that she earned a month's punishment. She wasn't allowed to smoke anymore pot since she obviously doesn't know how to handle it. Then I told her that if she touched my fucking jacket again, she would lose her membership to The Last Riders. She got my message. You, on the other hand, are still learning. That's okay, though, because I'm patient and I plan on teaching you to behave just the way I want."

As he talked, the whip began striking at her buttocks, the tingling now escalating to a slight stinging sensation that had first startled her, but now had small moans escaping her lips. The speed they were hitting her was so fast, she would feel the small sting then another would start before the other could fade away.

He stopped again and she felt his fingers slipping inside of her again, plunging deep before sliding away. His thumb caressing her clit with firm swipes before stopping suddenly.

"Shade…"

This time, when the whip struck, it felt thicker, making a loud thud sound, but it didn't hurt. It felt like when she had been given a deep tissue massage.

The whip moved back and forth across her shoulders. Lily moaned louder, her hips wiggling on the mattress. The whip stopped.

"Quit moving or I'll stop," Shade ordered.

Lily froze on the mattress, not wanting it to end. The

whip resumed. She did not understand how the loud thud against her flesh wasn't hurting.

Lily's body became boneless under the massaging rhythm of the whip as it began to feel harder against her bottom, moving back and forth across her buttocks as if he was now lightly spanking her. Lily felt the moisture between her thighs increase, becoming embarrassed that in her spread eagle position she was unable to hide her response to his strikes. The pressure in her began to build.

She tried to wiggle in her restraints again, and the whip immediately stopped. The now familiar feel of Shade stroking her pussy almost made her come.

"Do not come," Shade ordered, pressing down on her clit.

A broken whimper slipped past her lips. "Please, Shade."

"Do Not Move." Shade's hand left her and then he returned to tormenting her with his whip. The heavy thuds across her buttocks returned and his spanking continued. She heard him moving this time when the whip hit. It felt like the time he had put her over his lap and spanked her hard. The whip moved across her butt to just under the curve of her butt cheek.

"I'm sorry. I shouldn't have asked Rider for his jacket," Lily cried, wanting to come. The pleasure/pain of his strokes was driving her toward an orgasm and she didn't know how much longer she could hold out. Her body was being taken over by a frenzied need.

When she didn't think she could stay still any longer, she heard the thud of the whip as it hit the floor. Then Shade's hands were on the cuffs at her feet, unbuckling them from the hooks.

"If you want my dick, get on your knees."

Lily forced her shaking body to move as he un-cuffed her wrists. With the use of her hands returned, she was able to get onto her knees, her dark hair sliding forward, hiding her face from his sharp gaze.

She watched as he removed his jeans.

"Do you really believe I will cheat on you?" Shade's face was stoic as he stared at her, but the look in his eyes was easily readable.

"No." Lily released a deep breath, beginning to cry.

A tender look crossed his face, his hand reaching out to stroke her face. "Angel, I'm not Marshall. He made you think he was going to be a father to you and betrayed your trust. That's why when you felt Beth had betrayed you, you took it so bad. Beth didn't betray you, and I sure as fuck won't."

Shade moved to the bed, getting into position behind her. His cock brushed the opening of her pussy, just letting the tip of his cock enter her. His hand pulled her hair back, keeping it in a tight grip.

"You're going to give me everything I need from a woman." His cock slid through her tight channel then came to a stop.

Lily cried out. "Please, Shade. I can't take anymore."

"You are the woman I love. You're my wife. I never put my ring on another woman. I never gave them my love. I never gave them me. Not once. Only to you, my wife, have I given myself to. Don't you ever doubt that again."

"I won't," Lily cried out as he buried his length to her belly, his cock hitting her high, causing a brief flare of pain before his strokes changed direction, rubbing against the inside of her. It brought a fission of sensation unlike any she had felt before.

His hand gripped her hip, bringing her butt higher while he stroked downward. His other hand tugged at her hair, forcing her head back.

"I'm sorry, Sir," Lily moaned over and over again as his dick plunged inside of her with enough force that she heard each smack as his body hit hers.

The erotic sound with the music made her feel as if he surrounded her, that there was no escape from the control he had over the pleasure that was breaking her apart into tiny pieces. The orgasm struck with a climatic force.

Lily lost all control of her body as she fell, shaking, to the mattress with Shade following her down, pinning her under his weight as he continued to fuck her steadily. Lily's nails tore at the sheets as he showed no mercy, forcing another orgasm out of her rippling pussy. His hands reached for her hand interweaving them together.

"My wife." The relief and aching love in his voice and all it conveyed was shared with her in that moment of intimacy. Every minute and second he had waited had been torture for this man of hers.

Lily felt him shudder against her as his cock jerked his release deep within her. Lily lowered her head against the sheet, exhausted both mentally and physically.

Shade rolled to his side, pulling her to lay on his chest.

"Are you still mad at me?"

Shade twined a tendril of her hair through his fingers. "I don't get mad at you, Lily. I'm a—"

Lily laughed. "A patient man. I know."

"I didn't want my jacket on her either, but I was trying to be a nice guy." His words reminding her how often she had called him mean.

Lily lowered her head, ashamed. "I'm really sorry."

Shade grinned. "You can show me that temper anytime." His hand moved down to rub her bottom. "In private. I like to keep my business my own," he clarified. "Are you sore?"

"No." Lily shook her head, yawning.

Shade rose up with her, getting to his feet then carrying her to the bathroom. He sat her on her feet while he made a bath for her. She saw him pour something into the water.

"Rose and Lavender oils," he told her.

Lily sank into the warm water when it was ready, leaning back against the tub as Shade went to the sink. She watched as he shaved, looking at his tattoo covered body. She didn't know how she had gotten lucky enough to get

Shade, just grateful she had.

"What are you thinking?" Shade asked his now familiar question. He liked control, that was for sure. He constantly wanted to know what she was thinking. She thought it was his own insecurity showing itself.

She caught his gaze in the mirror. "I was thinking, now would be a good time to tell you that I offered to throw Sex Piston's baby shower tomorrow night."

* * *

Shade stood in the kitchen with Razer, Viper and Stud, wondering how in the hell he had been put in this position. His eyes went to the other men and saw the same expression on their faces.

"I take it you're having a boy," Shade said.

Stud grinned proudly, the only man in the group not ashamed to admit he was pussy whipped. "Thank fuck. If it had been a girl, I had my escape plan in place."

Shade watched Lily hand Sex Piston a blue stroller made of diapers that she had stayed up half the night to make. When he had asked why not just give her the fucking pack of diapers, she had looked like he had cracked his whip across her ass. After that, he had kept his mouth shut.

Shade heard Crazy Bitch question Lily about his tats. He reached in the cabinet by Viper's head for his liquor bottle then grabbed enough glasses for the other men.

He was pouring himself a glass when he heard a sudden burst of laughter.

"Shade helped you make my gift?" Sex Piston's disbelieving voice rose over the giggles.

"Yes, Shade brags all the time about how patient he is, but I never would have believed he would have helped like he did. He counted out the diapers, then made the wheels, and when I couldn't thread the ribbon through the top, he did it for me." His wife's damning words had the men looking at him with amusement on their faces.

He added another two fingers of whiskey to his glass.

"Patient? She actually thinks you're patient?" Viper almost choked on his drink.

"Shut the fuck up," Shade threatened, pouring himself another drink. It was a sad day when his brethren had the courage to laugh at him. The men at least were smart enough to smother their laughter.

"He's nothing like Train then." Shade winced for Train as Killyama dissected their fuck session. His fellow brother did not come out well.

When the women moved on to asking Lily questions, his hand was shaking as he poured the men their refills. It was a good thing he had wanted to wait a couple of weeks before he used his favorite toy on his wife again or she would have been complaining over the pretty sunrise pattern he promised himself she would receive for putting him through this torture.

Lily came into the kitchen, pulling out the large pitcher of tea she had made, stopping briefly to brush a kiss on his cheek. His eyes followed the jiggle of her ass as she went back into the living room.

His president put his arm around his shoulder. "Don't worry, Shade. It could be worse. You could be Train."

CHAPTER THIRTY-SEVEN
Friday

Lily walked down the pathway from her house, down to the parking lot. She still felt a thrill when she said *my* house, *my* husband. It had only been four days since their marriage, so she was sure it was going to feel that way for a while. She hoped it always did. She never wanted to take what she was feeling for granted.

Shade had to be at work two hours before she had to open the church store at nine. Curiously, she saw Shade, Razer, Rider and Train talking in the parking lot. It was unusual so early in the morning that all three were outside.

"What's up?"

"Nothing. We came out here so we could talk without being overheard. Georgia has several friends in there." Shade replied.

"What about Georgia?" Lily stiffened. Today was the first day back since the Christmas holidays. Both Shade and Razer had looked forward to firing the woman this morning, and she hadn't argued this time. Georgia had gone too far. She felt bad for her kids, but ultimately Georgia had to face responsibility for her actions.

"She quit. When she didn't come in this morning, I called her. She told me she wasn't coming in to give us the satisfaction of firing her. Then she told me what to do with the job, so I hung up on her." Shade's face showed how much he'd wanted to give the woman her filth back. She was proud he had handled it in a professional manner, despite it probably sticking in his gut.

"It doesn't make any sense to me," Lily said, blowing on her coffee.

"What doesn't? That she's a fucking bitch or that she quit?" Rider asked grimly.

"Both. Not a month ago, she was giving me heck because she thought I took her brother's job; now suddenly, she's calling one of her bosses' wives bad names in front of a large group who will spread it all over town so she wouldn't be able to deny it. It's almost like she wanted to get fired," Lily answered, blowing on her coffee again.

She reached up, giving her husband a quick kiss on his lips. "Later." She grinned, walking away, not paying attention to the stunned looks on the men's faces as she pulled out of the parking lot.

* * *

Lily unlocked the church store, going inside and then closing the door behind her.

"Morning, Mrs. Hunter," Pastor Dean said, coming in from the church entrance. "How are you this sunny morning?"

"Good. And you?"

"Can't complain, other than I've gained ten pounds over the holidays. I think if one more parishioner gives me one more casserole or cookie, I'm going to vomit."

"That bad?"

"The problem was that it was too good," Pastor Dean laughed. "I'm bursting at the seams."

Lily pulled two bags of clothes out from under the counter and another that had been shoved into a darkened corner. When she tugged the bag loose, it jarred a metal box. Lily dropped to her knees, reaching back, and with her fingertips managed to snag the box by the handle, sliding it free. She pulled it out from under the counter and then stood up, lifting the heavy box with difficulty onto the counter.

"What's that?" Pastor Dean asked, looking at the box curiously.

"Your guess is as good as mine. It looks like it's been shoved under there for a while." Lily pulled the two metal rings open then tried to open it. It was locked.

"It's locked," she said, stating the obvious.

"I have some tools in my office. I'll take care of it."

"Okay." Lily slid it across the counter toward him.

A customer came in and she moved toward the woman entering the store.

"I'll see you later, Lily."

She waved as Pastor Dean left, asking the woman what she needed.

Lily wondered what was in the box. She would have to remind herself to ask before she went home.

* * *

Shade was standing next to Razer in his office when his cell phone rang. The caller ID showed Dean was calling.

"Yeah?"

"Thought I'd let you know that your new wife found a lock box in the basement this morning. Want to take a wild guess what was inside?"

"Lily's adoption papers?"

"Yes."

"Fake?"

"Yes. I'll take them by Knox's office when I go to lunch."

"Thanks. Want to hear something interesting?"

"Hit me."

"Georgia quit this morning. Beat me to firing her ass. Thing is, Lily came up with this idea. She seemed like she wanted to be fired, so we checked it out. Seems the bitch had a chunk of money put in her checking account the day after Halloween."

"How much?"

"Fifty thousand. Not only that, another deposit of thirty was put in first thing this morning. This is the first day the banks have been open since Christmas."

"Someone paid her not only to start the fire, but to start an argument at the church," Shade concluded.

"Why start an argument at the church?"

"I think to try to rattle Lily into running out of the church. A month ago… hell, two weeks ago, it would have worked. Whoever wants her dead is getting desperate to try to get to her. We don't leave her alone, so someone was trying to make their own opportunity."

"I'll call Knox to come here and pick these papers up. I'm not going to leave the church from now on when Lily's here," Dean's voice was grim over the phone line.

"I'll call you if I find anything else out. Once Knox has the proof from the bank, he's going to arrest Georgia. I took him her coffee cup, so if the DNA matches the evidence found from the fire, we have her ass, and we may be able to find out what the fuck is going on," Shade's anger carried through the phone line.

"All right, I'll talk to you later, Shade."

"Later, Dean."

* * *

Lily locked the door to the church store, surprised to see Shade had picked her up from the store in Rider's truck. He always picked her up on his bike unless the roads were slick with snow or it was pouring rain.

It had been a long week and she was looking forward to the weekend to get some chores finished. She and Beth needed to clean out their house so it could be put up for sale. Almost all of the furnishings were going to be donated to the church store. They were both going to keep the few items that held sentimental attachment to them, though.

"Why the truck?" Lily asked, climbing inside.

Her husband's sunglasses stared back, hiding his

expression. "I wanted to talk to you on the way home," Shade said, making no effort to put the truck in gear.

"Is something wrong?" Lily questioned, becoming worried.

"Knox arrested Georgia this afternoon."

"Why? What did she do?" Lily's breath caught in surprise.

"She's the one who set the basement on fire."

"What? Why would she do something like that?" Lily asked. She knew the woman hated her, but she'd never dreamed it had been enough to kill her.

"Someone paid her fifty thousand dollars. The same person who probably tried to run you down on the street and attempted to break into your house.

"Who?" Lily tried to think of someone who could possibly want her dead.

"I don't know. Knox is questioning her now. He's going to be at the club tonight so we can find out more then."

She sat in shock while Shade drove them home. She and Georgia had attended the same church for years. The whole community would know she had been arrested. That would be a hard bit of humiliation for Georgia to bear.

"You better tell Knox to keep an eye on her. When she was younger, she tried to kill herself twice. This is going to humiliate her, Shade," Lily warned.

As soon as he parked the truck, Shade made the call to Knox. They went to their house to get changed before going over to eat dinner at the clubhouse. This was their first party since they had gotten married, and she wanted to look pretty for him.

Tonight she had dressed in one of her few short skirts. It came barely above her knees. Sex Piston had picked it out so it was tighter than she usually wore, as well. She had teamed it with a soft pink sweater that showed a faint hint of her breasts.

She had felt pretty and sexy until she walked into the clubhouse. Her sister was wearing a cute red skirt and a black vest.

"You look pretty tonight," Lily complimented her.

"You do, too. I might have to borrow that sweater," Beth said with envy.

"You can have it. It won't quit sliding down my shoulders." Lily pulled it back up in frustration.

"That's what makes it so pretty," Winter said, coming up behind her.

They ate dinner then decided to play cards, ignoring the men. Lily lost several games to Winter.

Sitting back in her chair, she watched as Winter picked up the huge pile of IOUs from the table. "I don't understand it. When I first started to play, I was good. Now I can't win a game." Lily's frustration with the cards had her throwing them down.

When the women burst out laughing, Lily looked at them suspiciously. "What's so funny?"

"You played with Train," Evie said. "He always cheats when he plays with women."

Lily looked at Jewell. "I didn't mind losing," she said unrepentantly.

"So they set me up?"

"Like a duck during duck-hunting season," Winter said shrewdly.

Lily looked at Winter at her comment. "You knew the guys set me up?" Lily's eyes narrowed on Winter. She had been set up both times she'd played cards. She had SUCKER written all over her.

Lily watched Winter smooth out her slips of IOUs. "I couldn't be sure."

Lily was willing to bet Winter had known; she hadn't played with anyone else since, and she was still gullible enough to believe she was good. The woman's name was listed under devious in the dictionary—Winter and Shade's.

She looked around the room to see the men were on a couch, talking quietly to themselves.

"I'm done for the night." She stood up, ignoring their grins. She would deal with them later; she was going to give her husband heck first.

She went to the couch where Shade was sitting on the end with his feet on the coffee table while Viper sat at the other end. Razer was sprawled on the chair next to the couch.

She started to say something to Shade then noticed they were having a serious discussion. Having seen her approach, they had quit talking. She turned to leave, giving them the opportunity to finish their talk when Shade caught her hand, dragging her down to sit on his lap.

The men began talking about their clubhouse in Ohio and the new recruits they had.

"Got one wanting to go for the patch here," Shade said, lacing his hand through hers. In that moment, she forgot she was mad over the cards, rubbing her thumb against his.

"Who?" Viper asked, his eyes going around the room.

"Dude against the left wall with the eight-ball tat," Shade answered without turning his head. Lily started to turn her head, but Shade's hand tightened on the hand he was holding so Lily remained still. This time it was his thumb rubbing hers.

"Name?" Viper didn't take his eyes off the recruit.

"Eightball."

"How original," Viper said wryly.

"I thought so. He had to think a couple of seconds when I asked," Shade said, his voice unemotional.

"Anything else?"

"He's good. Knows how to handle himself and his bike." Shade paused, looking at Lily. "Too good for someone not patched."

"Stud?"

"No. Stud doesn't play that game, but even if he did, he

wouldn't with us. He wouldn't want to take a chance on Sex Piston finding out; she and Beth are too tight. He's not going to get his old lady upset when she's carrying his kid."

"I agree, so who?" Viper asked in demand. Lily didn't think Viper wanted to wait when he wanted answers.

"Don't know, but I'll find out," Shade promised his president.

"Now," Viper commanded.

Lily expected Shade to get up; instead, he remained sitting.

"I'm on it," Shade replied, nodding his head toward Cash at the bar. Lily's eyes went to the bar, seeing Cash had his eyes on Shade.

At Shade's nod, he set his glass of whiskey down then said something to Nickel, who was standing next to him. When both men moved toward the left wall, Lily didn't turn her head; Shade's hand had tightened on hers once again. Lily started trembling and her bottom lip began quivering when she heard a scuffle going on behind her.

"Shade…" He leaned forward, brushing his lips against hers as his hand picked up his beer.

"Angel face, I like that sweater on you," he murmured against her lips.

"Don't hurt him," she pleaded softly back.

"Have to find out if he's here because of you."

Lily could tell the conversation was over when he lifted his mouth away from hers, leaning back against the couch and taking a drink of his beer. Train drew her attention away from Shade when he stopped in front of the couch.

"Lily, a buddy of mine gave me two pieces-of-shit bikes he wanted to get rid of. I fixed them up. Don't want them; none of the brothers want them. If you want them, you can have them to sell for your store, or maybe someone needs a ride for work."

"Thank you, Train." Lily jumped off Shade's lap, intending to hug him. She took a step toward him with her arms out when he froze like she had pulled a gun on him.

Before she could take another step, an arm around her waist swept her back down onto Shade's lap and she was staring up at a furious Shade.

"Stop doing that shit. Do. Not. Touch," he told her with his jaw clenched.

"What? But I was only going to thank him," Lily protested.

"Then thank him, but Do. Not. Touch. And quit kissing," he added as an afterthought.

"Quit kissing? But I like kissing you; I don't want to stop that," Lily protested, turning red when she heard Viper and Razer laughing. Train was still standing, unmoving.

"That's not what I meant." Shade's face gradually regained control. "I meant when you kiss men on the cheek."

"Who did I kiss on the cheek?"

"Viper." Lily's mind went back to when she had kissed Viper on the cheek outside the diner. She also remembered him being doubled over. Train was still frozen as she also remembered another incident.

"You scared Pastor Dean," she said in reproach.

"You do not touch anyone, especially Pastor Dean."

Lily looked at him. "Okay."

She relaxed against him, rubbing his chest with her hand until his breathing returned to normal.

"Thank you," he said, relaxing back against the couch.

"No problem." Lily smiled gently up at him.

"Thank God. At least we finally got that shit straight. I didn't think I'd have a brother left after Christmas."

Lily remembered when she'd given Christmas presents out. She had given each of the men a small peck on the cheek.

"You didn't?" She looked at him suspiciously.

"No, but it was close," Shade said unrepentantly.

She was shaking her head at him for his refusal to admit to being overly possessive when Knox came in with

Diamond. She was like Lily; she hadn't dressed overtly sexy either. She was wearing a dark jumper and a black pair of leggings with high-heeled boots that Lily really liked.

Knox took a seat on the couch next to Shade, pulling Diamond down onto his lap. Knox wasn't wearing his uniform, just jeans and a t-shirt. His huge frame crowded the large sofa. Lily had to sit up straighter, curling her legs on top of Shade's.

"I put Georgia on suicide watch. Had to hire an extra policewoman from Jamestown, but at least I don't have to worry about walking into her cell and finding her dead," Knox said, looking at Lily. "You were right. I saw the marks on her wrist."

"I wouldn't have ever said anything, but I didn't want her to hurt herself because she'd made a mistake."

"It's more than a mistake. She fucked up bad. She's going to do some hard time for arson unless she can come up with a name. Cash is trying to trace the account, but he said whoever set the account up knows what they're doing. He said it's one of the best he's ever seen," Knox informed them.

"Fuck," Shade exclaimed.

"Not only that, but Georgia says she doesn't know the man who gave her the money. Said she was at the grocery store and he drove a dark car up to her when she was putting groceries in her car. Handed her twenty thousand to do it then promised her the fifty thousand after it was done."

"Did you check the store surveillance?" Viper asked.

"Sure did. The store erases the tapes after a month. I looked through them just in case we got lucky, but no such luck."

"Damn," Shade said. "I was hoping she had more information than that."

"I'll see if she can remember anything more in the morning; maybe spending her first night in jail will jog her memory," Knox responded, adjusting Diamond on his lap.

"We need to catch a break somewhere before whoever they are makes another move against Lily." Shade's words frightened her. It was disconcerting to have someone so determined to hurt you and not know why.

"I like your boots," Lily said to Diamond.

"Thanks, I bought them at the shoe store in town. It sucks that store is on the way to the courthouse. I have to pass it every day. These were in the window. The manager knows what I like and I swear he puts stuff in the window he knows I can't resist."

"I like shoes, too. I have some new ones that I haven't worn yet. I don't get much of an opportunity to wear them and they're too large for Beth to wear."

"Really? What size are they?" Diamond asked casually, yet Lily was well aware of the gleam of avarice in her eyes.

"Eight," Lily answered with a smile.

"Damn, I wear a nine."

"Sorry about that," Lily apologized with a smile. She'd never had a girlfriend to share clothes with before.

"What size is the sweater?"

"Small."

"I'm a medium, but it looks big on you; it could work." Diamond reached out to touch the soft pink sweater. "I love pink, but it usually clashes with my hair.

"Let's dance," Shade interrupted them, his hand lifting her legs off his.

Lily looked around the room, seeing Train already had his hand between Bliss's thighs as she sat on a stool at the bar. Several of the women, who were allowed in the house, were dancing suggestively with the members on the floor. Nickel was standing behind one, pulling her breast out of her top. Lily looked away.

"I think the floor is crowded enough." Lily stood up.

"It isn't downstairs," Shade said, taking her hand. "Knox?"

"Coming."

Shade turned to Viper and Razer. "Later."

"Happy New Year, brother," Viper said, lifting his beer up.

"You, too."

Lily followed Shade downstairs. She was happy he understood she hadn't wanted to stay up there. This way she could stay and have fun without being uncomfortable watching the others.

Shade turned on a couple of the lamps then turned on the music. He pulled up the workout mats, placing them against the wall before holding out his arms for her. She stepped into his arms without hesitation.

Knox and Diamond came downstairs, closing the door behind them and then they began dancing next to them.

Lily had been around Knox the least of the members, so he was slightly frightening to her because of his size, though his gentle expression when he was with Diamond eased her fears. They spent a while on the dance floor before Shade went upstairs, getting beers for him and Knox, bringing sodas for her and Diamond.

After sitting and talking for a while, Knox and Diamond went to the dance floor to dance again.

"Are you having fun?" Shade asked, sitting down on the couch next to her.

"Yes. I like Diamond." Lily lowered her voice. "Shade, she really doesn't believe that zombies are going to take over the world, does she?"

Shade laughed. "I have no idea. I think she just watches too many zombie movies."

"See. That's why I don't watch scary movies." She gave him an I-told-you-so look.

"Why? Are you susceptible to movies?"

"Scary ones. They give me nightmares."

"Porno?" Shade leaned over her.

"No." Lily hit his shoulder, laughing. Her laughter stopped when she saw the look of desire in his eyes.

His mouth touched hers, parting her lips with a firm thrust of his tongue, demanding her response. She widened her lips, letting him have the control he wanted.

His hand then went to her shoulder, brushing the sweater off it. His mouth followed the path of the sweater while his other hand slid it off the other shoulder. Only her breasts now held up her sweater.

Shade's chest crushed her against the corner of the couch. His hand went to her thigh, sliding underneath her skirt, finding the edge of her panties. Lily felt a burning heat spread throughout her.

The music changed to a different song, bringing Lily back to awareness of where she was. She pushed Shade off her, sitting upright. Looking toward the dance floor, she saw that Knox and Diamond weren't paying attention to them. Knox was standing behind Diamond, grinding his hips into her ass, his arm around her waist to pull her back against him. Diamond was dancing with her eyes closed, listening to the music, and Knox was only looking at Diamond.

Shade stood up, pulling Lily to her feet before lifting her into his arms. He carried her back to the bedroom where he set her on her feet next to the bed then turned on the bedside lamp.

Lily was amazed he could see so well in the dark. She had noticed before he could walk in the pitch dark like he could see where everything was.

He took off his clothes then reached out, taking off her sweater and bra, his lips kissing each nipple when he pulled it off.

"Sit down."

Lily sat down on the edge of the bed. Shade bent down, pulling off her shoes and then kissing each foot he raised to his lips. Lily was charmed by his gentleness, thinking she was the luckiest woman in the world. He stood up, tossing her shoes out of the way. Then bending over, his mouth found hers again, giving her the passion she had been waiting for from him. His teeth nipped her bottom lip, giving her a small sting of pain, which he laved away with the tip of his tongue before he pressed her back against the mattress.

"Where did this furniture come from?" Lily tore her mouth away from his.

"I ordered another set. It came yesterday."

"Oh." Lily thought a second. "Why?"

"For when I want to play over here," he explained, taking a nipple into his mouth.

"Ohhh," Lily moaned as he bit down on the tip of her breast.

Just as her thigh came up, rubbing against his hip, Lily heard a sound and turned toward the doorway as Knox came in carrying a wiggling Diamond on his shoulder.

"Bed or couch?" Knox asked, pausing long enough to shut the door with his foot.

"Bed." Diamond and Lily both squealed, however Shade covered her mouth with his. Lily felt the lurch of the bed as Diamond was dropped onto the opposite end.

"Shade, I—" Lily started to protest.

"Lily, it's my turn," he said with a smile. "And I'm cashing in another of my IOUs."

Lily wasn't given time to think as Shade's mouth played with her breasts. As the mattress underneath her head shuddered with Diamond and Knox's movement, Lily could only guess he was undressing her from her gasps.

Shade straightened, standing up. "You got your cuffs?"

"Always," Knox grunted.

Lily thought she heard a whack against flesh at the same time she saw Shade reach into his nightstand, pulling out a pair of cuffs. Lily lay disbelieving as he slipped one cuff onto her wrist then stretched, snapping the other end to Diamond's wrist above her head. Shade then lifted her other wrist and she felt the snick of another handcuff close. Diamond and she were handcuffed together.

They started wiggling, and when Diamond tried to lower her wrists, it stretched Lily taut on the mattress. When Lily tried to lower hers, it stretched Diamond's body taut.

"Fuck." Lily heard Knox's groan of approval at what he was looking at.

Lily was sure she was red all the way to her breasts; she was so embarrassed. Then she remembered that, when Knox and Diamond had been dancing, Knox's eyes had only been on Diamond.

Lily looked up at Shade. He was staring down at her, his eyes filled with desire for her. Only her. Lily relaxed back against the mattress, coming to the decision she was going to let her husband play. Shade saw the resolve in her eyes and grinned.

She heard the rustling of clothes and automatically turned her head. The mirror on the walls reflected the four of them. She and Diamond lying on opposite sides of the huge bed handcuffed together, Shade naked, and Knox getting undressed. Her mouth dropped open, and she squinted her eyes to make sure she was seeing what she thought she was seeing.

She had never stared at Shade's cock the way she gaped at Knox's. Shade was big himself, yet Knox's cock was big and pierced. She looked at Diamond sympathetically then noticed the woman staring back at her, obviously embarrassed, though her eyes were twinkling in silent amusement at Lily for noticing Knox's cock.

Shade opened the nightstand again, pulling out several silk scarves and tossing a few to Knox. She felt Shade wind a scarf around the inside of the cuff so it wouldn't scratch her before he did the same to the other wrist.

Turning to the wall, he turned on the music.

"You have a thing for music, don't you?" Lily teased.

"It inspires me," Shade replied, smiling before stepping back between her legs and reaching for the waistband of her skirt. Lily then felt him lift her hips while he pulled her skirt and panties off.

Despite her wanting to please Shade, she couldn't help feeling uncomfortable being naked in front of Knox. She didn't even feel comfortable wearing a swimsuit in front of men. Only the remembrance of the way Knox had looked at Diamond reassured her. He looked at Diamond the way Shade looked at her.

Before she had time to ruminate further, Shade reached for another silk scarf, placing it over her eyes and tying it behind her head. Lily felt the movement at the top of her head and knew that Knox was doing the same to Diamond.

"I could jack off just looking at you like this." Shade's voice was hoarse with desire, and Lily relaxed again.

She felt Shade's mouth on the curve of her stomach, his tongue tasting her flesh. Then Diamond moved, bringing Lily's arms up, stretching her taut on the mattress. Lily gasped as his lips traced the bare skin of her pussy, his tongue dipping inside the slit, licking the top of her clit before sliding underneath, searching for the nerve endings that were screaming for attention.

Shade's hand cupped the back of her knee, bringing her leg up until her heel touched the mattress. Then he pressed her leg down sideways, the movement widening her. His tongue then slid through the opening of her cunt.

Her hands went down to his head, but she couldn't reach him. Diamond groaned, and Lily hastily put her hands back by her shoulders.

"Sorry," Lily mumbled.

"That's okay. You can do it again if you want to," Diamond moaned.

Lily couldn't help it, she giggled. A second later, the bed started shaking and Lily heard Diamond laughing, too.

"I think the next time I'll bring a couple of gags to the party," Shade threatened.

"I'll take care of it," Knox promised. Both of the women's laughter died immediately.

Lily felt the brush of his cock against her pussy a second before he thrust inside of her, driving himself into her with a single thrust. She reached up to his shoulders, sliding her hands to his chest and lingering on his nipples. With the scarf over her eyes, she felt the smoothness of his skin contrasted by the ridges, the skin of his nipples.

Her hands were jerked away and she was stretched as Diamond tried to reach Knox, her moans escalating, telling her she was enjoying whatever Knox was doing. Her screams confirmed that a second later. Shade began toying with her clit as he pounded his cock inside her slick pussy which was trying to adjust to the force of his thrusts.

Her thighs were lifted and pressed to her sides as Shade gave her more of his weight.

"Want to switch?"

Lily was about to climax when she heard Knox's voice.

"Fuck yeah," Shade answered.

"What!?" Diamond yelled.

"No!" squealed Lily, a coldness hitting her in the chest.

The men ignored them.

Lily felt Shade's cock slide out and felt the start of her climax die a sudden death. Shade put his hands on her waist then she was being rolled onto her stomach at the same time Diamond was. Lily had been turned so that her face was on top of the mattress, their hands now palm down on the mattress.

"Very funny," Diamond's irritated voice sounded over Knox's laughter.

Shade's hand went back to her hips, raising her bottom back in the air before sliding his cock back inside her in a thrust that had her screeching almost in Diamond's ear. The mattress shook as the men pounded the women. Lily's hands grasped the sheets.

"I've never seen something so hot," Knox groaned, and for several seconds, Lily thought that if Diamond and she hadn't been cuffed together, they would have bounced off the bed with the strength of the men going at them.

As Shade's hand went between her thighs, rubbing her clit, Lily could hear the slap of flesh against flesh filling the room. The erotic sounds heightened her arousal.

A second later, Shade's thumb pinched her clit, the pain lifting her ass higher against him.

"Fuck me back," Shade grunted.

Lily began thrusting her ass back at him as he thrust forward while he teased her clit, rubbing away the small sting of pain in a move that had her panting.

"Shade, I need to come," Lily begged, needing just a little more to bring her over.

He pulled his cock out so that only the tip was inside her. "You going to come by my office before you go to work Monday and give me this pussy?"

"Yes," Lily screamed when he filled her again.

Diamond began screaming, clutching Lily's hands. Lily grabbed her back as Shade's fingers reached underneath her, taking a nipple in his hand.

He began squeezing her breast until she felt it become tender and sensitive. When his fingers finally reached her nipple again, he twisted the nub. A burst of painful pleasure had her forcing the scream back in her throat, afraid she would hurt Diamond's ears.

Her control broke and she experienced her orgasm through a cloud of euphoria that held her senseless for several seconds. She came back into herself as Shade and Knox were unlocking the handcuffs.

Shade pulled off her blindfold, kissing her on her parted lips as her eyes opened. The love in his eyes had her raising her hand to touch his cheek.

"How do you keep your face so cleanly shaven?" The innocuous comment seemed normal to her.

"I shave a couple of times a day," he answered, lifting her up into his arms.

"Why so often?" she asked, laying her head on his shoulder.

"Because you like to touch my face." Shade carried her into the shower before setting her down.

"Why don't you do that for me? " Lily heard Diamond ask Knox.

She looked up to see they were in the big shower, but the only thing she could see was Shade's shoulders and Knox's back and head. Now she understood why the shower was so large. Lily was about to get out of the shower, but Shade turned the water on, handing her the soap.

Lily quickly washed then hurried out of the shower. Shade was right behind her, grinning as he dressed, watching Lily throw her own clothes on. She was about to rip a seam in her skirt when she realized Diamond and Knox were still in the shower.

Diamond was giving her the opportunity to get dressed. *She's probably as sensitive as I am*, Lily thought. She didn't seem to have much more experience at this than Lily did. Lily calmed down and finished dressing.

"Thirsty?" Shade asked.

"Yes."

Lily and Shade went back to the front of the basement. It was a while before Knox and Diamond came out. Knox threw himself down on the couch, pulling Diamond on his lap. Picking up his beer, he took a long drink.

"How is the new gismo Cash is working on?" Knox asked Shade.

"Waiting on the patent. As soon as it's approved, we can start selling it," Shade said, taking a drink of his own beer.

"Good. I need the cash. Diamond wants to turn our house into a fucking fortress." Knox grinned at his wife who threw him a dirty look.

Shade answered Knox's other questions on the factory, discussing several items that were making the highest sales.

Lily sat, sipping her now-flat soft drink, avoiding Diamond's eyes. Eventually, their eyes met, though, and they smiled at each other, silently laughing at their embarrassment.

"So, can I borrow your sweater?" Diamond asked.

"Yes."

* * *

Lily was almost asleep when Shade slid under the covers, pulling them over their bodies. When he tugged her to him, she rolled over, burying her face in his neck as she lay against his chest.

"Shade…" Lily began.

"Knox will always be a brother, but being sheriff he has to keep a low profile. Diamond is a lawyer. She's a good one. She's going to move up."

"I like to play; Knox likes to play. We all know how to keep our mouths shut. That's why Viper and Razer talked club business in front of you. You kept Georgia's secret even though that bitch trashed you all over town. The only time you talked was to protect someone else and to save Georgia's life after she almost killed you.

"I think Diamond's an attractive woman, but I don't want to fuck her. Do you understand what I'm saying?"

"Yes," Lily whispered.

She had briefly seen Knox naked. She thought he was handsome in a fierce kind of way, yet she would never be attracted to him.

"If you want to play sometimes with them and only them, we can. You don't, we won't. It's your call." Shade yawned, putting his arm behind his head. "I thought you and Diamond would get along since you're not close friends, but you can become friends. You're both kind of… sweet."

Lily lifted her head. "That wasn't what you were going to say." She glared down at him. "I don't know if you or Winter is the most devious."

"I am, but she thinks she is," Shade said smugly.

"Heaven help the person you two gang up on; they wouldn't stand a chance."

CHAPTER THIRTY-EIGHT
Saturday

Sawyer started the dishwasher, drying her hands on a dishcloth. The doorbell chimed and she laid the cloth down on the counter before going to the door. Her stomach sank at seeing Vida, Colton, Ice and Jackal.

She knew it was bad news when she saw their faces. Crossing her arms over her chest, she walked to the middle of her living room floor. She heard Kaden coming down the steps and turned to see him with an expression of worry on his face. He knew what they were going to tell her. She could see it in his face. Kaden came to her, standing behind her and wrapping his arms around her waist.

"Just tell me," Sawyer ordered. Staring at Vida's face, it was obvious she had been crying.

"Digger escaped," Vida said gently, aware of how upset Sawyer was going to be that the man who had kidnapped her and dozens of other women had gotten away.

"How?" Sawyer asked in disbelief.

Ice explained, "They were in the State's Attorney office. Digger had agreed to disclose the whereabouts of his houses, even tell where the women he had sold were at. He went to the bathroom before they started, and he managed to get away. Walked out the fucking front door. Both guards were killed. He had help."

"Oh, my God." Sawyer started crying.

Not only didn't they know where those poor women were, but he was on the loose where he could continue somewhere else, kidnapping even more women.

"At least he doesn't know about Callie." Sawyer's relief was cut short as Ice burst her bubble.

"He knows. When they checked his cell, they found information on Penni: where she lived, college, her half-brother. Digger had a complete dossier on her. The best we can figure out, he's known since his arrest from the date on the file. We think he recognized Callie's resemblance to King when he was in Penni's hotel room."

"We have to warn Callie," Sawyer said.

"There's more," Jackal broke into the conversation. "Rip, who was keeping an eye on Callie, has disappeared. He was supposed to check in last night. He hasn't. We will get our brother back." His menace-filled eyes showed the shadows of death.

Vida turned into Colton's chest.

"We can talk to Callie. They'll let him go." Vida tried to sound positive.

Ice took command. "This is what we're going to do. We're going to Treepoint to ask for a meet with The Last Riders and set everything straight. You can give the heads-up to Callie, offer to bring her back here under our protection. Digger won't touch her if we make a claim on her. If they give our man back, then we'll all be cool and leave in peace. If our brother is dead, then it's another matter. The brothers are on the way here. If you're going, get ready to ride."

Sawyer went upstairs to pack. She looked up when she saw Vida standing in the doorway.

"It's going to be okay, isn't it?" Her friend wanted reassurance.

"Pray, Vida. Pray hard. That's what I'm doing."

* * *

Jackal went to the door.

"Where are you going?" Ice asked, stopping him.

"I'll keep about twenty minutes behind you," Jackal told him with silent meaning in his eyes. "I'm going to get us some insurance."

Ice nodded his head, giving the okay.

They were ready to leave in thirty.

Kaden was riding his bike beside Colton's. Sawyer and Vida looked at each other, holding their husbands tight.

Kaden had called Alec; he was going to follow behind them in the Escalade. When the women needed breaks from the bikes, they could ride with him. They were going to drive straight through to Treepoint.

Ice held up his arm in front of over eighty bikers. They heard his voice in the back. "Predators, we ride."

* * *

Monday

Lily rushed to unlock the church store. She was late because she had stopped at Shade's office on the way to work, keeping her promise from Friday night. She almost spilt her coffee when she unlocked the door.

Carefully closing it behind her, she walked to the counter, putting her purse underneath.

Pastor Dean came in with a smile. "I called Shade to see if you were sick. You're never late. He hung up on me."

Lily turned red. "I'm sorry I'm late. I was…" Lily didn't know what to say. She certainly didn't want to tell the truth, but she didn't want to lie either.

"Busy?" Pastor Dean's grin widened.

"Busy." Lily nodded her head. "I'm sorry about Shade. He's a rude man. I'll have a talk with him."

"You do that, Lily. If anyone can straighten him out, you can." Lily's doubtful look had him laughing. "Lily, you brighten my day, which is a good thing since I'm doing the church accounts this morning. I'll be in my office if you need me."

"All right," Lily responded, looking over the paperwork on the bikes that Train was donating.

When the door opened, Lily smiled as a customer came in; a tall, broad-shouldered man with jet black hair.

Her smile began to fade as he came closer to the counter.

"Hello, Callie. Remember me?"

*　*　*

Shade was sitting at his desk when the first call came.

"You have something of mine and I want it back."

"And would this be Ice or Jackal?" Shade replied.

"You know?"

"I know something is going down and you know what it is. And you're going to tell us what we need to know, or you're going to have one less brother under your command."

"We need to meet."

Shade gave him the address.

"Bring my brother."

Ice could demand all he wanted; he wasn't getting anything until he produced the information he needed.

"You'll see Eightball when I decide you get him back." Shade emphasized Eightball's name to let Ice know they were aware it was as fake as shit and it had been a stupid fuckup to get caught by.

"Oh, you'll bring him and I'll bring that pretty little sister of yours." Shade didn't lose control of his temper. He had fucked-up himself; he should have expected the move.

"I'll bring him." Shade had no choice other than to relent.

"Now that's more like it. We'll be there in an hour." The line disconnected.

Shade got up from behind his desk, opening his door. "Jewell, take over. Rider, Train, you're with me."

They were halfway across the parking lot when the

second call came in. Shade paused to answer it. "Later, Dean. I'm busy—"

"Shade, it's Lily. She's gone. I was on my way to my office when someone knocked me out. When I came to... she was gone. I called Knox; he's on his way over."

Shade disconnected the call.

"Shade?" He looked at Rider.

"We'll talk in the house. Gather all the brothers and meet me in the kitchen.

They ran up the flight of steps. Shade found Viper in the kitchen. It took very little time to have the brothers gathered in the kitchen and the television room. The door stood open toward the living room so all the members could hear.

Shade quickly explained about the meet with Ice and that Lily was missing from the church.

Viper took control. "Razer, call Beth. Tell her to get here and stay here. Train, call the brothers in Ohio, tell them to haul ass here, then call Stud and tell him the same thing. I'm calling in my marker. We'll meet the Predators, we find out what they know and then we'll find out how to find Lily.

"We have to shut the town down so that whoever has Lily can't get away. We have to have someone that knows every way in and out of town. Call Knox and tell him to call the Porters for help. There's no place in town or the mountains they don't know. Everyone's got five minutes to get dressed and packed for war. We'll meet at our bikes. Move."

Shade went to his house and came back carrying a canvas bag. When he got to the parking lot, everyone was getting on their bikes. He threw his bag into Rider's back seat with Nickel. Unzipping it, he took out his .50 caliber Desert Eagle, shoving it in the back of his jeans. Then he reached in, taking several mags and putting them in his jacket pocket, zipping it back up. Slamming the truck door, he went to his bike, climbing on. Only then did Shade cut on his motor, ready to ride.

The brothers were all moving their bikes behind Viper and Cash at the beginning of the parking lot.

Viper's voice sounded strong and clear over the roar of the bikes. "Last Riders, we ride!"

CHAPTER THIRTY-NINE

Lily sat back against the wooden chair, staring at the man who had dragged her from the church store. He had shoved her into the backseat of a car before getting in beside her while a huge man drove out of the parking lot.

Lily didn't try to talk to the silent man, too busy watching out the window to see where they were going. She had to watch so that she could find her way home. They had driven several miles out of town toward Jamestown before pulling off the road and taking a small dirt road for a couple of miles. The car had then pulled inside a garage. Lily almost screamed when the light disappeared. Thankfully, another light flickered on.

The man had brought her to a room and told her to take a seat.

"Who are you?" Lily asked, staring at him.

The room was empty of furnishings except the chair she was sitting on. He stood, leaning back against the wall. He certainly didn't fit the house with his expensive suit and shoes.

A memory came back, reminding her of Rachel describing a man like him. She knew the answer before he spoke.

"My name is King."

"Why have you kidnapped me?"

"Now, Callie, kidnapping is such a harsh word." The man should know about harsh. It fit him. There was nothing soft about him. His body and face projected a ruthlessness that he seemed more than able to carry out.

"Don't call me Callie. My name is Lily. How do you know me?" Lily made herself sound more confident than she felt.

"Don't you remember?" He looked at her quizzically.

She did. God help her, she did. He was the man who had killed her mother, Marshall and the man who had been raping her and then set the apartment on fire, leaving a whole apartment building to burn down.

"You're the one who took me from my mother and gave me to my adoptive parents." She wasn't going to mention that she had seen him murder them, too, afraid that he would kill a witness to a crime he had committed years ago.

"That bitch was no mother to you. That slut should never have been allowed to have any children. She was evil incarnate."

"How did you know my mother?" Lily asked.

"She grew up in my neighborhood. We grew up together. I would see her around every now and again. I have several businesses; one of those businesses was to provide entertainment to men. She worked for me for a while until she started stealing extra cash out of the customer's pockets."

"My mother was a prostitute," Lily said, her face pale.

"Your mother was a slut. She would give it away for free as often as she sold it."

Lily winced at his cruel words.

"This is interesting, but I'm trying to understand what this has to do with you kidnapping me. If you're worried I was going to talk someday, I won't."

"I didn't think you would, Lily. It wouldn't be much

fun testifying, would it?" King said mockingly.

His words let her know he also remembered why he had killed her mother and the other men.

Lily shrunk in on herself, reminded of the treatment she had received as a child. She knew herself well enough to know that she would never be able to testify to what had happened to her when she was a child.

Lily heard King sigh, his hands going to his pockets. "I didn't mean to bring up bad memories for you, Lily, but I have no choice. I have an enemy who is determined to destroy me and he plans to use you to accomplish that goal."

"How? I don't understand. I don't want to understand. I just want to go home to my husband. He'll be worried about me. I want to go home." Lily refused to cry in front of this stranger. She had stopped crying all the time. She wasn't weak anymore; she had Shade, Beth and Razer, and she had The Last Riders. The weak woman she had been was gone.

"I can't let you go home until I kill Digger. He escaped a couple of days ago, and he's not far from Treepoint, if he isn't already there. I couldn't take a chance. I had to put you where he couldn't find you until I can find him. Don't worry; it won't be long then you can go home."

"Why would he try to use me against you? I don't even know you," Lily protested.

"Look at me, Lily. It's obvious." His eyes stared into hers.

"No." Lily shook her head, denying the possibility, squeezing her eyes closed as if she could make him disappear. She couldn't shove the truth away, though. Lily gave a bitter laugh. "So not only was my mother a prostitute, my father was her pimp?"

King nodded his head. "Among other things. I'm afraid being a pimp isn't the worst of my sins. You didn't stand a chance."

Lily lowered her head, her hair falling forward to hide

her face. "Do you even know that I didn't know that fathers existed? That when I found out, I cried for three days? Do you even know the things she did to me and made me do?!" Lily's eyes raised, the purple depths filled with hatred stared at King who went pale at her outburst.

His face quickly became an impassive mask; however, Lily saw the torture in the eyes that were so much like her own, and her hatred fell away, replaced with pity. She had suffered for eight short years while this man had suffered for much longer than that.

"I…" King cleared his throat. His impassive voice belied the eyes staring back at her. "I didn't know. My sister was violently murdered. She had been kidnapped and cut to shreds. I loved my sister. It was why I did some of the things I did when I began my business, so I could drag her out of the filth of that neighborhood. When she died like that, I swore I'd never let anyone hold someone over me like that again. The men I dealt with were too dangerous. The night they returned Ariel's body, I had to make the arrangements for her funeral and pick out the clothes they were going to bury her in the next day."

Kings hand ran through his dark hair. "I went back to my apartment, got drunk and did some coke. Brenda must have come by. I don't even remember the bitch being there. I remember stinking like sex the next morning, but I didn't remember anything from that night. I stayed out of the neighborhood Brenda lived in. It brought back too many memories.

"Then, one of my girls got hurt bad. I went there to settle a score and as I was leaving, I heard kids laughing— little girls. It's an unmistakable sound. I looked over at the playground and I saw you. You looked exactly like my sister had at that age. When Brenda came outside to get you, yelling at you to go inside, I knew what that bitch had done.

"I made her come to my office. She said she didn't tell me about you because she was afraid I would kill her. She was right. It was everything I could do not to kill her that day. The only reason I didn't was because I knew that I didn't want you hurt like Ariel. You were too beautiful to drag into my world.

"I gave her money for you. She had enough to move out of that rat hole, but she stayed there to be closer to her suppliers. I knew she was doing drugs, so I paid Marshall to move in with her to keep an eye on you, to protect you. Instead, he became another one of your tormentors.

"I had no idea what she was doing to you until that night when Marshall called. He was so mad at Brenda for letting another man have you that he called me. I don't think the dumb bastard thought I would ask you. I knew the son of a bitch wouldn't care if Brenda fucked fifty men." His voice was full of disgust.

"So you killed them then started the fire."

"I enjoyed it. I wish I could have brought them back to life and done it again." His eyes blazed hatred for the people he had so ruthlessly killed.

"How did Beth's parents come to adopt me?"

"Saul Cornett was my uncle. I called him and asked him if he would take you. He said he would, but he told me that if he did, I had to agree to stay away. He wasn't going to endanger his child. He knew Ariel had been killed because of me. I had an acquaintance in the morgue that falsified papers of a body there, showing you had died in the fire. I wanted to make sure no one would ever think to look for you."

"So, he was my great-uncle?"

"Yes. He was a religious fanatic, but I knew he wouldn't touch you." Lily didn't tell him that her adopted father had been a sadist who had tortured Beth. Lily wondered if he hadn't touched her because of Beth and the Sheriff's threats or because of King.

"You're the one who owned the house behind ours?"

King smiled at her ingenuity. "Yes. That way I could keep an eye on you. I would always vacation there during the summer because you were outside more often. You grew into a beautiful woman, Lily. I heard you got married during Christmas."

Lily nodded her head. "Small town gossip. I suppose you know everything about me, probably from just talking to a waitress at the diner."

King nodded his head. "All except one thing. Are you happy? When I would see you during my trips, you always seemed so reserved, I never could tell." Lily thought she heard a small break in his voice when he asked the question.

"Yes, I'm very happy. I couldn't have asked for a better sister. I have friends who I care about, and I love my husband, Shade. He's everything to me," she said softly, seeing her answer was important to him.

King nodded his head.

"Take me back to him. Shade and The Last Riders can keep me safe from whoever wants to hurt you."

"You've almost been killed twice because Digger has a hit out on you. I have to take care of Digger or you'll never have a normal life," King said resolutely.

"How do you plan to stop him?" Lily saw she wasn't going to change his mind.

"I have a meeting scheduled in two hours. I'm going to let him have me. Once he kills me, you become unimportant. Of course, I'm planning on taking the bastard with me to Hell."

* * *

When the Last Riders pulled into the parking lot of Rosie's bar, The Predators were already there waiting.

Viper and Cash pulled to the front while Shade rode his bike to the other side of Viper where the three waited.

Ice and Max rode their bikes forward, and the men faced each other down.

"Where's Rip?" Ice's cold eyes searched the riders behind them.

"You mean, Eightball?" Viper asked sarcastically. He

pointed to the mountain ridge to their left. Two men moved to the edge, one held with a gun to his head.

"Are you going to tell us why you planted a traitor in our club and what the fuck it's got to do with Lily? Or is your brother going to take a leap of faith?" Viper finished, turning back to Ice.

Ice gave a whistle and two bikes at the back of the lot moved. Penni stood with a gun to her head. The terrified look on her face made Shade want his rifle; however, he knew the men wanted their brother as much as he wanted his sister.

"Ice, man, this wasn't part of the plan." Two men toward the back got off their bikes, walking forward. Shade remembered the one with the goatee from the diner. The second one was recognizable to anyone that could turn a television set on.

"I told you I would let you talk, Colton. You got ten minutes before I do my own fucking talking."

The one named Colton walked a step closer to Viper before the large man next to Ice put an arm in his way, stopping him.

"My name is Colton, this is Kaden. Our wives were friends with Lily when she was a little girl. A man named Digger runs a sex ring; he kidnaps young women then sells them as slaves. Digger is in a power struggle with a man named King. Last year, my wife was kidnapped and held hostage by Digger to gain information to destroy King."

"What did she know?" Shade asked.

"That King had a daughter, Callie. Your wife, Lily. It was only when Penni started working for us that we discovered Callie was still alive. Unfortunately, so did Digger."

"That must be who's been trying to kill her," Shade said thoughtfully.

Shade saw the men pause and look at each other. "We weren't aware someone had tried to kill her yet. We didn't know until Friday, when Digger escaped, that he was aware of Callie. They found information that he had taken a hit out on Callie.

"Our wives have been tortured by this information. They love Callie and want to be reunited with her, but didn't attempt to do so because they didn't want to lead Digger to her. Ice was doing me a favor by trying to put a man in to keep an eye on Callie, and to be honest, make sure she was happy. That's important to them.

"If you bring Callie here, she can confirm that she knows them. She was just eight, but she should have been old enough that she would recognize one of them. We have them waiting. When you bring Callie, I'll send for our wives to be brought in."

"What're your wives' names?" Shade questioned.

"Sawyer and Vida. Are you willing to bring Callie?" Colton asked.

"There's a problem with that. She's missing," Shade said, carefully watching their reaction.

Shade could tell from their faces that they didn't have Lily. They had told them what they knew. Viper could tell, too. That was why he lifted his hand. The two men disappeared from the edge of the cliff.

"You can have your man back. Any idea where Digger would take her?" Viper asked.

"No. He's been in prison. We don't know where the houses he operates are or which routes he still has open. The FBI have been trying to find information and can't. That's why they didn't kill the bastard when they took him in custody."

The sound of a motorbike filled the air as Train pulled into the lot behind Viper. Rip got off the back of the bike, going to his brothers who started cheering.

"Aren't you forgetting something?" Shade's voice snapped out.

"Jackal!" Ice yelled.

The man holding the gun moved it away from Penni's head, and he gave her a shove forward.

She turned around and spat into his face. "Asshole."

The men around him broke into jeers as she walked through their midst. When she reached Kaden and Colton, Kaden reached out to touch her, but she jerked her arm away, going straight to her brother and climbing on the back of his bike.

"How long has she been gone?" Ice asked.

"Since this morning," Shade answered.

"Need some help?" Ice questioned, reaching his hand out for Viper to shake in truce.

Viper shook his hand. "Couldn't hurt. Tell us what you know about Digger?"

Shade listened to the men, gradually coming to the conclusion that only one man had the power to save Lily.

It was time to call Lucky.

CHAPTER FORTY

The knock came ten minutes earlier than he said he would be there, but Shade didn't have time to waste.

"Come in."

Shade walked into his office, seeing his brother standing by the window.

"Lucky, I wouldn't ask if I had a choice." Shade's harsh voice sounded hollow in the room.

"I've stood looking out this window for a lot of years, Shade. It took me over a year after your father opened the investigation into the pipeline going through here to find a connection. Then I had to find a way into the community, which wouldn't arouse suspicion. I'm a month away from closing down a pipeline that runs through nine states, carrying drugs and guns, and you're asking me to blow my cover for one woman when the men I'm getting ready to arrest have killed hundreds while I've had to sit and wait to get enough evidence to bring them all down. We have all the warrants, everything gone because of one woman."

"Lucky," Shade said, forced to do what he had never done before. "Brother, please. I can't lose her. I'm not like you and the others. I can pretend I have emotions, but they're not there for anyone. There's nothing inside of me except shadows. Lily drives the shadows away. She feels everything she can't even stand to crush a fucking flower under her foot and I don't feel anything unless I'm with her, I can't lose that. I waited so long for her, I've loved her for years; she's only loved me for a few weeks.

"When I first saw her all I could think about was fucking her. Then I saw her at the lake with Beth, I felt her fear but I saw the look she gave to Beth. She loved and trusted her, knew that Beth wouldn't let anything happen to her." Shade swallowed hard uncomfortable opening himself to anyone especially Lucky. "I wanted her to look at me that way, needed her to look at me that way. I wanted to give her a life away from the darkness that I saw had touched her beautiful soul." Shade's face twisted into a painful mask. "I've taken countless lives, and never felt an ounce of emotion that's why they recruited me in the military. One psychologist even joked after my evaluation I had been born without a soul, and it was true until that day at the lake. I fell in love with her that day, there is no other woman for me, there never will be. Lily is my gateway to Heaven without her the only thing left for me is Hell.

"You used to believe in something more important than that badge you carry. I'm begging you to save me brother because, as God is my witness, I will kill you if you don't help me."

"I wouldn't do it for anyone. Not my mother or any brother, not for a million fucking dollars, and especially not because of any fucking threat of yours. But, I will for Lily."

"Thank you." Shade's mind caught on something. "Wait a minute. You said you have the warrants? I think I know how we can get Lily back and serve those warrants at the same time. Call your boss."

* * *

They stayed in that tiny room, letting the day go by. At one point, Lily thought she heard a plane breaking the monotony for a few precious minutes until she could no longer hear the sound and the deadened silence returned. Her fingertips played with the red rubber band that she couldn't remember the last time she'd had to snap.

Lily saw King look at his watch. "I'm going to leave Henry with you. He's going to drive you back to your husband at nightfall. By then, it should be over."

"You don't have to handle it like this. I know the Sheriff here; he'll keep us both safe," she pleaded.

"In this little backwater town? Your town has never dealt with men like us who barter with life every day. As long as Digger is alive, he will chase you. The only way to stop him is if one of us is dead." King's voice was flat as he described a life that had been spent always looking over his shoulder.

King walked to the doorway, turning back before he went out the door. "I'm sorry, Lily. If it's any consolation, you were better off without me. I would have made a lousy father." King turned to walk through the doorway, leaving her without a goodbye.

One moment he was walking out the door, and in the next second, a gun blast and shattering glass sounded from the other room. Lily ran toward the sound, seeing King lying with blood pouring out of his chest.

Another gun blast sent glass splattering from another window, punching a hole in the plaster in the wall behind her. Lily screamed as more shots ricocheted into the house.

"Get down!" King yelled.

The big man, who had driven them to the house, came running into the room carrying a gun in his hand. He grabbed Lily's arm, forcing her to her knees.

"How many, Henry?" King asked, putting his hand to his chest.

Henry dragged her to a corner of the room, forcing her down onto her stomach. Then he scooted to a window facing the front of the house. He didn't say anything, just turned back to face his boss. For a second, the men shared a glance and Lily knew she wouldn't be going home to Shade again.

"I'm sorry, Lily. I always fuck up with you, don't I? I told you I was a lousy father."

As more shots were fired into the room, Lily screamed, covering her head with both her hand and arms. She started praying, over and over, hoping this time God was listening.

"What are you doing?" King's head turned on the floor toward her.

"I'm praying."

"Well, it's certainly the time for it. Say one for me. God knows I need it." He tried to sit up, finally managing to get up on an elbow, and then slid himself toward the window by Henry.

"Okay." Lily kept praying.

She heard him laughing, pulling a gun out of his suit coat. "Henry, did you ever think a daughter of mine or Brenda's would even know what a prayer was?"

"No, sir." More shots came flying into the room.

Lily stopped praying for a second. "How come you're not shooting back?"

Both men burst out laughing.

"I knew there was a part of me in there somewhere. We're not shooting because I want to save it for when they try to come into the house."

Lily started praying again when another round began.

"Come on out, King, and I'll let the girl live," a voice yelled from the outside.

"Digger, if you want me, come and get me. We both know you don't plan on killing her."

When a noise from the back sounded, Lily looked over at King; they only had minutes left. "Why didn't you just take me and disappear, instead of driving and leaving me with my parents? Why didn't you just keep me?" Lily asked with unshed tears in her eyes.

King turned from looking out the window to face her.

This time he made no attempt to hide his tortured expression. "Don't you remember what happened after we left the apartment?"

Lily shook her head.

"You were hysterical. You thought I was going to kill you, too. You didn't stop screaming until we got to Saul's house and you saw Beth. She rocked you until you fell asleep. I left while you were still sleeping. I didn't want you to wake up and see me."

Lily sat, staring at him, hearing the men coming from the back of the house. Knowing they only had seconds left, she said what she knew they both needed to hear the most before they died. "Daddy, I forgive you."

"What in the hell have you gotten yourself into now, Lily?"

Lily turned to look at the three men running hell-bent across the room, taking positions around it.

"Dustin, Greer and Tate? What are you doing here?" Lily found herself laughing in stunned disbelief.

"You've got everyone in the fucking country searching for you. The FBI, the ATF, even the motherfucking CIA. What shit have you stirred up?" Dustin gave her his usual shit-eating grin.

A shot rang out from the back of the house. "Got one," Lily heard Rachel's yell.

"Is that Rachel?" Lily asked.

"Hell, yes, there's nobody better with a twenty-two. If they try coming through that back door, they'll be meeting the undertaker in town," Tate said, taking a bead on someone outside and letting go with a shot. "Greer, you take the ones on the right. Dustin, the left.

"Which ones you going to take?" Greer asked, shooting again.

"I'm going to take the rest of the ones you two miss," Tate answered, letting go with several shots, one after the other.

As Tate stopped for a second as if he was listening to

something, Lily saw the black earpiece in his ear. He must have been listening to someone talking because moments later, she heard him tell them to send for an ambulance.

"They'll be here in five. Brothers, if you got them, shoot them. I don't want a motherfucker left standing. They'll laugh us out of the county if they hear the police had to help us."

At that, the men began shooting in earnest, and Lily had to put her hands over her ears.

Another round of gunfire sounded from the back.

"Got two more!" Rachel yelled.

Lily caught King's astounded expression. "What were you saying about my town dealing with men like you?"

"Hold up. They want us to quit shooting. They're afraid we'll shoot them. Pussies are scared to come any closer," Tate said, shooting once more before standing up. "Let's go see if any of them are breathing. Dustin, you stay here with Rachel and Lily."

Still more gunfire was coming from the back.

"Rachel, quit shooting. Get out here!" Tate yelled.

Rachel came running into the room, carrying a rifle in her hand. She was wearing jeans and a t-shirt, and Lily could tell she was having as much fun as her brothers.

She dropped down next to Lily on the floor. "I got a couple more. Did you keep count of how many you shot?" she asked her brothers.

Tate and Greer were opening the door. "More than you," Greer bragged before they went out the door.

She turned to Lily. "Did he?"

"I don't know. I didn't keep count," Lily replied, dumbfounded by her attitude.

Rachel flashed her a grin that was as full of it as her brother's. "They like to throw it up to me that they're better shots. I'll get a copy of the police report from Knox and count them up."

She turned and saw King. "You're the guy who broke down in town." She raised her gun to point it at him.

"He's okay, Rachel. He's my father."

Rachel lowered her gun. "He's the one who kidnapped you?" Rachel asked.

"Yes," Lily answered her question. She would tell her the rest of it later.

"Dammit," Rachel cursed.

"What?" Lily asked.

"That's strike three."

Lily heard several feet running from outside, and then the door pushed open for Shade, Viper and Razer to run in.

"Shade." Lily couldn't help her broken sob when she said his name. She'd been so scared she wasn't going to see him again.

"Lily."

If she'd ever doubted her husband's love for her, all she would need to do is remember his face when he saw her. He ran, picking her up and holding her tightly in his arms. All the fear he had suffered and the relief at finding her safe showed his love more than a thousand words.

"Are you all right?" he asked.

"I'm fine." She hugged him back then stood still. "Are you crying?" she asked, astounded.

"No."

CHAPTER FORTY-ONE

"Can we go home yet?" Lily asked again. She was sitting on a chair in Knox's office, waiting for Shade with Beth sitting next to her, holding her hand.

"They'll let us know. It shouldn't be much longer."

Knox had led Shade and her in here after they had left the house that King had taken her to. The ambulance had taken away King while two other ambulances had to be called along with the coroners from three counties to deal with the bodies.

"How did the Porters find me?" Lily asked.

"I have no idea," Beth responded as Knox and Shade came in.

"I can answer that question." Knox took a seat behind his desk.

Lily waited expectantly. "Well?"

"We're waiting on someone. We promised we would until he arrived." Shade walked to stand beside her chair, taking her hand. Razer came into the office then, shutting the door behind him. Lily could tell from their faces that the news they had wasn't going to be good.

"What's wrong?"

"Nothing, there's just a few things Razer and I haven't

told you. It's not because we didn't want to, it was because we couldn't," Shade answered her question as Razer moved to stare down at his wife.

A knock sounded on the door.

"Come in," Knox called out.

The door opened and Pastor Dean came inside, closing the door with a serious expression instead of the affable one he normally wore. He was also dressed as she had never seen him before. He was wearing jeans and a t-shirt, which was unusual enough, but the ATF jacket and hat was what had both her and Beth sitting in shock.

"Beth, Lily."

"Why are you wearing that?" Lily asked, standing up, her face tuning pale.

"Because I'm an ATF Special Agent."

Lily wanted to run from the room, but that was the old Lily who always ran away, afraid to face her nightmares. She wasn't going to run this time.

"I've been undercover since I took over your father's church. It's taken me this long, and over forty agents, to shut down a pipeline that carried drugs and firearms through nine different states."

Lily stood, listening to him, and all she could think of was how much she had confided in him over the years.

"When Cash joined the military, he never forgot you two. He was especially sickened with Beth's treatment and he knew it wouldn't be much longer before Lily would be receiving the same. Shade's father, Will Hunter, had retired, and so Cash asked him to stop by Treepoint to check on you two."

Lily's eyes flew to Shade at the mention of the former Sheriff.

"I was going to tell you when Dad came back into town next week. Think, Lily; why would I hide that from you when I've confessed to much worse than that?"

Lily nodded, believing him.

"When he stayed here those few days, Will decided he

liked it enough to stay indefinitely. He and his wife both were tired of moving around so much and wanted a break from it.

"They settled here, and as you both know, it wasn't long before he gained enough respect to become Sheriff. That's where his military training came in handy. He soon discovered the pipeline and notified the proper authorities." Dean walked further into the office, leaning against the corner of Knox's desk.

"This is where the conversation becomes confidential." He stared at both of the women with silent warning. "I had left the military and joined The Last Riders. I had been in the Seals and had served as a military Chaplin, but when I left the service, I no longer felt the call to serve as a pastor, so I left that part of my life behind. But I wasn't content. I missed the action of being in the military, so when the CIA approached The Last Riders to become a paramilitary group, we accepted.

"That's how we ended up in Treepoint to begin an investigation. The ATF offered me a position as a Special Agent to lead the investigation, but I had to go undercover to do so. The people who had begun developing leads ended up dead, so I waited for a way to enter the community that would be above suspicion."

"Our parents' death created the perfect opportunity," Beth said; her face had gone as white as Lily's as she gazed at Razer.

"Sadly, yes. I'm sorry." Dean paused then continued, "I became Pastor Dean and began my investigation. It's taken me all these years to gather enough evidence to win my cases. I was a week away from making my arrests. I even had the warrants ready to go, but it all came crashing down today. "

"Why today?" Beth asked. Lily watched her sister calmly asking questions while she just wanted to get out of there.

"Because of Lily. We pooled all our available resources

417

together, but to do that, I had to break my cover."

Lily felt sickened. She was hurt that Pastor Dean wasn't the man he'd pretended to be, but she didn't want his work to have been in vain, nor did she want the criminals, who were hurting others, to remain free.

"I'm sorry," Lily said.

"Thanks to Shade's quick thinking, we were able to serve the warrants in a two-hour mass bust and were able to arrest three-fourths of the people we were after, and we're confident we'll be able to locate the remaining ones."

"How?" Lily asked, relieved.

"We had interagency cooperation. It was one of the deals Shade made for The Last Riders. In return, they sold the pending patents' right to a technical computer system for pennies on the dollar than they would have made.

Lily and Beth realized what all The Last Riders had given up. They had sacrificed millions of dollars for Lily's rescue.

"One of the conditions was that they had to use their technology to help find you."

Lily remembered the plane buzzing overhead while she had been in the house.

"When you were located, the Porters were the closest. That's how they got there first. They're never going to let us live it down. They want Dustin's record expunged for their cooperation. I'll see they get what they want. They deserve it." Pastor Dean stood up straight, looking at Lily.

She honestly didn't know what to say to the man; she had admired him for years as a role model, as someone to look up to. She took a shuddering breath, stepping forward. She reached up, kissing him on his cheek. "Thank you."

She heard a chair scrape and she spun around, seeing Shade couldn't hide his expression fast enough.

"Don't you dare," Lily said, pointing a finger at him. Shade managed to control himself, taking a seat back in the vacant chair.

"I think you just returned the favor," Dean said, smiling.

When Beth would have gotten up, Razer pressed her back down in her chair with a hand on her shoulder.

"I have to go. I still have a lot of reports to finish today. I also have to find a new minister for the church."

Lily didn't know how anyone would live up to the standard he had set.

"You never know... you missed the military when you left it; you may miss the church," Lily said with hope.

Dean looked at both sisters briefly before going to the door and opening it. "Perhaps. I was blessed to meet two angels, so miracles can happen. We'll have to wait and see," he said, closing the door behind him.

"Show-off," Shade said, standing up. "I called you an angel first, remember that."

Lily laughed, breaking the tension. "Can we go home now?"

"Yes," Shade said, still irritated

"Can I make a stop on the way and see my dad?" Lily asked.

"Yes."

Lily laughed at his short response, reaching up to kiss him on his cheek. "Does that make it better?"

His blue eyes smiled down at her as he put his arm around her shoulders.

She turned to Beth, who had lost her paleness and was now giving Razer heck with her eyes for not confiding in her. He was going to have a lot of making up to do. Lily thought about suggesting a new shower; it might do the trick.

"Would you like to go, Beth?"

"Yes. I'm looking forward to meeting him. When I first saw him, when he brought you, Dad said he was from the adoption agency."

"That reminds me, Lily. That strongbox you found contained your fake birth certificate. Cash sent it off to a buddy of his, and they tracked down your real one. It came in the afternoon mail." Knox handed it to her.

Lily took the envelope, staring down at it. After all these years, she didn't need a paper to tell her a single thing. It had come too late. She already knew who she was.

CHAPTER FORTY-TWO

Lily was sitting on the side of the bed, brushing her hair, with Shade lying down on his side in the bed, watching her.

"What's going to happen to him?" Lily asked.

"Not much, since you've already told Knox that you weren't kidnapped, it was a family reunion. Several government agencies aren't very happy with you right now."

Lily shrugged her shoulders, not concerned. "How about that man who was after him?"

"He's a different matter. Since he believes in letting everyone do his dirty work for him, he wasn't hurt. He's in Knox's jail, waiting for the Texas Rangers to come and get him. I imagine he's planning more song and dance, holding the whereabouts of those women to himself."

"I hope not. I'm going to pray for him to let those women go tonight."

"You do that, Lily. I have a feeling he's going to need your prayers tonight," Shade said, stroking her back.

Lily set her hairbrush on the table then stood up, looking down into her husband's eyes. "It's my turn."

She watched Shade's grin widen as he scooted over on

the bed, patting the mattress. She knew exactly what he was expecting, what she always chose—him making sweet, passionate love to her where she felt like the most precious woman on earth. She knew she was blessed and would remember to thank God every day.

Lily shook her head. "Uh, uh. I want you to stand up."

Shade didn't try to hide his surprise. He scooted out of the bed, standing next to it. She went around the room, turning the overhead light off, leaving the bedside lamps on. Then she went to his cabinet, opening the side that was his. Turning, she walked to stand directly in front of him where she took off her robe and tossed it onto the chair by their bed.

Looking at Shade's astonished expression as she stood completely naked, she knelt in front of him, placing her hands on her lap, palms up. She lowered her head to her chest, giving him the complete submission Shade would never demand or ask from her.

He stood there in silence for several seconds.

"You did very well, Lily. Thank you." She heard him clear his throat. "The other night I told you that you were not allowed to kiss other men to show your gratitude, yet you did so today, didn't you?"

"Yes, Sir."

"I also said one man in particular you were not allowed to touch. Who was it?"

"Pastor Dean, Sir."

"Have you got anything to say for yourself?

"I'm very sorry, Sir. I won't do it again."

"Thank you for your apology, but that won't get you out of your punishment."

"I didn't think it would, Sir. I deserve your punishment for disobeying you."

As Shade went to his cabinet, she wanted to watch what he was doing, yet she kept her eyes forward.

"Lay down on the bed."

Lily immediately went to the bed and lay down. She

heard a package open and close then Shade was on the bed, bending between her thighs. She felt something cold and slick then Shade was sliding something inside of her.

"Sir?"

"I didn't give you permission to talk."

"I'm sorry, Sir."

She felt another cold object inserted inside of her and then Shade climbed off the bed, going to the bathroom. Lily heard the running water.

"You did very well, Lily. Since this is the first time I used them on you, I will tell you that I inserted two metal balls inside of you. They will add to our enjoyment tonight. Now, I want you to get up and get dressed."

Lily almost broke and spoke; instead, she dressed in the clothes that Shade handed her: a new pair of tight, black jeans and a sweatshirt then a thick jacket and boots. Lily dressed without talking. Shade also dressed and then waited for her by the bedroom door.

They left their house, walking behind it, down the pathway. When Shade got on the bike, she expected him to hand her a helmet, but he didn't. She couldn't hide her grin, getting on behind him.

The metal balls had generated a thrill of excitement as she had walked. She could already feel herself getting wet and warm. She thought sitting down would decrease the effect; she was wrong, especially when the throbbing, roaring motorcycle went wide open on a dark mountain road. She couldn't prevent her moans after five minutes. She didn't have an orgasm; no, it was a tease. The balls and the throbbing motorcycle drove her from one peak after another without letting her come. Her hands held onto the front of his jeans for dear life while all she wanted was to rip those jeans open and beg him to take her.

It was one of the warmer days of winter. It was cold but not unbearable. As Shade slowed his bike, turning into a clearing, Lily recognized they were in a private cove off the lake where she had first seen Shade and the other Last

Riders. Shade cut the bike off not far from the water. They sat there in the quiet for a few minutes, but Lily couldn't sit without moving around on the seat.

"I remember the day I saw you here in the lake. I've thought of how beautiful you were and how frightened you looked. I wanted to protect and fuck you at the same time. I thought the years I had to wait for you were a nightmare, but all those days and years combined didn't equal the torture of not knowing where you were today and that I couldn't protect you."

Lily didn't care if she got in trouble; she got off the bike, coming around to face him. She touched his face, rubbing her thumb over his smooth cheek. "Shade, I'm not going to say I'm not afraid of dying because I am. Everyone is. But today, what I was most afraid of wasn't dying; it was the fear of being separated from you. I prayed that, if I died, I would forget you because I knew, if I remembered you, I would be in Hell."

Shade jerked her to him, thrusting his tongue inside her mouth, exploring every part as if he was memorizing the feel and taste of her. When Lily's mouth broke away from his passionate kiss, gasping for breath—her hands full of his t-shirt—Shade was gasping as much as she was.

Lily leaned forward, placing butterfly kisses against his throat, tenderly kissing the curve. Her hands slid under his t-shirt as her mouth traveled to the base of his throat before tracing to the side where his neck and shoulder met, sucking a piece of his flesh into her mouth.

Shade groaned as her hand unzipped his jeans, pulling out his cock. Her hand slid up and down his cock as her teeth bit his shoulder, her tongue then brushing against the barely-there teeth marks.

She lifted her head as her hand began to slide even faster on his flesh. Lily bent over him, placing her mouth over his cock, sucking him deeply into her mouth as far as she could, then sliding her mouth up, letting her tongue tease the tip of his cock.

"Damn, Angel, quit teasing. Suck my cock," Shade groaned.

Lily quit torturing him, sucking on him harder as his hand buried itself in her hair, pushing her down on him as she used her tongue, feeling the slick flesh as it slid in and out of her mouth. Her hand went inside his jeans to play with his balls. She listened to the silent commands of his hands, determined to learn exactly what brought him the most pleasure.

His harsh intake of breath when she let the tip slip to the back of her throat had her smiling against him. When she went down further the next time, she knew she had him. His hand held her head in place as he came, leaning over her as his cock jerked in her mouth.

Lily straightened, smiling at Shade's expression. "Did I do okay?"

Shade put his cock back into his jeans, zipping himself up. "So good, I'm going to let you do it again in the morning," he joked, starting the motor.

Lily climbed on behind him, wrapping her arms around his waist. Shade turned the bike toward home and they flew back through the night. By the time Shade pulled into the parking lot, her pussy was on fire and she didn't think she would be able to make it to their house without having a screaming orgasm. The only way she did make it back was because she was afraid someone from inside the clubhouse would come running out to see who was getting murdered.

As she made it to the front porch, her steps were an agony of desire as the balls rubbed against her flesh and the tight jeans rubbed against her clit. Shade stood there, leaning against the doorway waiting for her.

She opened her mouth to let him have it then changed her mind when he arched his brow. She needed him to take them out before she lost her mind.

Shade closed the door as soon as she stepped through the doorway.

"Do you need anything, angel face?"

"Take them out or fuck me, Shade," Lily moaned, leaning back against the doorway, clenching her thighs, which didn't help with the seam of the jeans riding her clit.

"If you want my dick, all you have to do is ask for it." Shade said, his voice making her pussy clench even tighter. His husky voice sounded dirty and sexy and confident that he could deliver exactly what you wanted where you wanted it. All you had to do was ask. She had passed asking when they had driven into the parking lot. She was ready to beg.

"Please, Sir. Please, can I have your dick?"

"Come here."

Her sweatshirt was pulled off and dropped to the floor. Then Lily found herself pressed down over the back of the chair in her living room. It was waist-high; her belly was against the thick chair material. She felt Shade's hands go around her waist, unbuttoning her jeans and then tugging them roughly down her hips and legs before he stepped on the middle of them.

"Step out of them." His hand was pressed against her bare back, holding her down over the chair.

When she lifted her feet up, she felt him kick them out of the way. He pressed down harder on her back, making her ass come up higher.

"I'm going to give you what you want now. I can't give it to you hard because the metal balls are inside of you, but I'll give it to you hard later after I let you rest."

Lily felt his hand slide across the flesh of her pussy.

"You're wet, Angel. So wet. All I have to do is give you my dick."

He slid his cock in inch by slow inch, causing the balls to rub against the walls of her pussy with his cock sliding them up and down as he slowly fucked her. It only took a few strokes before she had an orgasm that had her screaming his name. His fingers found her clit, rubbing her as he slid his cock in and out. By the time he ground a second orgasm out of her, she was crying his name. When she lay too spent to move, he lifted her off the chair, carrying her upstairs to the shower and turning on the water.

"I love this shower," she said as he pushed her down onto the bench.

His hand brought her to the edge of the seat and his fingers delved inside her, pulling both balls out. He placed them in a small, plastic, red container, snapping it closed.

He then pulled her off the bench, washing her off. They took their time before getting out and drying off. Lily was asleep before her head hit the pillow. Shade slid into bed next to her, pulling the covers over them. He rolled over to turn the lamp off on his bedside table when a swatch of color caught his attention.

Sitting up in bed, he reached out, picking up the object. In his hand lay a red rubber band.

CHAPTER FORTY-THREE

"Are you nervous?" Beth asked.

"Yes. I feel like I'm going to be sick," Lily answered. "I'm excited and scared." Lily turned to look at her sister. "What if I don't recognize them? I was only eight. I'd feel terrible if I didn't recognize them."

Lily sat in her living room. Shade had gone to meet Sawyer, Vida and their husbands to bring them to her house. He hadn't wanted them to meet for the first time yesterday after she had left the police station, wanting her to wait until the next day to be reunited under a less-stressful atmosphere. She was glad she had listened. She didn't want anything to mar this moment.

Shade came in through the door, followed by two women and two men, then shut the door behind them.

She recognized Colton from the diner when he had introduced himself, but her eyes were drawn to the two women. Lily stood up as they walked into the room. They all three stood staring at each other after the introductions then, in the next second, they were holding each other, crying. It was several moments before any of them could say a word.

"We thought you were dead," Vida said, brushing her

tears away.

"You're so pretty," Sawyer commented.

"I was worried I wouldn't recognize you, but you haven't really changed that much. Sawyer, I recognize your nose and hair. Vida, your hair and face are almost the same. You're how I remember you. I was so scared I wouldn't recognize you."

The three friends sat down on the couch together, talking, asking about things friends ask about every day. Beth stood in the kitchen with the men after Lily had introduced them.

"We both decided to live in Queens City after we swore not to," Vida said, laughing. "I couldn't bring myself to leave, and Colton has his tattoo shop. I found a job, too, so we bought a house."

"I enrolled in culinary school. I wanted to travel, but after travelling on a tour bus for a few months, I decided I could learn about different cuisines just the way everyone else does, in a class or with a cookbook. When I do want to travel, we can do a few tour dates with the band. We're going to be in Lexington in a few weeks. You have to come."

Lily listened, enjoying the time together. Beth came over eventually, joining them, each taking turns telling Beth a different misadventure they had gotten into as children.

Sawyer and Vida both kept staring at her eyes.

"Why are you staring? Have I changed that much?" Lily asked curiously.

"No," Vida answered, taking her hand "You haven't changed. That's how we recognized you from Penni's picture." Vida indicated her eyes. "We went to see her this morning. She's furious at the Predators. When we told her we didn't know what they had done, she believed us. She said she wanted to stay here for a few days to figure out if she still wants the job."

"I hope you can stay for a few days, too," Lily said

hesitantly.

Both women nodded and said they would stay until the end of the week. Neither mentioned their mothers or hers. They also called her Lily, careful not to call her Callie. They kept staring into her eyes as if searching for something.

After dinner the women and their husbands started to leave.

"Just a minute. I'll be right back. There's something I want to show you." Lily went upstairs to her bedroom, picking up the quilt her adoptive mother had made for her. Coming downstairs, she sat on the coffee table in front of them as they sat on the couch.

"Beth's and my mother made me this quilt when I first came to live with her. I had terrible nightmares that wouldn't go away. When I came to live with them, the clothes I was wearing… she wanted to throw them away, but I wanted to wear them all the time. I didn't want to wear anything else. Our father finally got mad and cut them up and put them in the trash, but they couldn't get me to stop crying." Lily made a face. "Evidently, that's a habit I recently just outgrew. Anyway, my mother pulled them out of the trash and made them into this quilt for me. I slept with it for many naps and every night since. It's very special to me."

Lily spread the blanket out on all three of their laps. She pointed to the bright pink splashes of color. "Sawyer, that's the pink t-shirt that your mom gave me to wear when I spilt chocolate milk on mine." Lily pointed to a faded blue material. "Those are the pants that your mom gave me when my mom sent me to your apartment in shorts and it was freezing cold outside." Lily then pointed to a piece of green material. "Vida, this is the jacket you outgrew and your mom gave it to me when I was cold. And this white material is the socks she gave me when I had a bad cut on my foot and she didn't want me barefoot.

"When our mom gave me this quilt, my nightmares

didn't stop, but I would cover my face and pretend I was protected with a special blanket that had magical powers. It's funny how a child's mind can twist and turn and find what it needs to survive. I thought I had forgotten about you, but I hadn't. I never forgot. I kept you with me the only way I could." Lily swept her hand over the blanket.

"I made you my shield of love, always protecting me. Even now, all grown-up, you tried to protect me, Callie." Lily's hands reached out, one to each of her friends to take. Their hands grasped hers, tears falling from each of their eyes. None of them wanted to break the circle to wipe them away.

Lily looked at her friends. "I didn't forget you, Sawyer, or you, Vida. And I didn't forget Callie. I'm still here."

CHAPTER FORTY-FOUR

Lily stood on the snow bank, shivering though she had dressed warmly. She just wanted to see them one more minute.

She put out her hand, knowing how ridiculous it was, but it actually looked like she was holding the lights.

A warm blanket was draped over her shoulders. She hadn't even heard his footsteps in the crunching snow.

"What did I tell you about sneaking out of the cabin, Lily? I'm going to punish you when I get you back inside," Shade's seductive voice whispered into her ear.

"I couldn't resist, Shade. Isn't it beautiful?" Lily whispered reverently. "I didn't know anything so beautiful could exist."

"I didn't, either," he said, rubbing his cheek against hers, his tone just as reverent.

"All these years I've waited to see this. It's more spectacular than I ever believed possible."

He swept her up into his arms, packing her back inside the warm cabin, shutting and locking the world outside.

Shade had hot chocolate on the table in front of the couch and a warm fire blazing a few feet away. She sipped her chocolate from the mug as she watched him throw a log onto the fire.

He stood up, going into the bedroom then coming out with a small package, handing it to her.

Lily opened the tiny package. Inside she found the exact replica of the flower that Gaige had destroyed.

"Happy Valentine's Day."

"Thank you, Shade. I love it." She reached up, kissing his cheek.

"I'm going to go take a shower. Can I trust you not to sneak out again?"

"Yes." She curled her legs under her, sipping her hot chocolate.

She was still sitting and staring into the flames when he came back wearing sweatpants. His tats stood out in the firelight as he put some more logs on the fire.

He sat down next to her on the sofa, his arm on the back of the couch. "What are you looking so serious about?"

Lily shrugged, avoiding his question.

"Lily?" His blue gaze demanded an answer.

"Nothing, really. I was just thinking." She looked up at him.

His hand cupped her cheek, his thumb wiping away the lone tear clinging to her lashes. "About what?"

"It's just that I waited such a long time to see the Northern Lights… it would have been disappointing if they hadn't been as beautiful as I thought they would."

"I'm sure it would have," he said gently.

"I was just thinking that you said you had waited for me since Razer had met Beth, and then I thought that… what if I wasn't what you wanted. You might become disappointed."

"You did a lot of thinking while I was in the shower."

"I know." She nodded her head.

"Lily, you only saw the Northern Lights in pictures. It's different having expectations of something that you don't know anything about. I grew to know you over the years;

what a warm, loving woman you are, how you can't stand anyone hurt, and how strong you were to survive a childhood that would have seriously fucked up anyone else. Angel, I didn't have expectations. I knew I wanted that sweet girl whose beautiful soul I could see in her eyes. The more I grew to know you, I wasn't disappointed— I was captivated by everything I had learned. It was like unwrapping a pretty Christmas package and finding a work of art inside that's priceless. So, no, I wasn't disappointed."

Lily looked at her husband who always tried to give her what she needed. "You're definitely not what I expected. Giving me flowery speeches on Valentine's Day, a trip to Alaska to make my dream come true, even being a nice guy and giving Georgia's brother her job, so that he would be able to support his kids and hers while she's in prison.

"The first time I saw you, all I could think about was how scary you looked with all those tattoos. Then they ended up being the reason I fell in love with you," Lily said ruefully.

"You fell in love with me because of my tats?"

"I understood their meanings." She reached up, touching the stars on the side of his neck. "The stars are your guide so you always know what's important, the compass so you never lose your way home." Her fingertips brushed the one on his collarbone. "Strength and loyalty, meant someone strong enough to always protect me." Her hand glided down to the tat scrawled across his chest. "Only Death Can Stop Me—someone who will always be there for me. When I realized their meaning, I realized I had found him."

"Who?" Shade's tender voice was another reason she loved him. He gave her gentleness; not all the time, but when she needed it most.

"I knew I had found my cowboy." Lily's arm circled Shade's neck, touching his lips with hers in a kiss that expressed how much she loved him.

It had been a long journey from Queens City, Texas.

Behind her she had left a life that she would never forget; however, she had learned to forgive because each moment had set her on the path to Treepoint, Kentucky, where she had found a new sister and family who would protect her for the rest of her life. The Last Riders would be a force for anyone to reckon with. Most of all, she had found Shade; a strong, protective and gentle man who loved her.

She felt Shade lift her up into his arms, laying her down on the blanket in front of the fire. She smiled as she opened her arms to her husband. She had been right; God had heard her prayers better in the mountains.

* * *

Razer closed the bathroom door, seeing Beth standing by their bedroom window, staring out into the starry sky. He came to stand behind her, his arms slipping around her waist.

"What are you doing?"

"Saying thank you. There were times I didn't think my prayers were going to be answered, but they were." Her pale blonde hair shone in the moonlight coming through the window.

"I don't think Shade has ever been referred to as the answer to anyone prayers." Beth turned to look at Razer.

"He was mine. I prayed for someone strong enough to keep Lily safe and take away her nightmares, and he sent me Shade. Lily wasn't the only one who had her prayers answered; mine were, too. If Cash had left town and not looked back, I would never have met you." Beth looked at the still-arrogant man whose heart she had managed to capture.

"Divine intervention?" Razer said wryly.

Beth nodded her head while Razer shook his.

"I don't know if I believe that, but I'm more than happy with the way things turned out." His hands slipped the robe off her shoulders before they lifted her breast to his mouth. He sucked her nipple into his mouth, his hand sliding down across her stomach toward her... His hand caught on a piece of tape. He stepped back, looking at the gauze taped across her tat.

"What's this?"

"It's your Valentine's Day present," Beth said with a smile.

Razer went to his knees so he could take the gauze off. He saw the tat she had gotten on her hip when she first became a member—a razor blade cutting into her flesh and a tiny drop of blood that was in the shape of a heart with the date of their marriage inside. She had told him it represented him. When he had seen the tattoo, he had thought it was cool to have his symbol on her forever.

Razer swallowed hard when he saw what she had just had done. A tiny blue heart was underneath his.

Razer stood up, twirling her around before stopping and kissing her.

"I owe Cash a beer." He laughed.

"Razer, you owe him a couple of beers. The ultrasound didn't show the sex of the other one. I thought that I would wait and get their tat after they got here," Beth said, surprising Razer with her news that they were expecting not one baby but twins.

Razer buried his head in her neck, remembering how much of a jerk he had been when they first met. If she hadn't forgiven him, they wouldn't be standing here in their new home with two babies on the way.

"I'll be right back," Razer said, avoiding her gaze.

He walked out of their bedroom, leaving her standing naked. She bent down, picking up her robe. She had thought he would be happy. Doubt set in. She should have told him he was having twins more gently. He had gone from being a man who was determined no woman would ever have a hold over him to a married man and now a father in a few short years.

They had been trying to have a baby for the last year. She had let her excitement overrule her common sense. The reality for Razer must have been too much to handle.

She should have known that this was going to...

She slid her robe on, tying the belt. Upset, she started to move away from the window when a movement outside caught her attention. She moved closer to the window. A tender smile came to her lips. Razer was on his knees on the still damp, muddy ground with his head bowed. He had known who to thank after all.

EPILOGUE ONE

Digger sat, finishing his coffee. He was waiting to be moved to the next safe house.

The dumbasses were keeping him safe from the families who wanted revenge for those that had been returned and from those who had learned their women wouldn't be coming home again.

Digger stood, stretching. The worst part was the fucking boredom. He was used to his business or some bitch to keep him occupied. *I'll get that back again*, he promised himself. He would give it six or seven months for their anger to fade and get careless. They would forget all about him, and that's when he would make his escape and start over.

He would have to start again. He didn't have a contact left. He had burned them all to save his life; not from the fucking police, they couldn't wipe their own ass. No, he had to give up everything; the location of his houses, his contacts and the women. That was what had hurt the most; they were his moneymakers.

He had made a mistake going to that little town. If he had stayed out of there, he wouldn't have met The Last Riders. He sure as shit wasn't ever going to forget meeting them. They had nearly killed him without leaving a mark on him. He hadn't even known that was possible.

He had been locked up in that little piss-ant jail after that clusterfuck of a shootout, waiting for his ride back to Queens City, when his cell door had been opened by the biggest motherfucker he had ever seen, taking him into a holding cell.

He had known he would have another interview where he could play like he was going to give his bitches up then, not just to give them shit. He had taken a seat and waited. That's when they had come in. The meanest motherfuckers he had ever come across. Fuck, they were mean. King was mean, but those men, they had taken it to another level. They had given him one choice and that was to give up his information or he was going to die in that room. He had called their bluff. They couldn't hurt him; he was in police custody. The law was supposed to protect him.

That had been the second biggest mistake of his life.

They had spread him on a table. One of them had chains with padded cuffs, cuffing them around his hands and feet. Then they had nearly ripped him apart. He wasn't ashamed to admit he hadn't lasted long. When they had given him a chair and pencil and paper, he had started writing, making shit up to get him through the night until the Rangers could come and save his ass.

After the first two names, they had taken the paper away and left the room, and he had begun to sweat. Then they came back, throwing him back on the table; this time the one with brass knuckles went at him. He had begged to give them the names when another had come toward him with that long-handled razor.

He had given them names and places. Every so often, they would take the paper away and give him a clean sheet. He wasn't stupid, this time he knew they were checking and making sure he was still telling them the truth. He had given them most of his businesses, trying to hold onto enough so that he would have something to start fresh with when he got away. He had lied and said he had given them everything. That's when one had shoved a revolver down his throat.

He gave them the rest.

The next day, when the Rangers came to escort him back to Texas, he had almost broken down and cried. The big sheriff had warned him to keep his mouth closed, take the deal, and they would leave him alone. They had the information they wanted. Digger was no fool; he kept his mouth shut and took the deal the state offered. Now he was sitting sweet, away from The Last Riders and still breathing. He had kind of won.

He didn't have to see them again, and given time and his ingenuity, he would rise again. Digger laughed at his pun. The world was full of women, his for the taking, and he had one he was going to make sure he got his hands on. He would just be smarter next time.

King's brat would be his first bitch. He would make sure of that.

"It's a go. Let's move," the police commander gave the order.

They kept him in the middle—two men in front, two in back, three on each side—as they jogged through the hallway into the large elevator. They came out of the elevator into the underground parking garage, jogging in the same position just a few feet to the waiting SUV.

The ones in front slid into the vehicle while the others still kept his body covered with theirs. As he took a step up into the SUV, he didn't even hear the shot, only felt a millisecond of pain between his eyes, then complete and utter darkness descended.

* * *

"Do you think we have enough steaks?" his wife asked, worried there wasn't going to be enough for their guests tonight.

Ray pushed the buggy to his car. Opening the trunk, he

started putting the groceries in the back of his BMW, not worried about jarring the secret compartment hiding his equipment. He didn't make mistakes; well, except when he had paid someone to do a job he should have done himself.

When he had missed his target with the car and hadn't been given another opportunity to make it look like an accident, he had tried to get in her house. He had been planning to play with the woman before slitting her throat, but he had heard the bike of that scary fucker who was always watching her. He'd had to lay low after that. The one tracking him had almost caught him twice.

His mistake had been not to have hired someone smarter to start the fire. She hadn't even started a decent fight. She had been the one to come running out of that church.

Never mind. The next time he was out on a job, he would swing by and check on her. He couldn't let her live now; he had already spent his fee. Once paid, he made sure he completed a job.

When he rose up from putting the last bag in the trunk, Ray noticed his wife's horror-stricken face. It was the last thing he saw before darkness descended.

* * *

Georgia sat down at the picnic table at the minimum-security prison. Taking the cigarette out of her pocket, she lit it, taking a deep breath before releasing it.

She looked around the yard. Her eyes lit on the brunette sitting across the yard with a frightened look on her face. Fresh meat.

Georgia had seen them bring her in that morning. Georgia was going to have to introduce herself at lunch and make sure that, when that new bitch opened her commissary account, she picked up a few things for her. She would, too. She would be too scared not to. She reminded her of that mousey little Willa. Well, she would handle her just like she'd handled Willa—with an iron fist.

She took another deep draw of her last cigarette, inhaling the smoke as darkness descended.

* * *

When Rider's truck pulled to a stop on The Last Riders' parking lot, Shade opened the passenger side door, getting out. The other doors opened as Rider and Cash hopped out. Shade opened the back door, reaching inside and pulling out his canvas bag, looping it over his shoulder before slamming the truck door closed. He then moved around to the bed of the truck, reaching inside to help Cash pull out the big ice cooler.

"You go ahead; we got this." Rider grinned, coming around the back of the truck.

"You sure?"

"Yeah. Have fun." He smiled mockingly, reaching inside the truck bed for the fishing poles.

"Later," Shade said to both men, turning toward the path that led to his house.

He was halfway there when he saw her running toward him, her purple dress and black hair blowing in the breeze. Spring flowers she had planted lined the pathway.

His somber expression broke into a smile as he came to a stop, lifting his shades to the top of his head so he could see her clearly. When she got close, he held out his arms and Lily jumped into them, her mouth already turned up for his kiss. He gave her the kiss he knew she wanted; he'd take his when he got her inside their home.

"Did you have a good fishing trip? Did you catch anything?" Lily asked, gazing up at him with love shining in her violet eyes.

"Yeah, two big fish and a small fry."

"Was it fun?"

"Always." He looked down into her shining violet eyes. "Did you miss me?"

"Always."

EPILOGUE TWO

"Where is she?" Vida screamed from the bed.

"She's right here," Lily replied, setting her purse down on the chair. "My flight was delayed."

She went to the other side of the bed, grasping the hand Vida handed her and was immediately squeezed tight. Lily watched the midwife between Vida's legs and the nurse standing by the necessary equipment. Colton was standing on the other side of the midwife, looking ready to pass out.

Vida screamed.

Lily looked down at her in sympathy. "You do know they invented epidurals just for this purpose?"

"I wanted a natural childbirth. I did it with Lexi and Axel," Vida panted.

"I told you it wasn't a good idea then, either," Lily reminded her.

"I did, too," Sawyer chimed in.

"Will you two not pick on me when I'm in labor? I know I should have taken the fucking drugs, but it's too late now."

The three women looked at the midwife. She nodded back.

Vida's head fell back as she screamed in pain.

"I don't remember it hurting this bad," Lily said, biting her lip in worry for her friend.

"That's because you took the drugs," Vida said, grimacing in pain.

"And because your doctor was scared to death of Shade. I thought that doctor was going to have a heart attack by the time you delivered John. That's why he refused to deliver that one." She nodded her head at Lily's protruding belly.

"Shade's out in the waiting room. Do you want me to go get him?" Lily asked, only half-teasing. Her friend was in a lot of pain.

"No!" everyone in the room yelled.

"Okay." But if this wasn't over soon, Lily was going to give the midwife heck herself.

Three hours later, the three of them were fighting over holding the babies. Lily stood, holding one in her arms at the same time that Sawyer sat in the rocking chair, rocking the other one. Their husbands had taken the other children for dinner and were going to bring them all back to the hospital to say goodnight to the babies.

"Have you picked out names yet?" Lily asked, moving toward the bed to lay the baby back in her mother's arm.

"Yes, I have," Vida said, clearing her throat.

Sawyer brought the other one back, laying it against her mother's other side.

"This one," she nodded toward the baby who Lily had beside her, "is Callie and this one, Sawyer."

Lily stood, staring down at Vida as she lay on the hospital bed, holding her precious babies. She didn't know what to say.

Sawyer didn't have that problem. "That's going to drive you crazy. You'll have double tats with the same names."

Lily sat down on the side of her bed. "Or how about when we go on vacation and we're all together?"

"I already thought of that," Vida said ruefully.

"Then why?" Sawyer asked.

"Because I can have it again, and I don't want to miss that chance," Vida explained.

"What chance?" Lily asked, reaching out to cover the small, wiggling baby who had kicked off its blanket.

"Watching little girls grow up again together like we did. When I hear them giggling together, I'll think that's Callie and Sawyer. When they're driving me crazy, I'll think that's like Sawyer and Callie. But most of all, I couldn't think of two better namesakes."

Lily's finger touched the cheek of her namesake.

"She's a lucky girl to have both you and Colton as her parents.

"Both of them are," Sawyer said.

Lily watched as baby Sawyer grasped her namesake's finger in a tight fist.

"I have something for you, Lily. It's on the table there." Vida nodded at the table beside her bed.

Lily got up from the bed, picking up the thick, yellow envelope.

"I found it a couple of months ago when I was cleaning our spare bedroom out for the girls. I had put some stuff in there that was mine and Sawyer's from our apartment we'd shared. In one of Sawyer's boxes were her school folders. Her mom had saved all her school stuff. When I looked through it, I found that picture. I'll understand if you don't want it."

Lily looked at her friend to see Vida bury her face in her baby's neck. Her shoulders were shaking. Her eyes went to Sawyer's own pained expression.

Lily's eyes went back to the envelope in her hands, sliding the picture frame out. She gazed down at the picture in her hands. The picture was of the three of them when they were children, sitting at a small table at Sawyer's apartment. They were obviously playing school. Vida was cutting something, Sawyer was obviously gluing things together, and she was coloring. Sawyer's mom had taken the picture when the three had been chatting away.

When Lily looked at the picture, she didn't see the obvious neglect of her dirty hair, clothes that were out of season, or even the bruise on her cheek. All she saw was the love and affection the three little girls shared for each other at that brief second in time.

Lily walked back over, sitting down next to Vida on the bed. "Thank you, Vida. I'll treasure it. It was the best part of my childhood. Those days of playing with you two were very special to me. I learned everything any child needed from you two; what I hope to pass down to my children, and what I will always thank you for teaching me."

Lily lay the picture frame down on the bed, reaching for the sweet baby snuggled in Vida's arms. Her sleeve fell back, revealing the tattoo on the underside of her forearm. Clusters of forget-me-nots clustered around three white Easter lilies with her son's name, John Wayne; Shade's name; and Sawyer, Vida's, and Beth's, their children's names written inside the small forget-me-not flowers. Each Easter lily held a different word—Love, Hope and Faith. Only Colton could have given the tat the final touch it needed. Part of the tattoo was shaded, but the other half was enveloped in a golden light carrying the darkness of her pain away forever, leaving behind the birth of a new beginning to be shared with everyone she loved.

Also by Jamie Begley

The Last Riders Series:

Razer's Ride

Viper's Run

Knox's Stand

Shade's Fall

The VIP Room Series:

Teased

Tainted

Biker Bitches Series:

Sex Piston

The Dark Souls Series:

Soul Of A Man

ABOUT THE AUTHOR

"I was born in a small town in Kentucky. My family began poor, but worked their way to owning a restaurant. My mother was one of the best cooks I have ever known, and she instilled in all her children the value of hard work, and education.

Taking after my mother, I've always love to cook, and became pretty good if I do say so myself. I love to experiment and my unfortunate family has suffered through many. They now have learned to steer clear of those dishes. I absolutely love the holidays and my family puts up with my zany decorations.

For now, my days are spent writing, writing, and writing. I have two children who both graduate this year from college. My daughter does my book covers, and my son just tries not to blush when someone asks him about my books.

Currently I am writing four series of books- The Last Riders, The Dark Souls, The VIP Room, and Biker Bitches series. My favorite book I have written is Soul Of A Woman, which I am hoping to release during the summer of 2014. It took me two years to write, during which I lost my mother, and brother. It's a book that I truly feel captures the true depths of love a woman can hold for a man. In case you haven't figured it out yet, I am an emotional writer who wants the readers to feel the emotion of the characters they are reading. Because of this, Teased is probably the hardest thing I have written.

All my books are written for one purpose- the enjoyment others find in them, and the expectations of my fans that inspire me to give it my best. In the near future I hope to take a weekend break and visit Vegas that will hopefully be this summer. Right now I am typing away on my next story and looking forward to traveling this summer!"

Jamie loves receiving emails from her fans,
JamieBegley@ymail.com

Find Jamie here,
https://www.facebook.com/AuthorJamieBegley

Get the latest scoop at Jamie's official website,
JamieBegley.net

Printed in Poland
by Amazon Fulfillment
Poland Sp. z o.o., Wrocław

49928815R00270